SECRET
OF A
THOUSAND
BEAUTIES

SECRET OF A THOUSAND BEAUTIES

Mingmei Yip

KENSINGTON BOOKS
www.kensingtonbooks.com

KENSINGTON BOOKS are published by

Kensington Publishing Corp.
119 West 40th Street
New York, NY 10018

All Kensington titles, imprints, and distributed lines are available at special quantity discounts for bulk purchases for sales promotion, premiums, fund-raising, educational, or institutional use.

Special book excerpts or customized printings can also be created to fit specific needs. For details, write or phone the office of the Kensington Special Sales Manager: Attn. Special Sales Department. Kensington Publishing Corp., 119 West 40th Street, New York, NY 10018. Phone: 1-800-221-2647.

eISBN-13: 978-1-61773-322-2
eISBN-10: 1-61773-322-9
First Kensington Electronic Edition: December 2014

ISBN-13: 978-1-61773-321-5
ISBN-10: 1-61773-321-0
First Kensington Trade Paperback Printing: December 2014

10 9 8 7 6 5 4 3 2

Printed in the United States of America

To Geoffrey

*Our life together is like rich silk embroidered
with intricate, colorful patterns.*

ACKNOWLEDGMENTS

Although writing is hard work, I find out the more I write, the more I want to do so. Once at a writing conference I was asked by a reader if I ever get bored locking myself in a room and staring at a computer screen for hours and hours.

It was an interesting question. I thought about it, and replied, "No, how can it be boring? When I write I meet all sorts of people: the ones who inhabit my novels—adventurers, art collectors, courtesans, nightclub singers, magicians, spies, gangsters, even Buddhist nuns—whom in real life I would probably never meet. So, far from being bored, I find it exciting that I can live their lives, though just vicariously."

In order to continue to live this exciting life, first I have to thank my husband, Geoffrey Redmond, himself an excellent writer and my best critic. Without Geoffrey's support and compassion, I would never have had the chance to know any of my interesting characters, let alone give them the chance to live in my books.

I would also like to thank the fantastic Kensington group: my wonderful and supportive editor, Martin Biro; publicist Karen Auerbach; Associate Director of Communications Vida Engstrand; designer Kristine Mills-Noble, who graces my books with beautiful covers; Jacqueline Dinas, who has worked hard to have my books sold to ten countries so far; as well as Kensington President Steven Zacharius and Vice President Laurie Parkin, who have made me able to fulfill my dreams year after year.

Many readers have friended me on Facebook, bought my books, and cheered me along the way. I owe them my sincerest gratitude.

Dear Reader,

Like my other novels, *Secret of a Thousand Beauties* is about women determined to overcome great difficulties to make a life for themselves. It is set in 1930s Soochow (Suzhou in modern spelling) and Peking (Beijing) at a time when an imperial embroiderer might be your next-door neighbor. This was an era of great creative ferment, but also social turmoil with modernizers, revolutionaries, and gangsters vying to determine China's future. Women were attaining more freedom, but the old oppressions, such as the ghost marriage in the novel, persisted.

I have always admired people who can create delicate handiworks—seamstresses, knitters, quilters, jewelry makers, embroiderers—as well as those who arrange flowers and perform tea ceremony. When you work with your hands, your mind and senses come alive, and you have the chance to add something beautiful to the world.

China has a grand tradition of embroidery, carried out by many thousands of women, usually anonymous, often working under great strain. I decided to write about some of these women and the trials they endured to create the works that give us so much pleasure. Their skill was the result of almost inhumanly stringent training and bitter practice. Many were drafted to labor away in the imperial palace, serving the near-insatiable appetites of the rich and highborn for their elegant handiwork. To prevent distraction from their work, they were required to remain virgins during their years of service in the palace. Of course, the rule was flouted, but romance could only be pursued in secrecy and with great danger.

Aunty Peony, the head of the novel's small community of supposedly celibate women, was an imperial embroiderer schooled in the famous *Su* style of the Suzhou province. All five of the embroiderers in this novel belong to this 2,000-year-old tradition.

Many women trained in this school, like Aunty Peony, were taken into the palace to sew imperial garments, including the lavish dragon robes for the emperor and alluring undergarments for his many concubines. These court embroiderers had to compete for the emperor's attention, with their skill and sometimes with their bodies as well. They held great sway over the hundreds of concubines, from whom they extracted bribes in return for ever more seductive embroidered garments to entice the jaded emperor.

After the Qing dynasty was overthrown, all who had been employed in the palace were forced to fend for themselves. Some of the embroiderers succeeded as freelancers, but many were only a few commissions away from destitution. *Secret of a Thousand Beauties* is about the life of one of these women and her orphaned followers.

I learned a little about embroidery in elementary school when it was a required subject for girls—but not for boys, of course. The research for the novel was based mainly on Chinese sources including old embroidery displayed in museums throughout the world, scholarly books, and archeological finds (bone needles, thread, even bits of silk embroidered 3,000 years ago). I also made use of videos demonstrating *Su* embroidery techniques.

*When a skillful woman embroiders, it is like the spring breeze
across her tapering fingers.*

—Ancient Chinese saying

*If our love is forever like the first time we met,
No one would be abandoned like a fan in Autumn,
In an instant the heart can change,
But we never blame ourselves,
Instead, only the easy changing of our heart.*

—Nalan Shengde (1655–1685), "Ending Friendship"

*For me, if someone is dear to my heart
He and I would never part,
Even when our hair turn white.*

—Zhuo Wenjun (Western Han Dynasty), "Song of White Hair"

*Had I the heavens' embroidered cloths,
Enwrought with golden and silver light . . .
I would spread the cloths under your feet . . .*

—William Butler Yeats (1865–1939)
"Aedh Wishes for the Cloths of Heaven"

PART ONE

Prologue

It was my wedding day.

I was horrified.

Because my soon-to-be-lawful—and awful—husband was not even a man.

He was a ghost.

Well, a man, but a dead one! A sinister being, his cold hands reaching toward me from the *yin* world. . . .

When we were engaged, in accord with tradition, I'd never met him. In fact, *no one* had ever met him, because my ghost husband-to-be and I had been engaged long before we were even born. My mother and her best friend, my ghost husband's mother, lived in the same village and happened to get pregnant around the same time. Following the ancient tradition *zhifu weihun,* they pointed to each other's protruding bellies, and proclaimed, "If we give birth to a boy and a girl, they'll be husband and wife when they turn seventeen."

So, because of our extremely old and extremely unfortunate tradition, my fate had been decided even before I was born. I was going to marry a man I could never know, not even see, because he'd died before he could make it outside his mother's belly. Like a snake, her umbilical cord wound around his tiny neck and squeezed the tiny breath out of him.

"But, Spring Swallow," said my mean aunt, addressing me by name, "a promise is a promise."

It was my misfortune to have been raised by this very mean woman because both of my parents had died in a bus accident not long after their future son-in-law's failure to enter this life. It was whispered around the village that because the baby could not lure *his* parents to join him in hell, he dragged down his intended parents-in-law instead.

My heartless aunt went on. "You know, failing to keep a promise not only shames your ancestors, but will bring your husband's ghost back to haunt you. So, you have no choice but to marry him, dead or alive. Also, because not only your future husband but your parents also died, no man will marry you."

Before I had a chance to ask why, she cast me a malicious glance. "No man wants to marry a bad-luck woman!"

But I knew the real reason that Mean Aunt was so eager for me to marry a ghost. Not because I was bad luck, but because I would be good luck for her. My ghost husband's family was one of the richest in the village. Though the wedding would bring me no husband, it would bring her a bundle of cash and a heap of expensive gifts. But, of course, rich people do not give away their money just because they are nice. Once married to their ghost son, I would be obligated to take care of my mother-in-law until she died!

My aunt went on to threaten me. "You think any man would want to marry you? Born under an all-destroying star? Spring Swallow, you really have no choice. So don't even think of escaping. I won't let you destroy my reputation and ruin my life!"

Escape. That was exactly what I had in mind all along. I didn't care about my aunt's reputation and life. Because living in our remote village and being an old maid, she didn't have much of a life to begin with anyway.

❦ 1 ❦

The Ghost Wedding

Even though the groom was a ghost, it was a "real" wedding, with an elaborate evening ceremony in the Dragon Lake Daoist temple—only after dark would the dead wander into the realm of the living. Later there would be a gloomy celebratory banquet in the village's only restaurant.

At five in the afternoon, maids and helpers from the groom's family began to arrive at the temple's small room to make preparations. For a whole hour, I had to sit still on a chair while three hired women fussed over my hair, face, and hands, so I'd look my best for my groom. Where was he? Was he hovering invisibly nearby to appreciate me? But I could only see my mean aunt and a few of our close relatives milling around watching the preparations and offering uninvited suggestions for the wedding's *fanwen rujie*—trivial procedures and elaborate formalities.

The ceremony was to be held exactly at seven-thirty, the auspicious moment picked by our village's best—and only—feng shui master and fortune-teller. Auspicious, marrying a ghost? I might even have burst out laughing had a maid not stuck a candy inside my mouth for my future sweet happiness. Had my aunt not been keeping a strict eye on me, I'd have spat out that candy like it was dog droppings.

So far in my short seventeen years of life, I'd heard numerous prognostications but never bothered to find out if they were accurate. I'd come to realize that the only person I could depend on was myself—not a feng shui master, not my mean aunt, and not any of my relatives or neighbors. There was one exception: Father Edwin, the American missionary who ran a small church and school in my old village.

My aunt and her few confidantes were now ogling the lavish gifts from relatives, friends, villagers, and my soon-to-be Popo, my husband's mother. Nothing from his father, however, who was with his son in the Yellow Springs. Stacked high on the floor were bamboo and lacquered boxes storing clothes, housewares, jewelry, and maybe even red envelopes stuffed with lucky money. Bottles of the expensive Maotai and the famous local Half Moon Spring wine filled one corner, beckoning everyone to get drunk for this festive occasion. Displayed on the Eight Immortals' table in the middle of the room were the special wedding foods: candies, sugared olives, red-dyed buns, wedding cakes, spices and condiments, dried scallops, abalone, sea cucumber, cooked hairy crabs, and even a roasted baby pig.

On top of a string of sausages was a strip of paper with the words: "Wishing a marriage as long as the sausages." Another strip attached to a honey jar said, "Wishing the marriage as sweet as honey." Yet another strip attached to a bag of sour plums read: "Wishing you have many grandchildren." This last because the word *suan,* or "sour," sounds like the word for "grandchildren."

Even though my mood was entirely miserable, I let out a giggle at this last inscription.

My aunt looked up from counting the gifts and recording them in her notebook to cast me a mean look.

"So finally you're happy to have a husband and a big wedding? But don't act so crazy and make your Popo lose face! Behave and act like a proper lady, at least for tonight!"

I fought back. "What kind of face does Popo have anyway?"

"All right, you little ingrate, learn some manners and stop talking back to your elders!"

With a snort she turned to scold the maids who'd been listening and whispering to each other. Fortunately, my Popo, or soon-to-be mother-in-law, could not overhear this, for she was supervising preparations in the main hall.

Soon the maid who was doing my makeup yelled in my ear, "Done!"

Thrusting a mirror in front of me, she exclaimed, "See how beautiful you are? I'm sure the groom would be very happy to see you!"

The other two women echoed, "Yes, you two will make a happy couple!"

Did they imagine that a ghost can be happy? Or his bride? Thinking about it gave me the creeps.

After that, the maids went off to continue the preparations. In my embroidered red wedding gown, I walked around to look at the gifts and food. Although I loved roasted baby pig (especially its crispy, juicy skin) and soy sauce chicken (especially the drumsticks), now the sight of my favorite foods made me nauseous. My brain whirred, trying to focus on my dangerous plan of escape from my damned husband, damned wedding, damned village, and my whole damned life!

A little boy, probably seeing that I didn't touch any of the gifts or eat the food, came forward, and asked, "Big sister, can I have some of the candies?"

I smiled down at his round, eager eyes. "Of course, little one, take all you want."

Might as well, since I did not plan to be here much longer. But I'd definitely take some cakes and buns and chunks of the chicken and roasted baby pig to eat on the run. Most of the gifts would be of no use to me, so I would leave them for my mean aunt's satisfaction. One gift, however, I would not leave—a beautifully embroidered silk spread. Exquisitely colored, it depicted a dragon and phoenix surrounded by orchids, lotuses, jasmines.

At school all the girls were taught embroidery. So I knew a few things about needles and stitches, though I could not imagine attempting something as elaborate as this. Mean Aunt had told me this was a *Soo* embroidery, an extravagant gift, for embroidery of the *Soo* school is considered the best, and thus the most expensive and sought after. Although the dragon and phoenix symbolism of marital harmony seemed an ironic mockery, I found myself fascinated by the embroidery. Its complicated stitches and subtle color gradations made the dragon and phoenix seem to fly out from the red silk. How satisfying it must be to produce such beautiful work!

Half an hour later, Mean Aunt appeared and said in her harsh voice, "*Wah,* Spring Swallow, you're all decked out like a pretty doll!"

Or a ghost doll, I thought.

In a scolding tone, she said, "You better act right; this is the most important day of your life!"

She went on excitedly. "The ceremony is about to begin. The priest will lead you to sit next to the white cock, who represents your ghost husband. Then you must pay your respects to your dead husband, his dead father, his mother, and then to Heaven and Earth. After that, we'll ride in the rickshaw to visit the relatives who are too old to attend the ceremony. . . . You listening?"

She grabbed my elbow and pulled me along, trailed by the small entourage of helpers. We walked a few yards to the large hall where the ceremony would take place. Adults were already seated while small children wandered about, their eyes big and bright with curiosity. Women, young or old, cast me curious or pitying glances as we entered the hall. Smoke from the many burning incense sticks snaked into my nostrils, choking me and bringing tears to my eyes.

Below the many gods and goddesses arrayed on the walls and the expressionless head of the gaunt priest in his embroidered yellow robe stood a high-backed chair, to which was tied a white cock.

That miserable bird was going to be my husband!

As its bloody red crown gave me a chill, my aunt whispered in my ear, "The white of the bird symbolizes the purity of your and Wang Xing's union. The red symbolizes the virginal blood on your marital bed."

Right now my virginal blood was boiling inside all my arteries. What I'd like to do now was to slit that bird's neck so he'd bleed to death and end my bloody nightmare. But unfortunately my nightmare was just about to begin!

The somber priest signaled for my aunt and me to move to the altar, piled high with offerings—paper and bamboo furniture, houses, servants, and stacks of hell bank notes for the use of the dead—in this case, my husband. Why hadn't they also put some pretty paper women for him to enjoy so he'd leave me alone? I had to bite my lower lip to suppress a nervous giggle.

The priest ordered me to kneel in front of the altar beside the white cock and my mother-in-law, before the intense eyes of the guests. The bird looked as nervous as I. Could it be that my husband's spirit really inhabited it? I felt a chill crawl up my spine like a spider in a haunted attic.

Next, the priest performed the rite of purification. Walking around the hall, he dipped a willow branch into a bowl and flicked sacred water onto the four corners while reciting an incantation that I believed nobody could understand—except maybe that stupid chicken. When the drops sprinkled on the children, they giggled as if being tickled. The adults forced smiles onto their faces, trying to look as joyous as if this were a real, blissful union.

After the purification, the priest placed on the altar a handkerchief in which was wrapped a lock of my hair, fingernail parings, and a piece of paper inscribed with my name and birthday. These were so my "husband" could touch his new bride. I felt a wave of nausea. Was Wang Xing's ghost really going to touch me? Ugh!

The priest spoke in a far-from-comforting monotone. "Now I'll summon Wang Xing to ascend to the *yang* world to enjoy all these treasures and offerings. After he devours all this food, accepts all these gifts, and most important, takes home his beautiful wife, Spring Swallow, he should be so happy and satisfied that he will not come back here to make other demands."

Oh, Heaven, then what about me? What if Wang Xing would love me so much that he decided to drag me down to the *yin* world with him, or pull me so hard that only half of my body remained in the *yang* world while the other half became stuck in the *yin* realm? I cast a look at the wretched cock, and it returned a dirty glance, or so I imagined.

The priest continued muttering some Daoist sutras from thin, wrinkled lips as he performed equally incomprehensible hand gestures. Since it seemed unlikely that anybody in the temple hall understood even a single word he uttered, perhaps he was speaking in ghost language to my groom, and not to us, the living. Everyone watched with fascination, even the white cock. But he had no inkling that he was my groom, nor that I'd rather see him on my plate with black bean sauce than in my conjugal yet celibate bed!

As I felt a little relieved that the ceremony finally seemed to be at an end, I was hit by the priest's announcement that another ritual was about to begin.

His voice was thick and authoritative. "Now that Spring Swallow and Wang Xing are officially husband and wife, Spring Swallow should bear him a son. And since she will be banned from being intimate with any other man for the rest of her life, the only means to give Wang Xing a son is through adoption."

The guests clapped enthusiastically.

An old mother laughed. "Give Wang Xing a son!"

Another one yelled, "Yes, so the Wang family name can continue and prosper!"

A middle-aged man echoed, "An infertile woman is a barren land and is not welcomed in our temple!"

Didn't anyone realize if I didn't have a husband in the flesh, I would not have a son except through adultery? Yet everyone was clapping and shouting.

Waiting until all of the clamor died down, the priest spoke again. "Now we're going to start the adoption ceremony."

Wah, without a man and without any notice, I was going to be a mother.

But I had no time to reflect, for the priest had already placed a contract of adoption on the altar next to my dead husband's tablet. After some more gesturing and reciting, to my surprise, the priest announced the little boy who'd earlier asked me for candies and I were now mother and son. I almost threw up my lunch in shock! Oblivious to my emotions, the priest went on to read from a red scroll, announcing that from now on it would be the boy's duty to make offerings to his new father as well as the rest of the Wang ancestors.

Two hours later, the chilling ceremony drew to a close, leaving everyone satisfied except me. The tricycle rickshaw was waiting. It was now time to visit the elderly relatives who—either handicapped, sick, or too old—could not attend this big, celebratory occasion. Red ribbons hung from the rickshaw's small roof. If they were going to bring good luck to anyone, it wasn't me.

Mean Aunt asked me to squeeze into the rickshaw with her and my mother-in-law. My husband the white cock was cuddled against my heaving chest—not from excitement but from horror. I stared at his crimson crown and felt a wave of disgust as it reminded me of the nonexistent virginal blood and the equally nonexistent union. The bird gave me another of his dirty looks. Did he want to fuck me? Didn't he know that I'd already been "fucked," not by a ghost, but by fate?

Fifteen minutes on the road I turned to both my aunt and my mother-in-law, urgently rubbing my stomach. "Aunty and Popo, I suddenly have stomach cramps, can I stop to relieve?"

"Why didn't you go to the toilet before we left?" my aunt said with a scolding tone.

"Because I was too excited," I lied.

My plump, richly attired mother-in-law patted my head. "My good daughter, calm down. Don't you know by marrying into our house you'll have endless tasty food and nice, embroidered clothes?"

"All right." Now it was my aunt's turn to cast me a dirty look— obviously not believing in my "excitement."

However, she yelled to the cyclist in full throttle, "Stop! Our bride needs to pee!"

The man yelled back, "But there's no toilet around!"

It was my turn to yell. "Doesn't matter, just let me off where you see a knoll or tall grass."

Another few minutes had passed when I finally spotted a range of small hills. "Right here, let me off, I can't wait!" I screamed as loud as I could.

Without wasting a minute, I thrust the unfortunate bird onto my ghost husband's mother's lap and jumped off the vehicle.

The cyclist was discreet enough to pedal a few yards ahead of me so in case I had to take care of big business, the stink and the sight wouldn't reach them.

Perfect.

I immediately climbed over the small hill. When I was sure I was out of sight, I broke into a sprint as if pursued by a real, vengeful ghost.

❦ 2 ❦

Meeting an Embroiderer

Two days later, after anxious nights in deserted alleys and a ride on top of a northbound train, with a growling stomach and wobbly limbs, I finally arrived in the city of Soochow, feeling excited but mostly scared. What if I couldn't find a place to live or get a job, however menial? Would I starve to death, be caught by Mean Aunt and the villagers, or be abducted by bandits?

I remembered that when I was very small, my parents had taken me here once. Although I remembered little about the city besides its snake-like rivers, I felt somewhat relieved knowing that I had been here once before. And I was not totally unprepared, for I had started to plan my escape a few years ago when first told I was to marry a ghost.

The smartest thing I'd done to prepare for my escape was to continue my schooling even after Mean Aunt had stopped paying for it. She always warned me that "A smart girl can never find a husband. Men, smart or stupid, don't want to be outwitted by their wife. Not even a ghost-man."

Even though she'd refused to pay for school, whenever I could get away, I walked four miles to one run by Western missionaries. I'd heard about this school from an old neighbor, who boasted how generous the foreigners were there, how they gave out free food and clothes. However, food and clothes were not what I wanted, but learning. I didn't have the guts to ask for permission to take classes there, so I peeked inside a window and eavesdropped on lessons taught by a "white ghost." Not the dead kind like my husband, but the foreign kind. Strangely, this foreign, or barbarian, ghost called himself a missionary and, ridiculously, everyone called him Father.

Having spotted me watching his class and mumbling after him and his students, one day he invited me inside his school, which was, in fact, just one room. He asked me about myself and I told him that my mean aunt would rather die than pay for my schooling. Father Edwin listened sympathetically, then explained that his classes were free, and welcomed me to attend them anytime. Not only were the classes free, but the students were given books, notebooks, towels, toothbrushes, and small bags of rice. Eager to learn and get the free things, I went to all Father Edwin's classes: English, mathematics, geography, hygiene, even reading and writing Chinese. Whenever I was in his Chinese class, I couldn't help but giggle. How bizarre, a foreign ghost teaching Chinese to a ghost-marrying Chinese girl!

The reason I was eager to learn was because I knew his teaching would prove invaluable someday. If I wanted to survive, I needed to be able to read and write. With six years of elementary school education behind me, I could do both, but not fluently. The village school Mean Aunt sent me to was very bad—the teachers didn't care if you understood, learned, or even came to class.

But Father Edwin was different. An erudite man, he truly cared for his students and was eager to help and pass on his knowledge. From him I learned to read and write Chinese and English properly, and sometimes he would read to me from the ancient classics. Of course, we were all expected to study the Bible. Because I was such an eager student, he also gave me special lessons on literature, poetry, even philosophy.

My reading improved quickly so that when I had made my escape, I could read the road signs to find my way to Soochow. This city was close enough to my old village that I could make my way by foot and train in two days, but far enough away that no one here would recognize me. Even if my aunt and relatives visited Soochow, searching for me would be like "looking for a needle at the sea bottom."

Now, however, I was less concerned about whether I'd be found than how I was going to survive. I'd already eaten the roasted pig, chicken, and buns that I had stuffed underneath my wedding robe during my long, harsh journey. And being in a city, it was urgent that I find a place to stay. My hope was to find a place as a maid, so I'd be fed and given a roof above my head. Otherwise, if I did not starve to death, I'd be reported to the police as a vagrant by coldhearted city people, or even abducted by gangsters. I wondered if I would be better off sharing my bed with an invisible ghost every night, laboring for his mother, raising the little boy I had involuntarily adopted, and remaining celibate for the rest of my life.

My tired feet dragged along a cobblestone road beside one of Soochow's many rivers. I had arrived here before dawn, hoping not to be spotted in my red wedding gown. Under the pigeon-colored sky, everything—the rivers, houses, shops—seemed to be dyed gray. The waterways coursed here and there like dark, slippery water snakes. On the other side of the path were rows of stores with signboards above their doors, still blocked with wooden planks. The signboards announced the goods they would offer for sale: Old Gent's Tailor, Chen's Spicy Noodles, Big East Rice Shop, South-North Fabrics, Middle Harmonious Herbs, Auspicious Vinegar. . . . Could I get a job at one of these stores? I felt a surge of hope.

Fortunately, it was late summer and the early-morning sun, instead of burning fiercely, was warm and soothing. Feeling welcome and a little more hopeful, I continued to walk on the path, even though it was slippery and tortuous. As I surveyed my surroundings, in my peripheral vision I spotted a young woman hurrying toward the end of the street. Before I could decide whether to approach her or to hide, she had already spotted me. She had a kind face, so I braved myself not to turn and walk away. Maybe she worked as a maid for a rich family and could take me to work with her too. As we drew near each other, instead of talking, to my surprise, she pulled at my dress!

I flinched and started to turn away, when she said in a gentle voice, "Little sister, I'm not going to hurt you."

Before I could respond, she went on. "The reason I touched your dress is because I believe this is very fine *Soo* style embroidery, probably even done by one of us a while ago!"

"What do you mean?" I stared at her finely featured face.

"I, my aunty, and the other girls I live with are all embroiderers. Your dress looks like something one of us might have done."

She paused to give me a curious once-over, then asked, "Little sister, what are you doing out so early?" She paused again, then asked, "Why are you wearing this wedding gown, and where's your husband?"

I blurted out before I could stop myself, "My husband was dead before I married him. That's why I'm here!"

She looked puzzled. Not surprising since the whole thing *was* ridiculous. I couldn't think of any explanation other than the truth, bizarre as it was.

"Big sister, I ran away after my wedding to a ghost."

Her eyes were as round as two kumquats. "Oh, Heaven, a runaway bride! From a ghost! I've heard about that kind of horrible marriage. You better not be seen—both of your families are probably coming after you right now! So maybe I should be glad that we don't . . ."

As if thinking of something, she suddenly stopped.

I asked, "Don't what?"

"Nothing; anyway, what happened?"

Should I trust this total stranger? After I'd told her everything, would she report me to the police?

But I was already asking, "Big sister, can you keep a secret?"

She looked around even though the street was empty. "Of course I will." Then she chuckled nervously. "Since I assume no one knows you here, who would care about your secret anyway?"

"Please don't report me to . . ."

She stared hard at me. "But why would I do that?"

"So you'll get a big reward?"

"Little sister . . ." Now her eyes were filled with sympathy. "I am an ill-fated woman myself. Would I be so cruel as to betray an unlucky sister, or so stupid as to generate more bad karma for my-self?"

"Big sister, can you be as ill-fated as I?"

She didn't answer my question, but said, "Hurry, before some-one sees you or you'll be in big, big trouble! Follow me."

"Where are we going?"

"To my place so you can change. You want people to see you in a wedding dress but with no husband?"

"Of course not."

"Then put this on," she said, taking off her thin shawl and drap-ing it over my shoulders.

When we started to walk, she asked, "What's your name?"

"Spring Swallow."

She shook her head. "It's a pretty name, but not a very lucky one, I'm afraid. Just pray that your fate won't be a swallow who keeps flying, never finding her nest."

I was digesting her saying when she asked, "How old are you?"

"Seventeen."

"Good. My name is Purple and since I am six years older than you, you can call me Sister Purple. All right now, let's go to my place."

"Sister Purple, why did you come out so early in the city?"

To my surprise, she blushed. "That's none of your business, lit-tle sister."

"Sorry."

Maybe feeling bad for her abruptness, she smiled, and asked, "Are you hungry?"

I nodded emphatically. From my years living with a mean aunt, I'd learned never to pass up a chance to have food to warm my stomach—even if I was not hungry, or downright stuffed. One never knows where the next meal will come from.

"I'm now taking you to Aunty Peony's house and will get you something to eat."

"Who's Aunty Peony?"

"My and the other girls' embroidery teacher. Older than us and mysterious."

Either I was crazy or just desperate, because without any resistance, I followed her.

It turned out to be a very long walk. After leaving the store-lined street, we crossed a bridge onto a long and narrow path. The path led us by numerous alleys until we were outside the city. We stopped to rest a few times and eventually arrived at a two-story brick house. A short distance away rose a mountain. It struck me as very strange to build a house here, for there were no other houses or people around.

I inhaled deeply, then asked, "Sister Purple, why have a house here with nothing else around?"

She shook her head, smiling. "You're a little Miss Curious, eh? Aunt Peony likes to be left alone. But don't ask me why because I don't know. Also, don't worry, there's a very small village a short walk past the mountain. It's quiet here, but we can get what we need."

Since there was a nearby village, I was tempted to ask again why she was in the city so early in the morning. Instead, I swallowed my question with a big gulp of saliva.

Purple said, "Spring Swallow, the others should already be up and about." Then she looked hard at me, her tone serious. "Can you make me a promise?"

I nodded.

"Don't tell anyone that we met in Soochow. Just say it was in the nearby village that I told you about."

As Purple and I entered the house, three women were eating breakfast from a wooden table. Once they saw us, they set down their chopsticks and came over to stare at me.

The oldest one, a dignified-looking middle-aged woman, asked my rescuer, "Who's this, little sister?"

"This is Spring Swallow."

Purple turned to me. "Spring Swallow, this is Aunty Peony, our teacher and master embroiderer."

Then she gestured to a pretty girl about my age with a watermelon-seed face and curvy body. "This is Leilei."

After that, she patted the head of the youngest girl. "And this is Little Doll."

I bowed and softly wished them all a good morning.

The older woman acknowledged my greeting with a slight nod, exuding authority. She looked me up and down, then she turned to Purple, with a question. "Why did you bring this little sister here?"

Before I had a chance to say anything, Purple answered for me, lowering her voice. "She's a runaway bride—to a ghost." She lifted her shawl to reveal my wedding gown.

Aunty didn't respond to her but kept studying me with a critical eye.

Little Doll chuckled. "*Wah!* What a lucky ghost to marry such a pretty bride!"

Purple hit the girl playfully on her arm. "Stop that, Little Doll! We should be nice to our new guest."

Leilei, the prettiest one, didn't say anything but, like Aunty Peony, kept staring at me with her intense eyes like a wolf's. I had a bad feeling that she didn't want me here.

Aunty Peony spoke. "What's your name again? How old are you?"

"Spring Swallow, Aunty Peony. I'm seventeen."

She turned to Purple and asked again, "What made you think you should bring her here?"

Purple smiled, her tone apologetic. "Aunty Peony, I was in the village market and saw her picking leftover food from a stall. I went up to give her a bun and we started to talk. She told me she's a runaway bride from a ghost, so I didn't think anyone else would take her in. I hope maybe she can learn embroidery and give us some help here."

Aunty thought for a while, then said, "Let me see your hands."

Timidly I put out my hands.

She took them, then kneaded them this way and that. "Hmmm . . . they're a little coarse. Have you been doing menial work at your village?"

I didn't want to admit this but couldn't lie either, since she already held the truth right in her hands.

"Yes."

She didn't respond but told Leilei, "Go fix tea and heat up

some buns for our guest. Purple, you boil water, then take her to bathe."

After that, she turned to look me hard in the eyes. "You're lucky we found you." She paused, then spoke again. "Even doing menial work hasn't ruined your hands. So I guess you're not stupid. You seem to know how to protect yourself."

"Thank you very much, Aunty Peony." Of course, I would agree with anything this boss said since I needed a roof over my head and food in my stomach. I knew I was extremely lucky to have found a chance to stay somewhere so quickly after I'd arrived in the city.

I sat down and they watched me swallow the buns and down the tea like a woman caught in a famine. After I finished, Purple took a big pot of boiling water and led me inside the bathroom, which was a small space with a round wooden box for our dirty business. She moved an elongated wooden tub to the middle of the room and poured the hot water inside.

"Don't take too long. You understand that Aunty Peony didn't take you in just for you to enjoy a hot bath, don't you?"

"Of course I do, Sister Purple."

Her voice softened a little. "Go ahead, here are your towel and clothes. I know you must be very tired, so after the bath you can sleep in my room. I'll wake you up when it's time to eat."

After she left, I took off my clothes and got in the wooden tub. As I splashed the hot water over my bare skin, I sighed. Tears, as hot as the water, glided down my cheeks. What had I done? What would happen to me living with this group of woman embroiderers, all complete strangers? I scrubbed hard at the dirt that accumulated during my escape, hoping I'd also scrub off any remaining bad luck from the accursed wedding to an equally accursed ghost reincarnated as a cock!

When finished, I dried myself and put on the cotton top and pants. Purple was already waiting outside the bathroom. Without a word, she led me to her room and I collapsed onto her small cot. As soon as I entered my dream village, my ghost husband appeared. With a blurred face, dangling arms, and no feet, he stared hard at me, looking mournful.

"Wife, why have you abandoned me in the *yin* world, it's freezing here."

I answered defiantly, "You're not my husband but a ghost wandering in the *yin* world in search of victims. I'm not your wife, but a living person. So leave me alone, or . . . you'd better watch out!"

I didn't know where I got the courage to talk to a ghost like this—what if he was a bloodthirsty, vengeful one? Then I'd try my best to be an equally vengeful human!

But he didn't budge. "Dear wife, have some mercy, life here is very lonely and miserable. So please . . ."

Wah, a ghost intimidated by a human, a woman. I almost burst out laughing but suppressed myself.

"Please, my ass! Just get lost, won't you?"

Miraculously, he did, scurrying away on his nonexistent feet.

I woke up weary and chilled. Now awake, I thought that if my "husband" decided to visit me again, I'd better be nice to him, just in case. After all, everybody knows it is not smart to offend a ghost. I also decided I had better get along with everyone in my new home. If there was any mishap, I might find myself joining my "husband" in the *yin* world. Depressed by this prospect, I fell back into a deep, troubled sleep.

I didn't know how long I'd slept, but in my still groggy state, I heard someone push open the door. It was a smiling Purple.

"It's already six-thirty in the evening. Poor girl, you slept the whole day; you must be exhausted. Leilei and I have prepared some good dishes. Now come and have dinner."

She took my hand and led me to the living room and the long wooden table now covered with steaming plates of food. Everyone was staring at me as if I'd just returned from the world of the dead. After we sat down, I took the chance to get a good look at the house. Embroideries depicting landscapes, animals, birds, and lucky sayings hung on the four walls. Some were elaborate, others simple, but all looked refined and skillfully executed. One small table was filled with embroidering supplies—piles of fabric, paper on which faint drawings were traced, scissors, round wooden frames, bamboo baskets overflowing with spools of thread in a rainbow of colors, and other objects unfamiliar to me.

Against one wall was a wooden shelf with cubby holes crammed with more thread. On the opposite wall was an altar bearing a white Guan Yin statue, before which were placed offerings of tea, fruit, and flowers. The house seemed to be quite spacious, with several small rooms adjoining where we sat. A narrow staircase led up to another floor, which I guessed must be Aunty Peony's private quarters.

After I scrutinized the house, I examined my sisters as unobtrusively as possible. While Purple was thin and frail, Leilei was curvaceous with sharp, sparkling eyes. Though she was pretty, I was put off by her harsh look and sarcastic expression. In its own way, each of the women's faces, even Little Doll's, seemed to conceal a bitter story. I sighed inside.

Strangely, the oldest of the group, Aunt Peony, seemed to me the most beautiful. Her elongated eyes, slender figure, and, most of all, her regal manner and authoritative voice pulled my eyes toward her like metal to a magnet. Her aristocratic bearing led me to wonder how she came to be in this lonely, dilapidated house.

Aunty Peony directed each girl to tell me how she came to be here. Purple's husband had died six months after they'd been married at the age of eighteen. Her in-laws kicked her out of the house—accusing her of being the all-destroying star who'd brought the family bad luck, killing their first son, and depriving them of his grandchildren.

When she was fourteen, Leilei's parents lost all their money and sent her to learn embroidery from Aunty; she never heard from them again. Little Doll never even knew her parents; she had escaped from her oppressive orphanage and was found by Aunty foraging for scraps near a village temple. Although Aunty let her do some simple embroidery, her main jobs were cleaning and cooking. I spoke briefly about my life with my mean aunt and my escape from the ghost wedding. I kept waiting for Aunty to tell her story, but after a long silence she merely said that there was nothing interesting to say about herself.

Anyway, there were enough other tragic stories gathered in this house to fill the evening. I wondered what evil *qi* and ill fate brought all these unlucky women to this house, including me. It was as if it were a contest as to whose story was the most tear-jerking.

Purple's gentle voice interrupted my thoughts, explaining that Aunty Peony was the head of this small community of unmarried woman embroiderers. The work was done for a very famous store in Peking, which not only sold it to the locals, but also exported it to foreign countries like America, England, and France.

Purple complained that they were all underpaid for their hard work and skill, especially Aunty, who was the best even by international standards. The Peking company—Heavenly Phoenix—kept most of the money, even though the work sold for very high prices. However, all stayed because they had a better life here in this house than they'd led before. Here there was no controlling husband, jealous and abusive mother-in-law, or sexually harassing father-in-law. Here they could proudly live independent lives.

I was thinking that they were not so independent as they worked hard for not much money, but before I opened my mouth, Aunty said, "Let's eat. Tonight Purple and Leilei cooked two extra dishes to welcome our new guest, Spring Swallow." She gestured toward the table. "We have shrimp stir-fried with turquoise tea leaves and sweet-scented osmanthus chicken."

"Thank you all for your kindness and hospitality," I said, eyeing all the dishes as I sucked back my saliva.

Aunty went on. "We also opened a new canister of the best Dragon Well tea."

After that, everyone picked up their tea cup, took a sip, and uttered, "Welcome to our humble residence, Spring Swallow!"

Little Doll pulled my sleeve. "Sister Spring Swallow, can you embroider with us?"

"I'd love to."

I looked over at Aunty Peony, but she pretended she didn't hear anything. Purple put a few shrimp on top of my rice and watched as I chewed noisily. Aunty Peony cast me a disapproving look, took a small bite of her scented chicken, and chewed gently with her mouth shut. Swallowing quietly, she picked up her tea cup, holding out three fingers to imitate the shape of an orchid.

After taking a delicate sip, she spoke through her heart-shaped pink lips. "Spring Swallow, if you share our roof and our dining table, you have to do something to help bring in money, either housework or embroidery."

I felt so delighted to hear this that I blurted out, "I'd love to embroider!"

"Did you ever learn?"

I nodded. "Yes, in elementary school."

I'd say yes to anything to have a roof over my head, let alone to learn embroidery. Both my chopsticks and bowl were suspended in midair as I added, "My mother knew how to embroider, too, but how well I have no idea. She died when I was very small."

"Good. So you think you can learn fast?"

Good that my mother had died young? I was disappointed that this beautiful, older woman was not interested in my family or my life, only how quickly I could bring in money.

But I answered eagerly, "Don't worry, Aunty. I'm a fast learner. So, will you teach me?"

She remained silent as Purple put another pork morsel into my bowl under the jealous eyes of Leilei.

We busied ourselves picking up the food, putting it into our mouths, and sipping the fragrant Dragon Well tea.

Minutes later, Aunty put down her chopsticks and, her eyes suddenly fierce, said, "But don't think that I'll teach you just like that. You have to *baishi,* you know?"

I nodded. Of course I'd heard of *baishi,* "kowtowing to the master"—the ceremony cementing the relationship between teacher and a student. However, if the student does something to offend the teacher, she'll be kicked out. I'd also heard that for the rest of her life, whatever the student earns, she has to give some to her teacher.

Aunty cast me a suspicious look. "Since you're a runaway bride, do you think you'll have anything for your *baishi* ceremony?"

Part of the ceremony was the exchange of gifts between the new student and her teacher to commemorate the relationship.

"Sorry, Aunty Peony, I . . . don't think so."

Purple immediately came to my rescue. "Aunty, what about her wedding gown?"

"You think so? A wedding gown from a ghost husband's family? But I'll accept it if it's your only possession."

Of course I'd taken the precious *Soo* embroidery from the wedding gifts, but I was not going to let them know about this. Because it might be my lifesaver in the future. If my luck turned bad again, hopefully I could sell it for some cash. Anyway, I was more than happy to get rid of my wedding gown, which reminded me of nothing but misery. I hoped from now on that I wouldn't have anything to do with my old life, my mean aunt, my dead-in-the-womb husband, and my pathetic, greedy Popo, the one whose dead son was my ghost "husband."

"All right. Purple, you better help prepare for the *baishi* ceremony. Since you went through it yourself a few years ago, you don't need me to tell you what to do, right?"

"Don't worry, Aunty Peony; I'll have everything ready soon."

I wondered why Aunty Peony was in such a hurry, since I was still a stranger in this household.

Staring at her beautiful but haughty face, I felt too intimidated to ask.

3

Along the River during the Qingming Festival

Three days later, Purple lent me her embroidered pink top and pants with matching shoes for the *baishi* ceremony. I still couldn't believe my good luck that just a few days after my escape, I was wearing new clothes and having a new life!

Purple, Leilei, Little Doll, and I all gathered in the living room in front of the small altar. Fruit, flowers, tea, and an incense burner had been placed in front of the white Guan Yin statue. Next to the Goddess of Compassion was a small portrait of an elderly woman.

Soon Aunty Peony descended from her room and went to sit on a high-back chair with her back to the altar. To my surprise, she was elaborately made up and wearing a red silk gown lavishly embroidered with birds and flowers. Her hair was pulled back and tied up in a tight bun, highlighting her beautiful, mysterious face.

When everything was in its proper place, Purple told me to kneel in front of Aunty Peony. Leilei poured a cup of tea and Little Doll lit the three incense sticks in the bronze burner. Soon the room was filled with the fragrance of sandalwood, pleasing my nostrils and soothing my heightened nerves.

Aunty Peony spoke, her tone as serious as if she were conducting a funeral service. "I don't often take on students. But since Heaven decided to bring you to me just when I desperately need another pair of embroidering hands, I'll take you in. If you prove to be a good embroiderer, you'll embroider to bring in money. Do you accept?"

I nodded emphatically. I liked the idea of being an embroiderer, but anyway had no alternative. As she desperately needed help, I even more desperately needed to be housed and fed.

She cast a pitiful look at all of us. "I accepted you all as my students because I took pity on your dire situations—no money, no family, no husband. So besides being a teacher, I'm also your adoptive mother, you all understand?"

We all emitted a loud, "Yes, Teacher Peony!"

She turned back to me. "Now let me see your hands again."

Nervously I placed my hands on Aunty Peony's smooth-skinned, long-fingered ones. She flipped, squeezed, kneaded, and bent my hands as if they were two slabs of pork for New Year's dinner. Her hands kept harassing mine for several moments until a relaxed expression bloomed on her face.

"Good. Your bones are perfect for doing the different stitches and complicated patterns."

As I was about to thank her for this compliment, she spoke again. "Wait, Spring Swallow, don't be happy too early." She looked at me with her penetrating eyes. "Do your hands sweat?"

"No, Aunty Peony."

"Good. But don't lie to me. If I find out later that they do, you'll have no place here. Sweaty hands, no matter how pretty and skillful, cannot embroider. The threads will stick to them so they can't move smoothly. And the work will be stained and ruined."

Some silence passed before she threw me another harsh question. "You're not color-blind, are you? Can you tell the difference between colors?"

Before I had a chance to answer, she signaled Leilei to hand her a small basket filled with threads.

"Tell me quickly all the different colors."

I did. There were many subtle shadings of one color, but since I could tell the difference between the major colors, I passed Aunty's test.

"Good. But besides colors, you also have to learn the different threads like silk, cotton, fleece, gold, silver. Now, watch me."

She randomly pulled out one thread, then used her thumbs and index fingers to split it into four, eight, sixteen, then thirty-two miniscule filaments. My eyes protruded and my jaw dropped. It was like magic; how could she do that?

"See how my hands can produce rainbows thin as hairs?"

I nodded eagerly. "Indeed. It's beautiful, Aunty Peony."

Some silence passed, and she asked, "Can you do housework?"

It was a strange question because doing housework doesn't require much brains or even good eyesight. But I understood that the question was actually a statement telling me that I was not going to live here and consume their food for free.

So I nodded again. "No problem, Aunty Peony. Before I was wedded to my ghost husband, I waited on my aunt and my other relatives including my Popo."

"All right, but if you don't prove yourself worthy to be my student, you'll still have to leave."

My heart skipped a beat. "Then where would I go?"

"I can send you back."

"Oh, no, please, Aunty Peony, please don't!"

"Then you better work hard. Normally a student has to wait on me at least six months before I'll decide if I accept her. But since I just got a big order and we have to hurry, I'll shorten your trial period to one month."

She paused to clear her throat. "You're lucky. Before I was accepted by my teacher, I had to live with her and do all her errands for a whole year. But no one who is lazy and sloppy stays in this house, you understand?"

"Of course I do, Aunty Peony."

"All right, now let's start," she said, looking at Purple.

Purple immediately poured a cup of hot tea and handed it to me. "Spring Swallow, offer this tea respectfully with two hands to Aunty Peony and declare that you're willing to be her student and obey her."

Gingerly I lifted the cup to my head and handed it to her with both hands. "Aunty Peony, I, Spring Swallow, respectfully offer you this tea. Please accept me as your student."

She cast me a stern glance, then took a sip and nodded acknowledgment.

Next Purple handed me my wedding gown so I could offer it to Aunty as a token of my sincerity. Aunty accepted it, then passed it to Leilei.

"When a teacher accepts a disciple, no matter how poor the student is, her family has to offer the teacher at least five bags of rice. Spring Swallow, you're lucky that I exempt you from this."

Before I could say thank you, she was again speaking. "Now, I'm afraid we will have to feed you with many more than five bags of rice, ha!"

Upon hearing this joke, we all giggled, dissipating the tension that had been as tight as the bun on her head.

She went on. "If you had rich parents, they would hold a banquet with all the prominent local families, who would witness the ceremony. The teacher would be given sixty dollars as a deposit."

This time no one responded, because none of us could imagine this much wealth. Now Aunty Peony took out from her top a red lucky money envelope and handed it to me.

I took it with both hands, and she said, "All right, now you are officially my student. So from now on you have to do exactly what I say and never talk back or ask silly questions. You understand?"

Purple whispered to me, "Just say 'yes' or 'I understand' to everything Aunty asks."

So, like a parrot, I uttered, "Yes, I understand."

Aunty went on. "If you try to run away, say anything disrespectful about me, or work for another embroiderer, you'll not only be kicked out, your name will be forever disgraced and no other embroiderer will take you on."

"Yes, I understand."

"Do you understand that you cannot leak any secrets of our embroidery techniques?"

"Yes, I understand." I was getting tired of uttering this over and over.

"Do you understand that all the money made in this household belongs to me, and only I decide how much to give you?"

"Yes, I understand."

I was not happy to hear this, but her next demand jolted me awake. "Do you know that you can never be with a man or marry?"

This time I didn't say "yes" but asked instead, "Hmm . . . Aunty Peony, what do you mean?"

She pointed to all the other girls' hair. "See that we don't let our hair down like a loose woman, but either pull it up into a bun or braid it into pigtails?"

I nodded.

"This is a vow that we'll live a celibate life and never marry. You understand?"

"But, why . . ."

I'd run away from my village to escape a marriage to a dead man, but that didn't mean someday I didn't want to marry a good man and have children. Isn't this all women's heavenly duty? Now I wondered if my situation here was much better than my old one. Not to be a ghost's wife, but to be no man's wife. To work as an embroidery slave for the rest of my life. Suddenly, having found a roof over my head and the chance to learn embroidery didn't seem so wonderful.

Aunty went on. "Because a virgin's mind and body are pure so she is not distracted by improper thoughts. Besides," Aunty's eyes suddenly turned dreamy, "embroidery is our love. Even when the Sky is empty and the Earth old, this love never dies."

Before I had a chance to respond, she seemed to come back to reality, asking sharply, "I don't have time to waste; yes or no?"

"Yes, I understand, Aunty Peony."

"Good."

"Last question—can you read and write?"

"Yes, Aunty Peony." I'd already told her about this earlier. But I guessed she still didn't trust me. But why should she?

"Good."

Purple said to me in a low voice, "Now prostrate three times to Aunty Peony and the portrait of her teacher, now your grand-teacher."

Not only did I kowtow, I deliberately knocked my head hard on the floor to prove my sincerity. Whatever my doubts, I needed to be housed and fed.

When finished, I looked up at the portrait of the woman who was supposedly my grand-teacher and felt a shudder. Who was this dignified-looking, but long-dead woman with her hair pulled up as tight as a drawn bowstring? She stared down at me, as if mocking my naïveté and preparing to scold me for anything I deserved to be scolded for.

Purple handed me another cup of tea, and Aunty said, "Now offer this to my deceased teacher, your grand-teacher. After that, the ceremony will be over."

"Yes, I understand."

When the girls giggled, I realized I'd repeated this even when I wasn't required to. Even Aunty smiled, for the first time.

The next morning, I was awakened by a cock's crowing. Hearing the bird brought chills to my spine as I remembered my substitute groom and my escape, which still seemed to me like a dream—or a nightmare. Everything had happened so fast it seemed unreal. Were the villagers already trying to track me down to drag me back to a life of celibacy and drudgery as a half ghost? Could I really be starting a new life as an aspiring embroiderer? Or would this new life turn into another nightmare? All I could do was wait and see.

After a simple, yet hearty breakfast of rice soup, pickled radish, and salted fish, Purple, Leilei, and Little Doll all left for the nearby village to shop and have fun. But I was to stay with Aunty Peony.

I was hoping she'd tell me something about herself, the other girls, and their business with Heavenly Phoenix in Peking. But instead, with a firm voice and serious expression, she said, "Today is your first lesson; that's why I sent the girls away—so we would not be disturbed."

She asked me to sit by the same large wooden table, where the plates had been cleared and replaced with embroidery paraphernalia. Then she went upstairs to her room and returned holding an elongated, embroidered yellow box. The way she held it made me think the object inside must be of great value.

She set the box on the table, then sat down beside me. "Let's get started."

Even though she'd told me during the *baishi* ceremony that I shouldn't talk back or ask silly questions, I couldn't help but ask, "Aunty Peony, why are we in such a hurry?"

She cast me an annoyed look as if I was a nuisance like burnt rice sticking on the bottom of a cooking pot.

"All right, Spring Swallow, the company Heavenly Phoenix in Peking has commissioned us to do a very large piece of embroidery. If you learn fast and practice hard, you may be able to help out by embroidering easy things like leaves, branches, birds' feet, animals' whiskers."

She paused to inhale, then spoke as if she were going to divulge Heaven's greatest secret to the most insignificant person on Earth. "The commission is to embroider the famous painting *Along the River during the Qingming Festival.* I have already brushed this famous painting onto separate pieces of silk. We've started but have only a little more than a year left to meet the deadline. I'm embroidering the important parts while Purple and Leilei help with the smaller parts. Though a very complex painting, if you prove yourself to be worthy of my teaching, I'll let you be part of this project."

Not completely understanding what she was talking about, I asked, "What's *Along the River during the Qingming Festival?*"

She shook her head and the silver butterfly she used to hold her bun seemed about to take flight.

"Ignorant girl. Didn't your family educate you?"

"My aunt who raised me never bothered to teach me anything. She even refused to pay for my schooling when—"

"All right, enough. I have no time to hear about a girl's education, or lack of education."

She thought for a while. "Then how come you can read and write?"

"Later I attended a free school at a Western church. Besides reading and writing, the teacher there also taught me many other things." I smiled confidently. "Including English, you know those complicated letters, like a chicken's intestines."

"How come the teacher knew English?" Aunty's elongated eyes were now glittering with curiosity.

"Because Father Edwin is an American missionary, a foreign ghost." I smiled. "But he liked to think of himself as our father. So we all called him Father Edwin."

"Is that so? Before you came, even though I had only three girls here, I felt exhausted all the time having to teach and supervise them. So this Father Edwin is either really nice or very demanding."

"Father Edwin is very nice," I said emphatically, thinking of my missionary teacher and feeling nostalgic.

Now Aunty Peony looked at me admiringly. "Good for you, Spring Swallow. So you know how to read those curvy, dancing chicken's intestines?"

I nodded proudly.

"Let me hear you say a few words."

I tried to remember, then, "Ho do u do?"

To my surprise, my dignified, serious-faced teacher suddenly giggled like a teenager. "Oh my, it sounds so strange, what does it mean?"

"It means, 'Are you all right?' "

"All right? Oh, yes, I'm all right. What else?"

"Gud nite, gud dai, gud efan ning."

"Oh, Heaven, this sounds so complicated! What do these mean?" My teacher was laughing.

"It means have a nice night, a nice day, and a nice evening."

She tried to say these words. "Guuu ... d nite, guuud dai, guuud efunning ... hahahaha!"

She looked so much prettier and happier when her guard was down and she laughed so heartily. Especially about chicken's intestines, which cannot even be eaten. Then why didn't she laugh more? Why did she look sad and so serious all the time? She must have secrets that no one knew, not even the girls who lived here. Perhaps those secrets were upstairs in her own room where no one was allowed in. Or buried deep in her heart from her life a long time ago.

But her cheerfulness was short-lived. In a moment, she had resumed her dignified, authoritative look. Maybe now she regretted having laughed and said those silly words in front of a student. With her delicate, slim-fingered hands, she opened the elongated box and took out scrolls of silk. Carefully, she laid them on the table one by one.

"These scrolls are my copy of the famous painting by Zhang Zeduan, done a thousand years ago. It is enormous—about eighteen feet long, filled with scenes of people's lives in the city of Kaifeng."

She turned to cast me another suspicious look. "You know about the Qingming Festival, don't you?"

"Yes." How could I not, since my parents were dead. "It's the day when we go to sweep our ancestors' graves and pay our respects."

"Correct. But this painting is not sad, but happy—all sorts of people out and enjoying different activities."

Aunty Peony explained that *Along the River during the Qingming Festival* was a masterpiece because of its composition, with the famous Rainbow Bridge above a rushing river and the depiction of both city and countryside. She kept reiterating how beautiful and famous this work was, and how lucky I would be if she allowed me to help her work on it.

"Look at the beginning—here are farmers, pig herders, and goats. Do you feel the serene atmosphere?"

I nodded. Yes, it was calm but also boring, though, of course, I was not going to say that.

Continuing to unroll the silk, she next pointed to the city scenes. "Here in the busy capital are all sorts of people—peddlers, jugglers, fortune-tellers, seers, doctors, innkeepers, carpenters, government officials. . . . The peddlers are selling all kinds of things: wine, grain, medicine, paintings, fabrics, bows and arrows, musical instruments, gold and silver ornaments, acupuncture needles. . . . Name a business and you can find it in this painting."

When Aunty paused to sip her tea, I looked at her in a new light. Besides being elegant, she was also learned, a scholar, just like Father Edwin. Suddenly I felt proud to be the student of this erudite woman.

She went on. "I've counted everything in this painting. There are eight hundred and fourteen people, sixty-odd animals, twenty-eight boats, thirty-something buildings, nine sedan chairs, and one hundred and seventy trees."

Wah, it was very impressive. But didn't she have more important things to do with her time than count everything?

As if she'd already guessed what I thought, she said, "I spent several weeks studying this painting so I can do a perfect job. Mind you, our embroidered version has to be exactly the same as the painting in terms of size, color, and every other nuance. An excellent embroiderer must also be a good painter and calligrapher. So besides embroidery, I'll also teach you painting and calligraphy."

I kept my mouth shut and my ears open to absorb every sliver of knowledge that came through my teacher's lips. Though I was surprised and happy that she would teach me these things, I was also suspicious. Why was she so generous in giving free lessons to a stranger—was it just so she could work me to death in exchange? I hoped that she was just generous to her students, like Father Edwin.

Aunty Peony went on to tell me that embroiderers should be good at painting and calligraphy because the rich were willing to pay good money for embroidered versions of their expensive art collections.

"The embroidery of *Along the River* will be entered in a contest and, if it wins, is to be presented as a gift to an important American official scheduled to visit Peking next year. There are several copies of this painting, but this will be the first embroidered version. With such an honor, there must be no mistakes.

"Listen, Spring Swallow"—she looked at me with her penetrating eyes—"I don't make mistakes and you shouldn't either if you want to stay under my roof."

Frightened, I emitted an emphatic "Yes!"

Seeming satisfied, Aunty Peony went on to describe the painting, her long fingers pointing out details—paupers begging, coolies loading cargoes, monks asking for alms, a guard watching his barrack, a man with two donkeys pulling a loaded cart. . . .

Now Aunty unrolled the silk to the middle part where there was a bridge above a rushing river. A boat loaded with people and cargo was about to crash into the bridge. People on the boat and on the bridge were shouting and gesturing frantically.

I couldn't help but exclaim, *"Wah!"* fearing that some of the people, or the goods they carried, would be knocked into the angry waves.

Aunty cast me a curious look. "Good. You have a strong reaction, which shows you might learn to appreciate art one day. Not many people have this quality."

"Thank you, Aunty Peony, for your praise."

She didn't respond but pointed to the bridge and the boat. "This is the climax of the whole painting—the boat with its high mast about to crash. See how clever the painter was to create such drama right in the middle of the painting?"

"Such a complicated painting! How can we embroider it, even in a year?" I blurted out.

Aunty cast me an annoyed look. "Listen, Spring Swallow, only lazy people give up. The great painter Qi Baishi said the secret of success is that he never put down his brush. If you want to be an excellent embroiderer, from today on you never put down your needle, you understand?"

"Of course, Aunty Peony, and from now on I'll never put down my needle."

She sipped her tea, then said, "Good. I think introducing you to the famous *Along the River during the Qingming Festival* is enough for our first lesson. Now go do whatever you want, then come back in the afternoon to fix me tea and give me a massage. Just sitting here talking to you has given me a sore back."

So massage was part of our teacher-and-pupil relationship. But who was I to question her?

4

Watching the World Below

During the break, Aunty Peony went up to her mysterious private room and I went outside the house. I wanted to practice my characters in the mud, since I dared not ask Aunty to give me either paper, brush, or ink, for she'd already given me a roof, clothes, and food. So I broke off a twig from an ancient tree and attempted to "write" on the ground. When finished, I looked over what I'd written: ghost husband, funerary wedding, escape, famous embroiderer. I wondered about "famous embroiderer." Was I predicting my own future or was I merely thinking about Aunty Peony?

While I was pondering this, a flock of chicks that had been chasing each other in the distance now ran straight through the mud and smeared "husband," "wedding," and "famous embroiderer," whoever she might be. "Bad chicks!" I screamed, but they'd already scurried to the other side of the courtyard, emitting a triumphant "quuiik, quuiik, quuiik" sound, as if mocking my not having the heart to wring their necks. I reminded myself that soon, instead of messing up my writing, they'd end up on my plate—preferably covered with sweet soy sauce.

In my mind, I continued to relish the future dish of chicken, first sprinkled with generous pinches of scallion, ginger, sea salt, then fried in sesame oil and rice wine. Once they were fried into a golden sheen, I hoped they would be served with tender sweet potato. Sucking back gobs of saliva, I ventured outside the court-yard, hoping to find a place where I could practice away from the irritating little chicks.

After my struggles to learn to read and write back in my old vil-lage, I wanted to be sure I did not forget anything I'd been taught. Sadly, Father Edwin was no longer around to teach me. I was used to "dirt calligraphy" because my aunt had refused to buy me brush and paper. Of course I believed that if I had asked Father Edwin, he'd be happy to buy me writing tools. But I didn't feel comfort-able asking. Because he'd already done so much for me, I didn't want him to think I was greedy.

So I'd either practice using a stick to scrape on the soil or, if I wanted to remember something very important, I'd "write" it by using a small stone to scrape it on the rocky outcropping of a nearby mountain. When I had more time and was in the mood, I'd also write down my thoughts and feelings. I loved doing this, but sometimes also feared that my writing might be seen by a stranger—it'd be very embarrassing if I was recognized.

That was how I'd learned to climb mountains. When there was something I didn't want anyone to see, I'd climb higher to write, then higher and higher still. As I climbed, the village seemed to re-cede and this made me happy. From a high altitude, the world and my old village didn't seem to be so bad and miserable after all. On the mountain I felt that my sadness and troubles had been left below.

My climbs became longer and longer until one day I was able to reach the top. Here I found myself face-to-face with a better, more expansive world. The air was purer and the view uplifting. But my happiness could not last because I would have to come back down, then return home. To comfort myself, I remembered the famous saying "The virtuous love mountains; the wise love the sea." So, I must be a good person without realizing it. But was I also wise? I hoped someday I would be. Perhaps Father Edwin and his omni-scient God knew.

Maybe the advantage of not having parents was that I could do what I liked. My aunt didn't care—as long as I did the housework. She never stopped me from mixing with the street kids and going anywhere I wanted. And I became notorious in the village as a "wild girl." I truly believed that even if I did not come home for days, she wouldn't even have noticed until the house needed cleaning. I usually went around with the boys because the girls were afraid to climb mountains, or even trees, let alone sneak into cemeteries in the middle of the night.

So, whenever I could, after I finished Father Edwin's classes, I'd tag along with the village boys for all sorts of adventures: swimming, catching fish, grabbing lake crabs with our bare hands. We'd pick fruit from rich people's gardens, then run away as fast as we could. Once we visited a cemetery at midnight, walking on tiptoe and talking in whispery voices like ghosts. But among all these activities, I liked mountain climbing best.

Although I sometimes went with the boys, I was happiest during solitary climbs. Not only did I like to inscribe my thoughts on the bare rocks, I'd even talk to the mountain, especially when I didn't know the characters I needed to express my feelings. Since the mountain was huge, I believed it could absorb whatever thoughts, emotions, and fantasies I poured into it. Sometimes I even thought it responded to what I said through rustling leaves and falling pebbles. I did not want to share my innermost thoughts with the boys lest they deem me crazy, though they were no more normal themselves.

Though a "wild girl," I never let my adventures keep me from my studies with Father Edwin. One time when Father Edwin saw me practicing my writing on the ground, he generously gave me paper, a brush, and ink, so I could brush the characters in the proper way. Though I did not know many characters, when I saw a bird fly over the sky or a tiny flower peek from between rocks, I had an urge to write a poem about them. I knew about poems from hearing Father Edwin recite them in class. I even read some old ones in the books in his library.

I felt very proud that I could recite some that Father Edwin had taught me. My favorite was "Silent Thoughts at Night," written by Du Fu a thousand years ago:

The moon shines brightly before my bed,
Like frost on the ground.
Lifting my head I see the bright moon,
Lowering my head I think of my home far away.

At first I thought that I, or anyone, could write something just as good. But when I told Father Edwin, he laughed heartily.

"Ah . . . my dear Spring Swallow. You're too young to understand the depth of feeling beneath this poem's simple words. To really understand poetry, you have to first experience life."

"What am I supposed to experience?"

He smiled indulgently. "Ah . . . little girl, you'll have lots of experiences when you grow up. I just hope that your experiences are good ones."

"But, Father, so far most have been bad . . . but not all bad since you've let me into your class."

He smiled, his blue eyes filled with kindness. "Don't worry too much and don't thank me, Little Spring Swallow. Thank God for His blessing and protection."

"Can I write a poem about God someday?"

He cast me a curious look. "Of course, anytime. But you must realize that anything you do is because of our almighty and merciful Lord!"

Even when I pee and shit and spit and pick my nose, then flick it at a stranger passing by on the street? Of course I did not say this because I feared that Father Edwin would be embarrassed and his God furious at my rudeness.

Since that conversation with Father Edwin, the urge to write poems felt like an itchy rash on my back—which I could not reach to scratch. But the itch had become so unbearable that I felt I'd go crazy if I couldn't write out my poems—which were manifestations of God, according to Father Edwin.

I particularly wanted to write a poem about how I felt when I climbed to the mountaintop. When I looked up there were flocks of birds—floating, circling, calling. To me the birds meant the freedom that I wanted. Then when I looked down, there were small flowers squeezing between the rocks, seeking a taste of the sun.

After thinking for a long time I finally succeeded in putting my thoughts into a poem, which I scratched on the mountainside. But no one was around to say if it was good or bad.

> Fly fly, little bird,
> Fly over the mountain
> Fly over the sea,
> Fly over the village,
> And when you're tired,
> Fly home!
>
> Come come, little flower,
> Leave your dark, rocky home,
> Come out to see the bright sun and the beautiful world!

I felt pretty happy about my little poem, and I imagined that the little birds and the little flowers felt the same. But then I also felt sad, because even if I could fly, where would I go and where could I come back to? Finally, I decided to give this poem to Father Edwin as a gift to thank him for teaching me. He seemed happy when he read it, but when I asked if it was good, his answer was, "It's an innocent girl's true heart expressing God's greatness."

Whatever that meant.

Suddenly my mind came back to my surroundings and I realized I'd already wandered quite a long way from my new home and was standing facing the mountain I had noticed the day I arrived. The sun was getting lower in the sky and I raised my hand to shade my eyes. The mountain towered imposingly against the sky. I wondered if anyone had ever climbed it or if I would be the first.

An hour later, I was already halfway up the mountain. Although the sun was warm and the breeze soothing, I decided not to climb farther because I had to return soon. I eagerly awaited the day when I could savor my ascent all the way to the top. So I sat on a rock to watch the sky above and the world below. The few clouds seemed to be enjoying themselves as they drifted by. They could resemble anything they wanted: a smiling face, bunches of cotton, a graceful dancer. But what I really envied was how they moved aimlessly, without a care in the world.

Way below me, Aunty's house resembled a tiny beetle, by itself beside my mountain. Far in the distance was the city of Soochow with green patches of garden. Closer, but still some distance from the house was a small village—I assumed it was the one Purple had told me where they did their shopping. Of course I could not see them, but I was pretty sure that the girls were enjoying themselves there now, haggling in the market, eating, and gossiping. Instead, I had to listen to Aunty's talk about some thousand-year-old painting that meant nothing to me.

I wondered, since their embroidery was in such demand, why didn't Aunty Peony and her girls live in the city? They didn't seem to be rich, for the house had no valuables that I could see. I was puzzled by this little community that had just taken me in. My new teacher, the coldly imposing Aunty Peony, was even more puzzling. Perhaps I could fish out something from Purple about her. After all, it was she who had taken pity on me and brought me into the strange household. Purple seemed both kind and smart. Leilei was maybe even smarter, but seemed touchy and jealous, while Little Doll was a child. What would my life be like here? I had no idea.

Feeling a little worried, I took a deep breath of the refreshing mountain air and stretched my limbs. For the moment I was happy to be far away from the smoke and dust of the world. However, I had to go back to fix tea and give Aunty a massage. But since I was here, I wanted to leave a mark. When I'd escaped I had taken a knife from Mean Aunt's kitchen in case I ran into bandits. Now I took out the knife and on a nearby rock with a smooth surface I inscribed:

> *Today embroiderer Spring Swallow is here*
> *on this mountain watching the world below.*

I mused about the word *embroiderer*. Was I really going to become one? Anyway, I felt happy looking at what I'd just written.

But it was time to go back.

❧ 5 ❧

First Lesson

When I arrived back home, Aunty Peony told me she'd already eaten, then gave me two vegetable buns for lunch. She didn't ask me where I'd been or why I'd taken so long. As soon as I finished eating, she went to lie on the long wooden bench and I began to knead her shoulders, back, arms, and legs. I didn't resent doing this, because I liked my teacher's slim body. I hoped someday that I'd be as elegant as she.

After the massage, she asked me to sit by the table with her. On it had been placed a big bamboo basket containing the embroidery tools. Next to the basket, batches of colorful threads hung from a rack. Amazed by their variety, I also felt a little intimidated, even dizzy. However, I was comforted by the sight of a maroon ceramic teapot, two matching cups, and a small plate of sugared plums.

"Drink as much tea as you like—so long as you don't have to frequently slip away to the washroom."

I immediately poured tea into the cups, then handed one to my teacher respectfully with both hands. She nodded, acknowledging my gesture.

After Aunty took a delicate sip, she went on. "I never serve snacks during lessons, because eating is distracting. But good tea refreshes and keeps you alert. To be a first-rate embroiderer, you need to focus with your whole being."

I pointed to the plums. "If we can't eat these, then why are they here?"

"When we finish the lesson."

After a brief silence, she spoke again. "Spring Swallow, since you already know a little about embroidery, I hope it'll make my teaching easier. But there are many rules my late teacher taught me and which my girls must also follow. Rule number one is, don't ask questions, just listen. Even if you want to disagree with me, keep it to yourself. I won't waste my time arguing—I'm much older and more learned than you. And I am always right."

She looked at me with her penetrating eyes to see my reaction. I nodded without saying anything—since that was what she wanted.

Despite her stern words, her voice was clear as a sonorous bell. "You must have heard the saying that an older person has eaten more salt than you have rice, and crossed more bridges than you have walked on paths?"

I nodded again to please her.

But she cast me a stern look. "Questions are a waste of both the teacher's and the student's time. And in this household, no time can be wasted. There is too much work to do. You understand?"

I nodded once again.

"Good. Then pay utmost attention to what I have to teach you. Not just about embroidery, but about life."

Life—what about it? Most of what I knew about life so far was misery. What about hers? Was she my rescuer, or user?

"All right, let me tell you a few rules concerning embroidering. Before you start, you have to bathe, brush your teeth, wash your hands, and sit silently to quiet your busy mind. Have you done all these things?"

"Yes, Aunty Peony, and thank you for reminding me!"

"Good. I've shown you my drawing of the famous painting *Along the River during the Qingming Festival*. Now I'll explain *Sooxiu*, our school of embroidery. Have you heard of the *Soo* embroidery before?"

"I only know that it's famous; other than that, not much," I replied, feeling ashamed and ignorant. Not only had she consumed more rice and crossed more bridges than I, she also knew much more, seemingly about everything. Now I thought maybe she was even smarter and more knowledgeable than Father Edwin. But how could this be possible? Father Edwin was the son of an all-knowing God!

"Then I assume you also don't know much about China's four major schools of embroidery?"

"I'm afraid not, Aunty Peony." I couldn't even raise my eyes to meet her cleaver-sharp ones.

She sipped more tea and went on. "All right. The best embroideries in China are from Soo, Xiang, Shu, and Yue provinces. Our Soochow school is famous for portraying nature—flowers, birds, and animals. *Xiang* embroidery of Hunan is unique for its black, white, and gray coloration."

I was quickly realizing that embroidery was quite a bit more complicated than I had imagined.

Aunty Peony set down her tea cup and continued in her authoritative tone. "*Xiang* style emphasizes on light and shade, full and empty, *yin* and *yang*. *Shu* embroiderers of Sichuan like to portray flowers, birds, insects, and fish. *Yue* embroidery from Guangdong uses bright colors and light and shade, like Western paintings.

"Our school, *Soo,* is the oldest. During the Spring and Autumn era twenty-five hundred years ago, high officials wore our embroidered robes to meet with foreign ambassadors. In the Ming dynasty, there was a saying, "In Soochow, every woman raises silk worms; every girl embroiders."

She smiled proudly, her voice slightly rising. "Our *Soo* school is famous for the most refined needlework, stitching, and delicate coloration. When we embroider painting and calligraphy, we follow the principle that 'One brushstroke, one thousand threads.' "

Now Aunty picked up bunches of threads, caressing them as she would a baby. "This rainbow—in our hands it becomes magic. Each color has its own meaning. Black is mystery, red happiness, yellow power, and blue nobility. Only emperors were allowed to wear yellow and blue."

Before I had a chance to express admiration, Aunty went on.

"Our *Soo* embroidery has more than forty different stitches and hundreds of colors—"

"Hundreds?!"

She cast me a disapproving look but didn't scold me for interrupting her. I thought it was because she was very happy to show off her knowledge and boast about her school's unique style.

"All right, someday I will tell you more about the other different styles of embroidery. Now we will start to do some real work."

Instead of picking up the embroidery frame and needle, Aunty motioned for me to stand up and face Guan Yin on the altar.

"Before we start the lesson, we have to make an offering."

Aunty went on to tell me that by paying our respects to her teacher, my grand-teacher, and to the Goddess of Compassion, our hands would be guided to complete the work without mishap.

"Spirits and gods are everywhere watching us, so we shouldn't neglect any of them. We offer tea and food, even suckling pigs to our special gods. You don't want them angry at you."

After we had lit incense, offered tea, and bowed three times to the altar, we sat back down.

"Now while I sew, watch me, especially my wrists and fingers. Also pay attention to how I handle the needle and threads. Even when I'm not explaining, just keep watching. That's how you learn."

Aunty Peony selected a small piece of pale turquoise fabric, then carefully sorted through the bundle of threads, picking out a pale pink one. In a single motion she slipped it through the eye of a slender needle and began to stitch. Seemingly oblivious of my presence, she moved her hand deftly and a lotus flower blossomed on the fabric. As her hands continued their magic, other flowers bloomed in a proliferation of colors and shadings. The translucent blossoms looked as fresh as if they were covered with dew.

Mesmerized by her hands, I forced myself to look up at her face. Embroidering, she seemed completely transformed. Now, instead of looking stern and sad, she looked animated, even cheerful. It was as if she was no longer living in this world, but in a happier one filled with beauty and harmony.

She paused to look up at me from her work. "Another of our maxims is, 'A natural flower gives off a sweet scent for only a few days, but an embroidered one for hundreds of years.' That's how good and skillful an embroiderer must be. You understand?"

I nodded.

"This is just the beginning, Spring Swallow. Much work lies ahead before you can be worthy of learning my secrets of a thousand beauties."

I was tempted, but too intimidated, to ask about her secrets.

She said, "Now, go wash your hands again, then breathe deeply to quiet your mind. After that, you can—"

"Sew my first stitch?" I felt ecstatic to be finally able to start embroidering.

But my ecstasy was short-lived.

Aunty snickered. "Silly girl, you think you can do that in your first lesson? I mean grind your first needle."

She rose from the table and returned with a small cloth bag and an ink stone containing a few drops of water. From the bag she extracted a bundle of needles.

"All right, now grind all these needles to a sharp point like this one," she said, holding up the very thin one she'd just used.

"But, Aunty . . ."

"What?"

"I thought I'm supposed to learn embroidery, not grinding needles."

She swung her head back and snorted. "Ha! You think it's that easy? Everyone, even in the palace, has to grind needles first. After you have sharpened enough needles, then you can learn how to split the threads."

She thought for a while and spoke again. "Grinding also helps you quiet your mind before you start to embroider. All right, that's the lesson for today." She rubbed her eyes and hands. "Now get started on the needles. If you expect to stay here, you have to make yourself useful."

As I picked up the first needle, I glanced at the plate of sugared plums. But Aunty didn't seem to get my hint, or she didn't want to.

I had no choice but to swallow my saliva to keep it from dripping onto her exquisite embroidery.

‍6‍

An Invisible Mountain Friend

The following weeks went by slowly because Aunty Peony wouldn't even let me stitch a cat's whiskers or a dog's eyelashes. Every day it was needles and more needles. Finally, in the beginning of the second month, she allowed that my needles were almost up to her standard, and though I was unworthy, she would begin to teach me. But she also made it clear that in the event that I did not succeed at my lessons, if she did not simply kick me out of the house, she'd make me help Little Doll with the cooking and cleaning.

In between embroidery lessons, I had to try to get along with Aunty Peony and the girls. Aunty was the teacher, master, and absolute authority in the house, so if I listened attentively, acted submissively, practiced hard, and did as I was told, she'd probably keep me. Purple was older than me and quite easygoing, so all I needed to do was act friendly and appreciative. Little Doll was a child of ten and, as Aunty said, "a little slow," and so was easy to deal with. Leilei, however, seemed to take a dislike to me from the beginning. Though beautiful and talented, she was also bitter, which made her cold and aloof as if she was better than us and merited a much brighter future.

Whenever Aunty could not overhear, she'd say things like,

"Someday I'll leave this house and become rich and famous, while all of you are stuck here forever!"

One time I foolishly asked, "But how are you going to become famous?" I hoped she could tell me how so I also could escape to find fame and fortune.

"Sorry, Spring Swallow," she said, casting me a condescending look, "you'll never be anybody."

"Why not?"

"Why don't you wait and see what Aunty says about your embroidery, eh?"

Finally, after observing me grinding needles for more than a month, Aunty Peony deemed me hardworking and responsible enough to actually start teaching me embroidery. I was ready to show everyone that I was not as worthless as Leilei thought.

After my daily lesson, I was expected to practice for another five or six hours a day. First I was taught how to split one thread into many miniscule ones because only fine fibers can produce subtle effects.

Aunty Peony told me over and over, "You have to divide the threads until they are thinner than your hair."

Another challenge was being able to remember the subtle differences between color gradations. It was not easy, but I did my best to absorb everything she was willing to teach.

Finally, five months had passed and I was allowed to embroider simple items like hats, slippers, and children's stomach covers. My work, together with Little Doll's, was sent off to Heavenly Phoenix in Peking to be sold. We were given these undemanding jobs so the others could devote themselves to what Aunty planned as her masterpiece, *Along the River during the Qingming Festival*. However, Aunty left no doubt that she was the lead embroiderer and Purple and Leilei merely her helpers. So my two sisters, besides *Along the River*, still had to take time to embroider small items to bring in money.

I felt flattered that after only a few months my embroidery was good enough that people would pay for it. However, I wished I could work on the more ambitious scroll and so I practiced very hard. After I was done with the required work for the day, I also practiced painting and calligraphy. I did this in the hope of advancing myself, but also because there was really nothing else to do.

Aunty had some rubbings of the thick-stroked, big character steles of the Northern Wei dynasty. I copied these for enjoyment, but also because Aunty told me that writing big characters would help protect my eyes from the damaging effects of straining them while embroidering. However, no matter how hard I worked, how good my work looked to me, and even though Aunty praised my progress, I was not allowed to contribute so much as one stitch to *Along the River.*

When I asked my teacher when I would be ready, she'd say, "Not yet, Spring Swallow."

"May I ask why?"

"Because you were too old when you started."

"Old?" I couldn't believe what I'd heard. "But, Aunty Peony, I'm only seventeen and I had lessons before—"

"Your so-called lessons were barely better than nothing. Anyway, I started when I was eight. Seventeen is pretty old to acquire a skill like this." She looked at me directly. "Have you heard of *tongzi gong?*" It meant "begin as a little child," but before I had a chance to consider this, she was already explaining. "For any skill, it's best to learn when you are three or four, because children do not know the distractions of the adult world. And they have all the time in the world."

"But how can a little child concentrate?"

She chuckled. "Simple. If they don't, their teacher will starve them or beat them till their bottoms blossom. If they are too stupid to learn, they'll be sent back to their parents or get sold to someone else."

The corners of her lips seemed to lift a little. "But even I have to admit that you've made a good start, Spring Swallow."

I nodded emphatically.

She leaned close to me, and whispered, "That's why I don't spend much time teaching Little Doll; she's too stupid."

I was shocked by this cruel remark and could not think of any reply. I wondered how she talked about me behind my back. Although Aunty often said that Little Doll was slow and talentless, she still taught her to embroider simple items such as small purses, handkerchiefs, fan cases. . . . This way, Little Doll could feel good about herself and bring in pocket money by selling them in our neighboring village.

Aunty cast me a serious look and went on. "Even when I praise you, don't be full of yourself, you understand?"

I had no choice but to nod.

"Good . . . don't forget that you are still a beginner. Here's a story you should listen closely to. Wang Xianzhi, son of the most famous calligrapher Wang Xizhi, thought he could be as good as his father, maybe even better. So Xianzhi practiced very hard, wearing out countless brushes and using so much water to grind ink that he dried up the family's well. One day, Xianzhi finally finished a piece of calligraphy to his complete satisfaction. Happily he took his work to his father and expected accolades.

"However, after the father looked at the son's work, instead of exclaiming in praise, he remained uncharacteristically silent. Minutes passed before the father picked up his brush and painted a dot at the edge of Xianzhi's calligraphy. Then he said, 'Son, take this to your mother and see what she thinks.'

"The mother, after carefully examining her son's calligraphy, pointed to the dot, and said, 'Son, this dot is the only good thing in the whole piece.' Of course, this was the dot placed by his father."

I knew immediately what Aunty was trying to tell me with this story: "First, don't ever think you can surpass me. Second, it'll take long, bitter practice to even begin to master this skill."

Putting the second principle into action, she said, "All right, enough talking, now back to work."

I noticed for a long time that when Aunty Peony was not teaching me or embroidering, she seemed to slip into a state of melancholy. She'd either stare at her teacher's portrait on the altar or lock herself in her room upstairs, shutting out us and the rest of the world. Curious as I was to know what was inside her room and what she did there, I could not risk sneaking a look.

The four of us—Purple, Leilei, Little Doll, and I—each had a room of our own on the ground floor. Since I was the newcomer, I was given the smallest room, really just a closet. Aunty let us have our own room not because she was nice, but because she knew that if we shared a room we would pass the night snacking, gossiping, and laughing, leaving us too tired to work well the next morning. Of course, sometimes Purple and I would sneak out to the court-yard to talk during the night, but we had to keep it quiet so as not to wake Aunty.

During the day, Aunty Peony, Purple, and Leilei would embroi-der together on *Along the River* mounted on a long wooden frame. Aunty would work on the difficult—and interesting—parts while Purple and Leilei did the background, trees, minor figures, and whatever else was needed to fill up the space.

To better concentrate, sometimes Aunty would work on the most complicated sections upstairs in her room. I very much wanted to see her at work by herself, but none of us was ever invited. Only Little Doll was permitted into her private sanctum to clean it. No doubt she felt that the child did not interfere with her privacy. Curi-ously, neither Purple nor Leilei showed any interest in sneaking into Aunty's room—or maybe they already had but didn't tell anyone.

One time I asked Purple about Aunty's room, but she looked alarmed and warned me, "Spring Swallow, don't even think about this."

"Why . . . ?"

"Maybe you'd find out something you'd rather not know."

Seconds passed and I asked, "Sister Purple, did you ever go up there?"

She cast me a disapproving look. "Why are you so nosy?"

"Aren't you curious?"

"Spring Swallow"—she sighed heavily—"from now on, instead of thinking about going upstairs, you should stay in your room and work."

So, instead of going up to Aunty's taboo room, I went out and up the mountain. I didn't go there often because most days, after the hectic lessons and endless practice, I'd be so exhausted that the place I wanted to go was not the tall mountain, but my wobbly cot.

Aunty seemed to have too much on her mind to care what I did during my spare time. Though she never asked, sometimes I won-dered if she suspected that despite my oath of celibacy, I was going out to see a man. But I was sure she would be able to detect a man's smell on me. However, I had no man to meet and no interest. I hadn't overcome my fear and disgust at marrying a ghost. I wondered, though, what it would be like to be with a living man.

When I went up to the mountain, I'd wander around and reminisce about my mountain-climbing days with the village boys. But I had a special place I would go to with a large, flat rock where I would scratch Aunty's teachings onto the mountain walls. Despite her cold manner, Aunty was an excellent teacher—knowledgeable, meticulous, patient. What she taught me was so valuable that I wanted to write down as much as I could, in case I forgot. Aunty did give me a brush and paper but was very stingy with it and read everything I wrote. I knew she would not want me to record her teachings lest someone outside our group learn her secrets of a thousand beauties. I suspected one reason she kept such a close watch on us was so that no one could leave for higher pay somewhere else.

But, of course, Aunty would never suspect that on my walks I would climb the mountain and inscribe on the rocks some of the embroidery patterns that I'd learned. I'd also record some of the things that happened to me and what I thought about them. I used the small knife I had taken from Mean Aunt's kitchen and used it to inscribe the rocks. Making the scratches was hard, but so was everything else in my life.

I was lucky that this mountain was close enough to the house that I could walk here when I had a little free time. Although I felt happy to come here alone, I also wondered why there were never any other hikers. There was nothing special on my little mountain, so probably no one else was interested. Why come all the way here where there was no benefit? Maybe the reason Aunty had her house nearby was just because hardly anyone ever came here. Purple had said that Aunty wanted to be left alone. Or maybe, like me, she didn't want to be found. If my suspicion was correct, then what was Aunty escaping from? Maybe someday I'd find out, but for now I would concentrate on absorbing what she had to teach me.

One day when I was on the mountaintop and was about to

write, I was startled to discover that someone had written something next to my writing.

> Good day miss,
> Sorry to learn about your unhappiness. Maybe
> I can help you.
> Your calligraphy is very refined, so you
> must be from an educated family and of good
> character. I really want to know more about you.
> You have a hard climb to write your thoughts
> up here. And I don't understand your pictures.
> Though I am a stranger, I wonder about you.
> What do you do? Are you a student? Married?
> I hope you will answer me, but if not, I won't
> write on your rock again. Although we've never
> met, I am lucky that I had the chance to read
> about you.
>
> Shen Feng,
> A fellow lover of mountains

The writer was almost certainly a man, judging by his given name, *Feng,* which means "mountain peak."

This message from a man I had never met shook me up. It seemed to me now that no place is completely private and no secrets can be kept forever! Who was this Shen Feng, and what was he doing up here in this remote place? Although my mind was filled with suspicion, I could not help but admire his elegant calligraphy. But why did he leave a message for me? Could my own scratched characters attract a man's attention, when before the only man I could attract was a dead one?

I reminded myself of Aunty's admonition of not getting close to men and our vow of celibacy. I shuddered. Were all the women in our little group really prepared to die as husbandless old maids? Was I headed for a lonely old age with no children or grandchildren? Purple was the nicest of the group; was she really willing to give up the chance to have a family of her own? Even if I asked her, she might not tell me the truth. And Leilei, who was defiant, but also flirtatious? Anyway, she didn't really talk to anyone but her mighty boss, Aunty Peony.

I read the message again and again and felt fearful, but fascinated. If I responded, what would happen to me? But I would never know unless I answered him. So with an unsteady hand I took out my knife to inscribe.

> Dear Mr. Shen Feng,
> I'd thought no one but me would climb this mountain in the middle of nowhere, let alone read my humble writings and reply to me. I am nobody in particular. Someday I hope to be a skilled embroiderer.
> Wish me good luck.
>
> Spring Swallow,
> On the no-name mountain

During my descent, my heart pounded and my cheeks were hot as a wok. I'd just left a message for a man, a total stranger! Now I was happy because my mountain writing actually had a reader. But then worry seized me, since I had also inscribed some of Aunty's embroidery patterns. Would this Shen Feng copy them—or even sell them to other embroiderers? If Aunty found out, she'd definitely kick me out of her house. From now on I would hide my copies of the embroidery patterns—I had found a cave almost invisible behind a thick tangle of bushes.

But this Shen Feng seemed pretty curious, so maybe he would discover the cave.

7

More Lessons

A week passed. I dared not go back up the mountain because I'd be scared if Shen Feng had written a reply, but disappointed if he hadn't. Anyway, the weather had turned cold and so I was reluctant to return to the mountain.

The whole thing was very tense for me. I hadn't even met this mountain friend—what if he was not young and handsome as I imagined, but old and nasty? Just reading this stranger's words I felt like I was betraying Aunty Peony. I felt both excited and afraid that she would notice.

Though the days passed monotonously with lessons and practice, Shen Feng's words echoed in my mind over and over. I had to force myself to concentrate since I was at last being taught more difficult subjects such as birds and animals.

During a lesson, Aunty Peony asked, "Spring Swallow, what makes an animal come alive in an embroidery?"

"Their eyes." I knew the phrase "Eyes are the windows of the soul." But I wasn't sure animals have souls, or how to show them if they did.

"Good. Besides eyes, what makes long-haired animals like lions and horses come alive?"

"Their hair."

"Correct. Spring Swallow, you are smarter than I thought."

I smiled proudly.

But she responded with a disapproving look. "That doesn't mean you'll be good enough to work on *Along the River.*"

Her words made me feel as if I'd been splashed with chilled water.

"To embroider hair, animal or human, we have to use threads of different tone gradations."

I listened attentively, then asked, "Aunty Peony, what about our hair, since it's all black?"

She looked at me as if to ask, "How come you suddenly turned so stupid?"

"Under different light black has many gradations. Sometimes there are white reflections. That's why we need so many different colors. And that's why once in a while I need to go to Peking to stock up."

"*Wah,* can I go there someday?"

"Stop dreaming and let's continue." She rubbed her eyes for seconds before she resumed talking. "It can take up to twenty different color shades just for hair."

"Twenty! Can people really tell the difference?"

"Even if they can't tell the difference, we still have to do a good job. We are artists, after all. You understand?"

"Of course, Aunty Peony." But I was wondering why it had to be so complicated.

"Even if people don't notice the separate colors, they will sense the overall effect and feel happy. That's what makes it art."

"Yes, Aunty Peony."

"Now, watch carefully—I am going to use the 'wandering' stitch to show the mane of a galloping horse."

Again, I was completely fascinated by her fleeting finger movements as traceless as her stitches. As she worked, the horse came alive, with its mane flowing freely in the "wind." I wondered if I could ever learn to create something so perfect.

"Aunty Peony, how do you do that?"

"You need to learn the needle of no-needle, the skill of no-skill."

This did not help me understand at all.

"When you are really good, you don't need to follow any rule—that's the skill of no-skill . . . understand?"

Of course I had no idea what this meant, but I kept silent.

She went on. "Art has to have a pulse."

"Aunty Peony," I said, now that I had a glimmering of what she meant, "do you mean there's a spirit dwelling in the picture?"

"Hmm . . ." She cast me a curious look. "Yes, a masterpiece does possess something alive."

"What is this 'something alive'?"

She thought for a while. "I'd say that you can see someone's soul through it."

"*Wah,* isn't that scary?"

"Great art inspires fear."

I wondered about this fear. Was it why I was afraid of Aunty?

She continued. "All right, I've shown you the wandering needle."

"Can I learn that?"

"Maybe you can try. But you won't be able to do it properly until you have many months and years of training and bitter practice behind you, like me."

She raised her hands. "And as embroiderers, we have to protect our most important assets—our hands."

"They're beautiful, Aunty Peony."

"You think so? But before I became a great embroiderer they were even more so."

She waved her hands this way and that like a leisurely swimming fish or a lotus swaying gently in the breeze.

"It is said that 'embroidering is like spring wind blowing through the ten fingers.' And, 'When the needles fly, the threads run.' When an embroiderer is truly skilled, when you see her work, you can feel the gentle spring breeze."

Watching Aunty's running threads and flying needles was like watching a magician snatch a rabbit from thin air. I had seen her do it, but it still seemed impossible.

As if reading my mind, she said, "From now on I'll put three long sticks of incense on your table to help you keep time. You should not stop working until all the sticks are burnt. You understand?"

I nodded and she went on. "We embroiderers have a saying, 'Eyes focusing on nose, nose focusing on heart, heart focusing on hands.'"

It sounded like more gibberish, but I nodded obediently.

"Concentration is the first step. . . ."

"Yes, Aunty."

"Every stitch must carry an emperor's or a nobleman's heavenly power. That is the way to the secret of embroidery's thousand beauties."

My mind was wandering as I repeated, "Yes, Aunty," until I imagined I might turn into a parrot.

From that day on, I strictly followed Aunty's schedule of working until all three long incense sticks had finished burning. Sometimes I worked so long that my fingers swelled up and bled, and I was developing calluses on my fingertips. This was a great dilemma. I needed to practice long hours, but if I damaged my fingers I would have no future as an embroiderer. So, after I was done for the day, I would soak my hands in warm water mixed with medicinal herbs, then put on lotion concocted with fragrant oil. When I did chores like cleaning the table or taking out garbage, I wore cotton gloves.

Despite the long hours and the pain in my hands, I became more and more enchanted by the art of embroidery. And I was beginning to understand that Aunty was not only teaching me a skill but also about a way of life. There seemed always to be more to learn, not only the many colors of threads but their materials: silk, cotton, wool, fleece, silver, and gold. And many different ways to use the needle: not only parallel, crossing, slanting, braiding, but also wandering, hiding, jabbing, even nagging. . . . And these had to be properly combined. Aunty emphasized that whenever a new stitch is laid down, it should be hidden inside a previous one so the individual stitches would not show.

Aunty Peony rarely talked about herself, so I grew more and more curious about her life and what had brought her to this lonely place. I was pretty sure that, like me, she was here to escape some personal tragedy. Why else would she remain single and have only these homeless girls for companions? Surely she'd had a lover in the past.

One evening I invited Purple to take a walk with me outside the house. Once I was sure we could not be overheard, I asked her what she could tell me about Aunty.

Under the moonlight, my big sister's face took on a puzzled expression. "It's not only you, Spring Swallow, we're all curious about Aunty Peony. I think it's just because she didn't get married that she doesn't want us to."

"But why isn't she married?"

Purple led me to sit on a big rock under an ancient tree.

"Spring Swallow, I know you can keep secrets, but even so, you must promise never to let anyone know what I am about to tell you."

"Of course . . ."

She stared up at the moon for a few moments, then began. "Long ago, Aunty seemed very sad and drank a lot of plum wine. The other girls had gone to bed and she began to confide in me. She told me that her teacher was an imperial embroiderer at the Qing court. Only celibate women were allowed to be embroiderers. They were not supposed to have any obligations other than their work. Any girl who was an imperial embroiderer had to be a virgin so her work would be pure."

My big sister cast me a mischievous glance. "But I'm sure some only pretended to be virgins."

"Did she tell you that?"

"Not exactly. That night she was very depressed; that and the plum wine were why she told me about her past. But since then, she's never said anything more to me about it and I know better than to ask. But I believe she had lovers when she was young and eager."

"She told you this?"

"No, but I can tell."

"How?"

"Because she's extremely jealous whenever she sees any man

talk to us." Purple paused to stare into the distance. "A woman who's never had a man looks different."

"How can you tell?"

"Spring Swallow, you won't be able to tell."

"How come?"

"Because you've never had a man yourself."

I blushed. I sort of had men in my life, albeit one dead and the other invisible on the mountain—but basically she was right.

"Or have you, little sister?" She cast me a mischievous look.

"I was married, Sister Purple, but to a ghost, remember?"

She chuckled, then thought for a while. "Little sister, can you keep a secret?"

"Of course."

"All right, then let me tell you another one. One time Aunty Peony was in a hurry to go out and forgot to lock her door, so I sneaked into her room."

"Oh, Heaven, what did you see?"

"I'd always thought she must have kept lots of treasures there and that's why she never invited us in. But to my disappointment, there are only some of her embroideries. One is a portrait of her with a nice-looking young man. But I have no idea who he is."

"*Wah,* that's exciting! Tell me more!"

But she only smiled. Then she said, "Spring Swallow, you're blushing. So tell me your secret."

Just then thoughts of my unmet mountain friend had flitted across my mind. I hadn't gone back up there yet because of the cold weather. Had he checked to see if I had answered? Or had he already forgotten about me?

I asked her instead, "What secrets do you have, Sister Purple?"

She stood up abruptly, saying, "Let's go home, it's getting cold out here."

That ended our conversation—but not my curiosity.

The day after I learned that Aunty Peony might have a lover, I saw her in a different light. Now I could sense a sadness, even a vulnerability, that she did her best to conceal.

She resumed showing me how to do flowers and birds, but I

was not giving it my full attention. After a few stitches, the needle slipped and stabbed my finger.

"Oww!" I screamed.

Aunty immediately pressed a handkerchief against my finger to stop the bleeding. To my relief she did not sound angry, but concerned, asking, "Spring Swallow, where's your mind today, you left it somewhere?"

I lowered my head so as not to meet her eyes.

She picked up the bloodstained cloth. "Now watch me."

In minutes, Aunty had turned the dots of my blood into charming plum blossoms!

Before I had a chance to exclaim, she said, "This is one way to turn mistakes into something beautiful. Not only do we not waste a piece of cloth, we'll even be able to sell it."

She pointed to her temple. "Your head, it's your greatest asset. You understand?"

I nodded.

"Spring Swallow," she said, her voice turning sharp, "you're not giving total attention to your work. So I'll end our lesson today until you can focus again, you understand?"

"But, Aunty . . ."

She ignored me and went upstairs, shutting her door with a loud bang, jolting me.

I was alarmed that she'd noticed my distraction. Could she possibly have overheard Purple and me? Did she suspect I'd found out her secret—or did she know about my own secret, my mountain friend?

8

The Virtuous Love Mountains, the Wise Love the Sea

Eager to regain Aunty Peony's trust, instead of working for the length of three incense sticks, I started to do four. I desperately wanted to convince her that I was serious, that I really wanted to be a good embroiderer. As a result of my hard practice, now when I split the threads they never broke and when I worked on complicated patterns, my stitches left no traces.

As if what I did was never enough, Aunty would look over my shoulder and exclaim, "Practice more!" Whenever we were done for the day, Aunty would remind me that until I'd put in ten thousand hours of work, I'd never be good, let alone great. But because I was determined to master all her skills to maybe even surpass her someday, I practiced extra hard without her urging.

At last, one day after my lesson, Aunty Peony announced that I could join them in working on *Along the River.* I was elated at this promotion, even though I was only allowed to embroider clouds, distant trees, and anonymous figures. Purple and Little Doll congratulated me, but Leilei averted her face from me, scowling.

I was not surprised as Leilei never spoke to me unless I said hello or good morning to her first. A few times, she'd roughly pulled aside my room's curtain, plunged in, and closely examined what I'd been working on. A naturally jealous and spiteful person, she constantly spied on the rest of us, fearful that anyone else's work might surpass hers. She was skillful but did not seem to improve further, perhaps because she was so content with her skill that she no longer bothered to practice.

Once she peered over my shoulder when I was working and sneered. "It's only because we are in such a hurry with this big commission that Aunty lets you embroider with us."

I retorted, "So you think my hard work doesn't count?"

"Everyone works hard here, not just you."

"Leilei, why are you so mean to me? How about if we try to get along or even be friends?"

"I live my own life and I don't need friends," she huffed, then walked away.

I didn't know what was wrong with Leilei but was not really interested in finding out. She meant nothing to me. Aunty Peony's secrets aroused my curiosity, but most of all I wanted to know more about my mountain friend. Since Aunty now seemed to trust me more, I felt I could safely go back to the mountain, especially since spring was finally here.

After such a long absence, I was eager to inhale the fresh air, absorb its liberating energy—and, of course, see if there was a reply from Shen Feng.

So one day when I finished work, I walked over to the mountain and began to ascend so rapidly that I was a little out of breath by the time I reached the top. When I finally walked to our secret writing place, I was surprised that Shen Feng had left not one but four messages. I read them one by one.

> Dear Miss Spring Swallow,
> I'm so happy that you responded to my writing. I'd feared I offended by writing to you without any proper introduction.
> I come up here to have a few moments away

from the harrowing world below. The mountain opens the mind and elevates the spirit.

Your mountain friend,
Shen Feng

Dear Miss Spring Swallow,
I was hoping to read your writing once again, but nothing from you. Now it's quite lonely up here.

Your mountain friend,
Shen Feng

Dear Miss Spring Swallow,
Now it's even longer since I have seen your writing. It is my hope to read something more from you soon.
Can it be that you've moved away or lost interest in our mountain? But, of course, you needn't write to me again if you do not want to.
Perhaps you are too busy with your embroidery. I hope it is going well.

Your mountain friend,
Shen Feng

Dear Miss Spring Swallow,
I noticed that you scratch your words onto the rock instead of using a brush and ink. So, I left you some of mine. They are in a sack under a rock. I hope now it will be easier for you to write to me.

Your mountain friend,
Shen Feng

I found the canvas sack easily and took out a brush, a small bottle of ink, and a small, round ink stone. Tears filled my eyes at the generosity of this person I had not even met, who had never even seen me. His rock messages had also touched me. Somehow, I sensed that he was a decent man. Once again I thought of Confucius's saying, so often quoted by Father Edwin:

The virtuous love mountains and the wise love the sea.

Father had explained that the virtuous love mountains because they are solid and unmovable, just like the steadfast qualities of a virtuous person. On the other hand, wise people love the ocean because of its unfathomable depth.

But I was a mountain climber and Father Edwin was not, so when I looked at mountains I also thought of the hazards: being eaten alive by wild animals, falling off a cliff, or being captured by cruel bandits. . . . You may like mountains because you are virtuous, but the mountain doesn't care about your integrity. Maybe my life had been so harsh that I tended to worry about dangers more than virtues.

But then Father Edwin had also told me the Chinese fable *Old Fool Removing a Mountain.* An old man moved to his new house, saw a mountain in front of his gate, and decided to remove it. For this he was ridiculed by the other villagers who called him Old Fool behind his back. But Old Fool's determination was stronger than the mountain. Every day he, his sons, relatives, and friends dug diligently from morning till night. Finally, three generations had passed and the mountain was removed.

Inspired by Old Fool's courage and determination, I wrote back to Shen Feng.

> Dear Mr. Shen,
> I'd never imagined that a learned man like you would write to a simple girl like me. I have been so busy embroidering that I could not come here. Now that my teacher has finally approved my work I can come back.
> Also, thank you so much for the brush and ink.
>
> Spring Swallow

Finished, I stared at our writings and reflected on my short life. Here I was, living in a house with four celibate women, exchanging messages with a man who liked to climb mountains. Not long ago, I'd been a runaway bride from a marriage to a ghost. I hoped that the future would hold better things for me. Would this stranger play a part in it?

I felt my cheeks burn. I had not even met this man! He might be old and married with children. Suddenly disheartened, I covered over our correspondences with weeds, then began my descent.

By the time I reached home, it was nearly dark. Aunty Peony, Leilei, and Little Doll had already retired into their separate rooms. Sister Purple, who was writing something under the oil lamp, looked up as soon as I entered. Immediately she set a book on top of her writing paper, put down her brush, and stared at me.

"Spring Swallow, where have you been? Your face is flushed. Next time don't go away so long. I was worried about you."

"No need to worry, Sister Purple, I just went for a long walk."

"It's almost nine. So you must have gone very far."

Of course I was not going to tell her my mountain secrets.

"I guess so."

She stood up. "Are you hungry? Let me cook some leftovers for you."

Right after she left the room, I quickly lifted the book, peeked at her writing, and read:

> *My Dear Jiang,*
> *I miss you day and night like a child misses her mother.*
> *I fear our situation is hopeless. What will happen if I tell Aunty about us? She makes us take a vow of celibacy and is very serious about it. But if I cannot be with you, what's left in life for me? What I really want is to have a family with you, but I must continue to embroider since we will need the money.*
> *Whenever I see other lovers together my heart bursts with envy. Why must we hide our love like a disfigured face?*

*Maybe I should just tell Aunty Peony about us and
if she decides to kick me out of here, so be it. Then I'll
just follow you like the Chinese proverb says, "Marry
the chicken, follow the chicken, marry the dog, follow
the dog, marry the monkey, hold on to its tail and follow it up mountains and down valleys."*

By the way, there's a new girl here who . . .

Damn. It was just at this crucial moment that I'd interrupted
Purple's writing. So now I wouldn't know her opinion about me—
I must be the "new girl." So Purple had a lover—maybe she had
been hinting at this in our talk the other day.

Purple came back to the living room with a tray of rice soup and
a bun. "Eat something. Then we'll talk."

Was she about to confide in me?

"Thank you, Sister Purple."

As I was slurping my soup and chewing on the bun, I was well
aware of my big sister's anxious eyes drilling holes in my face.

She finally spoke, lowering her voice. "Spring Swallow, are you
happy living here with us?"

I nodded.

"Tell me the truth. You can trust me."

I also lowered my voice to match hers. "It's better than being a
ghost's wife and serving his mother for the rest of my life. Anyway,
I like embroidery very much and am lucky to have such an excellent teacher as Aunty Peony."

"You like Aunty?"

I thought for a while. "She's very good at what she does and I
learned a lot from her."

Now Purple whispered. "But do you *like* her?"

"Hmm . . ."

"Go ahead."

"She can be very harsh sometimes. . . ."

"That's what I think too. It's very oppressive here, all the rules,
the endless work, and hardly any pay."

We blurted out simultaneously, "But we have a home."

Silence passed before I gathered up courage, and asked, "Sister Purple, you have someone in your heart?"

"Why do you ask?"

"Just curious."

"Spring Swallow, no one voluntarily enters the world of celibacy, only to escape from a greater misfortune. Like all of us here."

She looked sadder than I had ever seen her, so I had no heart to ask her to tell me more.

PART TWO

✦ 9 ✦

Peking, Capital of the North

Father Edwin liked to quote the Chinese saying "Time flies like a horse jumping over a valley." The scent of spring was in the air. In the ten months that had passed since I'd joined this small community of supposedly celibate women, I had become very good at embroidering. This was the result not only of Aunty Peony's intensive teaching, her relentless scoldings, and the burning of countless incense sticks—but also my fear of being sent back to my old village.

I felt somewhat relieved that so far I hadn't run into anyone from Old Village, or seen any ad of "Missing Person" with my photo. But, of course, we rarely left the house, and if we did, we only went to the neighboring village. So if Mean Aunt was looking for me in Soochow, pasting ads on walls, lampposts, even in newspapers, I wouldn't have noticed. But I still reminded myself to be careful. However, even if they did find me, could they do anything if I refused to go back?

Having thus reassured myself, I felt more relaxed. I was exultant that Aunty Peony finally let me work on her intended masterpiece *Along the River*. But I thought it would be even better if Aunty would let me make my own copies of her stitch patterns and drawings of famous paintings. When I asked her, she looked at me suspiciously and adamantly refused, saying that they were not to be borrowed or copied. Period.

"I never give my patterns to anyone. What makes you think you'll be an exception?"

But, like the Old Fool who removed the mountain, I was determined. So I gathered up courage and challenged her.

"Aunty Peony, if you won't let me copy them, what about if someday they get lost or stolen?"

"You think I never thought of that?" She pointed to her head, her voice as sharp as her needles. "I have them all here. Anyway, neither I nor Heaven will ever let you copy them, you understand?"

So I just kept my mouth shut and my needle flying. But I realized something important from Aunty's rejection. She'd memorized all the patterns, so maybe I could too. If Heaven would not grant my request, I would grant it to myself. This was to satisfy my pride, but also so someday I could go out on my own, escape her constant scolding, and make money for myself.

So, from that day on, I secretly concentrated on putting all the patterns to memory as I worked on them. When I could get a little time free, I would climb to the mountaintop and write them on the walls inside the hidden cave that I had discovered. Since the entrance was small and hidden behind rocks and shrubs, I didn't think anyone would notice it. No one but an embroiderer would know what the patterns meant anyway. And who would come all the way from Soochow to climb the mountain and find my cave?

Then one day, unexpectedly, Aunty announced that we were all going to Peking. We wondered why we would be so lucky as to go with her, but none of us dared to ask, lest she change her mind.

Little Doll exclaimed, "*Wah,* the famous capital! So we can eat Peking duck, fried meat pancakes, and sugared fruits?"

We all laughed at our little sister's enthusiasm and naïveté.

Except Leilei, who said condescendingly, "You never had Peking duck before?"

I was sure Little Doll had only heard of the dish but never tasted it. But before she had a chance to respond, Leilei spoke again. "If you don't know, it's roast duck wrapped in special dough smeared with sweet sauce and scallion. I've eaten it many times!"

Purple tried to keep Little Doll in her happy mood, telling her, "Besides eating Peking duck, maybe we'll also buy all kinds of toys and some nice fabric to make new clothes. And we will meet Mandarin-speaking locals dressed in the latest fashions! How's that?"

Finally, when all the chatter died down, I asked timidly, "Aunty Peony, why are we going to Peking?"

"You don't want to?"

I quickly said, "Of course I do. We're all very excited, but we're curious too."

"I'm going to take you to visit the stores at Lotus Street. That's the most famous place for embroidery since the Qing dynasty. When you look at this Peking-style embroidery I want you to study it carefully."

When Aunty finished, Purple was the first to ask, "When are we leaving?"

"Day after tomorrow, so you all better start to pack soon."

The train ride was very long, so after we became bored watching the scenery, we passed the time chatting, snacking, and sleeping. Finally, we arrived and embarked into the huge station, filled with shouting, jostling travelers and thick with the odors of cigarettes, cheap perfume, sweat, and even urine. With her head held high over her bamboo-straight body, Aunty Peony confidently led us through the crowds. When we reached the street at last, she hailed two tricycle rickshaws and gave them directions to our destination: the Middle Hall Inn in the Front Gate area.

That evening, we were all too exhausted to start to explore the big city. So, after a simple dinner of spicy noodles and pork dumplings in the inn's dining room, we all went to sleep. Aunty Peony had her own room while the rest of us all shared another one.

The next morning, we each gulped down a plain breakfast of fried doughnut and soy bean soup, then went out together.

Aunty Peony said, "We are going to Lotus Street first. My teacher worked there. Embroidery thrived on that street because the foreign invaders had a military base here. The blue-eyed, blond-haired white ghosts loved silk embroidery, and it's easy to trick them into paying too much. That's why many Chinese businessmen keep shops in that street. We're going to walk there, so let's get moving."

At first sight this famous embroidery district seemed unexciting: an ordinary street flanked by grayish, two-story buildings. But then the proliferation of shop signs caught my eyes. On the ground level were Chang's Silk Fabric, Lotus Street Lanterns, Elite String-Bound Books, Wang's Noodle House, a bank, an herbalist, even the ironically named Lucky Pawn Shop. From the upper-story windows, clothes were hanging out to dry, suggesting that these were the homes of the shop owners' families. Along the street ancient trees spread their umbrella-like foliage. Banners and red lanterns hung from rooftops. Here and there bicycles and rickshaws waited patiently for their owners' return.

As we had arrived quite early, most of the shops were still closed. At tables set up outside little restaurants, middle-aged men sipped tea, smoked, and read their morning newspapers. Housewives in cotton tops and pants carried fishnet bags or bamboo baskets in one arm and held a small child in the other. Smoke from cigarettes mixed with the pleasant smell of dim sum frying in woks.

Walking together and dressed neatly in embroidered outfits, we got a lot of attention from the Pekingese, especially the men. A few young, muscular ones raised their heads from their food, stared at us as if we were the only women left on Earth, then whistled and whispered to each other.

Leilei, instead of looking annoyed, smiled flirtatiously as she twisted her hips—deliberately, I supposed. Did she really feel flattered by the attention of coolies? More likely she was that kind of girl who liked to tease men. Among us, she was the tallest and caught the most glances. She could be quite attractive—when she was not bitchy. But I had to give her credit for working hard and being good at what she did. Still, it was hard for me to believe that she would follow Aunty's celibacy rule. Surely she had at least one lover.

My thoughts were interrupted when Purple asked, "Aunty Peony, where are we going?"

"I'm looking for embroidery shops. There used to be many right here. But if we don't see any nearby, I'll ask around."

Suddenly, Little Doll exclaimed happily, jumping up and down. "Aunty Peony, here's Lotus Embroidery Shop!"

I found Little Doll very likable, but unfortunately there was hardly any chance for us to talk, let alone be friends. Aunty would never let Purple, Leilei, or me get too close to the young girl, whom she was always criticizing as stupid and slow. I guessed that for Aunty she was only cheap labor and so she didn't want us to keep her from her work.

Now we all stared through the shop's window, admiring the many embroideries, some mounted on wooden frames, others on panels, yet others framed behind glass. Spread around the display were other items, such as handkerchiefs, robes, slippers, pillows, round fans, even eyeglass cases.

"Wow, so beautiful!" we all exclaimed.

Aunty cast us a stern look. "I'd call it skillful, but not exquisite."

"How's that?" I asked.

"These are not art, only craft."

"Hmm . . . what's the difference?"

"They try too much to please."

Leilei asked tentatively, "What's wrong with being pleasing?"

"Because when work is slick, the connoisseur will reject it."

No one had anything to say to this.

"Why do you think I brought you here—so you will learn and open your eyes."

She cast another disapproving look at the merchandise. "These works have no souls. The embroiderers see only the glitter of gold and smell only the stink of money."

But what's wrong with that? I thought. If I had tons of gold and loads of money, I wouldn't have ended up being a ghost's wife, then a runaway bride, then a celibate embroiderer. On the contrary, I would buy a big mansion, hire maids to help, a chef to cook me delicious, nutritious food, maybe even a chauffeur to drive me around. Then I would have even more time free to do embroidery. But if I were so rich, would I lose interest in embroidering since I would no longer need to make a living? I hoped not.

Aunty's voice cut off my gilded dream. "None of the work here shows any sign of 'eyes focusing on nose, nose focusing on heart, heart focusing on hands.' "

She sighed. "*Hai,* how the world has changed and art has declined! Where have the fine embroiderers gone?"

None of us dared to respond to Aunty's remark. I still thought that the works in the shop were beautiful.

"All right. The shop won't open till eleven o'clock, so let's stroll around a bit and get something to eat."

So we continued to walk along the street amidst the curious glances of the locals. Aunty Peony seemed to be an object of admiration. She was dressed in a fancy silk top with floral embroidery and matching pants. Her face was delicately made up, enhanced by a silver flower dangling from her tightly braided bun. I realized that this trip was very important to her.

When we were passing a photography shop, Aunty Peony stopped. Behind the window were framed photos: young newlyweds smiling happily at the camera; a naked baby boy posed to reveal his little thing because his parents were so proud to have a son; twin sisters with missing teeth, arms around each other's shoulders and giggling; an old man smoking a pipe, the wrinkles on his spotted face matching the curves of the smoke. Though all the people in these photos must have been real, there was something illusionary about them.

We all appreciated the photos for a while before Aunty said, her expression nostalgic, "After breakfast, we'll come back here to have our picture taken together."

"*Wah,* I've never been in a photo before!" Little Doll exclaimed with pleasure.

I didn't know if Purple and Leilei had pictures of themselves, but I had none of myself. I remembered having a few taken when I'd been younger, but they must all have been lost. My mean aunt might have kept one or two, but she never let me look at them, let alone give them to me. Or she might have thrown them away a long time ago.

The next street was filled with restaurants; Aunty picked one out and we all entered and sat down. She seemed to be in a good mood and ordered lots of food—porridge, marinated eggs, scallion pancakes, fried doughnuts, soy bean soup, pickled vegetables. Since this was a novelty for us, our appetites seemed insatiable as we devoured the food with gusto. Finally, when all the plates were wiped clean like mirrors, Aunty announced that we would go back to the Lotus Embroidery Shop, then later we'd have our pictures taken at the photography studio.

Once we stepped inside the shop, we were greeted by a plump, middle-aged woman with an obsequious smile.

"Good morning, ladies. Can I help you pick some embroideries? What are you looking for? Gifts? Decorations?"

Aunty smiled back. "We'll look around first."

"Of course, please."

We all milled around the spacious store, *oohing* and *aahing* at the beautiful work. There was a peacock spreading its many-eyed tail, a tiger staring at me fiercely through trees, butterflies floating over clusters of flowers, a glittering dragon and phoenix chasing each other among colorful clouds. . . .

The plump woman expounded to us in a pompous tone that *kingxiu,* Peking-style embroidery, is very famous because it came from the Qing dynasty imperial court's embroidery department.

"That's why our work is all first-rate, because we use the best material like silk fabric, gold, and silver threads. But especially because it possesses the emperor's noble *qi.*

"You see"—she made a sweeping gesture—"every single thread sparkles royalty. That's why *Peking* embroidery is also called Court Embroidery."

Aunty glanced at the embroideries. "Are these the best in your store?"

Plump smiled. "I see you really know embroidery. We have a few very special items that we reserve for connoisseurs like yourself. Please wait here, I'll be back." She hurried to the back of the store, opened a drawer, then dashed back.

She showed us a piece depicting a soaring crane above colorful waves. "See? This is an antique piece from the robe of a high Qing official."

Obviously hoping Aunty would splurge, Plump went on excitedly in a high-pitched voice, her cheeks flushed a lively pink.

But Aunty seemed unimpressed. "Not bad. But do you have something better?"

"Of course, we have the very best work of any store here."

Again, she disappeared into the back of the store, then quickly returned, this time with a flat wooden box. She opened it very cautiously, as if she were afraid to find out what lurked inside. With a flourish, she lifted off a swatch of yellow cloth, revealing a folded fabric with a proud dragon on the chest.

Plump lifted the object from the box. "Who knows what this is?" she asked, eyes challenging us.

Leilei beat us to the answer. "An emperor's robe!"

"Correct." Plump pointed to the different images on the robe and pedantically explained to us what they were—"Dragons are symbols of the Son of Heaven's absolute power; colored clouds are auspicious; the sun, moon, stars represent the resplendent light of the throne. . . ."

"*Wah,* how beautiful!" we all exclaimed—except Aunty.

She seemed preoccupied, as if remembering something sad and dark.

Suddenly she blurted out a question. "Have you heard of an embroiderer by the name of Qiu Niang?"

Plump looked deep in thought for a moment, then answered, "Hmm . . . the name sounds familiar. I think I might have heard of her, but why do you ask?"

"Just curious. She was very famous for a while, but then her fame faded. Now no one knows where she is. I just wonder if she's still alive."

"Hmm . . . Yes, Qiu Niang. Now I remember. I think I heard that she became a nun. Or maybe she jumped into a river and the nun is someone else."

"Where did you hear this?"

"Oh, I can't remember. You know, there are so many people coming in and out of our store gossiping every day—"

"Do you have any of her work here?"

Plump scratched her round head. "Hmmm . . . I'm not sure. I can go back to our storage room a few miles from here and take a look. But then you may have to wait a day or two. That's if you want to buy her work, if not . . ."

"I understand."

"You want me to show you our other works here?"

Aunty waved her hand. "Oh, no. We do not want to trouble you anymore. Thank you for showing us the work, especially the dragon robe."

And that ended our first glimpse into the life of the emperor's court.

As we all made our way out of the Lotus Embroidery Shop, we didn't have the heart to see the disappointment on Plump's face.

Once we were some distance away from the store, I asked Aunty, "You never mentioned this Qiu Niang. Who is she?"

She cast me a disapproving look. But then said softly, as if to herself, "She's a very special woman—one of the greatest embroiderers."

"Even better than you?"

But seemingly lost in thought, Aunty ignored my question. Or maybe she didn't want to say that someone could be a better embroiderer than she. Soon we were again in front of the photography shop. Aunty was not in a good mood, so maybe she had changed her mind about the picture-taking.

But then she suddenly exclaimed, "That dragon robe is a fake!"

"Fake?" all the girls asked simultaneously.

"Yes, how could anyone get an emperor's robe and have it in a store just like that?"

Purple said, "That's true, how come we never thought of that?"

"Then how come the sales woman never thought of that?" I asked.

"Because the world is full of ignorant people who can't tell a fake when it's as obvious as the nose on their face," Aunty hissed.

Now it was Leilei's turn to ask. "So it's just a copy?"

"Yes, and it's a very bad copy."

Leilei said, "It looks pretty good to me, though."

Aunty cast her a disgusted look. "You think you have better eyes than me?"

"Of course not, Aunty, I'm sorry."

"Ignorant girl, it's at most mediocre. Worse, one symbolism for emperor is missing. It has the sun, moon, stars, and fire for brightness, mountains for steadfastness, bronze vessels for offerings, rice for nourishment, and opposite-facing bows for justice, and, of course, dragons . . . But there is no seaweed!"

"Seaweed?" we all asked at once.

"Haven't any of you heard the phrase, 'Following the sea's rising and falling currents'?"

Of course we hadn't, so Aunty went on triumphantly. "Because all emperors hoped they would ride forever over the ups and downs of fortune."

Leilei blurted out, "Aunty Peony, how do you know about all this?"

Our teacher simply ignored her question and continued. "The emperor didn't just wear one robe, but had many for different occasions, such as meeting with high ministers at court, leading his soldiers into battle, and especially important rituals, such as honoring Heaven and Earth at the Temple of Heaven."

Just then Little Doll piped up. "Aunty Peony, are we going to have our picture taken now?"

Aunty's voice softened a bit. "Of course, Little Doll."

∽∾ 10 ∽∾

Memory Lane
Photography Studio

The Memory Lane Photography Studio was a small space filled with photography paraphernalia. Tripods supporting large, accordion-like cameras were scattered around. Framed black-and-white pictures and hand-colored ones hung on the walls. Yellow film boxes spilled from shelves. However, one corner was neat, primly decorated with stiff, high-backed chairs, a vase with flowers on a carved stand, and landscape paintings on the wall. Aimed at these decorations were two large lamps with black covers.

Aunty Peony told the skinny, fortyish photographer that we wanted group pictures with her sitting in the middle, the three of us standing behind her, and Little Doll squatting in front. After fussing with his strange equipment, the photographer finally asked Aunty to sit and us girls to gather around her. After that, he carefully instructed us as to how to arrange our heads, hands, and legs into the "just right" positions.

Then he yelled, "That's it, don't move. Now, smile!"

We did what we'd been told. But I also thought: *What is there to smile about?*

He pressed the button repeatedly, resulting in a series of crisp *click, click, click.* After that, he announced that the pictures were taken and we could all relax. He said it'd take a couple of weeks or even longer for the pictures to be ready. But since we were not going to stay that long, either the store would have to send us the pictures or one of us would come back here for them. I secretly hoped Aunty would choose me, but knew this was unlikely.

Our stay in the famous city lasted only six days. We visited a few more shops, which gave Aunty the opportunity to criticize everyone else's work. In the evenings she would treat us to Peking duck and other special local dishes at an elegant restaurant, then walk us back to the inn and admonish us to go to sleep early. Although we heard the door of her room close, I was pretty sure she would go out alone, but where and for what I had no idea.

Finally, the day before we went back to Soochow, Aunty said she'd take us to the Forbidden City. She said since we didn't have much time, we'd only see a small part of it—the emperor's throne room. I wondered why, among all the treasures of this famous place, all she wanted to see was a chair, not where the Empress Dowager had slept, or her huge collection of jewelry.

The Forbidden City was conveniently within walking distance of where our inn was located. When we arrived at the enormous palace, Aunty seemed to know exactly where she was going—the Grand Hall of Ultimate Harmony, the site of the dragon throne. There were not many tourists around, so we were able to get quite close to *the* chair. It was impressive, indeed, with its high back, gold cushions, and many dragons.

The mythical creature was everywhere—on the chair's back, arm rests, and the screen behind it. There were also other auspicious creatures such as cranes, tortoises, and elephants. Strangely, instead of feeling awed by this chair's grandeur and beauty, I found it oppressive. The dragons running around with its dazzling gold made me dizzy. It was so overwhelming that I could hardly breathe. I guessed I was just not emperor or empress material.

But Leilei *oohed* and Little Doll drooled over its sumptuousness, sparkling gold, and elaborate carvings that only the emperor was permitted.

With a smug expression, Leilei exclaimed, "If I were the empress, I could ascend this throne with my husband the emperor!"

"Me too!" Little Doll echoed. "If I were their daughter, I'd be a princess!"

"I'd have maids and servants to wait on me hand and foot," Leilei added.

"Me too!"

Since Purple and I remained silent, Aunty asked, "What do you two think?"

Purple spoke first. "It's beautiful, but none of us will ever be an empress. We can only admire it from a distance."

When she finished, I said, "It's too much for me."

Leilei said sarcastically, "Spring Swallow, *you* will certainly never be an empress."

As I was trying to think of a retort, Aunty said softly, as if to herself, "I do like this throne. It's truly beautiful."

Her eyes lingered on the chair for long moments. After that, she said, "Let me tell you a story."

We all quieted down to attend to our teacher's words.

"In 1908, the three-year-old emperor was seated on this same chair next to the imperial minister for his coronation. Startled by the loud drums, cymbals, and bells, the little emperor burst out crying hysterically. The minister tried to comfort him, saying, 'Don't cry! It's going to be over soon.' And it was. Three years later, the whole Qing dynasty was overthrown."

When we were all trying to digest the story and its message, Aunty added bitterly, "If it's not your destiny, it's not going to happen."

What was she trying to tell us?

The following morning, I wondered about the little emperor's fate as I helped pack for our trip back to Soochow. When we were done, we went into Aunty Peony's room to tell her we were ready.

Then I wondered aloud, "Aunty Peony, how come you didn't take us to where our embroideries are sold—the Heavenly Phoenix store?"

Now all the girls asked simultaneously, "Yes, Aunty Peony, how come?"

Aunty cast us a penetrating look. "Because Heavenly Phoenix only has business with me, not you girls, that's why. Don't think you're so special just because I let you work on *Along the River.* I am *the* embroiderer, you girls are only helpers, you understand? Remember, without me, you'd all be homeless nobodies!"

Now enlightened to the fact that we were not only homeless but also nobodies, we girls left behind the North Capital, the Forbidden City, the dragon throne, and the doomed little emperor to accompany Aunty back to nowhere, where we lived. . . .

Soon we were back to reality: our house near the mountain, our long hours of embroidering, our celibate lives. For me, I was happy enough to be back to work, because only with embroidering did I feel any sense of accomplishment. Seeing Aunty back at work after our visit to the imperial capital, I wondered anew why she had chosen such an improvised life. Aunty rarely took us out to have fun, nor—as far as we knew—did she go out for lavish meals or entertainment for herself. Though she continued to teach us, she seemed depressed. Lately she would finish working early and go upstairs to rest. She must have made a lot from our work, but what did she spend it on? And why the trip to Peking? I knew my teacher well enough to know that the trip was not just to be nice to us.

Now that she was spending more time by herself in her room, I was more curious than ever what her room was like and what she did there.

I asked Purple about it again, but she would not tell me anything more, warning me, "Don't do it, Spring Swallow. Aunty would disown you. Besides, some secrets are best left secret."

I had my own secrets, so I knew what she meant, but I still asked, "Why is that?"

"It's bad luck to pry; it can be dangerous."

But I had never heard that knowing others' secrets could bring bad luck.

"You think Leilei ever snuck into her room?"

"I really don't know. Leilei is weird and she is nasty to everyone, except Aunty, of course. I think she's very cunning and won't be here much longer. Like Aunty, she never really tells us about herself or anything. She might already have broken into Aunty's room and snooped around, but she'd never tell anyone, certainly not me."

Bad luck or not, I did plan to have a look at Aunty's room if the opportunity ever presented itself. I went up a few times when Aunty went out, only to find her door was locked as tightly as a virginity belt. What was she so afraid of? Since I couldn't go upstairs, the next time she went out, I went to the mountain. With the Peking trip and catching up afterward, it had been nearly a month since I'd had the chance to visit my writing place.

In my thick-soled cloth shoes, I climbed as rapidly as I could, not even pausing to rest or look down. Once at the top, I found myself alone in my little sanctuary, sharing the warm sun and soothing breeze only with the birds, trees, and the flowers peeping through the rocks. As I breathed in the pure air I felt my frayed nerves gradually relax. I wasn't even sure what I was so nervous about.

From the distance, I'd already spotted what looked like a new "letter" from Shen Feng and hurried to the rock.

> Miss Spring Swallow,
> I haven't seen your writing for a while and that worries me. Are you all right? I hope that soon you will have a chance to enjoy the mountain air—and write to me again.
> I have been hoping to run into you here. It would be an honor to meet you someday. Up here together we can have a better view of the world.
> Do you know Wang Zhihuan's poem?

> "The white sun descends down the mountain,
> The Yellow River rushes into the sea.
> If you want to see beyond one thousand miles,
> You must ascend one more level."

> Your mountain friend,
> Shen Feng

By the time I finished reading, my heart was pounding. How could he be so interested in me even though we'd never met? I read the poem again, then sat down on a rock to think. How could this man, who had never even seen me, read my mind? He seemed to know I climbed mountains to be alone and to expand my vision. And he knew I would love his poem about mountain climbing.

I remembered Father Edwin had read me a poem about ascending mountains. I loved the way he recited it so much that I kept nagging him to repeat it. Looking up at the clear, blue sky, I recited to myself the lines he'd taught me:

> Shadows of geese on the Autumn river,
> With a bottle of wine I go up the green mountain.
> In this dusty world, smiles are rare.
> Walking down, I cover my head with flowers.

Father said the Tang dynasty poet Du Mu was telling us that life is short and harsh, so we should grab happy moments as we can. I knew that life is harsh, but I disagreed with Du Mu that life is short. To me, it was pretty long and tedious. But who was I to argue with the erudite Father Edwin—or the famous poet!

Another poem he had taught me was by Wang Wei, also from the Tang dynasty.

> Now a stranger in a remote country,
> With whom can I enjoy this holiday?
> Crowds climb this mountain with me,
> But not the one I miss.

Father Edwin said that if we keep warm in our memory of the friends who are gone, then life is not so sad. I wondered who was the missing person in this poem. I also wondered why most Chinese poems are sad. But Father Edwin said when I was older, life's experiences would make me understand a lot of things, both sad but also happy. Then he said that nothing is sure in life except God's love. So we should always have faith in our Creator. But I was pretty sure that Wang Wei was not thinking about God's love when he composed the poem. Still, Father Edwin was the kindest person I had ever met and I hoped that someday I would see him again.

Though feeling sorry for myself, my spirit was again lifted when I remembered this poem by Du Fu.

When you have reached the top of Mount Tai,
The other mountains seem small.

I looked down and thought that perhaps someday I would climb a mountain much higher than this one. I took out my brush and ink and wrote this simple poem next to Shen Feng's letter and also a reminder for him to write inside the cave next time. After that, I picked a few wildflowers, put them on my head, then hummed a tune as I headed down the steep path.

Once I was home, however, I started to worry that Shen Feng might think me boastful to want to climb the highest mountain. Would he think I was so conceited as to fancy I could be on top of the world? Maybe I'd get to the top someday, but for now it was back to hour after hour with needle and thread. I knew I had not much chance in life, except by learning embroidery.

During the next few days Aunty Peony would catch me staring into space—fortunately I was sure she could not know I was day-dreaming about a man I had never met. But she must have had a secret preoccupation of her own because two weeks later, to all of our surprise, Aunty Peony announced that she was about to take another trip to Peking to collect the photographs, but that she would only bring Little Doll.

Purple asked timidly, "Can't they send us the photos?"

Aunty said, "We don't have a real address and the photos might get lost. We won't have many chances to get pictures taken together like this, let alone by a photographer in Peking."

The three of us, Purple, Leilei, and I, cast each other questioning glances, but none of us dared to ask why only Little Doll was so lucky.

Aunty must have already guessed what was on our minds. "Don't be jealous of a little orphan girl."

But I thought, weren't we all orphan girls?

Aunty spoke again. "We'll leave tomorrow and be back in a week."

That evening when the others had gone to sleep, Purple took me into the courtyard and whispered, "I bet Aunty has something else to do in Peking besides getting the pictures."

"We can probably find out from Little Doll when they come back."

She shook her head. "I'm sure Aunty will tell Little Doll not to say anything. Or she may just leave her in the inn when she goes out. Since she wouldn't take us to Heavenly Phoenix, I guess this trip has to have something to do with the store—secret deals that Aunty doesn't want us to know about."

She sighed. "*Hai,* I've lived with her for five years, but Aunty Peony is still an enigma to me."

I nodded in agreement, but besides Aunty, I also found Purple an enigma. She was quiet, kind, resigned—very different from the jealous and sarcastic Leilei.

"Sister Purple, you're an enigma to me too. Why don't you tell me more about yourself?"

"Spring Swallow, I don't talk about myself because I'm afraid I'm not a very interesting person."

"You have been good to me, though. Without you, I wouldn't have a roof over my head, let alone learn to be an embroiderer."

She sighed under the pale moonlight. "I have a sad life. We all do, otherwise we wouldn't have ended up here."

"You miss your husband?"

I remembered the first day I was here, Purple had told us her husband died shortly after they'd been married. Her in-laws blamed her, calling her an all-destroying star, and cast her out of the house.

"I hardly knew him. It was an arranged marriage, and we'd only been together for six months before he died."

"How did he die?"

"On the way to pick me up on his bicycle. He was trying to avoid hitting a dog and got hit by a car."

"I'm sorry." I thought for a moment, then asked, "Is it hard to keep the vow of celibacy since you were married before?"

"But I haven't . . ."

"Haven't what?"

Purple remained silent, but I pressed her for an answer. Anyway, I'd already guessed because I'd read her unfinished letter to her lover.

"I know you have someone in here." I pointed to my chest.

She looked totally shocked. "What more do you know? Have you been following me?"

"Never, Sister Purple. But the way you reacted . . . you must have someone."

She looked relieved. "All right, maybe I do."

"You're afraid Aunty will find out?"

"Yes, but the power of love overcomes everything."

"*Wah,* is that so?"

"You've never been in love?"

"Of course not, Sister Purple, my husband was a ghost. I never even met him!"

She nodded. "Then you don't even know what you've missed."

Actually, I thought I did know, at least a little. Even though I had not actually met Shen Feng, I imagined what it would be like if we did meet.

"Sister Purple, what if Aunty finds out?"

"She won't have any sympathy for me. She must have been hurt so badly by love that she won't fall again."

"Why not?"

"She's beautiful and talented and she must have some money, so lots of men would want her. I have no idea why she ended up working for a greedy factory many miles away, and probably lies about how much they make from our work."

We remained silent for a while before I asked, "Who's the man?"

"What man?"

"The man in your heart."

"I'll tell you, but you must promise to keep this secret until you are in your grave."

She looked around to make extra sure no one was eavesdropping. Then she whispered into my ear. "He's my dead husband's brother."

"Oh, Heaven!"

"Shhh . . . Jiang gives me great comfort after my husband's death. He told me he'd been in love with me since the day I'd come home with his brother. Now, whenever I can, I sneak out to see him. Of course, we live in fear that sooner or later his parents will find out. They would never give him permission to marry me. I can live without embroidery, but I can't live without Jiang."

"*Wah,* you love him so much?"

She nodded, looking sad yet hopeful.

"Where do you meet him?"

"As you know, as long as we do our job, Aunty Peony doesn't bother us much. So sometimes I can steal away, even in the middle of the night, if I am very quiet. He knows that on Tuesdays I will sneak out if I can, so he waits for me."

"How come I never notice you're not here?"

"You still need to learn to observe things, my little sister." She paused, then spoke again. "Remember when we met?"

I nodded.

"I'd just finished seeing him—that's why I was out so early in the morning."

"You still haven't told me where you meet."

"At an old dilapidated temple."

"*Wah,* you're not afraid someone will see you there?"

"No one goes there—everyone is afraid it's haunted."

"Is it really?"

"We don't care. We just want to be together. But we always burn incense to appease any wandering ghosts who might be around.

"I hope someday you can meet Jiang. I'm sure you'll like each other." She sighed. "*Hai,* it's late now. Let's go to bed and maybe we'll have some sweet dreams tonight."

～ 11 ～

First Encounter

The next morning when we woke up, Aunty Peony and Little Doll were gone. The three of us discussed our situation while we ate our simple breakfast of congee and fried donuts. Aunty had left a note telling us what to do and what not to do while she was away. She warned us that we must continue to embroider and, in any free time, practice painting and calligraphy, because she'd check on what we'd done when she got back. If we did not finish *Along the River* on time, we would not get any more orders from Heavenly Phoenix and we would either become prostitutes or starve to death.

"Wah!" the three of us exclaimed in disbelief.

Leilei scoffed. "I don't believe we'd end up in such a dire situation. That old witch just wants to threaten us, but I'm not scared!"

Purple cast her a disapproving look. "Leilei, watch your spiteful mouth and show some respect for your teacher!"

"Ha, respect, why should I? We work day and night and all we get in return is a pittance. She took us to Peking but wouldn't let us visit the company we work like dogs for. I'm sure she's been pocketing most of our money—"

"That's enough, Leilei, don't say something you're going to regret."

"I'm regretting my life, which has been in the gutter all along. Maybe you two have nothing to hope for, but I plan to be rich and famous. And I will. You two just wait and see!"

After this outburst, she stormed off.

"Where're you going?" Purple yelled after her.

She flung her head back and spoke defiantly. "To see a man! You will never know what it's like to have a man in you. No man will ever want either of you, you understand?"

She dashed outside the house, slamming the door with a loud bang.

Purple turned to me. "I don't like Leilei, but I admire her defiant spirit. *Hai,* she'll be lucky if she gets what she wants in life, because most people don't. But for you she's a bad influence, so don't listen to her."

"But why not?"

"Because she's nothing but trouble. All right, let's finish our breakfast and get back to work."

Suddenly, with Aunty, Little Doll, and Leilei gone, the house was very quiet. I'd gotten used to hearing them talking, eating, laughing, bickering. Purple had gone into her room and, sitting by myself, I imagined the little household was itself an embroidery, with each of us, even Leilei, an indispensable part of this special fabric.

I worked long hours that day, until I fell asleep with the needle and cloth in my hands. When I woke up, it was eight in the evening. I hurried to knock on Purple's door, but there was no answer. So she was either sound asleep or had taken her work into her room and was so engrossed that she didn't hear me. Finally, I got impatient and pushed open the door. But her room was empty!

I hurried to Leilei's room and found that hers was empty too. But, of course, in the morning she'd said she was going to see a man, so maybe he was inside her right now. Realizing that I was completely alone, I felt a wave of panic. Had even my one friend, Purple, deserted me?

I took deep breaths to calm myself, then looked out the window. The sky was already dark and I could see the distant lights flickering in Soochow city. Except for far-off barking, the night was quiet. Feeling acutely lonely, I went to the kitchen and cooked myself some noodles, then sprinkled them with chili powder and scallions. My loud slurping echoed eerily in the empty house—even the hot soup gave me no comfort.

I wondered what it would be like if none of them returned and I would be alone all night. Purple might be at the deserted temple, so I could go there to look for her. But what if it really was haunted? Hoping to distract myself from all these scary thoughts, I took out my embroidery tools and spread them on the table: scissors, threads, needles, cloth, wooden frame, and metal finger protector.

But as soon as I had arranged everything neatly on the table I suddenly lost my desire to work. So instead I went to brush my teeth and wash my hands. Then I burned incense and offered tea to Guan Yin and my grand-teacher, both looking down at me from the altar with pity—or so I thought. Finally, feeling a little calmer, I plunged into my embroidery.

As the hours passed, I was happy to see the two bright-eyed tigers stare back at me from the pair of red children's shoes I was working on. I felt a surge of pride. Skillfully done, the tigers would not only entertain the child, but also keep his feet warm and guard him from evil. I imagined a cute little boy running around, asking his grandmother for candies, his mother for affection, and his father for a piggyback ride. But when the child grew up into a young man, he would have forgotten these little tigers that had tirelessly protected his little feet. Then I felt sad. I'd embroidered so many shoes for other people's children; would I ever have children of my own to make little tiger shoes for?

I did not realize that I had fallen asleep until the first light woke me up the next morning. I hurried to knock on Purple's and Leilei's doors, but there was still no answer. They must be having too much fun to bother coming home. Feeling restless, I gulped down some leftover soybean soup, changed to a thin cotton top and pants, went out, and headed directly toward the mountain. I hoped the fresh air would soothe my nerves and clear my mind. Unlike the women whose home I shared, the mountain never failed me. It was always patient as I poured out my troubled emotions.

During my ascent, the sky was as gray as a pigeon's belly. Through the thin soles of my shoes I could feel every clod, pebble, and twig. Whenever I started my climb I would think of Father Edwin's favorite quote from the great sage Laozi, "A journey of a thousand miles begins with the ground under your feet." Father reminded me of this whenever I had to start a difficult task.

As I continued to climb, the mountain breeze gently massaged my face and body, as if blowing away all my worldly troubles. As I neared the top I heard, faintly, the bittersweet tones of a flute. I didn't feel fear, only curiosity. I wondered who would be up here so early, trespassing on my mountain sanctuary?

As I ascended farther, I could see, silhouetted in front of the rising sun, the figure of a man, his fingers trembling on the flute as the music flowed out. As I came closer I saw that his silk clothes covered a well-formed, muscular body. With the sun no longer in my eyes I could see that his hair was neatly cut. So he could afford a barber, unlike most of the villagers, who had zigzag or seesaw haircuts, as if the strands had been hacked off by clumsy wives or fuzzy-eyed mothers.

Somehow I knew he was not a ruffian or a bandit. To create such refined music, he must be a learned man. I remained very quiet, enjoying his melodic playing, as if he were greeting the rising sun. Then he stopped, exhaling a melancholy sigh. I realized that he was standing right in front of the steep rock cliff and suddenly feared that he was contemplating suicide. Perhaps he had experienced some great tragedy and was playing his favorite tune one last time before . . . But if he was really going to jump, I didn't think I'd have the strength to pull him back. Even if I screamed, there would be no one else to help, not even a ghost. Suddenly I felt dizzy and fell.

A loud *"aiiiya!"* involuntarily flew from my mouth.

The man turned, saw me, dashed down, and helped me up. Then he led me to sit on a rock. Seeing him face-to-face I was certain he was not a bandit. And seeing him smile at me reassuringly I was sure he was not about to jump. He had the look of a scholar with intelligent eyes, square jaw, and determined expression.

I felt too stunned to say anything as he looked me over with great interest, his eyes lingering.

Finally, he asked, very gently, "Miss, you have cuts on your knee"—he pointed to my torn pants—"but don't worry, they're not deep and you'll be fine."

Next he took out a handkerchief and pressed it to staunch the oozing blood. I noticed that his brows were thick and black. In his strong presence I felt comforted, but also still a little afraid.

"Are you all right?" he asked.

I nodded, still feeling confused.

He smiled. "Miss, may I ask how does a young girl like you come to be on this mountain just as the sun is rising? You know, it might be dangerous—wild animals, mud slides, maybe even bandits. Shall I bring you home to your parents?"

In my daze I feared that he intended to take me back to my old village, so I blurted out, "Oh, no, please don't! I only come here to be alone and write."

"Poor girl, don't be frightened. Of course I won't tell your parents. I can just walk you to your door, or part of the way. How's that?"

"But I don't have parents. I live with my embroidery teacher."

Suddenly his face took on an excited expression. "Hmmm . . . could you be . . . Spring Swallow?"

Before I could think, I blurted out, "How did you know?"

"Oh, Heaven! I've been hoping to meet you for a long time!"

By now I had guessed who he was.

He laughed. His thick black hair reflected the glancing rays of the sun like fishes' scales.

"I am Shen Feng, your mountain friend! So we finally meet!"

I felt my cheeks burn. I could smell the mountain on him—a fragrant blend of grass, breeze, and mud. The moments crept by like snails as we both tried to think of what to say.

Finally, I gathered up my courage, and asked, "Mr. Shen, were you really . . . waiting for me?"

"Yes, for a long time I have been coming up here to practice my flute. Since I first saw your writing I have been hoping to meet you."

"I like your playing . . . but it is sad."

"Yes, indeed."

I didn't feel I should ask him what he was sad about, so instead I asked, "Why so early in the morning?"

"I like to see the sunrise. And I've been worried about you, especially when it's been so long since you wrote anything. Of course, during the winter it gets very cold up here."

"Worry about me? We don't . . . even know each other."

"It's true we hadn't met, but I already feel I know you. Maybe we were close friends in a past life."

Actually, I felt somewhat the same but was too embarrassed to say so.

He went on. "You know, you are almost exactly as I imagined you."

"Are you clairvoyant?"

He laughed. "I don't think so. I'm so happy that we met."

A few silent moments passed, and I said, "Mr. Shen, it was nice of you to quote the poem for me."

"I like your writing too." He smiled. "I can tell it is from your heart. How are you learning embroidery? Is it very difficult?"

I told him about Aunty, that she was a good teacher but also hard on us. But I loved doing embroidery.

Now he knew something about me, but I hardly knew anything about him, except that he liked mountains.

So I asked, "Do you live nearby, Mr. Shen?"

His answer surprised me. "No, but this place is special for me. I come here to remember my sister."

"To remember her? Did she move far away?"

But his answer was, "Her life was very sad."

"Sadder than marrying a ghost?"

He looked puzzled for a moment, then nodded.

"Did she . . . die?"

"Yes, five years ago."

"How terrible. Can you tell me about her?"

"She and her lover, an elementary school teacher, committed suicide by jumping down the cliff here."

"Oh, Heaven! What happened!?"

"My family had arranged with a matchmaker to marry her to the son of a rich merchant. But my sister was in love with this penniless teacher. Unfortunately, the wedding had already been arranged and the dowry sent."

"So she did not love the merchant. . . ."

"I told her she should run away with her lover, but she could not bear to disobey her parents. . . ."

"How unfair of them. Were you close to your sister, Mr. Shen?"

"Yes . . . it's been many years. We grieve, but life goes on. Since the tragedy, my parents have been very regretful. They hardly talk to each other . . . or to me. That's why I like to come here by myself to remember her, and also to calm my mind."

I was unable to think of anything suitable to say.

He changed the subject, asking, "Have you noticed that there is almost never anyone else on this mountain?"

"Yes, and I always wonder why."

"It's because of my sister and her lover. People fear it's haunted. You're new here, and no one ever told you this?"

Aunty must have known. Either she did not believe in ghosts or she did not care about what might happen to us when we ventured outside.

He spoke again. "Only up here do I find peace. When I saw your writing, I felt as if struck by lightning. What sort of person, especially a woman, would come up a haunted mountain? So I thought we must have a karmic connection from a past life."

Feeling very touched, I hesitated, then said, "Mr. Shen, I'd like to be your friend . . . but Aunty Peony would send me away if she finds out that I've befriended a man."

"But how would she know. She doesn't follow you, does she?"

"I don't think so. But you know the saying that 'If you keep going up the mountain, one day you'll run into a tiger'?"

He smiled. "Yes, but you seem to be a girl who is not afraid of tigers."

"I can run fast. A tiger—or a bandit—I can get away from either."

He laughed out loud. "I see you are brave, Spring Swallow. But I am not so sure you could get away in time. Anyway, now you have me to protect you. Will you tell me more about yourself? I am sure you did not grow up here. How did you come to be in this isolated place?"

I told him about my mean aunt, Father Edwin, and my wedding to a ghost.

He looked shocked. "You're married?"

"Yes, but to a ghost or a chicken, not a man." I went on to explain how I had gotten into this trap.

"Poor girl. Lucky you could escape. If my sister had your courage, she might be alive today. That's why China needs to be modernized, to get rid of its feudal poison."

"I'm sorry."

I was afraid he would get tired of hearing about my troubles. And I wanted to know more about him. So I asked, "Where do you live?"

"In Soochow."

"And you come all the way here?"

He nodded. What I really wanted to know was why he didn't have to work, so I asked about his job.

"I coach some university students, so my working hours are up to me. I come up here before or after I give my lessons," he replied.

He paused to look at his watch. "Actually, I am going to be late for my first lesson today so I need to go back now. Spring Swallow, tell me where you live. I'll walk you home."

"The only house near this mountain."

"I've seen that house and always wondered who lives there."

"But, Mr. Shen, I can walk home by myself. I can't let Aunty see me with a man."

"I understand. But China is now modern. Men and women are equal and can freely mingle."

"But my aunty made all of us take a vow of celibacy before she would teach us embroidery."

"You're serious?"

I didn't know how to respond.

"I hope not. Since you're so pretty and, I assume, also very talented."

Again, I remained silent. So we turned and descended the mountain together.

When our feet set on level ground, Shen Feng asked, "Spring Swallow, when can we see each other again, since I don't think I can send or deliver you a letter."

"I never know when I will have the chance to come up here."

"Then if we do not see each other when we come, let's keep writing each other on the cave's walls, all right? Anyway, I'll be here tomorrow morning, so I hope you can come then too."

I hoped so, too, I thought, but felt too shy to say it out loud.

∽ 12 ∽

The Secret Chamber

As I dashed back in the house, my heart was fluttering like Aunty's embroidering hands. I checked Purple's and Leilei's rooms, but neither had returned. Since it was only seven-thirty in the morning, I imagined that Purple might just now be waking up with her lover in the haunted temple, and Leilei perhaps with her man in one of the inns along one of the Soochow rivers.

Would they imagine that now I had a male friend too? Weren't they worried that Aunty would come back early and put two and two together? But it didn't seem likely. To go back to Peking again so soon, she must be doing something very important for herself, something other than simply picking up the photographs.

Then I realized I had the opportunity I had been waiting for so long—to go up to her forbidden room to snoop. I tiptoed upstairs and knocked softly on the door and, as I expected, there was no answer. I twisted the knob back and forth and, also as expected, it was locked as tightly as her lips were when asked about her past. But my instinct told me she must have a spare key hidden somewhere.

I searched underneath a large vase and carpet on the stair landing, but no luck. Then I had an idea and dashed downstairs, hurrying across to the altar. I picked up the ceramic Guan Yin statue, shook it, and turned it over. But to my great disappointment, there was no key. Finally, my eyes landed on Aunty's teacher staring back at me from her photo. I lifted off the framed photograph and turned it around. Sure enough, a little cloth pouch had been sewn on the back. I reached inside and pulled out the key, being careful not to tear the cloth.

The key turned smoothly in the lock and I swung the door open. Sunlight streamed in through a window high up on the wall. The room was modestly furnished with a plain wooden bed, a large chest of drawers, and a bookcase. What immediately attracted my attention was the embroidery covering all four walls. If the works downstairs were excellent, these were exquisite. I turned my head to survey them: brightly colored carp swam in schools; lotuses bloomed on a rippling pond; white cranes spread their wings above undulating waves; bats—to symbolize good luck—flew in the four auspicious directions; dragons undulated through colorful clouds and lightning flashes. . . .

Looking at these beautiful images, I felt myself transported to another world. Finally, when I came back to reality, I noticed a small writing desk on which stood a wooden frame enclosing an embroidered portrait of a young couple. The man had a high, shiny forehead, neat crescent-moon brows, single-lidded eyes, a knobby nose, and thin mouth. A handsome man. The woman was wearing an elegant, high-neck embroidered silk *cheongsam.* As I studied the young woman's image I realized with a start that it was Aunty Peony herself! What was she doing with a man? Or perhaps it was merely her younger brother—but he did not look like her.

The work was painstakingly done. Every single hair on their heads, even their brows and lashes, was visible. Their faces were shown with colors ranging from pink, to brown, to deep brown, all depicted with invisible stitches.

I remembered when Aunty had taught me how to embroider portraits. She said, "If you use only threads of one color to embroider eyes, they'll look like a dead fish's. To make them look alive, you must choose threads with many gradations of white, split the threads as thin as possible, then sew the brighter and darker areas according to the light. This way, the eyes will be round and realistic."

In Aunty's portrait, the couple's eyes appeared so alive that I imagined I could see into their souls. I felt a little uncomfortable, as if Aunty herself were watching me invade her private life.

Calligraphy ran down the right side of the portrait. *Qinse hexie, huahao yueyuan,* meaning *qin* and the *se* music played together harmoniously and the flowers beautiful and the moon round. This was a popular celebratory saying for married couples. So was this man Aunty's husband? This was a shock. If she had been married herself, then why our celibacy vows? I'd never seen this man, of course. Perhaps he was a ghost, like my own husband.

Inadvertently, I knocked over the portrait, and as I leaned over the desk to put it upright, I slipped and fell hard against the desk. I felt a little dizzy as the wall behind the desk seemed to shift. After rubbing my eyes, I looked again, only to find that the wall was really moving. Then I pushed myself up and, to my complete surprise, part of the wall swung open like a door.

Before me loomed a secret chamber, a mystery within the mystery of Aunty's room. Gingerly, I stepped in. In the dim light I could make out many shelves and drawers. Something bright was hanging on the wall—a dazzling yellow robe. Everything else was in shadow, so I ran as fast as I could down to my room and brought back my oil lamp.

The robe resembled the one in the Lotus Embroidery Shop in Peking that Aunty had declared a fake. Now I could see why—this one was of a completely different standard.

Countless laboriously layered threads gleamed in the light of my lamp. There was a fullness in the way the fabric hung, almost as if it were still inhabited by a living, breathing body. I'd never seen threads, silk, and craftsmanship so fine. Not one coarse surface or sloppy stitch was to be seen. The nine dragons embroidered with threads of gold seemed about to leap out at me. Their eyes and whiskers seemed to follow me as I moved around admiring them.

I remembered an expression for extolling masterpieces, *qiaoduo tiangong,* which meant "cleverly robbing Heaven's skill." Then I realized what had been at the edge of my mind: This masterpiece must be the robe of an emperor! Could this really be so? It must be, because the emperor's symbols mentioned by Aunty were all here: sun, moon, stars, mountains, arrows, ax, bronze vessal, fire, rice—and the seaweed missing from the fake one. The dragon's robe in the middle of nowhere? And in Aunty's possession? Had she made it herself or been given it—I did not want to think that it was stolen.

But there was much more here, so I walked around the secret chamber to glimpse the rest of her hoard. I spotted a Guan Yin embroidery in a corner. Its craftsmanship was flawless, but it seemed rather dull because the embroidery was all against a white silk background. Something was different about the threads, however, and, with a start, I realized the entire work was made from human hair, likely the offering of a very devout lady, maybe Aunty Peony herself.

She had told us about the use of human hair to embroider religious figures as offerings. But if she had cut off her own hair to create this goddess, she must have done it because she wanted something back from the goddess. What it was I had no idea.

I was getting nervous that Purple or Leilei would return soon, but I could not resist looking at another piece, a simple one, showing yellow butterflies with translucent wings hovering over blue flowers. I turned the frame around to see a completely different picture—orange-spotted carp swimming in a weed-strewn pond.

I realized this was the famous double-faced embroidery for which Soochow was known. Aunty—though frequently boasting that she was teaching us the secrets of a thousand beauties—never mentioned these techniques. She was holding these back for herself, like many teachers. This way the students will never excel over their masters and they will keep coming back, hoping to learn the ultimate secrets of the craft.

Now I was even more nervous, so I started quickly opening drawers, hoping to find more of my teacher's secrets. There was no embroidery work in the drawers, but instead I found piles of notes, patterns, fine silk threads, and expensive embroidery tools.

So here were the things that Aunty held back for herself. There was no time for me to memorize the designs to inscribe in my secret cave. And though I would have loved to take them to my room to study, as soon as Aunty noticed they were missing she would quickly search everyone's room. So I reluctantly set down the sheets, doing my best to arrange them exactly as I had found them.

Next, I stroked the threads, enjoying the cool feel of the little rainbow. When I picked up the last few bunches of threads, I spotted a thick book bound with brocade. I assumed it contained more patterns and notes, but when I opened it and started to read Aunty Peony's tiny, very neatly brushed characters, I quickly realized that it was her diary. It seemed that, after all, she did confide her thoughts, not to us, of course, but to a notebook. I felt guilty intruding on her private life, but my curiosity was too much. Besides, she knew my secrets, so why shouldn't I know hers?

I thumbed through the notebook. Much was about embroidery, but then I spotted a more interesting entry:

> *I was a fool to believe that the Son of Heaven was truly in love with me.*

I gasped out loud. Could Aunty really mean the emperor? Was this just her imaginings? I continued to read.

> *He probably did love me, but he also loved many other women. After all, officers from the palace scoured the empire to find the most beautiful and seductive and, when possible, talented women. Unfortunately for me, these men were all too successful in their quest and so the palace was filled with ladies seeking the emperor's favor, at least for a night.*
>
> *The Buddhists teach that everything is impermanent, even love. I came to realize that we girls were like chickens—to be consumed for a pleasant time. He picked both us and the chickens very carefully. Before they were cooked, he'd meticulously check each bird's crown, eyes, muscles,*

*feathers, and feet. The bird would be cleaned, then
seasoned with precious herbs and condiments to make
it as tasty as possible. After his dinner, nothing was
left except the bones.*

*With his concubines, once he'd feasted on our
virtue, we would be discarded like the chicken bones.
Would he remember the chickens who warmed his
stomach, or the women who warmed his bed? Of
course not. Because the next night, and the next after,
as long as he ruled, there'd be a new chicken and a
new girl.*

*The palace is the biggest whorehouse, and the
emperor the best customer.*

*But still I let myself hope I was special and that he
really loved me. And he did treat me differently from
the others—for a while. But the day came when he
had to choose between me and earthly power and
possessions, even including the robes and
undergarments that took me years to embroider,
slowly ruining my hands and eyes.*

*I know he greatly valued my embroidery work. He
provided maids to attend my every moment. I never
had to lift a finger to get wine or food or whatever else
I wanted. He said that I must care for my hands. So
every day I washed them with warm fragranced water
soaked with precious herbs and rubbed on nourishing
oil concocted from flowers and honey so I wouldn't
burn or stain my hands, or twist their tendons. I was
not allowed to wash fabric, lift heavy things, or even
pick flowers from the imperial garden. But I still
injured my fingers a few times with my own needles.
So I learned you're never completely safe in life.*

*My hands were precious treasures because only I
was allowed to embroider formal clothes for the
emperor.*

I gave him not only his dragon robes, but a dragon seed—I bore him a son. But sadly he never even reached his first birthday.

But it is said that good times never last. Mine ended because of a gift from the empress. When the eunuch arrived, holding it in his outstretched arms, at first I'd thought there was some mistake—I knew that her jealousy had made her hate me. When I opened it, I found an embroidered silk scarf—the very one that I had made for the emperor. It was one of my best works and the emperor loved it so much that he wore it under his gown all the time. Enclosed with it was a poem:

> *Everything comes to an end in this world,*
> *So what's the difference going to the underworld?*
> *As if you are wandering in a foreign land.*

I was puzzled that a scarf and a poem could bring misfortune. I continued to read.

The empress gave me my embroidered gift to the emperor to hang myself! How ironic that I also was supposed to thank her for granting me this favor— ending my life by my own hands with my own scarf, instead of suffering extreme tortures and, finally, being beheaded.

But I chose a third option—escape.

Sometimes when I think about these things, I fear I'll go crazy. Perhaps it does not matter what happens to me, because my embroidery will survive.

I have no regrets leaving all the luxuries behind. But I do grieve that I had to leave behind with him my love, my youth, my dreams. My departure from the palace was not glorious but sordid. I faked my own death. A girl had just been murdered by some of her fellow concubines, so I was able to bribe two eunuchs

*to steal her corpse. After dressing her in one of my
gowns and putting the scarf around her neck, they
threw her down a well.*

*Later, when the body was discovered, it was
assumed to be me. No one could tell who it was, since
her face and body were swollen beyond recognition.
Meanwhile, I had been hidden away by the two
eunuchs, waiting for the empress to think I was dead.*

*In the imperial household filled with hundreds of
people, someone was always dying. Since an elderly
maid had passed away at this time, the eunuchs
dumped her body in a wooded area outside the palace,
then sent me out in her funerary carriage, announcing
that it was carrying the old woman's body for burial in
her village.*

*So I found myself alive in the outside world and
not at a loss for money because I had taken with me
many imperial treasures. But most important, I had
the protect-the-embryo herbs given me by the imperial
physician, for I was pregnant with the dragon seed.*

*I guessed that the gossip about my suicide would
die down quickly. After all, concubines killed
themselves from time to time, and the loss of one
woman was not that important—there were always
others to take her place.*

Reading this, I felt dizzy and sank down onto the floor. That my
own teacher, so stiff and prim, had been the emperor's lover! And
she had escaped the empress's wrath by pretending to be dead. . . .
It was hard for me to match this story with the prim teacher I knew.
However, it did explain her authoritative air . . . and her sadness.
Although I felt ashamed of my curiosity, I could not keep myself
from continuing to read. . . .

*I think sometimes I am like Emperor Xuanzong's
beloved concubine Yang. Of all the beautiful women
in the inner palace, the emperor cared only for her. I*

often think of Bai Juyi's poem about their love, "Song
of Everlasting Sorrow":

> *Wishing to be birds flying together,*
> *Or on earth, intertwined roots.*
> *Heaven and earth will perish someday,*
> *But my regret knows no end.*

But what's the use of regret, Emperor Xuanzong?
It was you who lifted her to the heights and you who
gave her the white robe to hang herself. Just to
appease your soldiers who deemed her the femme
fatale who would doom the Middle Kingdom. In the
end, you chose power.
After that, you felt so lonely that you called upon
all sorts of shamans and diviners to speak to her. But
she never answered. And so you died a lonely and
loveless old man, surrounded by willing concubines
for whom you felt nothing.

I knew about concubine Yang, but had never thought much
about her; it was just another sad love story. There were no more
emperors anyway. But my teacher had known one—more than
that, had loved one. And become pregnant by him. Now I wondered again who the man was on the embroidery portrait—he must
not have been the emperor as he did not wear a yellow robe.

All this seemed so strange to me that I really did not know what
to think. Somehow, though, I had known that Aunty Peony was not
an ordinary embroiderer, not even an ordinary person. She was
linked to something big. Very big—and scary. My eyes inadvertently landed on the imperial robe and suddenly it was obvious to
me that she had stolen it when she'd escaped from the palace. Had
she been caught, she would have been killed in the most horrible
way imaginable. The realization was so disturbing that I had to slap
a hand over my mouth to keep from screaming.

I thought I heard a sound somewhere. Panicking, I quickly put
everything away as best I could and stuffed the diary back to the

bottom of the drawer. Trying to make as little sound as possible, I came out into the bedroom, pushed the table back, then tiptoed rapidly down the stairs. Seeing no one in the living room, I went to knock on Purple's, then Leilei's door, but got no response. Realizing that I had not been caught snooping, I heaved a great sigh of relief and slipped the key back safely into its little pouch behind the picture.

I was still worried, though, now about why Purple and Leilei had not come home. Was I to be abandoned, leaving only Aunty and me to complete *Along the River*? But I tried to reassure myself that they knew Aunty would not be back tonight.

Exhausted and with a headache, I went into my room and lay down. I kept imagining Aunty hanging from her embroidered scarf, eyes and tongue protruding, as if she had not escaped. Questions revolved in my mind like a merry-go-round. Why did the emperor allow the empress to try to eliminate Aunty?

I wanted to go back up to read more of her diary, but knowing what I did, I felt scared to find out more. My teacher was obviously tougher than I'd realized. Would she have me killed for knowing her secrets?

❧ 13 ❧

More Secrets

It was not until the next night that Purple finally came home. She looked flushed and happy, no doubt from tasting the elixir of love. After we greeted each other, she went to take a bath, and I headed to the kitchen. Soon we were noisily slurping spicy noodles and crunching stir-fried vegetables.

I said, "Sister Purple, you look happy."

"Well, because I *am* happy."

"You went to see him?"

Her face bloomed with a mischievous smile. "Spring Swallow, you must promise never to tell anyone about this; otherwise, I'll tear your lips off!"

"Trust me, Sister Purple, my lips are sealed as tight as a coffin."

She poked me playfully with her chopsticks. "Don't joke about unlucky things."

"Sorry. So how was it?" What I really wanted to ask was, how did *that thing* go?

Her face flushed as red as the chili in the noodles. "As good as it can get."

Did she mean just meeting him, or *that thing,* or both?

"Hmmm . . ." I was chewing and thinking. "Why don't you tell

Aunty about this and maybe she'll give you permission to leave and marry him?"

"It's not that easy." She sighed, putting down a bok choi that she'd just picked up.

"How come?"

"Because I know Aunty Peony. She took me in, has been housing and feeding me for almost six years. I owe her for all that and I don't have any money. I can't just walk away like going out to the market. But, of course, I could . . ."

She paused, but I'd guessed what was on her mind. "You plan to run away with him?"

She cast me a sharp look. "Shhh . . . no one should know."

"I won't tell, Sister Purple."

She looked around as if there were a third person in the house. "Jiang and I have been thinking of this for a while, but I've been trying to get up the nerve. . . ."

She distractedly chewed her food, then suddenly blurted out, "Spring Swallow, you want to run away with us? To Peking?"

I was confounded by this unexpected offer. Of course I had thought of leaving, too, but had no answer to the countless questions that would whirr in my mind: Where to live? How to make a living? What would happen to the unfinished *Along the River*? I often felt oppressed by Aunty's severity. We worked long hours to supply goods to Heavenly Phoenix but never saw any money except the pittance she doled out to us at the end of each month.

Despite Aunty Peony's faults, now that I knew about her past life I felt some sympathy for her. She did teach us, even though she held back her best skills. But she'd never trusted us. She wouldn't lend me her patterns to copy, no doubt assuming that I'd sell them. Or that someday I would try to go out on my own. Of course, she was right about that. But I still had much to learn; so even though Purple's offer was tempting, I felt that I needed to stay with my teacher. I still hoped that someday she would pass on to me her imperial skills, especially the exquisite, double-sided embroidery.

Also, I really had no idea what I would do if I left. So I asked, "Sister Purple, why do you want me to leave with you?"

"Because we can help each other out, maybe even start our own embroidery shop."

"What about Leilei?"

"I have a feeling that she'll run away with her man soon. Anyway, I don't want her with us. She's a troublemaker."

"Then what about poor Little Doll?"

"She's so young, it's better that she stay here with Aunty."

It sounded like Purple had already thought everything out.

I asked, "You think Aunty Peony is really that bad to us?"

She thought for a long while. "Hmm . . . I wouldn't say so. She's had a hard life, so we shouldn't expect too much from her."

"What kind of hard life?" I asked, although I already knew some of the story.

She hesitated. "I don't know if I should tell you."

"I'll nag you until you do."

"Can you keep your mouth shut, Spring Swallow? Promise not to tell anyone, even your lover, when you have one."

"Promise."

"Swear by Guan Yin over there."

I stood up, bowed to the statue, and swore in a loud, vehement tone that I would not ever tell anyone Purple's secrets.

"You're sure you mean it? I guess you do. You've never lied to me before."

She leaned over toward me, and declared in a dramatic whisper, "When Aunty was young, she was an embroiderer in the Forbidden City!"

Of course I already knew not only this, but that she had been the emperor's lover. But I thought I would get more out of Purple if I played dumb. Besides, I didn't want any bad consequences from opening my mouth.

Had Purple also been inside Aunty's secret chamber and read her diary? Should I confess that I had? But she'd told me she was afraid to sneak into our teacher's room.

"Sister Purple," I tried to sound calm, "how do you know this?"

I could not have been more shocked when I heard her say, "I got it from Aunty's own mouth."

"What?!"

"That was before Leilei and you came. I was alone with Aunty. Sometimes she would get in a horrible mood and start downing her plum wine. This night she drank even more than usual and was so drunk she could hardly stand up. I was going to go to my room to sleep, but she asked me to stay with her.

"Aunty started talking as if I were not in the room with her. She said, 'I was the best—except my teacher Qiu Niang, who also worked in the palace.' "

I asked, "Qiu Niang?"

"Yes, the one Aunty asked about at the embroidery shop in Peking."

"So what about Qiu Niang?"

"I'll tell you later. Let me finish telling Aunty's story first."

Purple stopped to take a sip of tea, probably to soothe her nerves, and I did the same.

After setting her cup down with a clink, she went on. "Aunty Peony told me that the emperor . . . you're sure you won't tell anyone, Spring Swallow?"

I nodded vigorously. I had a pretty good idea what she was about to reveal, but I wanted to be sure.

"Anyway, she told me that the emperor was enamored with her, that she was very beautiful in that day. But, of course, the empress sensed this. She did not care about the other concubines, but because the emperor loved Aunty she went crazy with jealousy."

I asked eagerly, "Sister Purple, Aunty really told you all this?"

"Yes, I think she'd never dared tell anyone, but she was so drunk she let it out."

"Then what happened?"

Purple hesitated before she resumed. "Oh, Spring Swallow, I believe horrible things happened then. The empress ordered her to kill herself! Somehow she escaped, she didn't tell me how."

"She was lucky?"

"Of course, but she is more crafty than we think."

I nodded.

"But I found out why she hides in this desolate place that is so boring."

I had often wondered about this, but now it was not so boring to me, since I had met Shen Feng. But this was certainly not the moment to tell Purple about him.

She continued without waiting for me to respond. "They're after her!" she announced melodramatically.

"Who—"

"I better look around."

I assumed this was to be sure that Leilei had not chosen this moment to return. Purple opened the door, stepped out, and looked all around the house, before returning with a relieved expression.

"There are men from the Qing . . ."

"But there's no more Qing dynasty."

"That's just it. They want to bring it back."

I was puzzled by this, but, of course, had not much idea about politics—and didn't want to.

"Aunty told me that when she escaped from the Forbidden City she was pregnant!"

I had known this, but had no idea where he might be buried. Or if he was really the son of the Son of Heaven.

"That's why they are after her. There is a secret group that wants to restore the Qing dynasty—they know about her son and have been searching for him, to make him emperor."

"But, Purple, why didn't Aunty tell the empress that she was pregnant? Because of her dragon seed, the empress wouldn't harm her and maybe even let her remain in the palace."

Purple shook her head vehemently. "No, the empress would be more likely to kill her!"

"Why?!"

"If Aunty were out of the way, the empress could raise the son as her own."

"What about the son? What happened to him?"

"Aunty would never tell me. She must have given him to another family—or maybe he died."

"How sad."

But what was really on my mind was whether, as Purple feared, Aunty was really being chased by those crazy, leftover Qing dynasty officials. Whether or not there was still a dragon seed who could reinstate their imperial glory. If they found Aunty, I was sure they would kill all of us. A panic seized me because I knew something that Purple didn't—that Aunty had stolen many of the imperial treasures, and even had the emperor's gown. If these men were so fanatically loyal to the Qing, they would kill her for this. The gown represented the emperor's presence and power, so anyone who possessed it other than the Son of Heaven would be punished by death! I dared not say anything to Purple about the stolen gown because if word leaked out, it could be the end of us all.

The headache I'd had after reading the diary with all its terrible events was coming back.

Hoping for reassurance, I asked Purple, "Do you think they are really looking for her, even now?"

"Spring Swallow, that's why I asked you to come with me and Jiang. Since I know Aunty's story, I never feel safe here."

"But those officials, or eunuchs, or whoever they are, should be very old by now, maybe even dead!"

"*Hai,* you really don't understand, do you? First, I don't think they're *that* old. They are Manchus and very vengeful that their dynasty was overthrown. They want their power back, so they will do anything to restore the Qing and the imperial system. Aunty's son is the only possible one who can occupy the throne."

"But you think he's dead?"

"I think he must be, but I don't know for sure. And they don't know."

I leaned my throbbing head on my hands. I had been so curious about Aunty and now I wished I did not know what I knew.

I did not want to hear any more, but Purple had more to tell me. "You know about Qiu Niang?"

"You mean her teacher, the one on the altar next to Guan Yin?"

"Yes. They had a falling out. Qiu Niang taught Aunty everything. But then the emperor fell for Aunty and sent Qiu Niang out of the palace. I suspect Aunty manipulated the emperor into doing this and later felt guilty about it. That's why now she makes offerings and makes us pay respect to her as our grand-teacher—to appease her ghost."

"Then why did she ask about Qiu Niang when we were in Peking?"

"I believe Aunty is afraid she died after being sent away from the palace."

"Did Aunty also tell you this?"

Purple sighed. "Ever since that night, Aunty has been cold to me—she never tells me anything anymore. I think because she spilled her secrets to me, she fears that I'll report her to get a reward. But I would never betray my teacher."

Purple rubbed her eyes. "All right, no more talking about inauspicious things. Let's go to bed. If we are going to leave here, we need to get ready."

My head throbbing on the pillow, I kept thinking about whether I should leave with Purple. She was my only friend, but what if we had a falling out and I ended up homeless. I might have a bright future living in the big city of Peking, but if it did not go well, Aunty would never take me back. And if it got back to her that I was doing embroidery in Peking, she would do her best to ruin me. Yet, I did not want to be stuck working for her for the rest of my life. But something else was pulling at me—Shen Feng, my mountain friend. Could I say good-bye when we had barely met?

Finally, I fell into a troubled sleep.

∽ 14 ∽

The Masterpiece Disappears

When I woke up the next morning, Purple had already made breakfast. Neither of us said anything for a while.

Finally, I asked, "Sister Purple, when do you plan to leave?"

"Before Aunty comes back with Little Doll. We need to pack soon."

Suddenly I thought of another important question. "What about the embroidery; after we leave, who's going to finish it?"

"Don't worry, Aunty can work very fast if she has to; she'll finish it without any help. Right now she needs us to also make small items to bring in money quickly."

But I did not ask her about what was most on my mind: my friend on the mountain.

Exhausted from the revelations of the night before, we did not talk much during breakfast. After a period of awkward silence, Purple announced that she was still very tired and needed to take a nap. Feeling restless rather than tired, I picked up my embroidery and worked on it absentmindedly. Lunchtime came and went without Purple reappearing. Finally, worried about her, I knocked on her door, but as loudly as I knocked there was still no answer. Alarmed that she might have left without me, I pushed the door open to discover that Purple was lying unconscious on the floor. A puddle of blood had formed between her legs.

I knelt down beside her and raised my voice. "Sister Purple, what happened? Are you all right?"

She didn't answer. I grabbed her mirror and put it underneath her nostrils. Relief washed over me when I saw mist appear on the glass. I grasped her shoulder and shook her until she opened her eyes.

"Sister Purple, please tell me what happened. Should I bring you to the hospital?"

She moaned, weakly waving her hand. "No, just help me get back on the bed."

After I helped her to settle on the bed and propped her up with pillows, she began to sob. I put my arms around her, not knowing what to say. Not long ago we'd been discussing leaving together with her man and now she seemed to be bleeding to death.

"I'm pregnant, but I was afraid to tell you. But now I am having a miscarriage."

"What . . ."

"Miscarriage. I just lost my baby."

"What do you mean?" I felt confused; my mean aunt had never told me about this sort of thing.

"I was carrying Jiang's baby. But I just lost it." She pointed to the huge bloodstain. "It's gone. Baby, I'm so sorry. I failed to bring you into this world."

She turned to me. "Maybe this is my punishment for breaking my vow of celibacy."

I was at a loss to find words to comfort her, but finally said, "Stay here and rest, Sister Purple, I'll get a cloth and some water to clean this up."

I helped Purple wash and change into a new set of clothes. Then I cleaned the floor, washed her bloodstained pants as best I could, and hung them up. Then I found her some rags to soak up the blood. When I finished, Purple was still moaning in pain.

"Purple, I need to take you to a hospital. I'm scared; you're very pale."

"But then the house will be empty, and if—"

"Purple, you're still bleeding!"

"All right. . . ."

Before we left, I grabbed a few necessities, along with some money and a few embroideries I hoped I could sell. Then I tied everything up in a square cloth and went back for Purple, pulled her arm over my shoulder, and struggled through the door with her. Outside a woman was hurrying toward the house—it was a disheveled and irritable-looking Leilei!

I yelled, "Leilei, where have you been?"

"Am I allowed to have some fun, eh?"

Before I had a chance to reply, she pointed to Purple. "What's wrong with you? You look like a ghost."

As I was wondering what to say, Purple piped up weakly. "I'm sick. I have a severe stomachache. Maybe it's food poisoning. Spring Swallow is taking me to the hospital."

A sly smile flitted across Leilei's face. "Sorry to hear that; hope you feel better."

I asked, "Leilei, please come and help me with Purple. She can hardly walk."

"I'm sorry. . . ." Her pretty brows knitted. "I'm not feeling very well myself. See you when you get back."

"We need to go to Soochow, to the hospital."

"Well, when you get back I'll cook dinner, how's that?"

"Sure, thank you," I said.

Leilei looked at me as she smiled meaningfully. "Take your time. Purple, I hope you recover. Don't worry about the house. I'll be here keeping an eye on it."

She waved good-bye and went inside.

I had a bad feeling about Leilei being left to herself in the house, but I had to get Purple to the hospital. I half-carried my big sister to the outskirts of the nearby village, where we hired a donkey cart to bring us to the hospital in Soochow. The ride was slow and bumpy, and I was terrified that Purple would die before we could get to the hospital.

When we arrived, the emergency room was crowded with moaning and shouting patients. Fortunately, a nurse cast one look at Purple and took her into a room. I was told to wait outside. I paced the floor worriedly until about an hour later, when the nurse came out and told me that Purple was in surgery but would be fine. I stayed with her that night.

The next morning, the doctor came to check on Purple, said she could be discharged and admonished that she should be married before getting pregnant. I helped her up and together we walked to the lobby.

When I stopped at the front desk and opened my cloth bag to pay, the woman said, "We do not ask for money. We are missionaries at this hospital. But please come back to our church."

In the donkey cart back to the village, Purple said, "What if Aunty is back. What are we going to tell her?"

"Sister Purple, please don't worry too much. How can Aunty blame you if you're sick?"

"Spring Swallow," she sighed, "the reason I was so eager to run away is because I didn't want Aunty to find out I was pregnant."

"Sister Purple, why don't you just tell her the truth and marry Jiang?"

She shook her head. "I've made lots of money for her over the years, so she won't let me go that easily."

"If she has a lot of money, how come she's living in a run-down house instead of a grand mansion?"

"She can't risk attracting attention because of her past. I believe she's hoarding her money somewhere."

I didn't see any money in Aunty's secret chamber, so I agreed that it must be hidden somewhere else.

Despite the uncomfortable ride, Purple dozed off. My mind wandered to my mountaintop and Shen Feng. Then I dozed off, too, only to be awakened with a start by the cart driver's loud shout of, "Get off now. Pay!"

I opened the door to the house, helped Purple to enter, then called out, "Leilei, we're back!"

There was no answer and in the silence the house suddenly seemed eerie. Leilei was nowhere in sight.

I yelled again, "Leilei, where are you? We're home and Purple is all right!"

Still no answer. I helped Purple to the bed in her room, then looked in the other rooms, but there was still no sign of Leilei.

Purple said, "She must be out with her lover again. She won't be back until it's time for Aunty to return."

Something was bothering me; I assumed it was Purple's condition. Then back in the living room I realized with a start what it was. The long wooden frame where we sat to work on *Along the River* was empty! Heart pounding, I dashed over to it hoping my eyes had deceived me. I hoped I would find it lying on the floor under the frame. But, no. *Along the River* was gone!

I tried to think quickly. Aunty could not have come back for it. It had to be Leilei. She must have stolen it while Purple and I were at the hospital.

I dashed back to Purple's room and shook her shoulder. "Sister Purple, wake up. Leilei has taken *Along the River*!"

"What are you talking about?"

"Our embroidery. It's gone!"

Purple was awake, but confused. "How can it be gone? You're sure?"

"Leilei . . ."

She sat up straighter. "Yes, you must be right."

"Sister Purple, this is terrible. When Aunty Peony comes home she'll blame us, even if we tell her Leilei stole it. She'll say it's our fault for being away."

"We can't tell her I was in the hospital. . . ."

"We have to tell her. We'll just say it was food poisoning. But she'll blame us anyway."

Purple shook her head. "*Along the River* is Aunty's biggest commission. She'll be ruined and we will too. *Hai,* now I'm afraid I have to change my plan."

"What plan?"

"Now I've lost the baby, Jiang won't be in a hurry to marry me. So I'd better stay with Aunty for the moment. Even though she'll be angry, she needs us now to try to redo the embroidery."

"What about Jiang, what are you going to tell him?"

"He's already left for Peking. All I can do is send him a letter."

* * *

When Aunty finally returned with Little Doll in tow, Purple was nearly recovered. They brought back sacks filled with thread, silk and cotton fabric, needles, and, best of all, snacks—sugared pears, rice cakes, pea-flour cake. And, of course, our group pictures from the photography studio. We munched the snacks while looking at the pictures. Purple and I acted enthusiastic, but this was somewhat forced as we knew there would be an explosion from Aunty.

It would be soon because Aunty was already looking around suspiciously.

It was Little Doll who blurted out, "Where's Sister Leilei?"

Aunty asked sharply, "Yes, where is she?"

Purple and I looked at each other for seconds before she said, "Aunty Peony, I'm afraid Leilei is . . . gone—"

"What do you mean gone?"

"She's left. We don't know where she is."

"So she took advantage and went out to play. Leilei is wild, but she'll be back. She has nowhere else to go."

I blurted out, "Aunty Peony, Leilei is not coming back. Because *Along the River* is gone, too, and we think she took it."

Suddenly Aunty's face turned white as bleached silk, but she still managed to act calm. "When did you find this out?"

Purple told Aunty that she'd had a severe stomachache and so we went to the hospital in Soochow. When we came home, both Leilei and the embroidery were gone. Aunty didn't say a word.

A long silence passed until I said timidly, "Sister Purple believes we can redo the whole thing."

Aunty finally lost her cool. "Redo! Do you know what you're saying? We have only five months. Five months!"

Purple said very gently, "We have to try. I think we can do it, Aunty Peony."

But she seemed frozen in her anger. According to tradition, it was the master embroiderer who must lay down the first stitch. And until Aunty calmed down and picked up her needle and thread, we could not get to work.

She always emphasized the importance of the first stitch. "Pause to think for a moment before you sew your first stitch—since the next thousand stitches all derive from this first one. Placing the first stitch is like laying the first brick of a house. If it is done wrong, the structure will be slanted and collapse. In the past, the student was expected to hold a banquet just to celebrate the teacher's laying down this first stitch, and another for the last one."

Purple and I woke up very early the next morning and mounted a new piece of silk on the frame. Then we waited anxiously for Aunty to come downstairs. Of course, before she could lay down the first stitch, she would have to draw the outline, or at least the first section of it. But we had started the mounting anyway to show her that we were determined to re-create *Along the River*.

We waited and waited, but Aunty didn't come down. Finally, we dared to go knock on her door. We knocked until our hands were sore, but there was still no answer.

I asked, "Sister Purple, should we go in?"

"But how, we don't have the key. Unless we force open the door. . . ."

"I know where the key is." I regretted my words as soon as they were out of my mouth.

Purple stared at me with rounded eyes.

I had no choice now but to tell her how I had found the key . . . and that I'd been inside Aunty's room. But not about the hidden chamber.

"How long did you intend to keep this from me?"

"I'm sorry, Sister Purple. I was just too scared to tell you."

"All right, then get the key now!"

I dashed down to take the key from behind the portrait, then back upstairs. I handed it to Purple, who quickly opened the door. Gingerly we stepped inside, but there was no sign of Aunty. I did notice, however, that the portrait of her with the young man was not in its place on the desk. However, the desk was still blocking the secret chamber, so I knew she could not be inside.

Purple said, "Let's go look for her."

"But where?"

"I don't know, maybe on the way to Soochow. . . ."

"Why there?"

"Where else would she go?"

I suspected that Purple was thinking the same thing I was—could Aunty be so upset that she might try to kill herself? But neither of us wanted to express our fear out loud.

There was no sign of Little Doll. Aunty must have taken our little sister with her.

I was starting to be really scared. I'd heard that high palace officials never went anywhere without their servants—even into death.

Purple pulled at me. "Let's not waste any more time and go."

"Sister Purple," I stalled. "Three people are missing now, shouldn't we call the police?"

"Are you out of your mind? You want Aunty's identity revealed?"

At the neighboring village we rented bicycles, then rode as fast as we could to Soochow. But Purple tired easily and so we had to stop several times for her to rest. When we finally arrived at the city it was late afternoon. We rode around the streets looking for Aunty and Little Doll, but they were nowhere to be seen. Now we really worried that they might have tried to kill themselves. So we biked along the river, looking fearfully for any floating objects that might be bodies. We also kept calling out Aunty's and Little Doll's names. A few passersby cast us curious glances. Most simply hurried along, oblivious to our anxiety and fear. A few small children looked at us curiously as their mothers waited on benches.

Soon Purple and I realized searching for them like this was futile. We didn't even know that they had come to Soochow and even if they had, they could be anywhere. But we were not willing to give up either. Finally, feeling completely drained, we bought some buns and washed them down with tea from our thermos as we sat under the cool shade of a willow tree. After that, exhausted from our journey, we both dozed off. When I woke up, it was already dark. Purple was still sound asleep next to me. Luckily, our bicycles were still there, leaning lopsidedly against a tree like two battered war horses. No other people were within sight.

I gave Purple's shoulder a slight push. "Wake up, Sister Purple, wake up, it's already nighttime!"

She jolted awake, exclaiming, "How long did I sleep?"

"We both slept for hours."

As I was about to tell Purple that we'd better go back, she uttered softly, "Maybe Aunty doesn't plan to kill herself but . . ."

"But what?"

"That's what puzzles me, why would she just go away and abandon us?"

That made me think she was really going to kill herself and Little Doll.

"Oh, no!" I blurted out.

Purple was also screaming. "Look!"

"What?"

"There's something strange in the river over there."

"You're sure it's not just garbage?"

"I'm not sure, so let's go take a look."

When we got closer to the "object," we both screamed at the same time.

It was a woman lying with her back up, undulating in the current, her long hair stuck on a tree branch. I was sure we both feared this might be Aunty Peony. But what about Little Doll?

I asked, "Should we call the police?"

Purple gave me a sharp look. "No, if it's really Aunty, the police will come and search our house. They may even arrest us. I think we should just jump on our bicycles and get out of here."

"But then we'll never know if it is Aunty."

"Whoever it is, will her ghost come after us?" Purple looked almost as if she had seen one right in front of her.

"I was married to a ghost; I'm not scared of them. Besides, maybe she's still alive. I think we should take a look." Of course I was just as scared but did my best to hide it.

Hands shaking, we used some thick branches to pull the body toward the shore, then got a closer look. To our utter relief, it was not Aunty Peony. But our relief was short-lived.

It was Leilei!

Purple started to scream, so I slapped a hand over her mouth. But I let go as she vomited. We stood together in silence.

"How could she be dead?" Purple asked.

I was wondering the same and had no explanation.

Feeling a wave of nausea myself, I asked, "What should we do?"

"Spring Swallow, don't ask me . . . we need to think. Oh, Leilei, how could this happen to you?"

Then she covered her face and sobbed, her shoulders shaking violently. I held on to her and started sobbing myself.

When we finally calmed down and wiped away our tears, Purple said, "Listen, we can't just leave Leilei here . . . we have to give her a proper burial to appease her soul."

"But we can't stay here . . . it's dark now. Someone might come here and find us."

"But we can't carry her back either."

Then I had an idea. "We'll find the coolie with the donkey cart—the one who took us to the hospital. He can come here and take Leilei's body back."

"But what if he tells the police?"

"He won't want to deal with the police either—they might decide he murdered her. We'll just pay him extra."

It was very late when we finally arrived at our small village. Shops were closed and the streets were empty. In the background the mountain loomed dark against the darker sky. We soon spotted the cart, with its donkey and driver asleep under a tree.

Purple and I hurried over to him, shook him awake, and told him we'd pay him a lot to go to Soochow to carry something back. When he saw the money Purple took out, he didn't bother to ask what that "something" was. So we were soon on our way back to the city.

Purple and I whispered to each other about how to break the news to the coolie that it was a dead person he would have to carry back. But it turned out that we did not have to explain—when we arrived at the spot where we had left Leilei's body, it was nowhere to be seen. We jumped out of the cart and looked around as best we could, then asked the driver to take us downstream while we continued to search. But there was no sign of her body.

We went back to where we had originally found her body for a last look. Of course we did not find her, but I spotted something familiar a few feet out from the shore that was stuck on rocks. I took some cautious steps out into the river, leaned over, and grabbed it. It was the cloth sack Leilei had used to carry her things around with her.

Inside was a roll of soggy fabric. To our astonishment, it was the embroidery we had all worked so hard on—*Along the River*—completely destroyed. As I had feared, she must have stolen it to sell. But now it would find no buyers in its ruined condition.

Purple and I set the waterlogged bag in the cart and headed home. We dozed on the way back, but now we were worried that there might be a second tragedy—Aunty Peony. My hope that we would find her home with Little Doll was disappointed. The house was dark and empty. But for the moment there was nothing we could do, so, exhausted, we both went to our rooms and fell asleep.

I woke up first and was cooking our usual congee when Purple appeared, looking haggard. We sat down and ate silently.

Finally, Purple said, "We can't bury Leilei, but we have to do something for her. Let's go up on the mountain and make a little shrine for her. That way her spirit will have a resting place."

I agreed, and added, "We can bring some of her favorite foods to offer along with her favorite top and pants to bury."

Moreover, we decided to bury what was left of *Along the River* with her clothes. After all, she too had worked hard on it. Also, it was best that Aunty, assuming she would return, would not see it in its ruined state. Once we'd made the offerings and buried Leilei's things, we'd recite a sutra to comfort her soul.

After arriving at the mountain, we climbed for a few minutes to find a location that would not be visible from below. Purple picked a spot facing south. She said that even though this was traditionally the privilege of emperors, perhaps it would help Leilei to a better rebirth into a wealthy household where she could live the pampered life she had always desired. And this way the sun would shine on her.

Even though it was daylight, the moon was visible as a crescent. In my depressed mood it looked to me like thick, crying lips. A few pale wisps of clouds floated across it like incense smoke in a funeral home. I wondered if, like us, Heaven was mourning Leilei's short, tragic life.

We dug a hole into which we placed her clothes and the ruined *Along the River,* covered them over with earth, and marked the spot with two smooth stones. We poured a cup of tea from our thermos and prepared two plates, one with her favorite snacks and the other with a few coins. This was so that Leilei would not get thirsty, starve, or run out of money in her long journey to the other realm. And, of course, a tip for the King of Hell so he would let her cross over.

We lit candles, burned incense, and picked a few wildflowers for her little shrine. After that, we knelt down, lifted the incense respectfully with both hands, and bowed to Leilei's pretend burial site.

Purple began her prayer. "Old Heaven, please have mercy on our sister Leilei and grant her a smooth journey to the *yin* world. We also pray that you'll let her have food in her stomach and money in her pocket, so she won't be harassed by hungry ghosts. She had a hard life in this world, so please grant her a better next one. Also, please help us find out if she just fell into the river or was murdered. Leilei, our dear sister, may your soul be appeased and you'll soon reincarnate in your next life as a rich man's daughter, or wife."

After Purple finished, we held up the tea and the two plates as a gesture to offer them to both Heaven and Leilei. Then Purple recited the Heart Sutra: "The Goddess of Observing Ease entered the realm of wisdom and saw that all the five *skandhas* are emptiness, transcending all sufferings. . . ."

Back at the house, Purple and I were so drained that we went straight inside our rooms and collapsed on our beds.

~15~

Inside the Mountain Cave

The sun was just coming up when I awakened the next morning. I found Purple sitting at the table, staring through the window at the distant mountain.

"Sister Purple"—I sat down by her—"why are you up so early?"

"*Hai,*" she sighed. "You think I can sleep after all this? Anyway, I prepared some tea and noodles for you. Eat quickly and we'll go out."

"Go out where?"

She chided. "We'll burn more incense and make another round of offerings to Leilei. That's the least we can do for her. Don't forget, she just died, so her spirit is still hanging around her body. After that, we'll try again to find Aunty and Little Doll."

"Where are we going to look for them?"

"We didn't find them in Soochow. Let's try the mountain."

At the spot we had chosen, we bowed again at Leilei's shrine and recited the Heart Sutra once more. Then we continued to ascend. Purple was still weak and I am naturally a fast climber, so I had to slow down several times to wait for my sister to catch her breath.

On our way, we kept shouting, "Aunty Peony and Little Doll, where are you!?"

But the only response was our shouts echoing back from the rocks.

As we stopped about halfway up, Purple asked, breathing heavily as she pressed a hand over her heaving chest, "Spring Swallow, how did you learn to climb so fast?"

"Back in my old village I mixed with the street kids. Dangerous places were our playgrounds—mountains, cliffs, ponds, cemeteries. . . . Sister Purple, you look tired. You want to go back?"

But I was actually trying to find an excuse. I feared that when we reached the top, she'd learn all my secrets—my "diary," Shen Feng, and, worst of all, my copies of the embroidery patterns inside the cave.

She shook her head. "No, I will keep going to the top. We must find them."

I couldn't possibly argue with this. So we rested, drank our tea, and ate a light lunch of buns and preserved eggs, then resumed our climbing. Finally, we reached the top. Purple sat down on a rock, looked all around, then got up and gingerly approached the edge of the cliff to look down. After that I was alarmed to see her walk in the direction of my secret cave.

"Sister Purple, I don't think there's anything over there."

Purple pointed, and said eagerly, "Spring Swallow, looks like there's a cave hidden by bushes and vegetation, let's go take a look."

"But I don't think there'll be anything inside. . . ."

"You never know."

"What if there're spiders, or snakes, or a tiger?"

She cast me an annoyed look. "We can't be that fearful if we want to find Aunty and Little Doll. Let's go."

I was trying to think what to tell her when she saw my notes and embroidery patterns on the cave wall.

However, when we stepped inside, I screamed, "Oh, Heaven!"

"What's wrong, you see Aunty and Little Doll?"

I was shocked, not because of what I saw but because of what I didn't. I stepped toward the wall to have a better look.

"Spring Swallow, why do you look so shocked, there's nothing here."

Yes, exactly. All my writings, embroidery notes, and patterns were gone, scraped clean from the walls!

Purple studied the cave for a while before she signaled that we should leave. As she was stepping outside, she stumbled on a rock and I grabbed her arm to keep her from falling.

Then she saw something. "Look, Spring Swallow, here's a piece of cloth!"

She picked it up and we examined it closely. It was embroidered.

Then we called out simultaneously, "From Aunty's robe!"

The cloth had a brown streak on it—it looked like dried blood.

Purple's voice trembled. "Aunty was here—she must be hurt. I wonder if Little Doll . . ."

We looked at each other, afraid to say what we thought—that Aunty had come here with Little Doll and took her over the cliff with her.

Purple spoke, still breathing heavily. "Since they aren't here, why don't we go down the other side of the mountain and see if we can find them there?"

Or their bodies, I silently added. But at the base of the cliff was an expanse of water, so if they'd jumped I didn't think we'd find them—or their bodies.

We hurried down but saw no sign of either Aunty or Little Doll.

Purple smiled faintly. "Spring Swallow, if we don't see them, that means there's still hope." Then she looked at me curiously. "You realize that there's no one else on this mountain?"

I knew why but was not going to tell her.

She blurted out, "It's haunted, that's why! I didn't say anything before because I didn't want to scare you. People have been coming here to kill themselves since the first girl and her lover jumped to their death."

"Then why did Aunty build her house nearby?"

"Because no one would think to come here to look for her, that's why. Except for having to look for Aunty and Little Doll, I'd never have come up here to inhale all the bad *qi*. Promise me you'll never come here by yourself, all right?"

I nodded, having no intention to keep the promise.

Purple complained of feeling chilly, so we quickly walked down the mountain and back home.

That evening I lay awake, unable to blink an eye. Endless questions whirred in my mind: Aunty and Little Doll's whereabouts and their possible suicide; Leilei's stealing of the masterpiece and her sudden death; the destroyed embroidery notes and patterns that I had spent months memorizing. . . .

I was distraught that my drawings of Aunty's patterns were gone. So I'd thought of stealing them from her secret chamber when Purple was asleep. But I quickly abandoned the idea. Probably she had taken her treasures with her. And even if I was able to find them, I did not want to carry them to a hiding place and attract more bad *qi.* Or even get caught by the police.

The next morning, Purple told me she was not feeling well and needed to stay in bed. I asked her if she wanted me to go out and buy her some medicine.

"No, I just need more rest. Anyway, I still have the medicine from the hospital. Spring Swallow, don't worry about me. Why don't you go out and get some fresh air? I'm sure I will feel better tomorrow; then we can continue to look for Aunty and Little Doll."

"Where else can we look for them?"

"We didn't find her where the piece of her robe was, so I am still hoping that she and Little Doll are alive. But I don't know where. Maybe after I have some rest I'll think of something. Or you will."

After I left Purple in her room to sleep, I gathered up my ink and brush and headed back to the mountain. I wanted to examine the cave more carefully to see if there were any traces of my writings and patterns left. Without Purple to slow me down, I quickly reached the top. I was eager to see if there was a new message from Shen Feng on the nearby rocks—I had avoided the rock yesterday because I did not want Purple to notice the messages.

> Miss Spring Swallow,
> I came up but didn't see any message from
> you. In the cave were some drawings that I think

you did, but a few days later, the drawings were
gone!

When I went out of the cave I found a woman
and a young girl staggering around. I asked who
they were and what happened, but they seemed
completely confused. I took them both to the
hospital in Soochow.

If you read this, please let me know you are
safe.

Your mountain friend,
Shen Feng

I ran down the mountain and dashed home.

"Purple," I shouted, shaking her shoulder, "wake up, I think I
know where Aunty and Little Doll are!"

She rubbed her eyes, then, realizing what I'd just said, jumped up.
"Did you see them?"

"No, but they were taken to the hospital in Soochow. Hurry,
let's go!"

Two hours later, after another bumpy cart ride, we arrived at the
same dingy hospital, waiting in line at the same reception counter.
We described Aunty and Little Doll, and were directed to a room
on the second floor. We dashed up the stairs and entered a large
ward crammed with iron beds. Some patients were lying still, others wandering around or talking with visitors. On the floor next to
the beds were used food bowls, chicken bones, piles of clothes, and
chamber pots. The noise and smell were overwhelming. We looked
around and finally spotted Aunty Peony and Little Doll.

When Purple and I hurried to their bedsides, we saw that both
were sleeping and Aunty's head and hands bandaged. However,
Little Doll, except for a few small scrapes on her arms and legs,
looked quite all right.

I whispered heatedly to Purple, "You think Aunty is seriously
injured?"

I called out "Aunty Peony," as Purple gently touched her shoulder. Our teacher opened her eyes, saw us, and tried to sit up. I

reached around her to help her sit upright, then put a blanket behind her back and head.

"Aunty Peony, how are you and Little Doll?" Purple and I
asked.

"How did you find out we're here?" she asked, her voice as
weak as cheap tea.

Reluctantly, I told Aunty about Shen Feng and my secret cave.

She didn't say anything but glared at me.

Purple gave me a dirty look, and said into my ear, "You little
fox, how come you never told me about this?"

My teacher continued to glare at me, so I asked again, "Aunty,
are you and Little Doll all right?"

"Can't you see we're still alive?"

Silence passed before Purple asked, "What happened?"

Without looking at us, she said, "What do you care?"

I said, "We came all the way here to find you."

"Then why didn't you come sooner?"

"Aunty, we didn't know you were here. We've been searching
for you for days."

In a dull tone she said, "I tried to kill myself. . . ."

We both exclaimed, "But why?!"

"Why? Because Leilei's gone, *Along the River* is gone, my reputation ruined, and there will be no more business from Heavenly
Phoenix. So pretty soon we'll be homeless and starve to death!"

Now she cast me a sharp, angry look, but didn't say anything. I
was pretty sure this was about my copies of her patterns on the cave
walls.

Just then a middle-aged woman from a nearby bed yelled at us.
"Shhh . . . lower your voices, you gossipy women! This is a hospital, not a teahouse!"

Aunty looked furious. It took a few seconds before she shot
back, her voice suddenly turned high. "I don't care if it's a hospital
or a teahouse. I came from the palace, so I don't listen to people
like you. You miserable, pathetic lowlife!"

The woman laughed like she'd just been transferred to a mental hospital. "Hahahaha! From the palace! Maybe you peeked at it from outside as a child! Or looked at a picture of it!"

Aunty looked too angry to respond.

The woman shook her head, sighing and talking to herself. "*Hai,* crazy woman, maybe she should be in a loony bin instead!"

It seemed just when Aunty was about to fight back, she suddenly shut her mouth. She must have realized she'd carelessly leaked something to us—her imperial background. Purple and I exchanged understanding glances.

Purple immediately changed the subject. "Aunty Peony, how are you feeling now? And what happened to your head and hands?"

Aunty didn't respond to her but stared at me with eyes like daggers. "What happened, Spring Swallow, is that you who stole my patterns and wrote them in the cave?!"

"Aunty, that's not stealing. . . ."

"If it's not stealing, what is it?"

"I didn't steal, just memorized them—"

"That's still stealing! What if they were seen by other embroiderers?"

I didn't think anyone would ever find them, or even know what they were, if they did. But I was not going to pour oil onto her fiery anger.

She sneered. "But I have to praise both your excellent memory and your accurate rendering of *my* patterns."

Now it was Purple who looked at me with upset and disbelief. "Spring Swallow, you memorized those patterns and wrote them on the mountain walls?"

I nodded.

Aunty said, "That's why I had to scrape them off, and that's how the falling rocks hit me in the head and hands."

I gingerly asked my teacher, "Aunty Peony, I hope that your hands . . ."

She raised her hands and examined them, then spoke sarcastically. "Yes, my hands are ruined! You happy now?"

"Of course not, Aunty, but I'm sure they'll recover."

"How do you know, are you a doctor now or a clairvoyant?"

Neither Purple nor I dared to say anything.

Finally, Purple asked, "What happened?"

Aunty said without looking at us, her eyes blank and her expression sad, "When I went up the mountain with Little Doll I planned to end both our lives. Little Doll had no idea what was on my mind, but I knew she could not survive without me. Thinking that I took her out to have fun, she climbed happily in front of me, even humming a tune.

"When we reached the top, she stopped, pointing and shouting, 'Look, Aunty Peony, a cave!' My eyes followed the direction of her finger but saw only rocks and bushes. Before I could stop her, she'd already dashed inside. I heard her exclaiming, 'Aunty, come look at all the drawings!' So I hurried inside. Of course I was puzzled to see embroidery patterns inside a mountain cave. Then when I realized they were *my* patterns, I was furious!

"So I picked up a big rock and worked like crazy scraping off everything. Suddenly an avalanche of rocks fell on me. Then a big boulder tumbled down onto my right hand. . . . Then I woke up in the hospital here, with Little Doll."

Purple said, "Aunty Peony, we're so sorry for what you've gone through. Do you know how you got here?"

"Now I think I remember that a young man helped us, but that's all."

Purple and I cast a glance at our little sister. "How's Little Doll doing?"

"The doctor says she'll be all right. She has some bruises and shallow wounds, but she is still in a state of shock. So they are giving her sedatives, that's why she's asleep."

Purple pulled me aside. "Aunty's pretty depressed. We need to be sure she does not plan to try to kill herself again."

I agreed but had no idea of what to do. After all, Aunty was blaming me for the whole thing.

Purple walked back to the bed, and said, "Aunty, we think that Heaven has decided that you should live. So you must follow Heaven's will."

Aunty's eyes suddenly brightened and she looked happier. But then her happy mood deflated like a punctured balloon. "I don't think I can embroider, at least not for a very long time. . . ."

We both tried to comfort her by saying that she'd recover sooner than she thought.

"But *Along the River* is lost. Leilei's gone. It's hopeless." She turned her head away from us, tears welling up in her eyes.

We had no heart to tell her that Leilei was, in fact, dead.

After some silence, Purple said, "We can work faster. We'll just spend all our time embroidering so we can finish in five months."

Then, to my surprise, my teacher turned to me. "Spring Swallow, do you think you can finish this in five months?"

"We'll try our best," Purple said.

"But Spring Swallow will be the lead embroiderer."

Face turning pale, Purple protested. "But why?!"

"You know why—because Spring Swallow is already better than you."

Before Purple had a chance to react to this, my mountain friend suddenly appeared by Aunty's bedside.

Aunty cast him a sharp glance, then looked at me. "Who's this young man?"

"Aunty Peony, he's Shen Feng, the one who rescued you and Little Doll and brought you here."

With curious eyes, she studied Shen Feng from head to toe and made a few repeated rounds. "Is that so?"

Shen Feng nodded. "Yes, Aunty."

Aunty turned to me. "So you know him?"

"Yes, he's the man I told you about."

"So you broke your vow of celibacy!"

I hastily told Aunty that he and I had just met, nothing else. Shen Feng cast me an amused look.

"Young man"—Aunty regarded him sternly—"my girls are not allowed to make friends with men. Only if necessary for business. There's no pleasure in my house, only dedicated work! So, Mr. Shen, I advise that you stop seeing my girl. You think I don't know why you go to that haunted mountain where nobody goes?"

Now Shen Feng looked shocked. "But, Aunty—"

"There's no 'but.' Please leave now, young man, I need to talk to my girls in private. Thank you for bringing me and my little friend here; I am grateful to you for that. But you needn't come see us again. We are fine without a man, young or old."

I was astonished to hear Aunty treat her rescuer in such a cold, ungrateful way.

As Shen Feng was leaving, he winked at me. I hoped that this meant he would ignore Aunty's prohibition and keep meeting me.

Just after Shen Feng left, a Western doctor came to Aunty's bed.

The foreigner said to Purple and me in accented Chinese, "Don't talk too much and disturb the other patients."

Purple asked, "Doctor, when will my Aunty's head and hands recover?"

"Her head is fine. Her hands, she used them to fend off the rocks . . . it's too early to tell. She has a fracture in her right metacarpal. This will take time to heal. But she's all right otherwise, only bruises and abrasions on her shoulders, back, and legs. The little one is just in shock, no serious injury. Please, they both need to rest, so you can go now and come back tomorrow."

We thanked him, then said good-bye to Aunty. When we came downstairs into the lobby, Shen Feng was waiting, pacing restlessly. He came up, effusively thanking Purple for being so loyal to Aunty, while at the same time thrusting a slip of paper into my hand. As he was leaving, I told Purple I needed to use the bathroom. Once alone, I took out the paper and read.

> Spring Swallow,
> I want to see you again soon. I hope you can come to the mountain tomorrow, as early as possible. I will be waiting for you, but I don't have much time.
>
> Shen Feng

❧ 16 ❧

The Pledge

The next morning over breakfast, Purple asked, "Spring Swallow, how do you know this man?"

"We exchanged messages on the mountain. He saw my writing and answered."

She sighed. "*Hai,* nothing can fight human nature. You love him."

"But Shen Feng is not my lover—"

"Not your lover? I saw you together; it's very obvious."

"Really?"

"Of course, since I'm in love . . . you can always tell when a woman's in love."

"But, Sister Purple, we haven't done anything, not even hold hands. . . ."

"Have you heard of the Peony Pavilion story?"

"You mean about Aunty Peony?"

"No, it's a famous play. The woman met the man only once, and only in her dream. But she fell in love with him so deeply that she ended up dying of a broken heart. Not only did they never even hold hands, their only encounter was in a dream. This is the force of love, Spring Swallow."

"Do you love Jiang?"

"Yes, we love each other."

I gathered up my courage, and declared, "I love Shen Feng too."

"How do you know about love? Your only lover was a ghost."

I had not expected this—it was not like Purple to be mean.

She went on bitterly, changing the topic. "Are you happy that Aunty assigned you the job and not me?"

"What job?"

"You know what," she said, then went inside her room and slammed the door with a bang.

But I had no time to worry about her feelings, because I needed to hurry to meet Shen Feng on the mountain.

Once I reached the top, I saw Shen Feng silhouetted against the rising sun, playing the flute and looking tall and powerful. A bittersweet tune filled the mountain air, tugging at my heart. Purple had said I did not know what it was like to love a live man. But I thought what I was feeling must be love. It made me happy just to look at his back.

Hearing my footsteps, Shen Feng turned and smiled at me. He lowered his flute, then extended a helping hand. I willingly took it, even though I didn't need help. His hand felt different from Purple's or Little Doll's; it was big and very warm. Then I was surprised to feel myself being pulled into his arms, and even more surprised that I let him. He said nothing and I felt content absorbing his body's heat in the pure mountain air. Seconds later he let go of me, looked in my eyes, and kissed me, at first tentatively, then, sensing that I didn't resist, more urgently.

I had never been kissed by a man before. My emotions were a jumble—but I liked it.

When he finally released my lips, tongue, and body, he asked, "Did you really take the celibacy vow?"

I nodded.

He remained silent for a while, then spoke again. "Spring Swallow, I really like you."

I didn't know what to say to this. Of course, I really liked him, too, but was not sure if I should say so.

He shook his head. "Your vow doesn't mean anything. China is changing and women can decide for themselves. It doesn't matter what your Aunty tells you to do. Now, for me, if I really want something, I'll get it—at any cost. And I can't wait—because I have to go away tomorrow."

The thought of him going away now left me desolated. "Why . . . ?"

He sighed, his eyes surveying the mountain and the sky. "Here I coach university students part time." He paused, then said proudly, "But my real work is as a revolutionary—"

"A revolutionary? What does that mean?" I'd heard there was a revolution, but all I knew is that it was something political.

"We are working to overthrow the corrupt government that is stopping China's progress."

"But we already have a new government since the Qing dynasty is gone."

"But there are still evil warlords. . . . Anyway, I've just been assigned to leave Soochow for another city." He sighed. "I'm so sorry, Spring Swallow, I . . . don't know when I'll be back."

"I'll wait for you."

"It's not that."

"Then what is it?"

"Because this time I may . . . get killed."

My voice shot up. "Killed? Then why are you going?"

I remembered Father Edwin once quoted Confucius's saying, "The superior man would never stand under a crumbling wall," meaning we should avoid dangerous situations.

"Spring Swallow, I love my country and will do anything to help build a modern China so that my sister and her lover will not have died in vain. They were destroyed by the feudal system. I swore to oppose the evil forces until my last breath. That is what it is to be a revolutionary—we are China's future."

I stared in bewilderment at the man who'd just kissed me passionately. If he was going to get killed, why had he kissed me? To be his last memory?

Shen Feng held me, and said tenderly, "But don't worry, Spring Swallow, I promise I'll come back. For you."

Can one *promise* to come back from a dangerous mission?

"How long will you be away?"

"A few weeks, if not months. I really don't know. It all depends on headquarters."

"Where are you going?"

"Sorry, but I can't tell you—our revolutionary plans are top secret. Spring Swallow, I like you very much. More, I'm in love with you. Before we met, I already felt we were destined to be lovers just from reading your writings . . . that maybe . . . we were husband and wife in a past life. I hope you have the same feeling for me."

I liked Shen Feng very much, but everything seemed to be getting so complicated so quickly that I was now completely confused. He'd just said he was in love with me, but then he also was about to leave me. What did he really want?

As if guessing what was on my mind, he said, "I wish I could stay here with you forever, but sadly I cannot. So we must make the most of the time we do have together."

He tilted my chin so he could look into my eyes. "So, Spring Swallow, if you feel for me as I do you, we'll make a pledge and take Heaven, Earth, and this mountain to witness our love. Please tell me you will."

"But . . ."

"There's no time. Just say yes or no."

Feeling too embarrassed to say yes, I nodded while avoiding his gaze.

Shen Feng untied the flute from his waist and put it on my palm.

"Accept this—it is all I have to give you to remember me by."

The bamboo felt cool and comforting in my hands, but the tears coursing down my cheeks were warm and bitter tasting. I thought of Father Edwin telling me that Chinese think of bamboo as one of the three winter friends, together with pine and plum blossom. Bamboo is the noble person because it always grows straight and can survive the harshest winter. I was hoping that our love would too.

He leaned down to kiss me on my cheek, then wiped my tears with his flute-playing hand. I wanted to give him something in return but all I had was a small embroidered handkerchief. I handed it to him. He looked at it carefully, smiling as he appreciated the lotus flowers swaying above a pond. Then he put the handkerchief to his nose and deeply inhaled the scented herbs.

"Spring Swallow, what a beautiful piece! I'll take this with me wherever I go. Whenever I touch it or look at it, I'll remember your beautiful face."

"Feng"—I touched his face—"whenever I touch your flute I will think of when I first heard you playing it up here."

He kissed me again, took my hand, and led me to kneel on the ground facing north. From his bag he took out three incense sticks, lit them, then inserted them into the ground.

I looked down at the vast expanse of green veiled by the mountain fog. Rivers coursed in and out between red-roofed houses. After we silently appreciated the scenery looking in the distance like the land of the immortals, Shen Feng started to speak in a solemn tone.

"Heaven above, Earth below, and the mountain on which we stand, we respectfully ask you to witness Spring Swallow and me, Shen Feng, pledge our vows to be husband and wife."

I felt a jolt. I had no idea that he was going to "marry" me! Besides, I was already married. But since I was never going back to my old village, no one would know. So I put this worry from my mind.

Shen Feng went on. "We will always love and respect and take care of each other until our brows turn white."

After that, he led me to bow three times looking up at Heaven, three times looking down to Earth, and then the same to the mountain. When we finished, he took out a small knife and cut off a strand of my hair, then of his. He tied the strands together into two knots, then handed one to me and kept the other for himself.

"Spring Swallow, with these two-hearts-as-one knots, we'll be united forever. So we are now *jiefa fuqi*—hair-tied-together husband and wife."

Everything had happened so quickly that my mind couldn't catch up.

But it didn't have to, because my just-wed husband took me

into his arms. He pulled me to him so tightly as if he feared the slightest mountain breeze might blow me away from him into the mist below.

We remained silent for moments; then, as if hypnotized, I let Shen Feng carry me inside the cave. When he laid me down, I felt frightened, but also aroused by this man's love, passion, determination. Revolutionary or not, for the moment he was just my husband. Shen Feng moved on top of me and started to kiss my eyes, lips, and neck. . . . Warmth slowly rose up from between my legs as Shen Feng's hand joined his lips in discovering my body.

I'd never had sex with a man. This would be my first time, but I didn't dare to ask if this was his first. Once I had let one of the street kids kiss me and pull down my pants to see what was underneath. But this was different—now I felt awkward and shy as Shen Feng began to gently remove my clothes. I turned onto my side to try to hide my naked body.

"Please, Spring Swallow, let me . . ."

"But, Feng . . ."

"Please . . . time is running out, always . . ."

Now his big hands reached up and loosened my pony tail so my hair fell free on my naked shoulders.

I let myself go completely, kissing and touching him back, giving myself to this man I'd met only three times and who'd be leaving tomorrow. . . .

"Feng, promise me you'll be back soon. . . ." I murmured as I felt his lips brushing against my breast.

"I love you, my dear wife Spring Swallow, you must wait for me."

As his hands got more adventurous, I writhed uncontrollably under his strong, revolutionary torso, while feeling helpless, vulnerable, and, for the first time, deeply loved. . . .

～∾ 17 ∾～

Redoing the Masterpiece

That night I had a very disturbing dream. I was making love to Shen Feng in the mountain cave, but after we finished and he got up from me, I saw that he was not my mountain husband, but my ghostly one!

His blurry face split into a cunning, sharp-toothed smile. "So you think you're someone else's wife now, eh? That's just a dream! Because you're my wife till death and then for eternity! If you make out with another man again, I'll come back every night to haunt and fuck you!"

I jolted awake with a scream, sweating profusely. Though I knew immediately it was just a dream, it took me some time to calm myself. I wondered if my scream had awakened Purple. So I put on a shawl, slipped on my slippers, and walked to her room. I wanted to tell her everything about Shen Feng and the dream of my ghost husband.

I knocked on her door many times, but there was no response. I thought she must be completely exhausted from all the recent events—her miscarriage, Leilei's death, Aunty and Little Doll's attempted suicide and injuries. So I went back to my room and softly closed the door.

The next morning, I awoke to the distant sound of roosters

crowing. I went to knock on Purple's door, but there was still no answer. I feared that something was very wrong, so I pushed open her door and found that her bed was empty, and her embroidery tools, normally on the top of her small table, were gone. Alarmed, I dashed into the living room to see if there was any sign of Purple. A piece of paper was lying on the altar, in front of Guan Yin. It was a note from my big sister:

> Dear Aunty Peony, Spring Swallow, and Little Doll,
> I must depart without saying good-bye. I've stayed in this house a long time, but I've also done my share of bringing in money.
> Now it's time for me to move on. Aunty Peony, I'm leaving because I've found love and I want to spend my life with someone who truly cares about me. I'm breaking my celibacy vow and I hope all of you can break yours too. I wish you all a happy life with a loving husband and fat, healthy children.
> Please don't try to find me; you'll just be wasting your time. Spring Swallow, you need to get to work redoing *Along the River.*
> I don't think I'll be needed, or even missed, in this house. Sooner or later we all have to say good-bye. That's the sad truth about life.
>
> Respectfully and regretfully,
> Purple

When I finished reading, I collapsed on the chair and sobbed, feeling sick and dizzy. Leilei was dead. Purple had left for good. Aunty and Little Doll were still in the hospital. Shen Feng was off somewhere fighting his revolution. And I was left in a deserted house next to a haunted mountain. But the real haunting was not by the dead but by the living. Were there any more disasters waiting to happen?

I poured myself some tea and felt steadier after I took a few sips. I pondered why Purple had left without me, especially when earlier she'd asked me to escape with her. All I could think was that she felt bitter that Aunty had promoted me to be the lead embroiderer for *Along the River*. Maybe she also thought I should have declined and given the role back to her. But no one else cared who was the main embroiderer in this now-broken household.

Actually, I didn't care myself whether I was the lead embroiderer and felt sorry that Purple had taken it so hard. I decided to make offerings to Guan Yin and my grand-teacher for them to protect my big sister—wherever she went and whatever she did. Of course, I'd also ask Guan Yin to bless and protect my newly-wed-and-left husband, Shen Feng, the injured Aunty Peony, and shocked Little Doll. So I knelt in front of the altar where the Goddess of Compassion and my teacher's teacher Qiu Niang sat regally. I poured tea, lit incense, and bowed three times with utmost sincerity and respect. Then I went to bed.

The next morning, I dragged myself out of bed with heavy feet and arrived with an even heavier heart to begin the journey back to Soochow to pick up Aunty Peony and Little Doll and bring them home. I feared that Aunty would despair when she arrived home, now empty except for the three of us. On the way home, I finally told Aunty that Leilei was dead. I couldn't tell how she took the news because she was scowling the whole way back and said nothing.

Back home, Little Doll seemed oblivious and ate her hot soup and almond cakes with relish. With Aunty, however, I had to press her to eat anything at all. I felt affection for both, even though Aunty was cold and mean and Little Doll a little "slow."

Soon Aunty asked, "Spring Swallow, where is Purple? Why didn't she come to the hospital with you?"

Little Doll noisily slurped her soup as she looked around. "Yes, where's Sister Purple, how come she's not here?"

"Aunty Peony . . . Purple . . . has left."

She asked calmly, "For good?"

I nodded.

But Aunty kept her cool. "Hmmm . . . another one left. But how do you know she's not coming back?"

"Because she left us a note," I said, then took Purple's letter from the altar and handed it to Aunty.

After she read it, her face turned pale.

Little Doll put down her spoon and started to cry. "I want Sister Purple and Sister Leilei back!"

Aunty cast her a shut-up glance. "Stop fussing, Little Doll! We have enough trouble already!"

Seconds later, when both seemed to calm down, I asked tentatively, "Aunty Peony, what about Purple?"

"What about her?"

"Should we try to get her back? We could place a missing person ad in the newspaper."

"Absolutely not. What's the point? She left us a note saying very clearly she's leaving us and won't come back. She doesn't want to be with us anymore, you understand? You think she'll come back just because she sees an ad? Don't be naïve, Spring Swallow. Anyway, I already assigned you to do the work; she's not needed in this house anymore. Ungrateful bitch!"

Having no courage to respond to her anger, I continued to eat but without tasting the food.

When we all finished, Aunty said, "Spring Swallow, if Leilei's dead, what happened to the body?"

I'd been dreading this question, but I quickly explained how we'd discovered the body, only to find it gone the next morning. Aunty lowered her head, weighed down by all the misery. I thought she also looked scared—nothing made ghosts angrier than lack of a proper burial.

So I quickly added that Purple and I had made a shrine to her on the mountain and already made offerings to her spirit.

"All right, then we all better go to pay respects to her now, even though she betrayed us. We have enough troubles without being haunted. Let's go prepare offerings."

Then she turned to Little Doll. "You stay home and keep an eye on things. Clean or embroider."

"No, Aunty, I want to go with you and Sister Spring Swallow!"

"Stop whining. It's not the place for a little girl. You understand?"

When we were on the way to the mountain, I asked my teacher, "Aunty Peony, what if Leilei did not drown but was murdered?"

She looked shocked. "Spring Swallow, no more talk like this. Why would anyone do this to her? She must have gone wading in the river and drowned."

"I hope you're right." I knew she did not want any rumors that might lead to an investigation.

"Anyway, she's gone and when a person leaves, the tea cools."

Nobody wants to drink cold tea, so it will be poured away and forgotten.

Aunty went through the ritual quickly, yet respectfully. After we displayed the offerings—Leilei's favorite tea, snack, and embroidery—in front of her shrine, we lit incense and kowtowed.

Aunty said a prayer: "Leilei, we're all very sorry that you had to leave us under such a circumstance. But I promise we'll come here to make you offerings, especially on the Qingming Festival and other special days. We hope you're now in the Western Paradise surrounded by fragrant flowers, melodious tunes, and flavorful food. In your next life, we hope you'll reincarnate into a wealthy household. . . ."

Over the next few days, we settled back into our normal routine, or at least as much as we could without Leilei and Purple. But I did not yet start working on *Along the River*.

Finally, I asked, "Aunty Peony, can you give me the drawing of *Along the River* so I can copy?"

"There's no drawing."

"Then what are we going to do?"

She hesitated a long time, then, "All right, I'll draw it out on silk for you. I don't need a copy"—she pointed to her head—"it's all in here."

"But, Aunty, how can you remember all that?"

She looked at me as if I was stupid—like she sometimes looked at Little Doll. "Haven't I taught you that nothing is impossible if you put all your effort into it?"

"But your hands . . ."

"My right hand was injured, but I can use my left, which is still fairly agile."

I was stunned to hear this. "You can embroider with both hands?"

"There're lots of things you don't know about me. All first-rate court embroiderers had to be able to do this."

"But then why can't you embroider *Along the River*?"

"Because I don't want to go through that again. Drawing is easier than embroidering." She rubbed her eyes. "And I don't want to strain my eyes with the different colored threads. You understand?"

Before I had a chance to reply, she had dashed upstairs and closed her door with a bang.

Except for coming down to eat and bathe, Aunty Peony stayed by herself in her room for several days. Then one day she descended the stairs triumphantly, arms around bundles of silk fabric. She laid them on the table and asked Little Doll and me to sit beside her.

As she unrolled the scrolls, we were amazed to see her beautiful drawings of *Along the River* with all detail shown. I suspected that Aunty did not really reproduce the entire work from memory, but if she had the original imperial drawings hidden in her secret chamber I had failed to find them.

"Spring Swallow," Aunty interrupted my thoughts, "before you start to embroider, take several days to study the drawing. Then I'll lay the first stitch and help you with the difficult parts."

So the following days I did nothing but study *Along the River,* with Aunty pointing out important details and warning me about pitfalls. I needed to depict both serene rural villages and bustling city scenes. Aunty had not bothered to discuss the work with me in such detail before, and now I appreciated her genius more than ever.

Finally the day came to officially begin. Aunty Peony reminded me to bathe my entire body, especially my hands, and rinse my mouth with herb-scented water. Then she led me to offer incense, tea, food to her teacher, my grand-teacher, and Guan Yin.

When we finished, she said, "Spring Swallow, listen, you must live like the famous embroiderer Yu Chunhui, who locked herself in her room and would not come out until she finished her work."

I nodded as she used her left hand to carefully put down the first stitch onto the waiting silk cloth.

From that moment on, all I did was embroider, eat, and sleep. Not only my hands but my mind was strained. There were so many things to consider: the selection of just the right shades of colors, the thickness of the different threads, the various sized needles, and the kinds of stitches to lay down. Different details required different stitches to come alive—flat, realistic, wandering, cross, braided. . . . It all had to come together as a harmonious whole, a balance of dark and light, *yin* and *yang*. All this and keep the viewer interested as the energy gradually intensified to its climax— the chaotic scene depicting people gesturing and shouting as the boat is about to crash into the Rainbow Bridge.

To keep my interest as I worked, I imagined myself as the different people living in the prosperous metropolis one thousand years ago. I'd walk in leisurely steps along the crowded streets, passing a teahouse, a wine store, a butcher shop, a pawn shop, and a temple filled with devotees making offerings. I imagined entering a store selling musical instruments and plucking the four strings of a *pipa,* pretending I could hear the bittersweet melodies filling the air. I'd also enter a fabric and brocade store, my hands caressing the smooth silk. . . .

Every day when I finished work, Aunty Peony would look at what I'd done and give her opinion. She was unsparing; nothing escaped her cleaver-sharp eyes. If there was a flawed stitch, I had to take out the threads and redo it on the spot. Sometimes I would make more important mistakes and she would undo the whole area with an annoyed expression and re-embroider it herself, though I could tell that this was painful for her.

When I'd started to work on *Along the River,* I feared that I could not possibly execute such a sophisticated and complex masterpiece, even with Aunty's guidance. However, I kept telling myself that this was a test from Heaven. Either I'd finish it perfectly within the short deadline and prove myself a master embroiderer, or I'd fail and always remain a slave to Aunty.

Though I was grateful to Aunty for teaching me her skills, I couldn't help resenting her constant rebukes. Now that my chance of escaping with Purple was lost, my only hope of leaving Aunty was if my *Along the River* would win the contest.

When I felt overwhelmed by the daunting task, I'd remind myself of Father Edwin's quote from the sage Laozi: "A journey of a thousand miles begins with the ground under your feet."

He said, "Just keep walking and never stop, and one day you *will* reach your destination, however long the journey."

He told me about how hard it was for him, as a white ghost, when he first arrived in China to spread the word of God.

"I had to learn to speak Chinese, and also to read and write it. Every day I would wake up to study before the cock crowed. I studied so hard that my Chinese dictionary fell apart and I had to tie it with string so as not to lose any pages.

"Even when I could speak Chinese, no one listened. Chinese don't trust foreigners, and they think God is just another barbarian, only bigger and meaner. Sometimes when I spoke to someone, he would answer with a slew of dirty words, even spit on the ground. So I told myself it was God teaching me to be patient and kind. During the most difficult times, I reminded myself of Laozi's saying. And finally I succeeded in opening a church and a school. God's power is truly amazing, don't you think?"

I felt confused. Which power is truly amazing, God's or Laozi's? But, of course, I nodded enthusiastically. Not only because I truly liked Father Edwin, but also because it was he who made me a learned woman—for free.

Days and nights blurred into one another as I spent every waking moment working. Even though I tried to force myself to think of nothing but the work in front of me, my mind kept going back to Shen Feng and Purple. Thinking of them made me feel vaguely guilty; after all, here I was safely doing embroidery when Purple might be lost, or even abandoned, and Shen Feng might already be in battle. One was my husband and the other my big sister, and yet I was doing nothing for them.

With Leilei my feelings were mixed. Though she had never made even a friendly gesture toward me, I knew she did not deserve her tragic fate. In the end, her beauty did nothing for her, yet like the rest of us she only wanted a chance at a happy life. Such a pretty, ambitious girl, just to end up abandoned, her body dumped in a river. I still wondered how she had died. Yet I could not bring myself to feel sad that she was no longer part of the household. I hoped I would not become as cold and unfeeling as Aunty.

Months went by, each day being like the last except that more and more of the scroll was filled in. Hour after hour, Aunty was watching me, usually silent but quick with rebuke if I made any mistake. Little Doll was occupied running back and forth fetching us whatever we needed—tea, snacks, bowls of warm water for us to soothe our hands—occasionally being scolded by Aunty for making too much noise.

Then finally one day, it was finished. Or almost. According to tradition, the work was not considered complete until the teacher, that is, Aunty, placed the final stitch. She did this with a flourish of her now mostly healed hands, then led the three of us to pray in front of the altar. We then sat down to a sumptuous dinner with roast pig and sweet and sour fish from the Soochow River—all carefully prepared by an old woman from the neighboring village.

When we finished eating, Aunty Peony announced, "Spring Swallow, I'll be taking this embroidery to Peking. There will be a big fair where many people, including foreign ambassadors, are invited to appreciate Chinese arts. This embroidery will be part of the exhibit. There will be a prize for the best work. If *Along the River* wins, it will be donated as a gift to the American ambassador and he'll take it to be displayed in the famous New York City. If that happens, our work will be famous, not only here, but in Peking, even in America."

"Wow! I'm so happy to hear this, Aunty."

Little Doll clapped enthusiastically. "Yes, yes, Sister Spring Swallow, when it wins we'll have another huge celebration!"

I could feel the corners of my mouth rising higher and higher, like me climbing the mountain. Now maybe this was my chance to move up from being an unknown apprentice to a master embroiderer. Maybe I would even get invited to America to demonstrate my skill!

"When are we leaving for Peking?" I asked eagerly.

Before Aunty could respond, Little Doll clapped again. "I love Peking! I want Peking duck and sugared *hulu* and to buy kites and lanterns!"

Aunty gave her a sharp look. "Quiet down, Little Doll." She paused for seconds before she announced in her authoritative voice, "I'm going to Peking by myself. I'm going to be gone for nearly two weeks, so you two better stay here and not fool around or go off to Soochow or anywhere else."

Her declaration shocked me, and Little Doll looked as if she was going to cry.

"But why, Aunty Peony? It took me five months working non-stop, day and night to finish this for you."

"Because I said so. You two stay home and take care of each other. And you, Spring Swallow, stay away from that man. If you've been with him, I'll smell him on you when I get back and you'll be sorry."

I wasn't sure how she would make me sorry, but I tried my best to hold in my anger at this intrusion into my private life. Aunty had only me now and so could not kick me out even if she wanted to. But it did not matter because Shen Feng was off fighting his revolution.

Now Little Doll started to cry. "But, Aunty . . ."

This time Aunty didn't even bother to scold her or ask her to shut up. She just walked away.

✺ 18 ✺

The Opera Singer

Two days later, Aunty Peony left with two large bags and my embroidery wrapped around her waist under a loose long top. I had a bad feeling about this, because when Leilei's body had been found, she also had *Along the River* with her. Of course, I was not going to mention this to Aunty. It was bad luck, and talking about bad luck only makes it worse. The good thing for us was that Aunty would be away again, leaving the house to ourselves. For a few days we would be free of her prying eyes. Of course, I had something planned: entering Aunty's secret chamber for a longer look, this time without fear of being caught.

So the next day I gave Little Doll some money and told her she could spend it on whatever she wanted in the neighboring village. As soon as she disappeared down the road, I picked up my oil lamp and went up to Aunty's room, then entered her secret chamber. I wouldn't dare steal any of her imperial treasures, but I could now copy the embroidery patterns I liked, since Aunty had destroyed those I'd written on the cave walls. I still had these in my memory, but there were others I had never seen, so I wanted to copy as many as possible.

After a few hours of copying in the dim light of the secret chamber I was worn out, and so I picked up Aunty's diary and began to read at random:

> *Now that I am on the run, I don't know how I can keep from going crazy—if I don't get caught first. I am not me, but someone I had to make up.*
>
> *If I reveal that I was a court embroiderer, I'll be in great demand and get paid a lot, but I don't dare, lest some busybody pry into my affairs and discover that I stole the emperor's embroidery. So, here I am. The best imperial embroiderer stuck in a dilapidated house by a haunted mountain. Instead of creating for the Son of Heaven, I am reduced to selling my work in Peking. Though I never told the shop owner that I'd been in the court, he suspects something.*
> *That's why I adopted all these ill-fated girls in the hope that it will neutralize my bad karma. I had my years of glory; now I just want a few peaceful years.*
> *My youth has passed with every stitch and thread!*

Of course, I had no idea that Aunty had led such a sad life. Now I could understand her coldness and meanness, even sympathize with her a little. I continued to read.

> *In the palace, the emperor's concubines all favored embroidered gauze. They needed to look sexy and mysterious to compete to seduce the emperor. But not everyone who wore gauze would succeed in bewitching the Son of Heaven, only those who could attire themselves in the very best. So a concubine had little chance unless she could befriend—or bribe—the best court embroiderer.*
> *But the best embroiderer in the court was me, so I was the one who bewitched the Son of Heaven.*
> *Not only did I embroider my own seductive gauze,*

*I also embroidered the emperor's robe, and even his
undergarments. For just one elaborately adorned robe
was not enough for the Son of Heaven. He was clad in
many layers, each the product of immense labors on
the part of embroiderers, mostly myself. One inner
robe in particular, on which our names were placed
together inside where no others could see, he seemed
to love above all the others. When I escaped I took it
with one of his dragon robes as souvenirs.*

*So important was weaving embroidery for women
in the court that our methods were referred to as the
secrets of a thousand beauties. Secrets that the
emperor's women would kill each other for. . . . The
best embroidered gauze in which women "move
mysteriously like smoke and fog."*

I set down her diary and looked around. But I hadn't seen any
undergarment in the secret chamber, only the dragon robe. So I
went back out to the outer room and began to search—inside the
closet, her writing desk, a large ceramic vase—but still nothing. I
sat on her bed to think, and noticed her luxurious pillow embroidered with a pair of Mandarin ducks. On a small expanse of water
the two ducks were swimming leisurely among lotus flowers. I was
touched by the way the bigger, more colorful, male's wing was
placed lovingly and protectively on the female's shoulder. The work
was clearly by her hand and I was surprised that Aunty, always so
cold and distant, should be able to depict such tender emotion. But
once she'd had lovers, at least two, I was sure. She must have been
so enamored of one of them that she'd embroidered this to commemorate their love. The all-powerful emperor, or the ordinary
young man?

Examining the pillow, I noticed a specific stitch Aunty used to
embroider the waves that she'd never taught me. This was yet another technique she had held back from me. I decided to take off
the cover to see if the inside would reveal the secret of this stitch.
But what I found was totally unexpected.

The emperor's undergarment!

Touching such a beautiful, intimate—and dangerous—object made me dizzy. It had some of the same images and designs as the dragon robe, but was much lighter and smaller. Folding over the hem I saw the two names Aunty's diary had referred to. Rendered in thread that was the same color as the silk, they were nearly invisible. Though it was less overwhelming than the more splendid dragon robe, I was fascinated by the undergarment's delicate intimacy. I imagined the needle in Aunty's beautiful hand move tenderly in and out of the yellow silk, putting in each stitch with love, tenderness, and hope. I stroked its smooth surface, imagining Aunty doing the same when in bed with the Son of Heaven.

Of all her creations, it was this that most appealed to me, much more than the ornate dragon robe. I was tempted, but did not have the courage, to take the garment. I could stuff some plain cloth back into the pillow so Aunty would not notice, but I had no place to hide it and would be burdened carrying around something so valuable. Trying to sell it would be extremely dangerous. The buyer could accuse me of trying to pass off a fake, or report me for possessing imperial property. So after running my fingers over the delicate needlework one more time, I reluctantly put it back inside the pillow.

I went back to Aunty's secret chamber a few more times to copy patterns but was afraid to touch any of her treasures again for fear of leaving stains or other signs of my intrusion. I also checked as carefully as I could to be sure everything was back in its original place.

Since Shen Feng's departure I had not had a letter from him, so I had no idea if he was thinking of me, or was even alive. One morning I went up the mountain, hoping that somehow he had left a message for me, but of course there were only the old writings outside the cave, now starting to fade. So, feeling very lonely, I walked slowly back to the little house.

Another week had passed and Aunty returned. To Little Doll's delight, she'd brought us many things. There were snacks—fried butter cakes, almond bean curd, crispy sugar-coated water chestnuts, and minced meat with sesame cake. There were also toys for

Little Doll—a stuffed tortoise embroidered with a big flower on its shell, a clay figurine of the woman warrior Mulan, and a small kite in the shape of the Moon Goddess. For me there was a round, colorful needle cushion surrounded with small children, and a jade *pixiu* amulet. Little Doll was very happy with the gifts. Although I joined her in thanking our teacher profusely, I felt melancholy, missing my lover and feeling aimless, now that *Along the River* was finished. Also, Aunty's sudden generosity made me uneasy—the little jade creature looked expensive and this was not like her.

That evening, my little sister and I cooked a welcome-home dinner for Aunty to "wash off the dust from her journey." After our lips were well greased with meat and our bellies as bulging as a rich man's wallet, Aunty asked Little Doll to brew the before-the-rain Dragon Well tea she'd brought back from Peking. Soon the three of us were enjoying tea as exquisite as Aunty's embroidery.

While we sat quietly sipping, our teacher took out two thick red envelopes and placed them in front of Little Doll and myself. "This is to reward you both for your hard work."

"Thank you, Aunty Peony," we said in unison.

I asked, "Aunty Peony, did the embroidery win—"

She cut me off, her slender fingers massaging her temples. "It's quite late now and I'm tired, so let's go to sleep."

I wondered why she was avoiding talking about the embroidery. My work must not have won, not even an honorable mention. So maybe she was trying to spare me embarrassment. But I needed to know the outcome, not be left in suspense.

Since Aunty's return I could only feel unhappy energy emanating from her. She acted even more distant and cold than usual. I knew something was weighing on her mind but had no idea what.

One morning Aunty told us she was going to Soochow to shop for silk and thread and that she might return late so we didn't have to wait for her. She looked so glum and serious that this time I dared not ask her to bring us along. I doubted that her real purpose was to shop for threads and silk since she'd just brought a full supply back from Peking. Maybe she was not going to Soochow at all. But if I questioned her, as always she would tell me to mind my own business. And my business in this house was to embroider, not to ask questions.

A few hours after Aunty's departure, I was practicing calligraphy when Little Doll came to me carrying a pile of papers.

"Sister Spring Swallow, I've been cleaning and found some newspapers in Aunty's room. You want to read them, or should I throw them away?"

I was surprised to hear this. "Little Doll, how come you could go inside her room?"

"Sometimes she asks me to clean her room and it wasn't locked this morning."

So Aunty must have left in a hurry for something very important. Something strange seemed to be going on.

"Did you see anything else in her room?" I asked.

"Nothing. Just these newspapers on her bed. You want to take a look?"

Little Doll was the only one whom Aunty would allow inside her room once in a while, because she thought Little Doll was slow so it didn't matter. Also because there was "nothing" in her room.

"All right, Little Doll, let me have a look at them."

Little Doll handed me the newspapers and went off humming to herself.

We never had newspapers in the house—nothing important ever happened here—so Aunty must have brought these back from Peking. My curiosity piqued, I started to read with great relish about happenings in the North Capital. When I turned to the arts section, I saw this headline:

PEKING INTERNATIONAL ART AND CRAFT FAIR. FIRST PRIZE WENT TO EMBROIDERY

Winner of the much-coveted grand prize at the Peking International Art and Craft Fair contest is Miss Lilac Chen. Miss Chen, a Peking local, beat the other fifty contestants from different provinces with her stunning work *Along the River during the Qingming Festival.* Judges said that this work, based on the Song dynasty masterpiece with the same title, is most exquisitely and skillfully executed, attaining both a realistic and spiritual quality. Miss Chen gives the city of Kaifeng a new incarnation in silk and threads. Besides a gold statue, she was also awarded one thousand dollars, the highest prize in any of the city's contests so far.

The lower right corner of the article was a picture of a woman receiving the award from a foreigner. She looked like Aunty, but I couldn't be sure from the fuzzy photo. However, the winner's name was given as Lilac Chen, not Peony, and she was said to reside in Peking. I thought hard. Was this Aunty's real name? Or was it a fake name and Peony her real one? Or, maybe neither was real? It suddenly hit me that I really had no idea who my teacher was. My head started to pound, so I rested it on my arms for a few minutes, then took several sips of tea to calm myself.

If Lilac Chen was Aunty Peony, then she had taken the credit for my embroidery and even kept the gold statue and the one thousand dollars for herself! Actually, more than one thousand. She must have also been paid well for the work by the Heavenly Phoenix embroidery shop.

My mind was in turmoil. I was pretty sure it was my work that had won the contest and that Aunty had simply kept the money. But I could not be absolutely certain that Lilac Chen was Aunt Peony. And if I falsely accused her, that would be the end between us. But how likely was it that someone else, who even looked like Aunty, had embroidered the same painting? I was confused, but one thing was certain, if I had won, Aunty now had the money and the credit.

I needed to do something, but right now my brain didn't seem to be working. So I listlessly flipped through the newspaper until I saw this gossip column:

OPERA SINGER IN TROUBLE

I've been a great fan of the famous opera singer Soaring Crane. He had the kind of sonorous voice that only can be heard once in a hundred years. But his recent performances were one disappointment after another. His voice has lost both its brilliance and its stability.

We have learned that he is addicted to gambling and his debts are getting bigger and bigger. That is why he performs so much—to pay the gambling house and the loan sharks.

We have also learned that he is infatuated with a well-off, older woman with a mysterious past. This is the woman who embroidered all of his gorgeous costumes that helped him attain fame. Some say that he is still alive only because this woman has paid some of his debts.

We all hope that these rumors are unfounded. But, unfortunately, the deterioration of his voice is happening before our very ears.

Who else could this older woman with a mysterious past be but Aunty Peony? Were her trips to Peking really for trysts with Soaring Crane?

Maybe Little Doll had seen something without knowing what it meant, so I called her over, and asked, "Little Doll, what did Aunty Peony and you do when you two were in Peking?"

Her answer surprised me: "Shopping and watching Peking opera."

"You like it?"

She nodded. "Aunty explained all the stories to me."

"What operas did you see?"

"Many. *Farewell My Concubine, The Empty City Strategy, Peony Pavilion,* and . . . I don't remember."

"Do you remember the actor's name?"

"Aunty really likes the one called Soaring Crane."

Soaring Crane. So I was right. Aunty *was* the mysterious embroiderer mentioned in the same paper. In spite of all her talk of chastity, my teacher had a lover, just like the rest of us. But an opera singer was a big step down for the woman who'd been loved by an emperor!

"Little Doll, what does this Soaring Crane look like?"

She thought for a while. "Long face, single-lidded eyes, and a knobby nose."

Her description seemed to fit with the man on the embroidery in Aunty's room.

"How old do you think this Soaring Crane is?"

"Old, but younger than Aunty Peony."

"That means how old?" I was a little annoyed at Little Doll's vague answer.

"I really couldn't tell. But, Sister Spring Swallow, why are you so interested in this crane?"

"No reason, Little Doll. Just forget about it."

My teacher, after returning from her mysterious trip to Soo-chow, continued to seem troubled. I was puzzled by this. Since she now had fame and wealth after winning the contest, why should she be depressed? When she embroidered, her hands seemed to have lost their magic. They moved stiffly and her stitches were less sure.

Also, since *Along the River* had won the best embroidery contest, Heavenly Phoenix should be flooding us with commissions and we should be very busy by now. But, on the contrary, she never mentioned any new work.

Once during dinner I asked her about this, and she replied, "Don't worry. There's a lot of work waiting to be done, but I decided to take a long break after we worked so hard on *Along the River*."

Of course she didn't really need the money now, but she also didn't know that I knew.

I was suddenly tired of keeping up a façade. "But, of course, Aunty, you're rich now because *Along the River* won the first prize of one thousand dollars at the Peking International Art and Craft Fair!"

She looked stunned, but then quickly regained her calm. "What do you mean? I don't know what you're talking about. I told you that it didn't win."

"I read the newspaper you brought back from Peking."

"So?"

"You're Lilac Chen, aren't you?"

Finally, she said, "Yes, *Along the River* did win the first prize."

Little Doll turned to me and clapped. "Congratulations, Sister Spring Swallow!"

She cast Little Doll a sharp glance. "It's my embroidery, not your sister's."

This was too much for me. I was not going to hold in my anger any longer. "What do you mean it's yours, Aunty Peony? I stayed up and worked nonstop for five months and my hands still hurt—"

She cut me off sharply. "It's my work, my honor, and my grand prize. Period."

This time I was not going to back down. "Aunty, you didn't do it, I did. It's my embroidery!"

"Your embroidery? Your embroidery! I taught you everything you know. I corrected and re-corrected all your mistakes. If I hadn't put down the first and last stitch, you couldn't even begin to work or finish it. If I hadn't taken you in, fed you, accepted you as my student . . . you'd still be a ghost's wife whom people would avoid like a leper."

She paused to inhale sharply, then, "And now you want to take the credit from me, you ungrateful brat?"

After that, she stomped upstairs and closed the door so hard the whole house shook. Maybe what she said had some truth in it—but I *did* do *Along the River* and she had cut me out completely!

Aunty and I didn't talk to each other for days. Though my mouth was at rest, my hands began to get busy again with some minor embroideries that were waiting to be completed. If I wanted to continue to live here, I had to embroider to bring in money. I was thinking again of running away. I desperately wanted to join my husband, Shen Feng, but he had never sent a letter and I didn't know his family, so there was no one to ask. Though I missed him very much, I decided to try to put him out of my mind. His silence had turned sweet memories into painful ones. Now I couldn't bear to look at, let alone touch, the flute he'd given me as a token of our love. It was underneath my bed, probably feeling my weight every night.

I often thought that maybe I should have listened to Purple and run away with her. But it was too late now. Even so, I wondered, would I ever meet my big sister again in this life? On this Red Dust?

One evening after Little Doll had gone to bed, Aunty Peony said to me, "Tomorrow I want to be left alone in the house to rest and think of our future. So I want you to take Little Doll out; you can go to the village or even Soochow."

I found this a strange offer. "Aunty, why . . ."

"I want to be quiet so I can think. I can't stand Little Doll's constant babbling and giggling. Just do me a favor and take her to the city, won't you?" She took some money from her pouch and handed it to me. "This should be enough for a day's trip."

PART THREE

✸ 19 ✸

A New Life

The following day, I had no intention to take Little Doll with me to Soochow, because whatever was on Aunty's mind, it wouldn't be anything good. I feared she might be contemplating suicide again. This seemed less likely now, however, because she had the money from the contest and a lover, even though he had just gotten a devastating review and was up to his ears in debt. I was still worried, though. I didn't want our little group to dwindle away completely. Even though she had cheated me out of the credit and money that was rightfully mine from *Along the River,* she had been my teacher and I certainly did not want her to take her own life. But I had no idea what to do about it.

Little Doll and I woke up at six, ate breakfast, then said goodbye to Aunty.

Our teacher's face was pale and she looked worried. "Have fun and come back for dinner."

After we left the house, I told Little Doll that we'd first go to the mountain to pay respect to Leilei, then pick wildflowers to wear on our heads before heading to the city. After rushing through our little ritual for Leilei, I told my little sister that we had to go back to the house.

She stamped her feet. "But Aunty said we can go to have fun in the city!"

I smiled and cooed to her crestfallen face. "It's a long trip and I forgot to bring snacks and drinks—"

She didn't take my bait. "But we can get food and drink in Soochow!"

"Sorry, Little Doll. I also forgot the amulet Aunty gave me to protect us. You don't want us to have an accident like Sister Leilei, do you?"

My trick of offering snacks did not work, but the threat did, so Little Doll followed me home dejectedly.

But Aunty was not to be seen, nor did she answer our calls.

Little Doll started to cry, asking, "Where's Aunty?"

I was wondering that, too, but I needed to look around without my little sister watching me. I told her to go outside to pick flowers to give Aunty when she came back. As soon as she was out the door, I hurried upstairs to Aunty's room but was surprised to find the door hanging open. This alarmed me, as she had never left it open before, even for a few moments. I looked around to find the room in disorder and the portrait that had always been on her desk missing. I was even more astonished to find the door to the secret chamber ajar.

When I stepped inside, yet another surprise awaited me. Everything was gone! The drawings, the embroidery, even the imperial treasures . . . gone.

My teacher had vanished without a trace. But then I saw she had left something for us—a note on the bed. I picked it up and read.

> Spring Swallow,
> Smart as you are, I'm sure you found a way to get inside my room.
> You've seen my treasures, but not anymore—I have taken them all with me and left this house forever. But you'll survive because I taught you to embroider almost as well as the court embroiderers. There are many embroidery

stores in Soochow. If you show them your work, someone will hire you.

I've left some money for you and Little Doll, enough for a few months—if you are careful not to spend it all at once.

Don't try to find me. We'll never see each other again. If we do, I'll pretend we never met. I have my own plan and my own problems.

Don't feel any regret. When you came to me you were a nobody; now you are an award-winning embroiderer. I'm the one who has regrets.

Take care of Little Doll for me.

Good-bye and good luck,
Aunty Peony

I was so stunned that Aunty would leave us forever that the letter fell from my hand. If she didn't want to see us, she'd be able to find a place to hide so that we could never find her. I sat on her bed and leaned against her pillow to think. I guessed that if she was not coming back, she'd most likely go to Peking to be with Soaring Crane. So she might still be at the train station right now.

I pushed myself up against the pillow; then it suddenly came to me that this was where the imperial undergarment had been hidden. I snatched up the pillow and pulled off the cover. The gown was still there. In her haste, Aunty had left it behind!

I wondered how Aunty could have forgotten this, the most intimate of her connections to her past lover, the emperor himself. But maybe she now loved Soaring Crane so much that she had no interest in this token of an earlier love. But I knew Aunty better than this. She would not leave something so valuable behind unless, under the stress of the moment, she had simply forgot.

I sighed. I hoped the love between me and Shen Feng was not fleeting like Aunty's. But with Shen Feng gone so long without a word from him, I found I was thinking of him less. Though not by my choice, my life was going on without him. Thus lamenting, I took the imperial undergarment and walked out of my teacher's room, for the last time.

Back in my own room, I stuffed the garment inside my own pillow, then went to look for Little Doll. She had fallen asleep in her room with the bunch of flowers next to her on the bed. I quickly wrote a simple note telling her I was out looking for Aunty and would be back soon.

When I arrived at the train station it was crowded with people, some lucky ones sitting and the rest milling around. This made me think the train to Peking had not yet arrived and so Aunty might still be here. Looking for her was not easy, however. The hall was packed with families with boisterous children, lovers saying their tender farewells, businessmen puffing on cigarettes or cigars. Eyes sore from the smoke, I walked around the big hall but didn't catch sight of Aunty. Suddenly the din of conversation was drowned out by the approach of the locomotive as the crowd rushed toward the platform.

Despite my efforts to reach the exit I was borne toward the tracks by the rushing crowd. Just then, I spotted Aunty—she was on the platform, hanging on to the arm of a thirtyish man. I thought he might be Soaring Crane, but then they were hidden by the puffs of smoke coming from the train engine.

I pushed hard through the crowd until I was only a few feet behind them, hoping to hear what they were saying to each other. But the train station was too noisy for me to hear anything useful, as vendors engaged in a shouting competition.

"Braised pork!"

"Salted duck noodle soup!"

"Sugared plum and fried peanuts!"

Just then, Aunty and the young man climbed up and disappeared into the train. In a moment they would be on their way to Peking. I thought of hurrying up to try to stop her. But if she was determined to leave, she would, no matter what I said. Even if I could lure her back, she could still leave tomorrow, the day after tomorrow, or the day after that. It was the young man who held her interest now, not me and not Little Doll.

In a few minutes the train chugged its way out of the station en route to Peking, and the great hall was quieter. Feeling frustrated that I'd failed to catch up with Aunty, I bought a cup of hot tea, then went to sit on a wooden bench. Next to me sat a young couple intoxicated with each other and in their own world, making me feel lonelier than ever, with Aunty gone and Shen Feng anywhere or nowhere.

I thought the man with Aunty must be Soaring Crane, which meant he had come all the way here to accompany her back to Peking. Either he really loved her or he wanted something very important from her. Did he know about her imperial treasures? For the first time, I realized that Aunty, for all her severity, might be as vulnerable as the rest of us.

While I was mindlessly sipping my tea without tasting it, I felt a hand on my shoulder. I raised my head and saw—Shen Feng!

"Feng, what are you doing here?" I was happy to see him, but startled.

He squeezed down beside me, then took my hand into his. "Spring Swallow, I just came back. But what are you doing here? Are you going away somewhere?"

I studied my husband's surprised and happy expression, suppressing an urge to kiss him. "Feng, why did you suddenly come back?"

"I'm so sorry to startle you like this. But we revolutionaries are not allowed to write letters. But, anyway, here I am."

"I'm so glad. . . ."

"Why are you here, Spring Swallow? Did someone tip you off that I was coming?"

He seemed to look worried at this possibility. I was beginning to find it tiresome that everything had to be secret with him.

"I never expected to find you here. But Aunty just decided to run away to Peking and I was trying to catch up with her to see if I could stop her."

As Shen Feng sat beside me on the hard wooden bench, I told him about all the miserable things that had happened since he had left, and that Aunty's household was no more. I didn't say anything about Aunty's secret chamber and her imperial past. He might be my husband, but actually, I hardly knew him. But studying his manly face I felt love warming my body.

"Feng, what happened? Are you back for good?"

"Just a short time."

"I am so glad you are here, but I need to go home and see how Little Doll is doing. Why don't you come with me?"

He sighed, then went on. "I came back to see you, of course, and my ailing mother. But I also have . . . revolutionary business. It is possible that I am being followed. And if you are seen with me, it would put you in danger. So we should not stay here. But know that I love you and also work very hard to build a better future for China."

He took something out from his pants pocket and stuffed it into my hand. "Here's some money."

"But I don't need your money; Aunty has left us some. Take it back; you may need it more than I do."

But my husband wouldn't take no for an answer and that warmed my heart.

He took my hand. "We should go. Let's meet on our mountain tomorrow morning."

I nodded, too overcome by this tumultuous day to speak.

Shen Feng led me outside the train station to a corner hidden by trees, then kissed me passionately. I returned his love by kissing him back while holding his strong revolutionary torso tightly against mine. In the distance I could hear another train approaching.

"Until tomorrow," he said, and disappeared into the crowd.

Back home, I reluctantly broke the bad news of Aunty's departure to Little Doll. Though I tried my best to comfort her, she could not stop crying. It occurred to me at this moment that she was now entirely my responsibility. What this meant for me I had no idea, but since I still had Aunty's and Shen Feng's money, we wouldn't be starving for a while.

That night my body thrashed like a fish inside a dry bucket. My husband had come back, but he couldn't even spend one night with me. This secret revolutionary—and extremely dangerous—business must be very important that he'd leave his newly wed wife for it. I shuddered, then finally fell asleep.

* * *

The next morning when I saw Shen Feng on the mountaintop, I had the feeling that our meeting was but a dream. As soon as he caught sight of me, he kissed me on my lips, then led the way into our secret cave.

He took out a blanket, spread it on the ground, and we both lay down. Face-to-face, he cupped my face with his large hands and studied me like a mother her newborn baby.

"Spring Swallow, we have so little chance to see each other and I miss you so much."

"I miss you, too, Feng."

Gently, but eagerly, my husband unbuttoned my top, lifted it off my shoulders, then slid down my pants. He studied my body and gently ran his hands down my sides to my feet. Then he began to unbutton his shirt. Suddenly I felt shy and turned away so as to hide my blushing face. When I saw that all his clothes were in a pile on the floor, I tried to cover my face. But then I felt his hands on my wrists, pulling my hands away and kissing me. Somehow we found ourselves lying on the blanket. Then I felt his hands on my cheeks, my neck, my breasts. . . .

I felt I should stop this dangerously joyful act, but it was like trying to stop a starving tiger from devouring a lamb. . . .

Shen Feng was as passionate a lover as he was a revolutionary. His lips and hands were like beggars, always wanting more, unwilling to give up. When he finally entered me, I let out an animal cry loud enough to shake the mountain and maybe awaken its dwellers, living and dead.

That evening I could not help but relive our lovemaking over and over, despite my efforts to concentrate on my embroidering. Fortunately, Aunty was gone or she would have realized that my mind was not on my work and demanded to know why. In my narrow bed I squirmed restlessly, anticipating meeting Shen Feng again in the morning. I knew he would soon leave again for the revolution that was my rival.

Early the next morning I eagerly climbed to the top of the mountain to join Shen Feng again, but all that awaited me was his scribbled letter:

Dear wife Spring Swallow,

I just received a hand-delivered emergency letter ordering my immediate return to headquarters. So I sneaked up here in the middle of the night to write this for you.

It would not be safe for us to be together now. I'd never forgive myself if you were hurt because of me.

Take very good care of yourself and don't worry about me.

After you've read this letter, scrape it off.

They may have seen us together at the train station. So you must get Little Doll and leave your house right away.

How I wish I could hug, kiss, and make love to you one more time. I love you, my dear wife.

Yours,
Shen Feng

When I finished reading, I looked up at the sky, and exclaimed, "Oh, Heaven, why are you so cruel to me?! First my embroidery patterns were destroyed and my teacher has left me. Now my husband is gone, too, and I can't even keep his letters!"

But Heaven had no answer for me.

So I hurriedly scraped off our writings and stared at the newly blank space, wishing my mind were just as blank. I started to wonder if my "marriage" to Shen Feng was any more real than my marriage to a ghost. He was almost as invisible.

I collapsed on the ground and sobbed. I still loved him and now was more afraid for him than ever. If those people succeeded in finding Shen Feng, what would they do to him? And would they come after me too? I kept asking Heaven to protect my husband as tears coursed down my cheeks as I ran down the mountain.

It was only eight in the morning, so once I was back home I quickly packed, taking my money, my embroidery tools, my best work, Aunty's amulet, and Shen Feng's bamboo flute, and squeezed everything into my cloth bag. After that, I hurriedly sewed the emperor's undergarment underneath my loose top so it'd travel securely with me. Then I went to Little Doll's room to wake her up.

Rubbing her eyes, she split a big smile. "Sister Spring Swallow, I'm glad you're home! I'm hungry; can we have something to eat?"

"Little Doll, how about I take you to Soochow for lunch?"

She sat up and clapped. "Good idea, Sister Spring Swallow!"

Good. Of course I didn't tell her that our departure was forever.

Walking on Soochow's cobblestone streets, amidst people hurrying about, the nearby river glittering under the sun, I felt almost happy. For Little Doll this was an exciting outing, but there were practical matters to be addressed. First was finding a place to stay for that night. Since I'd been here a few times, I was able to quickly find an inexpensive inn in a decent area. Little Doll didn't question me about it, so we left our things there, washed, then got ready to go out again. At the hotel desk I borrowed a worn guidebook and read that among all the streets in the city, the one called Shantang Street was most popular because of its many stores. The guide gave the following description:

> Shantang Street, located in Jin Chang District, Soochow, is a walking street constructed during the Tang dynasty in 825. Popular with natives and tourists alike, it runs along the Shan Tang River crossed by many ancient bridges.

I decided to try our luck there.

Half an hour later we arrived at Shantang Street. It was quite narrow with ancient arched bridges joining the two sides at frequent intervals. Trees spread their wide branches across the sparkling turquoise water, shading the pedestrians and spilling pink petals everywhere. Boats adorned with red and green roofs ferried passengers and goods. Along both banks were shops adorned with colorful lanterns, embroidered banners, and signboards covered with elegant calligraphy.

I bought some roasted nuts from a vendor for Little Doll so she would stop her chatter for a few moments and leave me in peace.

We continued on, walking and eating, passing a knife-sharpening stall where the vendor yelled at the top of his scratchy voice: "Scrape scissors and polish knives!"

Another vendor was busy repairing pots and plates. A signboard erected next to him said: ANY POT OR PAN YOU BREAK, I CAN REMAKE.

We continued to walk, past a barber shop, a pawn shop, its entrance covered by a thick curtain, and stores selling herbs, condiments, and toys like kites, dolls, and clay animals.

Little Doll tried to pull me inside a store selling little animal toys, but I shook my head.

Seeing that she was about to cry, I said soothingly, "Little Doll, why don't we play a game?"

She immediately stopped chewing and asked with excitement, "What game?"

"See who'll spot an embroidery shop first."

My trick worked, because in less than fifteen minutes, I heard my little sister exclaim, "Sister Spring Swallow, look, there's the Golden Thread Embroidery shop right over there!"

"Good, Little Doll; let's go."

Inside the store, its cleanliness and tasteful décor implied expensive products and brisk business. The walls were covered with skillfully executed embroideries with auspicious motifs: peony for wealth and nobility; a peacock spreading its tail for good luck; a ferocious tiger oozing virility. . . . My pleasure in these beautiful works was soon interrupted by a high-pitched voice.

"Miss, they are beautiful, aren't they? Would you like a closer look at any of them?"

I turned and saw a young, round-faced woman studying me and Little Doll with suspicion.

"I'm not here to buy anything. . . ."

"Then is there some way I can help you?"

"I'm looking for . . . can I see your manager?"

"Let me see if he's free. Please wait here."

Soon she returned with a fiftyish, skinny man with a long face. I told Little Doll to go look at the different embroideries and, fortunately, she happily obliged.

The young woman said, "This is my father, Mr. Li. He's the owner and knows everything about anything here."

After that, she sat down behind the counter and picked up a magazine.

Mr. Li looked us over suspiciously. Fortunately, we'd put on our best tops and pants with nicely embroidered edges.

"Young Miss, can I help you?"

I gathered up courage to take out my best embroidery and laid them on the counter in front of him.

"Mr. Li, I'm an embroiderer. I want to know if your store would be interested in hiring me. . . ."

The old man studied my works with interest. "Hmm . . . pretty good. So you're looking for work?"

I nodded.

He cast another glance at my work. "You're very talented, miss. But unfortunately we have our own embroiderers and don't need extra help."

I blurted out, "Please, Mr. Li, have mercy, I need to work to feed my little sister and myself!"

The daughter looked up from her magazine, and piped up, "Father, they look neat, so maybe they can work here as maids, maybe even help with sales? Then I can have more time free to study as you're always nagging me."

Her father's tone held a scolding edge. "Study? That'll be the day."

But she ignored him and looked back at her magazine.

Mr. Li turned to look at me for long moments. "Hmmm . . . maybe that's not such a bad idea after all. We can't pay you much, but you can live here in the store and we'll give you food."

That was exactly what I wanted! So maybe Heaven finally decided to grant us some good luck! I nodded enthusiastically.

"Good. But I need to talk to your parents first."

"Mr. Li," I lied, "our parents don't live in the city, but a village far away from here."

"Then what are you two doing here?"

"To find jobs in the city so we could send money home."

"How old are you and your sister?"

"I'm twenty and she's fourteen," I lied again.

"Fourteen? She looks quite small for that."

"But she works hard." This time I told the truth.

"Good. Maybe you and your little sister can do the cleaning, keep an eye on the store so no one can steal, maybe even help with sales when it's very busy. Can you do these things?"

I couldn't help but smile. "Of course, Mr. Li."

"Can you read and write—add and subtract?"

"Yes, Mr. Li."

Now he smiled. "Good. What are your names?"

"I am Spring Swallow and my sister is Little Doll."

"When can you start work?"

"What about tomorrow?"

"All right, come at six in the morning with your belongings. Don't be late."

∽ 20 ∽

A Proposal

The next morning during breakfast at a street stall, I broke the news to Little Doll that we were going to settle in Soochow and work for Mr. Li at Golden Thread.

To my surprise, instead of feeling sad or making a fuss, she clapped. "Good, I love Soochow! And I'd like to work at that store; it's so clean and beautiful!"

So Little Doll and I began to live and work at Old Li's store. To my surprise, it was our luck that he actually treated us better than Aunty Peony. Every morning, we woke up at six to clean the store—sweeping the floor, then rubbing it with rags, dusting the glass cases, making sure all the products were neatly arranged—and then we would boil water to pour into the big thermos. With the hot water ready for tea, we'd eat a simple breakfast, then pull up the big shutter that covered the shop window and door.

Before long Old Li and his daughter, Ping, would arrive and check to make sure everything was ready. Li would go into his office, a tiny room in the back, and shut the door. We would hear the drawer open where he kept his account book locked up; then his abacus would click for a few minutes. When he had done his sums and the account book was safely back in its locked drawer, Old Li would come out and eat the breakfast we had bought for him and his daughter. Then all was ready for the new day's business. Since there were few customers at the beginning of the day, we would often be sent off on errands such as mailing letters or buying supplies.

During the work day, Ping was supposed to help the customers, but she almost never knew how to answer the questions, so she was always summoning her father from the back. Pretty quickly I learned the stock and so ended up being the one serving the customers. In the afternoon, Ping or Mr. Li would often slip off to nap, but of course Little Doll and I had to remain in the shop waiting on customers.

When evening came and the shutter came back down, Ping would usually dash off somewhere, while Mr. Li would sit quietly, puffing on the water pipe I would prepare for him. Sometimes Little Doll would massage him after dinner.

The way we worked and lived was called *qianpu houju,* "front store work, back store sleep." Most out-of-town workers, unable to afford housing in the city, worked and lived this way. Shop owners were equally happy about the arrangement, for they'd hire one person to do the work of two—daytime salesman and nighttime guard. In addition to lodging, shop owners would also provide their workers three meals a day. Some days, if business had been particularly good, the happy owner would reward his workers with a special dish at dinnertime, like roast duck or crispy fried fish.

For the moment, this live-in arrangement was best for me and Little Doll. Not only did we make a little money, we did not have much expense. However, we didn't have much freedom either. Little Doll and I were allowed only one day off each month. We could do whatever we wanted, but of course had no time to go very far.

I could tell that Little Doll was not very happy. But she also knew that Aunty and her two other sisters had gone and probably would never come back, and I was her only sister left. She would be very nervous if I ever went anywhere without her. When I could, I bought her candies and toys, and did all the hard tasks like scrubbing the floor and the bucket we used for a toilet. To be ready for our unknown future, I spent only what we were paid by Golden

Thread, which was not much, so that the money that Aunty and Shen Feng had given us remained untouched.

Though life was not altogether unpleasant, I hadn't forgotten that this was not the life I wanted. I didn't mind the hard work, like putting up and taking down the heavy shutter or crawling on my hands and knees to polish the floor. I put up with it because I was determined I would not live like this for the rest of my life.

I was an embroiderer, an excellent one, whose work had won first prize in an international art fair. Even though Aunty had stolen the credit, it was still my skill that had produced the work. But if we left Golden Thread, where would we go? It was unlikely my husband would find me here and anyway, I could not go with him to fight his revolution.

Often I would think of Aunty Peony and how she was able to look after us four girls, teach us embroidery, and run the house and our business smoothly. From time to time I thought of trying to find her, Purple, and Shen Feng, so we could all have a happy reunion. But where to find them? Underneath it all, I knew this was an impossible dream.

I had no choice but to stay here for a few more months, maybe even years, to save a little more money and hope for a better opportunity. However, as the Chinese say, "Life has a thousand twists and a hundred turnings." And so fate was about to steer us onto a different path.

I found out I was pregnant—from the forbidden pleasure with Shen Feng in the mountain cave.

I couldn't decide if this was good news or bad. But I did know that if I stayed here, my belly would keep growing bigger and bigger. Not only would I be kicked out of Golden Thread, I would be shamed, avoided, and jobless. For the moment I decided not to tell Little Doll. If I did, she'd ask who the father was. But no matter what would happen in the future, I couldn't suppress my happiness that I was carrying Shen Feng's baby.

But then fate was about to twist again. One day during breakfast, as I glanced through a newspaper dreaming of the handsome son who would soon be born, my eyes landed on this headline:

The Fate of a Revolutionary

A group of revolutionaries were executed in Peking for trying to bomb the legislative building. The six men, believed to be members of the communist party, were caught and hanged.

The rebels were Chen Anguo, Huang Ruoshui, Liu Dewei, Fan Xinru, Ma Donghe, Shen Feng. . . .

Seeing the name Shen Feng, I dropped both the paper and my bowl of soy bean soup to the ground, and with them shattered my dreams and hopes. . . . I felt so devoid of hope that I could not do anything but sit and feel miserable. I told Old Li that I was sick and had to take off from work. To my surprise, he wasn't angry and even asked Ping—with Little Doll's help—to cook me nutritious herb soup to speed my recovery. So for the next few days I just slept myself to oblivion.

I said nothing to Little Doll about the real reason for my "sickness." Every night I would wait until she fell asleep, then burn incense and say a prayer for Shen Feng. I hoped my prayer would send him off smoothly on his next journey, so that he'd finally live a happy life in the Western Paradise or be reincarnated into a rich household.

I knew that I had to seem to recover so that Old Li and Ping would not suspect that I was just avoiding work, so as soon as I could, I buried my unbearable grief inside my heart and tried my best to act and work normally. In the middle of the night, I'd take out Shen Feng's flute to caress, then try to play it, but I could only produce a few broken notes.

When I was at my wits' end about my expanding belly, life twisted yet again—Old Li asked me to see him in his office.

After we sat down, without much ado, he asked, "Spring Swallow, do you like working here so far?"

I nodded. "Yes, Mr. Li, very much. Thank you so much for taking in Little Doll and me."

He waved a dismissive hand. "I've been observing you for a

whole month and long enough for me to trust you. You have an alert mind, quick hands, and kind heart, especially judging from how you help your sister by taking on all the hard work. Even my daughter, Ping, who is very hard to please, speaks well of you."

Of course Ping liked me—because of me she could goof off and take all the breaks she wanted. However, I did not want to live my life as a maid, but to become a famous embroiderer. I dreamed of my work being so admired I'd be invited all over the world to have it displayed. Of course, I knew reality always paints a very different picture. So now it seemed I'd stay a maid—until I was kicked out because of my big belly.

Old Li spoke again, interrupting my thoughts. "So I'd like you two to continue working here, permanently."

"But—"

Li cut me off. "All right, Spring Swallow, let me be direct. My only son, Li Wenyi, will come back from Peking soon and I want him to learn my business so he can run it after I am too old. You learn fast and already know how this place runs. I want to offer you the chance to marry my son so someday you two can run the business together."

I was stunned by this unexpected offer. I'd already married a ghost, then Shen Feng. . . . Now was I to be married for the third time? At nineteen? It was ridiculous—probably not even legal!

I blurted out, "Mr. Li . . . marry your son?"

He smiled, patting my shoulder. "Calm down, Spring Swallow, I know this is an unexpected, even shocking, request. But think about it. First, sooner or later you have to get married. It's much better if you marry my son and continue to work and live here than marry into a family you don't know anything about. Because the in-laws of those wealthy families out there would surely ill-treat you and your sister."

"But why would they do that?"

"Because your family is too far away to protect you—if you really have one. Also"—he watched me intently with his small, flickering eyes—"if you become my daughter-in-law, sooner or later you'll be the boss's wife and this store will be partly yours when I retire. And then as my daughter-in-law, you and your sister will no longer have to sleep on bunk beds, but will live with us in our nice house with maids and a cook. Wouldn't that be wonderful?"

I remained silent, weighing his offer in light of my present situation.

He went on enthusiastically. "Besides, my son is a very nice-looking young man who's just about to graduate from Peking University. You can't possibly find someone better than him."

This was much more complicated than he realized.

"All right, I know this is a surprise. Take some time to think it over. Right now Wenyi is busy with his studies. Although I'm old, I'm also a modern, open-minded man. So if you agree, we won't need to waste money on a matchmaker, or a fortune-teller to compare your birthday to my son's, or even receive a dowry from your family."

Wah. He made it sound like this marriage was a bargain for me, just like when he told his customers they were getting a big discount on his overpriced goods. But if his son was such a great catch, why would he choose me to be his future daughter-in-law?

I asked him why he would choose me, a simple village girl.

He replied, "All the young girls in the city are so spoiled that they care only about enjoying themselves and living a pampered life. I haven't met any as hardworking, smart, and honest as you. So"—he split a cunning smile—"I am sure I've made a good choice for my son!"

He took a photo out from his pocket and handed it to me. "Here's Wenyi. Think about my offer and I hope you'll say yes."

After that, he abruptly stood up and went back to the store.

I looked at the picture and saw a stranger staring back at me. A young man, not bad looking. So, I should feel lucky to get this "bargain." But instead of feeling happy, I was sad. It was Shen Feng whom I loved, even dead.

That evening, after much thought, I accepted that Old Li's offer was my only option. Otherwise, once Aunty Peony's and Shen Feng's money was spent, I'd be shunned and destitute. Married to Li Wenyi, I'd be a respectable matron, helping to run a family business and, most important, my baby would have a father. So I decided to marry Li's son—for my baby's sake, so he'd be born with a father and a family. Maybe for once my fate was twisting in the right direction. But now that my mind was made up, I burst out sobbing.

The next day when I told Old Li about my decision, he looked delighted.

"Hahaha, this is my happiest day! All right, Ping and I will prepare for the wedding. We'll have it as soon as possible. No point to waste time. To celebrate I will give you and Little Doll the next two days off."

It bothered me a little that he acted so happy. And this was pretty quick. What about Wenyi—had he been consulted? What if he hated me at first sight?

Soon Old Li announced the engagement at the family's ancestral hall, making it official. I wasn't included in this ceremony, which was just as well because I had had enough of ghosts at weddings.

As the wedding day approached I felt more and more anxious because my future third husband was still nowhere to be seen. Mr. Li said that something unexpected had turned up, and Li Wenyi was forced to postpone his return from Peking. But he was vague about what that business was, only assuring me that the son would definitely arrive in time for the wedding. This seemed to be my fate with men, either being dead or not showing up, or both. But Wenyi was not a revolutionary, so I wondered what was more important than his wedding.

That night, my ghost first husband came to me in a dream to scold me. I couldn't see his expression, because his face was blurred by smoke and dust.

But he pointed a long-nailed finger at me. "You unfaithful wife! Just one man after another. Shameless woman of depravity!"

After that, he disappeared into smoke and dust, leaving a trail of ghostly curses.

I woke up, sweating heavily. I was getting a bad feeling about Li Wenyi. Could I pull out now? I didn't think so, unless I ran away— *again.* Old Li and Ping had already booked the wedding banquet, sent out invitations, and gotten everything ready—clothes, wine, dried seafood, red wedding cakes, lucky money, firecrackers, celebratory banners. . . .

Two weeks later, a red curtained *huaqiao,* a "flower palanquin," carried by several muscular men arrived at the store to take me to the wedding hall. Servants marching on both sides of the palanquin held up red signboards with the character "Happiness." The clashing of gongs and cymbals deafened ears and animated the already busy street.

Two middle-aged women who had been hired to supervise the rituals helped me into the enclosed red palanquin. Little Doll and the others were to take another one following mine. To my surprise, the man I had been waiting so anxiously to meet, my about-to-be husband Li Wenyi, was already inside. He smiled happily and I smiled back, lowering my head. I couldn't help but feel delighted that he was as handsome as he was in his picture.

"Spring Swallow"—he took my hand—"sorry for my late arrival. I've been eager to meet you. You are even prettier than I expected. I am a very happy and lucky man."

I didn't know how to respond to this, so I just kept smiling and letting him hold my hand. Soon the palanquin was lifted and we were on our way. A large group of people followed us, children laughing and screaming, while the adults shouted good-luck sayings.

"Your good karma from previous lives. Happy union this life!"

"One-hundred-year blissful union!"

"Happy marriage, hearts forever linked together!"

When we finally arrived at the wedding hall, a few maids appeared to steer me inside, with Wenyi following behind. Then we were led to kneel in front of the family altar, watched silently by the Li family's ancestral portraits. Old Li, his daughter, Ping, all the relatives, staff, and servants smiled happily, except Little Doll—to my surprise. I gave her a stern look to remind her to behave properly and act happy.

After Li Wenyi and I kowtowed and made offerings to all the

ancestors, and to Old Li and Ping, a maid and a servant helped us to stand back up.

Suddenly I understood everything: Little Doll's strange expression; Old Li's urgent arrangement of the marriage; lack of a matchmaker and dowry; Wenyi's non-appearance until this moment.

For my new husband's left leg was severely damaged, bending at a very awkward angle. He could hardly walk. I sighed inside. Though I was very young, life was continuing to teach me that nothing is what it seems. . . .

That evening, during the banquet, I drank one cup of celebratory wine after another. Everything was a blur until Wenyi and I entered the bedroom, when I immediately passed out.

The next morning I awakened with a terrible headache and no memory of what had passed during our dragon and phoenix night. I even hoped it was all a bad dream, but as I looked around the room, tall red candles, sweet buns dyed red, and piles of red-wrapped gifts were everywhere, leaving no doubt that a wedding had just occurred. And to remove any possible uncertainty, my new husband was snoring beside me.

When he finally woke up, it turned out that Wenyi and I had little to say to each other. After a few minutes of desultory conversation he left me alone and went off somewhere.

When the maid came to fix the marital bed, I saw lotus seeds underneath our pillows.

I asked her about this and she said, "Young mistress, you don't know? That's for you to have babies!"

The word for lotus seed, *lianzi,* also meant "continuous births of sons." The Li family put them underneath our pillows so I'd bear the family many sons, not knowing that now I did not need lotus seeds to be pregnant.

I'd thought that in my current condition almost any husband would be better than none. But I was wrong. It wasn't that Wenyi was a cripple, for I didn't think I was much better considering that I'd been a wild child, a ghost wife, a runaway bride, and was now married despite a vow of celibacy. The cause of our troubles together was simple: He was a bad husband and a bad person.

Not long after the wedding, I heard two maids gossiping and found out what was behind Old Li's haste in marrying off his son. Wenyi was a compulsive gambler. His main subjects of study in Peking were whores and roulette. When he had frittered away all of his father's allowance each month, he would borrow more from loan sharks and promptly lose it all in the casino. He promised to pay it all back when his lucky day came, but it never did. The loan shark's men finally came after him and beat him severely, smashing his kneecap with an iron club.

Old Li hoped that if he brought his son home where he could keep an eye on him and married him off, perhaps he would reform. But word of his dissolute lifestyle had reached Soochow, and none of the local families would consider him for their daughters. So though I may not have fitted their social aspirations, I was handy.

That Wenyi had little to say to me did not mean I was excused from my nightly duties. Whenever he demanded the "pleasure of the fish in the water," I blew out the candle and did my best to shut down my mind. I kept telling myself I had to be patient until my baby was born. Then I would figure out something.

❧21❧

Rain Flower Pavilion

A month later, I announced my pregnancy to the Li family. Everyone was overjoyed, especially Old Li, who was desperate for a grandson and heir to carry on the family line. I did feel a bit guilty that the heir would not really be his. But then he'd also tricked me into marrying his good-for-nothing son, so I thought our scores were even.

As the saying goes, "It's easier to change mountains and rivers than a person's character." Old Li's hopes that marriage and a wife who was expecting would reform his son were disappointed. Wenyi did hang around the Golden Thread salesroom under the pretense of learning his father's business, but he mostly read the newspapers and chatted with the women who came into the shop, at least if they were young and pretty. One other thing at Golden Thread did hold his interest and that was the cash drawer. There was no doubt that he was stealing from his father, and I often heard Old Li berating him about the missing money, but to no avail.

Finally, Old Li seemed to give up on his son and instead gave his attention to the "grandchild" in my belly. He encouraged his daughter to cook me all kinds of nutritious foods and tasty soup to boost both my and my baby's energy. Though I had a good appetite, I couldn't possibly consume all the food: bird's nest to smooth my skin, abalone to nourish my *yin* parts, fish maw to provide me with protein, albizia flower and licorice soup to soothe my nerves.

Little Doll was even more devoted to me now, following me everywhere and making sure I did not lift anything heavy or otherwise tire myself. I no longer had to wait on customers, but in the afternoons, when my morning sickness had worn off, I would help Old Li with the sales records and bookkeeping.

As the days and weeks passed, my belly kept getting bigger, but my husband was around less. Although Wenyi never told me where he went in the evenings, I heard rumors from people going in and out of the store. He now spent his evenings drinking, gambling, smoking opium, and visiting other women. Though I didn't like this, the truth was, I was more than happy to be left alone.

Whenever I asked Old Li about his son's whereabouts, all he ever said was, "Don't worry, just take good care of my grandson."

I greatly missed my baby's father—my true love, Shen Feng. Whenever I felt movements in my belly, I would think about Shen Feng and our days together—which were so few—on the mountain. Someday, when my child was old enough to understand, I would explain how its brave revolutionary father had died helping build a better China.

One evening I decided to follow Wenyi to see if the rumors were true. As he was dressing to go out, I asked, "Wenyi, why don't you have dinner with us first?"

"I wish I could, but I'm having dinner with a businessman from Peking."

I lowered my head submissively, and said, "Then please don't drink too much and come back early."

Wenyi grimaced and pushed through the door without saying good-bye. As soon as he was about ten feet down the road I also left, following him. I knew his mind was on his plans for the evening and he would not look behind him. I assumed he was on his way to gamble away whatever had stuck to his sticky fingers from that day's sales. Nothing made me think he was honest, but I needed to know for sure.

Soon he hailed a rickshaw and I immediately hailed one to follow him. His rickshaw traveled straight for minutes, then began to turn corners and alleys until it finally stopped in front of an imposing mansion. He got off and walked in as quickly as his twisted leg would allow. I waited until the door had closed behind him, then paid and alighted.

The building was two stories high, with red ribbons wrapped around its balconies and red, yellow, green lanterns hanging from the roof. Over the door was a plaque with the words "Rain Flower Pavilion" in gold characters against a black background. A muscular man stood guard at the gate, looking bored. I stayed under the shadow of a large tree, where I would not be noticed.

Over the next few minutes, several guests were admitted, all well-dressed and all male. Then a big carriage arrived and several men started to climb out. They were laughing loudly but walking in a tipsy fashion, so the guard went to the carriage to help them out. While the guard was engaged with these clients, I hastened through the door.

Inside, the lavish décor spoke wealth and decadence. No one paid any attention to me, so I was able to conceal myself behind a thick pillar to observe the strange scene that presented itself to my eyes. The walls were decorated with large paintings of flowers and calligraphy with good-luck sayings. Fresh flowers in ceramic pots gave out pleasant fragrances. Men were sitting around tables enjoying a sumptuous banquet, while beautiful ladies in elegant gowns hovered over them. At other tables, mahjong was being played, accompanied by laughter and shouts, while other women, equally beautiful, encouraged the gamblers to raise their bets. A few women worked the crowd, bearing trays laden with drinks, snacks, cigarettes, hot towels.

Then my attention was drawn to a small stage in the center from which lively tunes spilled out over the audience. Almost everything on the stage was decorated in pink—curtains, tablecloths, carpets, even the pretty young woman who was playing the *pipa* and singing.

When I was taking in this scene, a harsh voice next to my ear demanded, "Miss, what are you doing here?"

I turned and saw a middle-aged, big-bosomed woman staring at my belly.

I stuttered. "I'm looking for—"

But she cut me off, smiling excitedly. "Miss, if you're looking for a job, you're in the right place."

It wouldn't be a bad idea to have another place to work in case things didn't work out with the Li family.

"You need someone for accounting and bookkeeping? I can do that."

"Come with me so we can talk quietly." She chuckled, then led me to a hidden corner with a table and two chairs.

After we sat, she spoke again in her rough voice. "Miss, you really come at the right moment."

"What do you mean?"

"Because people like you are in demand and are hard to find."

"So you have work for me?"

She smiled, her eyes lingering on my stomach. "Recently a few of our customers ask for sisters like you. . . ."

I was getting confused and nervous. "What sisters like me? I have no idea what you're talking about!"

Now she cast me a sharp glance. "What's the matter with you? You came here . . . and now you want to play games with me? People in Rain Flower Pavilion are not to be messed with!"

"I'm not messing with anyone; I've just come here to look for my husband."

"Ha! Don't make me laugh! Most respectable pregnant women wouldn't come here, let alone to look for her husband, if you really have one!"

I didn't know how to respond to this.

"All right, this is how it is. We'll pay you a lot because a very rich customer's been asking for a pregnant sister."

"But what does this have to do with me?"

"It'll have everything to do with you if you know how much this salt merchant is willing to pay."

"Pay for what?"

Finally, she studied me with a different expression. "Huh, are you *really* that naïve?" She paused, then exclaimed, "Don't you know this is a prostitution house?!"

Now I suddenly saw the lavish décor, flirtatious women, and fierce-looking guards in a new light.

"But I'm not a prostitute!"

"Then what are you doing here?"

"I told you I'm looking for my husband."

"Your husband, what's his name?"

"Li Wenyi."

"There's never a Li Wenyi here."

"But I saw him enter this mansion."

"Huh, then either he entered the neighboring establishment or he uses another name here. Smart, hahaha!"

She cast me another glance, then said, "All right, I believe you, so you better leave right now. But when you go home, think about my offer. Come back and let me know if you want a big bundle of cash, huh, little pretty? And forget about your husband. If he goes to a prostitution house, then it's fair that you work at one, right?"

She winked and walked away abruptly.

I still wondered if Wenyi was here. But there were so many rooms both downstairs and upstairs, and I couldn't just go around peeking into all of them. And one of the mean-looking guards was eyeing me, so I was getting frightened and decided to get out as quickly as I could. But just as I was heading toward the door, I felt a hand on my shoulder.

I turned and saw the singer. "Come to my room, we need to talk," she said in an insistent whisper.

I didn't have a chance to say no, for she'd already pulled me inside. The room was nicely decorated with a *luohan* bed, an Eight-Immortals table with tea utensils and plates of snacks, flower and bird paintings on the walls, and fresh flowers in large, ceramic vases.

After we sat down, she looked at me intently. "You don't know who I am?"

"You're the musician who's just played and sung."

She shook her head. "You really don't recognize me, do you, Spring Swallow?"

I was startled that she knew my name.

But before I had a chance to say anything, she exclaimed, "I'm Purple, your big sister!"

"Purple?"

"Yes!"

Now I looked at her carefully and could discern her familiar features under her heavy makeup. Instead of the two pigtails she'd always worn, her hair was now piled up high on her head, held up by hairpins with tasseled jewels and adorned with flowers. Instead of the simple cotton top and pants I was used to seeing on her, she wore an elaborately embroidered, high-collar pink jacket over a matching long dress.

She looked very excited, but I really didn't know whether I was happy to see her. All I could think was that my celibate embroidery sister had somehow turned into a prostitute.

"Sister Purple, how come you work in a . . . I thought you would be married to Jiang by now and living your new life in Peking."

She sighed heavily. "*Hai,* it's a sad story, if you want to listen."

"Of course I want to."

But she stared at my bulging stomach. "Spring Swallow, don't tell me that you are. . . ."

"Yes, I'm five months' pregnant."

"So you're . . . married—I hope?"

I nodded.

"Then what are you here for?"

"To find my husband."

She sighed again. "Hmm . . . that doesn't sound good. Tell me about him."

I shook my head. "Please, Sister Purple, tell me about you first."

"All right, but let's have some tea." She picked up the teapot and poured us full cups.

After we sipped for a while, she began. "I'm sorry I left without a proper good-bye. I had planned to stay to help Aunty redo *Along the River.* But she asked you instead of me to be the lead embroiderer.

"After I left, I went straight to the train station and boarded the next train for Peking. When I arrived at Jiang's address, the landlord told me he'd moved out—with a young woman—and hadn't left any forwarding address. At that moment my whole world collapsed. Then, because I had almost no money, I came back. If I died, better it be in my hometown."

"But, Sister Purple, I thought the two of you were truly in love."

She tilted her head and laughed without humor. "That's what I thought too. But now I think it was only I who was *truly* in love."

Silence passed and she went on. "After I came back, I felt too humiliated to ask Aunty to take me back."

She paused, looking at the floor. "Spring Swallow, I really had no place to go, so here I am."

"Do you regret being . . ." I couldn't say the word *prostitute*.

"An entertainer? If you want the truth, it's yes and no. No one wants to be this kind of woman, even at an expensive establishment. But working here numbs my mind and feelings so I don't have to think of Jiang and his cruel betrayal.

"The truth is"—she looked at me with teary eyes—"even if I'm not happy here, I make good money from my many wealthy admirers."

"I didn't know that you can play the *pipa* and sing."

She laughed. "The Mama here said I look different from the other girls, because I have an artistic temperament. So I can attract certain customers like scholars, or vulgar men aspiring to be artistic. So she made another girl teach me. I learned fast. Anyway, if I make mistakes, the men here don't care."

"Sister Purple, do you have any other plans?"

"Now I know that it's pointless to plan for anything. Heaven decides, not us."

We remained silent for a while, absorbing each other's presence.

Then she asked, "What about you, Spring Swallow, what happened to you after I left?"

I told her everything—almost. I told her about Shen Feng, but not that I was carrying his baby, not Wenyi's. Nor about my finding Aunty's secret chamber and taking the imperial undergarment.

Purple took my hands in hers. "Spring Swallow, I'm so sorry to hear about Shen Feng's death, and, of course, about Aunty's troubles. But I'm glad that Little Doll is with you and that she's doing well. It's good luck that you married again so soon and got pregnant quickly. Your husband—maybe he will change after the baby is born."

I smiled but didn't reply. It was a kind thought, but I knew that Wenyi was rotten beyond salvation. I wondered about Purple and Jiang, if there was more that she hadn't told me. But whatever had happened, the result was that she now worked in a prostitution house. So in comparison to her, maybe I should consider myself lucky.

I asked, "Sister Purple, do you plan to leave here someday?"

She sighed. "Yes, but I need to make more money first." She laughed sarcastically. "Problem is, after one has tasted the goodness of money, then what you have is never enough."

I had no answer for this. Purple had changed. So I got up, squeezed her hand, and said, "We should see each other again soon."

"Of course, Spring Swallow. Bring Little Doll too. I miss her."

❧ 22 ❧

Our Lady of Sorrows

But I didn't bring Little Doll to see Purple, for everything soon changed.

I lost my baby. The whole family, even Wenyi, was in deep grief, not for me, but for the baby. It was a boy. Without knowing he was a Shen, not a Li, the Li family buried the tiny body and hired monks to conduct a ritual in the ancestral hall to appease his equally tiny soul. Every night I sobbed, burned incense, and recited the Heart Sutra for him and his father.

But the worst was yet to come. Instead of leaving me alone, Wenyi demanded sex almost every night, even when I was sick.

"Now give me a son this time, a living one!" he'd yell, his face red, his breathing heavy, and his arms prying apart my legs. Although Wenyi was a cripple, his torso and arms were strong, so I had no choice but to yield.

To take my mind off my miseries, I thought of taking up embroidery again, even redoing *Along the River*. But soon my life took another unexpected turn.

One morning I overheard a conversation I was not supposed to hear. The maid was talking to Old Li in a puzzled tone. The two must have thought I'd already left to work at the shop, so I stayed in my room to listen.

"Master Li, when I was cleaning the young master's room, I found this jacket wedged between the sofa cushions and the frame. Young mistress must have left it there when she lay down to rest. I saw a gold thread sticking out, so I looked underneath and found this."

Even though I could not see what was happening, I knew the maid had found the emperor's undergarment.

"Master Li, I thought I should show it to you."

I heard a gasp from Li, followed by a brief silence before his voice piped up again. "All right, you were right to show this to me. I'll take care of it; you can go back to work."

That day Old Li seemed preoccupied and I wondered what was on his mind or if he would confront me about what the maid had found. But I didn't find out until that evening. As usual, Wenyi was out somewhere. To calm myself, I went to the backyard to look at the moon and the distant mountain peak, muttering a prayer. What was I going to do with my wretched life? What would Old Li do to me, now that he knew about the imperial undergarment? As tears coursed down my cheeks, I heard Ping's voice behind me.

"Spring Swallow," she said softly but firmly, "I hate to tell you this, but I think you better leave this house as soon as you can."

Of course I immediately understood why she'd said this, but I wanted to hear it from her mouth. "Why?"

"Because my father may report you to the police. If you're caught with the stolen imperial garment, you might even be executed!"

I felt too frightened to speak.

"How did you get it?" she asked.

"Sorry, Ping, but I can't tell you."

"All right, I didn't expect you to. Spring Swallow, I like you, you work hard in the store, and you're my sister-in-law, so I want to help you. My advice is, you better leave before my father makes up his mind."

Tears coursed down my cheeks. "But you know I have no place to go. . . ."

She replied, "There is a Buddhist temple a few miles south of Soochow. I suggest you try your luck there. At least the monks and nuns will not send you away—or report you to the authorities. You can stay there for a while, but it's not safe for you to remain in Soochow."

She took out a small pouch and gave it to me. "Here's some money—just pack and leave before it's too late."

"But . . ."

"There's no 'but,' Spring Swallow. You have no future with my brother now that you lost his baby."

"Then I need to tell Little Doll—"

"No, you don't have time. Anyway, you don't have to worry because we'll take care of her. She'll continue to work here, fed and housed, so she'll be fine. You can write to me and I'll let you know when things cool down, then you can come back for her."

When I was about to leave, she took out an envelope and handed it to me. "I've worked out everything for you. This is Wenyi's *xiuqishu*. Keep it; maybe it will be useful."

The *xiuqishu*, "letting-go-the-wife" letter, was a document to dissolve marriage from the husband's side so he doesn't have to go through long, costly legal procedures. It's also a huge humiliation to the wife. But I still thanked Ping profusely, not only for alerting me, but also for giving me this letter, insulting me in the process but also freeing me.

After she left, I quickly packed and wrote a note for my little sister telling her I had to leave the Lis' house but promising that one day I'd be back for her. I also said I'd try my best to find Aunty and Purple and get our family back together. I regretted not having a chance to say good-bye to Little Doll, but thought that Old Li and his daughter would not treat her badly, because she'd continue to help with chores both at the store and in the house for a pittance.

I almost collapsed with despair when I heard the soft *click* of the closing door. This was not just the closing of a chapter in my life, for what lay before me was unknown—and terrifying. I feared I was now cut off from all who had ever shown me any kindness— Shen Feng, Old Li, Ping, Purple, Aunty Peony, even Little Doll, whom I might never see again in this life.

Being on the run yet again made my earlier life—with my mean aunt, Aunty Peony and the girls, Shen Feng, even the Li family—

seem no more than a dream. Now I had to wake up. However, I didn't want to think Shen Feng was a dream too. I wanted to embrace his strong body and kiss his warm lips one more time. . . .

I decided that before I left Soochow for good I would stop at Rain Flower Pavilion to say good-bye to Purple. Then I'd have to find a temple that would take me in for the night. What I really hoped was that I could persuade her to come with me.

It was already evening and the sun's fading light dyed the street golden, making my surroundings seem unreal as floating in the air. I hailed a rickshaw and was soon dropped off in front of the pleasure house. A group of richly attired men strode in with happy expressions. A few feet down the road was a skinny woman with stooped head and long, tangled hair. In front of her was a chipped begging bowl with only a few coins inside. So business must be bad.

Before I entered Rain Flower Pavilion, I took a few coins from my pocket and threw them inside the bowl.

She mumbled, "Thank you," but did not lift her head, so I could not see her face.

I still had Aunty's money and so I felt I could help another woman whose fate was even worse than mine. But I knew my savings would not last forever.

Feeling comforted that I'd done something good, I entered the pavilion in better spirits. Inside, the mood was completely different. Men were devouring expensive food with relish or gambling large sums with abandon, attended by pretty girls pouring tea, lighting cigarettes, preparing water pipes, even picking up food and putting it in the men's mouths. My eyes sought the stage where Purple had performed but found it empty.

When I craned my neck to look for her in the crowded hall, I saw a familiar figure approaching me—the same woman who wanted me for customers interested in pregnant sisters.

"Young miss," she smiled happily, "you came here a while ago, right? I'm glad that you've finally decided to join us!"

"Madame, I'm only here looking for Purple."

She cast me a curious glance. "Purple? Sorry, but we don't have a Purple here—nor a Pink, nor a Lavender, hahaha!" As she appreciated her own joke, the corners of her eyes wrinkled.

"But I talked to her when I was here last time!"

"Then your friend must be a wild chicken who sneaked in here to make a few bucks."

"No, she played the *pipa* on that stage!" I pointed.

She rolled her eyes and made an annoyed expression. "Ah, the *pipa* girl, why didn't you tell me earlier? But her name is Chrysanthemum, not Purple, unless there are purple chrysanthemums. Why are you looking for her? She left a while ago."

"Do you know where she has gone?"

"You think I know or care? Girls come and go here, like a merry-go-round."

I asked, "She didn't tell you where she was going?"

"No. You think if she's going to work for another house, she'll leave the new address for us?"

She cast a look at my now smaller stomach. "Guess you're not pregnant anymore . . . but you can be a regular sister. For less money, of course. Otherwise, you better leave now. But wait—" she looked me over appraisingly. "Or maybe *you* want another sister. I can recommend one for your taste."

Her leer made my skin crawl. I thanked her and hurriedly left the rain, the pavilion, and its flowers.

Though Ping had suggested I should find temporary refuge in a Buddhist temple near Soochow, I decided to go to Peking instead. I wanted to put as much distance as I could between Soochow and myself. Old Li might still decide to send the police after me. Also, this place had become *shangxin di,* "heartbroken land." So I needed to make a new start as quickly as possible while my money lasted.

I took a rickshaw to the station, boarded the next train, and a few hours later arrived in Peking. Fortunately, I'd been in the capital before with Aunty, so I did not feel completely lost. I immediately took a tricycle rickshaw to the same inn we'd stayed in last time. By the time I was settled into my room, it was past midnight, so I went straight to sleep.

Next morning after a simple breakfast at the inn, I went to a nearby bookstore to buy a guidebook, then back to my room. Sitting on the bed in my cramped room, I studied it carefully. Ping's suggestion to take refuge in a temple made sense because not only would I be housed and fed, I'd be safe. Soon I learned that the biggest temples were on Wutai Mountain—far enough that I would have to hire a car. Of course I knew that even if a temple took me in, I would need to work in exchange for their compassion since I could not offer them a big donation.

As I continued to read, I realized that in addition to Buddhist temples, there were Western churches here. With great curiosity, I savored the exotic names: Saint John's, Saint Michael's, Saint Teresa's, Sacred Heart Cathedral. Some were named for the four directions—East Church, West Church, South Church, North Church—I guessed to attract people from all corners of the world. Or, as the Chinese say, "From the five lakes and the four seas."

When I saw the name Immaculate Conception Cathedral, I was amused. Couples who are childless call up the Baby-Giving Goddess for help, so why would anyone want an Immaculate Conception? Father Edwin had told me that the Virgin Mary did just that—giving birth to baby Jesus without a man to do that thing. But why would any woman want to have a baby without a husband, a man she loves? And how could it be possible?

I resumed reading when yet another name caught my attention—Our Lady of Sorrows. Reading these words, I suddenly burst into tears. I had a feeling the church was meant for us—Aunty Peony, Purple, Leilei, me, and even Little Doll. Weren't we all ladies of sorrow? Because this name struck a chord in me, I decided to go there first. It would not be entirely strange because of the lessons I had taken with Father Edwin in his little church back in my old village.

Our Lady of Sorrows, rather than looking sorrowful, appeared forbidding, with two towering steeples topped by two huge crosses. As I walked toward the building, I heard music coming through its colorful mosaic windows. Enchanted by the beautiful melody, I quickened my steps until I reached two thick wooden doors. I knocked for seconds, but no one answered. I guessed the wood was too thick for those inside to hear. Or maybe the heavenly music completely obscured my earthly knockings.

As I was wondering what to do, a man's gentle voice rose next to me. "Miss, no one will hear you because the mass is going on right now."

I turned to face a tall, blond man in a black robe who was speaking to me in fluent Mandarin. His fair skin seemed to reflect the bright sunlight.

Not knowing what to say, I asked, "A mass?"

He smiled as he pushed open the door, held it, and signaled me to get in. I stepped into a courtyard with trees and two reddish brown brick buildings. He followed me in.

"Have you been to our church before, miss?"

"I was just passing by, saw the name of the church and decided to take a look."

He cast me a curious glance with his grayish blue eyes.

"May I ask why you're so curious about the name of our church?"

"Because I'm a lady of sorrow myself!"

He looked surprised. "But you're too young to be sorrowful. What are you sorry about, miss?"

What a naïve question! Had this man's life been so smooth that he had no idea about women's sorrows? Then why did he come to work at a sorrowful church?

"Mister, I'm afraid you won't understand."

He smiled, revealing neat, white teeth. "I can try, so why don't you tell me?"

I hesitated.

He said gently, "I am sure that your troubles are only temporary—all problems can be solved with God's help. If you pray earnestly to Him, He will answer your prayers and direct you back onto the right path. As the Bible says, knock and doors will be opened."

This white ghost sounded pretty naïve to me. In my life, many doors were opened for me without me even knocking. But mostly they opened onto disasters.

Then the tall foreigner pointed to the doorway. "Miss, please come in and join us for mass. I'm sure after hearing Our Lord's blessings, your heart will be eased."

Smiling, he went on. "Let me introduce myself. I'm Ryan

McFarland, a seminarian in this church. I studied Chinese in America before I came here. In one more year, the Lord willing, I'll be fully ordained as a priest. You can just call me Ryan."

Now I looked at him with curiosity. Why would a total stranger tell me so much about himself just minutes after we met?

I didn't know what to say until finally he asked me my name, and I replied, "Spring Swallow."

"What a beautiful name, as if you are free as a bird," he said, blushing, or so I thought.

"Thank you."

If only he knew what kind of "freedom" I had—usually on the fly—away from trouble. I did like my name, but I thought it might be bringing me bad luck. Because a swallow is always flying, I feared I would never have anywhere to settle.

"Spring Swallow, please go in now. I hope you will find peace here, and return often."

Inside, the pews were mostly occupied, so I found a place for myself in the last row. The worshippers were mostly Chinese, but a few foreigners were sprinkled through the audience. Shafts of colored light from the stained-glass windows fell across the long nave. In front of the altar stood a man in a red and gold robe, intoning in a strange language. On the wall above him I could see the tall pipes of the organ, from which emanated the music I had heard outside. I wasn't sure what the priest was saying or doing, but the swelling music began to relax my taut nerves.

Then the organ was silent and the priest went up to the lectern and read in a solemn voice from a huge black book. After a few sentences, he set the book down, looked up at the congregation, and began to speak in Mandarin.

"Remember, God always answers our prayers. But in His omniscience He sometimes answers in ways we do not understand. Do not resist hardship or suffering, they are God's way to teach us humility and charity. When you lose loved ones, remember they are now with God. . . ."

I was baffled that this God is actually blessing you when he makes you suffer, even strikes your lover dead. My mind began to drift. Then suddenly I realized that the voice with its accented

Mandarin was familiar. His hair looked a little grayer and his stomach now protruded a little, but it was Father Edwin! Here in Peking was the man to whom I owed my education, who had taught me to read and write Chinese, as well as English. He'd often told me about the love of God, but I never got this part. To me, this God sounded like a crazy old man who cared about us but was too frail to do much to solve our problems.

However, when I looked around, I saw believers listening in rapt attention with a devout expression. But I also saw a few Chinese children secretly reading comic books, or poking each other and giggling while their mothers shushed them. A few old people, mostly sitting off to the side, were reading newspapers or magazines. I guessed these were what I'd heard called "rice-bag Christians." For them, God's love was free food. But I realized that I was not much better . . . wasn't I also here for food and shelter?

When the mass ended, Father Edwin walked to the back doors, while the congregation respectfully waited for him. Then a long line formed, awaiting his blessing as they left the church.

Finally, I was standing before my former mentor and he said, "Miss, I haven't seen you here before. You are welcome."

I was surprised and disappointed that my mentor did not recognize me. Had I changed so much?

I smiled. "Father Edwin. Don't you remember me? I am Spring Swallow!"

Now he studied me with curiosity. "Can you really be my little girl from the old village?"

I nodded.

"Oh my, have you been well, I hope?"

I was tempted to tell him that since I'd last seen him I'd been married three times and pregnant once—and had also stolen imperial property. But, of course, I was not going to shock him during our first reunion.

"Do you live in Peking now?"

"It's a very long story, Father Edwin."

"Of course, let's go to my study so we can talk over a cup of tea and some cake."

I nodded, then followed him outside to a smaller building beside the church. Inside was a plain office with a large wooden crucifix on the wall over his desk. On the desk was a portrait of a young, bearded man looking upward longingly at something above the picture frame. I recognized him as Jesus, though he hadn't aged at all since I'd seen his picture in Father Edwin's office in the old village.

We sat across from each other at a small table, and Father poured us tea from a thermos and placed a plate of cakes on the table.

After sipping the amber liquid and nibbling the biscuits for seconds, he asked, "Spring Swallow, what brings you to Peking and our church?"

I hesitated and he smiled.

"Don't worry, only God and I will hear what you say."

With his experience aiding the troubled, he must already have realized that all was not well with me. Though I had never really understood this religion, I knew I could trust Father Edwin. So I told him my story, including my horrible ghost marriage and how I had learned to be an embroiderer, but leaving out a lot, too—including my secret marriage to a revolutionary. I explained how I had been tricked into marrying Wenyi without being told he was a drunk and a gambler, only to be kicked out after my son was stillborn.

After I finished, Father Edwin looked very sad. "What a life you've led at such a young age, Spring Swallow. But God has always looked after you too. He brought you back to me—and to Him. And don't worry about the ghost marriage. Christians do not believe in such superstitions. So you are free to have a real marriage."

He sighed. "I'm sure you need a place to stay, right? The house of God is always open for His children. So you're welcome here."

"Thank you so much, Father Edwin. I'll help out by cleaning, cooking, and doing errands for the church. . . ."

He thought for a while, then, "You said you can embroider?"

I nodded.

"Then maybe someday you can embroider some Christian themes

so we can sell them at auction to raise money for Our Lady of Sorrows. But for now take some good rest and get used to our church."

I was relieved and happy at these suggestions, relieved that I had a roof over my head and happy because I could put my embroidery skill back to use, and to help my mentor, who had done so much for me.

"All right, then, it's decided. I'll ask my assistant Ryan McFarland to arrange things for you. Tomorrow he can take you to shop for what you need. Your work here will be light and we will pay you modestly for it."

"I do need to shop, but there's no need to bother Mr. McFarland. I can do it myself."

"No, trust me, Peking is huge and full of cheats and thieves. You've had enough bad luck in your life. Ryan is a very trustworthy young man and a devoted Christian. He will look out for you. I'm very proud that he will be ordained as a full priest soon.

"Oh," he smiled contentedly, "Ryan is also an excellent cook. That's how I got my belly." He affectionately patted his middle part. "He has been God's gift to me. I really don't know what to do without this young man."

I felt very lucky that things had been settled so easily. I knew I could trust Father Edwin, even though the others I'd trusted had let me down—Mean Aunt, Aunty Peony, Old Li and his family—even Shen Feng had jilted me for his revolution.

23

The Storyteller

Now that I felt safe, I gave in to my fatigue. For the next two days I just slept and ate. Ryan McFarland was indeed an excellent cook and had extended his culinary skills during his time in China, producing not only fried chicken, black-peppered steaks with onions, and pan-seared pork chops with boiled potatoes, but also sweet and sour pork, crispy duck, kung pao chicken, and several other dishes. Even the church's regular cook liked the way Ryan prepared food.

Once I'd regained my energy, I went to Lotus Street where Aunty Peony had taken us to shop and sightsee two years ago. Seeing the same sights now gave me a melancholy feeling. In the intervening time I'd transformed from a novice to a master embroiderer. But also from a young girl into a woman, then a widow, then a married woman who'd lost her child, and now an outcast at the mercy of a Western church run by foreign ghosts, albeit kind ones.

I wanted to find the Heavenly Phoenix shop where Aunty sold our works but had kept secret from us. Since I didn't have an address, I went to the embroidery shop Aunty had taken us to, hoping they would give me directions. The same plump woman was still here, busy with customers. All she would tell me is that someone at a tea shop nearby might be able to tell me. I assumed she just didn't want to help me find a competitor, but since I had no other leads, I decided to find the teahouse.

She pointed, saying, "It's down that way."

The weather was fine, so I enjoyed walking along, feeling the city energy, while looking for the tea shop. All along the walls of the buildings were colorful posters—Movie Star Perfume, Twin Sister Cosmetics, Longevity Cigarettes, Great Wall Coffee . . . all with pretty women smiling at you, their eyes dreamy and their smiles intoxicated, luring you into their world of make-believe.

Soon I noticed a few wooden tables and chairs under a bamboo roof. In back stood a huge cast-iron stove with a big metal teapot emitting billows of white steam, hissing like a complaining old wife.

Hanging over the stove were wooden plaques announcing the varieties of tea available: Chrysanthemum, Hundred-Year-Old Pu'er, Iron Bodhisattva, Big Red Robe, Before-the-Rain Dragon Well, Turquoise Spring. Another horizontal plaque advised customers to "Meet friends through tea drinking."

Small tables were crowded into the space under the roof, all occupied except one. Intrigued by this cozy little sidewalk teahouse, I sat down at the empty table. It did not seem an easy place to make friends—everyone was absorbed in conversations within their own little groups. Nearby a young woman was feeding her baby, who occupied her entire attention. At another table was an amorous young couple. I sighed to myself, remembering my own lost baby and lost mountain husband. How come all of these people were luckier than I?

I ordered fragranced flower tea and peanuts. While I was sipping the scalding brew and crunching the peanuts, a stout, fortyish man materialized on the sidewalk in front of the tea shop. He lifted a drum and fastened it onto a wooden stand.

I leaned toward the young mother. "What's this man going to do?"

"He comes here every day to tell stories."

"What kind of stories?"

"Wait and you'll see." She fed and cooed to her baby, then spoke again. "We come here to learn the news from him so we don't need the newspapers. He's very good at telling any kind of stories, funny, happy, sad . . . depending on his mood."

A small group had now gathered around the man, eyeing him with anticipation. The storyteller spread his strong feet to root himself on the ground. Slowly he lifted his right hand, then brought it down on the drum with a loud bang. He then began in a sonorous voice.

"Honorable guests, welcome to my storytelling!"

A round of applause burst in the air.

"Today there'll be no news—but mind you, no news is good news. Instead, I'm going to tell you the story of Tiger-Head Shoes. . . ."

Hearing the words "tiger-head shoes," my ears perked up. According to Aunty Peony, these shoes were among the most sought-after items that I'd embroidered for Heavenly Phoenix. Because my tiger heads were so cute, both the toddlers and their mothers loved them. Babies, besides wearing the shoes, also played with them as toys, and they liked to kiss the embroidered tiger.

The storyteller continued. "Once upon a time in ancient China, there was a man called Yang Da who made his living by ferrying people across rivers. Though Yang was young and nice looking, he was too poor to get a wife and start a family.

"One day after he ferried an old woman across the river, she said she didn't have money to pay him but could give him a painting in exchange. Yang, always kind to his customers, accepted her offer. Once home, when he took out the painting, he saw a beautiful young woman sewing tiger heads onto a pair of tiny shoes.

"Yang became transfixed by the woman's beauty and skill, then was astonished to see her begin to move and step out from the painting. . . ."

A young man among the crowd asked, "*Wah,* where can I get this painting?"

His buddy joked, "But even if you had the painting, the lady wouldn't walk out for you!"

Everyone laughed heartily; some clapped and others booed.

The storyteller went on in high spirits, his hand beating the drum in a steady rhythm. "Soon Yang and the woman from the painting married in a simple ceremony witnessed by the god of the river where he made his living. Ever after, Yang's wife would hide herself inside the painting during the day and come down from the painting at night. To help bring in money, she did embroidery. A year later, their son Little Treasure was born and the mother sewed many tiger-headed shoes for him. She believed the tigers would protect her son and give him strength and courage.

"The evil village head heard about Yang and his mysterious wife and decided to pay them a visit. The next morning, when he arrived at Yang's house, both father and son were out working. So he stole the painting with the wife in it and left. Arriving home and shocked to learn that the painting was gone, Yang asked his son to retrieve it.

"Little Treasure went to the village head's house, saw the painting, and pulled his mother right out. Village Head immediately ordered his servants to tie up Little Treasure, but the child vigorously stomped his feet. Immediately, two ferocious tigers jumped out from his shoes. The terrified Village Head and his servants screamed and fled. Little Treasure then returned home safely with his mother inside the painting."

The audience clapped enthusiastically.

The young mother next to me exclaimed, "Good for Little Treasure!"

The couple to my left yelled, "We want a son just like Little Treasure!"

Now the storyteller recounted the moral of his tale. "That's why we embroider tiger heads onto the shoes of our children—so they'll be brave as a tiger!"

The audience yelled out, *"Hao, hao, hao!"* ("Wonderful!")

The storyteller set down a pair of tiger-headed shoes, which rapidly filled up with coins from the audience. After that, customers began to trickle out of the tea shop.

I went up to drop in a few coins myself and noticed something odd about the shoes, so I bent down to get a closer look. To my astonishment, they had been embroidered by me!

I approached the storyteller. "Sir, I really enjoyed your story of the Tiger-Head Shoes." I pointed to his—or my—shoes. "May I know where you got these from?"

He cast me a suspicious glance. "Why do you ask? They're my shoes."

"Because I believe I embroidered them."

"But they are from a shop here."

"But I'm the embroiderer."

"All right, since you are an embroiderer, we can talk. But I'm hungry, so I will order something to eat."

He led the way to another table in back, near the kitchen. After we sat, he pounded on the table and yelled orders to the cook. The wiry chef was leaning over his wok, which emitted a mouth-watering smell of meat and garlic.

He shouted back, "All right, all right. Hungry, hah?" Then the wok smoked and sizzled as he poured more oil onto it.

Soon fragranced tea with sugared ginger was placed in front of us. Then tasty dishes started to arrive: crispy marinated pig ear, pork intestine filled with soup, fried pancake with lamb and green onion filling.

The storyteller made a sweeping gesture with his rough hand. "Help yourself."

I wasn't hungry, but in order to show appreciation I picked up a piece of pancake and started to nibble. To my surprise, the food in this humble street stall was unexpectedly delicious. The pancake had been soaked in lamb fat, then pan-fried just right—crispy on the outside and juicy on the inside. The crunchy green onion teased my palate.

I sighed with pleasure, not just from the perfectly prepared food, but because seeing the cook in action made me think of Aunty Peony's teaching. She always said that to be successful at embroidering, or anything else, one must concentrate completely. "Even if a mountain collapses outside your window, you shouldn't look, but continue to work."

Aunty also emphasized thorough study. "If you embroider bamboo, you study it in all circumstances—sunlight, moonlight, summer, winter, rain, snow. . . . Only when you've become one with the bamboo should you begin to work. Then you will possess the secrets of a thousand beauties."

But Aunty had another rule that was not always possible to follow, though I tried. This was to look at and think of only beautiful things—so as not to defile our vision.

I often remembered what she had told me: "Try to avoid ugly things like a pock-faced man, a beggar in rags, a pus-oozing wound, a dying person, a stinking corpse. If unfortunately you run into something like that, you should immediately wash your eyes with clear water and look at a beautiful painting or scene in nature to neutralize the unpleasant images. Even the face of a crying baby is considered ugly. You understand?"

I challenged her once. "But I find babies cute, even if they are crying."

"That's why I don't like students to talk back, or ask stupid questions. If your embroidery looks like the face of a crying baby, will people buy it?"

I had no answer, but, of course, just as all babies cry, sometimes we all have to look at unpleasant things. Yet some can stay cheerful in difficult surroundings.

This street cook worked on the dirty street, amidst disorderly crowds. Like me he must have spent years of bitter practice perfecting his art. Yet, as I watched the unassuming middle-aged man sweating beside the fiery wok, he seemed to be enjoying himself and I felt great admiration. I looked around at the other diners, lost in their conversations, not even thinking of the cook who had made their enjoyment possible.

Finally, the plates were empty. The storyteller took a long sip of his tea, sighed with satisfaction, then cast me an inquiring look.

"All right, young miss, please tell me why you say these are your shoes?"

"Mister, they are not mine. I only embroidered them to be sold at Heavenly Phoenix embroidery shop, but then—"

"Did you say you embroidered for Heavenly Phoenix?"

I nodded.

"Then how come I never saw you there?"

"My aunty, three sisters, and I all embroidered for Heavenly Phoenix. But we all lived near Soochow, not Peking. Only Aunty went to Heavenly Phoenix—she never took us with her."

He looked surprised. "Who's your aunty, is her name Lilac?"

"No, Peony."

He murmured as if talking to himself. "But Lilac is the best embroiderer who sews for Heavenly Phoenix."

"Sir, how do you know about Heavenly Phoenix?"

His answer took me by surprise. "I used to work there."

If he worked at an embroidery shop, what was he doing as a street storyteller?

He went on. "But Lilac never mentioned anyone who worked with her, and I always wondered how she could work so fast."

By now I was pretty sure that "Lilac" was Aunty Peony. To find out, I asked, "Is Lilac the one whose *Along the River during the Qingming Festival* won the prize at the Peking International Art and Craft Fair?"

I kept my mouth shut about the real embroiderer being me.

"Yes, then Lilac must be your aunty!" He shook his head. "*Hai,* she ruined us!"

"What?"

"You don't know?"

I told him I had no idea what he was talking about.

"Someone told the police that the embroidery was based on a stolen imperial painting."

"I never heard anything like this." Actually, I knew Aunty had stolen from the palace but kept my mouth shut about it.

"Yes, that was the rumor. So one day the police came to search our store. They asked for Lilac, but we never knew where she lived. Now you tell me she lived near Soochow. Oh my, what a woman!"

He stared at me intently. "So, you know where she is?"

"She left Soochow several years ago, but she didn't tell any of us that she was leaving and we have no idea where she went. Aunty was always very secretive about herself—that's why she never took us to Heavenly Phoenix. And she used a different name with you."

"Good. Better that you and I have nothing more to do with her."

Actually, I did hope I would see Aunty again, but I knew it would be dangerous to suggest that.

"Did the police find anything suspicious?"

He shook his head. "Even though the police couldn't find anything, customers stopped coming—they did not want anything to do with a business that was watched by the police. And without Lilac's work we didn't have enough good stuff to sell."

He sipped his tea noisily, then spoke again. "We were delighted when she won the contest, thinking it would boost our business. But instead, it ruined us. My boss had to close up. He is still rich, but I ended up here telling stories."

"I'm very sorry, sir. . . ."

"All right, young miss," he said dejectedly, "I am happy to have met you. The shoes you embroidered are now my earning tools. And I really like the tigers."

He put some money down to pay for the food and got up to leave. "Good luck to you and your embroidery. If you want to chat again, you can always come here for my storytelling. Or someday bring your work to show me. Maybe I can introduce you to our rivals who are still in business."

In a moment he had disappeared into the crowd.

I didn't go back to the tea place to chat with him or show him my embroidery. In fact, I had no wish to see this man again—in case he might bring me bad luck.

Heavenly Phoenix's bankruptcy meant nothing to me, but in spite of everything, I was concerned for Aunty Peony's safety. There wasn't anything I could do for her so, as the days passed, I focused on my new life in Our Lady of Sorrows Church. Father Edwin only assigned me light tasks like shopping nearby, mailing letters, brewing tea, and setting the table, while exempting me from cleaning, cooking, and gardening where he had other help.

But as if my life had not been complicated enough, I found out I was pregnant, *again,* this time by Wenyi. I felt both happy and sad. Happy that a new life was kicking inside me, but sad that, instead of having a clean break from the Li family, I'd be forever entangled with them. I also agonized over how I should tell Father Edwin about this.

* * *

One day when I brought Father Edwin his tea, he signaled me to sit across from him.

"Spring Swallow, from now on I hope you will help Our Lady of Sorrows by embroidering works for our upcoming auction."

I'd been expecting Father to ask me this for a long time, so I nodded my head like a hungry chick pecking on rice. I was pleased that I would be able to pick up embroidery again, and that I would be doing something to return Father Edwin's many kindnesses.

"Of course, Father Edwin, thank you so much!"

He smiled. "I should thank you. I am happy that you have turned out to be such a hardworking, responsible young woman."

"It is because of your and Aunty Peony's teaching."

"Thank you. But I'm sure not all her students are as good as you. I suggest you embroider some small items first; if they sell well, then maybe you can do some larger works later."

From that day on I was back at my favorite occupation again. I felt pleasure as the needle in my hand moved smoothly in and out of the fabric. I did cute little things that I thought would be easy to sell: children's shoes, hats, bibs, stomach covers, blankets with lively animals like tigers, roosters, monkeys, sheep, or pretty flowers like lotuses, orchids, plum blossoms.

I also embroidered pillow covers for newlyweds with Mandarin ducks for marital harmony, dragon and phoenix for loving union, double characters for happiness, and one hundred children for fertility. Moreover, I did a few that would appeal to everybody: bats for good fortune, paired carps for abundance, and cranes for longevity.

But sometimes when I embroidered for weddings, I felt sad. Shen Feng's image and the memory of our all too few happy times on the mountain together would flit across my mind like scenes from a silent movie. I'd imagine him standing on the peak playing a melancholy tune on his flute and gazing at me with sorrowful eyes, as if mourning his tragic fate. Sometimes a tear or two escaped my eyes before I was able to put my mind back on my work.

But my mood lifted when, a few weeks later, my embroidery went on sale. As I'd expected, parents loved to buy things for their newborns, and most couples would splurge on the most important day of their lives. Encouraged by my success, I continued to embroider with great enthusiasm, branching out to other items such as shoes, purses, gloves, hanging decorations.

Though days in Our Lady of Sorrows continued to pass pleasantly, if uneventfully, some sorrows remained. I missed Little Doll and felt very guilty that I had let myself be intimidated into leaving her at the mercy of the Li family. For now all I could do was send small gifts to her at Golden Thread in Soochow. Of course I didn't attach any return address, so I had no idea if she received them. I'd been also thinking that since Ping had warned me that I needed to escape, maybe she would help me see Little Doll secretly.

Then one day as I was thinking back on these matters, I suddenly realized that I had been fooled. I set down the shoe I had been embroidering as the ground under me seemed to tilt crazily.

It was not I who had to worry about the police, but Old Li. Now he was the thief who had the imperial undergarment! Indeed, he would never report it to the police but keep it as his own. So Ping only pretended to be nice to get rid of me quickly so I couldn't confront her father and cause a big fuss. She'd never done anything for me before, so I should have known that she was not being my friend—but rather her father's accomplice in stealing from me!

I felt overcome with rage. But even if I'd known I was being tricked, it would have been to no avail. Old Li already had the garment and he'd rather die than give it back to me. So, though no police would have been called, I still had to leave—especially because I'd also lost "his" grandson.

Now I was pregnant again, this time with a child who was really his, but I would never tell him, so he would lose this one too. In fact, I decided I would never tell anyone who was the father as I did not want to take any chance that Wenyi could come back into my life.

It would be some time before my pregnancy showed, so I put off figuring out how I would tell Father Edwin and the others at Our Lady of Sorrows. For now, I threw myself into the church activities, including frequent ventures into Peking for errands. The young seminarian Ryan McFarland insisted on accompanying me to protect me from the perils of the big city. In fact, I was beginning to suspect that his interest in me went beyond saving my soul. He also liked to watch me embroider, during which he would help me practice my conversational English. Sometimes he would bring me small gifts, such as a fancy needle cushion or a potted bamboo to cheer up my bare room. He did seem a little nervous around me, however.

I liked Ryan, a gentleman with great compassion, faith, and devotion. But I sensed something with him that I never had with Father Edwin—that Ryan was a man and felt desire, no matter how strongly he wanted to be a priest. I didn't know if his infatuation was due simply to my proximity, or if he really appreciated my talent in embroidering. To him I must seem exotic, and perhaps he was also moved by my tragic background. Ryan was a kind and attractive man, but I dared not dream that I'd find love that might actually last. Let alone from a foreigner, though a decent one. But it seemed more likely that nothing would come of it—after all, I was competing for him with God.

But as my baby was growing inside me every day, I began to think in a different light. Since I couldn't possibly go back to the Li mansion, again, I needed a father for my little one. So, if I was to accept Ryan's love, I needed to tell him about this and ask if he was willing to be the "father." I'd lied to Wenyi and disaster struck, so I didn't want to lie again, especially not to an honest, loving man. It was bad karma.

But I quickly dismissed this preposterous idea. What could possibly be on my mind? To seduce a priest-to-be so he was willing to be my baby's father and take care of both of us?

❧ 24 ❧

The Infatuation of
a Foreign Ghost

One Saturday Ryan McFarland suggested we go out shopping together. His pretext was that because my embroideries were selling so well, we needed to replenish our stock of thread and fabric. Also, since I'd been working so hard, it would be good for me to have a break. But I could tell that he wanted another chance to be with me alone outside the church, since my embroidery supplies were not even close to running out.

I did like Ryan, maybe even very much. But like my revolutionary husband, he had his mind on something higher than a mere woman. Even if we became lovers, where would our future be? Ryan was going to be a priest—would he be willing to break his vows? Of course, I heard that seminarians, or even ordained priests, would sometimes renounce their vows for love. Anyway, who would stop them, God? Or Our Lady of Sorrows? But I was also well aware that scandal might accomplish what God could not.

After we finished shopping at the busy Wangfu Jing commercial area, Ryan took me to eat at an open-air food stall facing the busy street. We ordered Dragon Well tea, dan dan noodles, pan-fry chicken dumplings, and stir-fry spicy pork belly. We sat quietly watching the bustling crowds as people with anxious faces went about their errands, carrying bags of goods and haggling with street vendors. While the adults looked harried, their children skipped along happily with their parents, holding new toys or begging for candy. A few elderly people shuffled along with bored, blank expressions, as if they'd already seen enough of this world.

Not far from us a middle-aged woman sat inside an alleyway mending silk stockings. Straining her eyes through thick glasses, she nimbly moved her fingers to sew the delicate material. I was curious because from a distance, she could have passed as an embroiderer. I'd never even touched a silk stocking, but I knew they were the latest luxury imported from the West. But only beautiful, rich *taitai* who rode in shiny cars with white-gloved drivers could afford them. Did I wish for silk stockings? Maybe. But mostly I was tired of being poor, insecure, and on the run.

However, I knew that even being rich did not guarantee a happy life. There was the famous movie star Ruan Lingyu—she could afford all the silk stockings in the world but could no longer wear them because she'd killed herself. Her movie *Modern Women* made fun of vicious reporters and gossip columnists, but the press took its revenge by slandering her. Finally, she was unable to put up with all the lashing tongues. Her last words were *renyan kewei* ("words can kill").

I sighed inside. Although my situation was not close to Ruan's since I was not famous or a movie star, I could understand her hopelessness. Though the day was sunny, I could not clear the gloomy thoughts from my mind. Wenyi, Old Li, Ping, Aunty Peony, Leilei—was it my karma to always be among people like these? Were there any kind ones?

But then I looked across at Ryan, who seemed to sense my mood because he had an expression of concern. I did not want to appear unhappy in front of him, so I tried to push the unpleasant thoughts from my mind.

Nearby was a store displaying bamboo wares. A young, plain-faced woman was caressing a bamboo stroller with one hand and her bulging belly with the other. The jade green, half-moon-shaped pram was the cutest little thing I'd ever seen. Horizontal poles along the sides kept the baby from falling out. There were four wheels on the bottom and a long handle in back so the parents could push their little treasure when they were out for a stroll. I imagined curious little eyes darting around, taking in this new world. But like everyone, he would grow up and learn what this world is really like.

Now the young mother-to-be tapped on the pram, probably testing if it would be sturdy enough for her little treasure. A young man took her hand as he bent over to examine the pram with her.

As I watched, my hand moved to caress my belly, imagining *my* to-be-born little treasure. Would it be a boy or a girl? If it were up to me, I'd prefer a girl, so I could dress her up in my embroidery and someday pour out all my secrets to her. The last thing I wanted was a boy who resembled his father, Li Wenyi. Then I realized—he would be my baby, after all.

Ryan's gentle voice piped up, interrupting my reverie. "What's on your mind, Spring Swallow? You've been very quiet."

I blurted out, "Ryan, I'm pregnant."

He stared at me, chopsticks suspended in midair. The air around us seemed frozen, while the people passing by us kept talking and laughing, oblivious to our little drama.

"What do you mean?"

"I'm pregnant—carrying a baby."

He put down his chopsticks, cast a quick look at the young pregnant woman still checking on the baby carriage, then back to me.

"Are you serious?"

"Ryan, I'm sorry to disappoint you."

He didn't respond directly to my question, but asked, "Is that the reason you . . . came to our church?"

"Ryan, I had no other place to go."

He stared at me.

"Now you must think I'm a bad woman."

He shook his head, took a sip of his tea, and looked down at the table. Finally, he raised his head, asking, "Who is the father?"

"It's the store owner, Old Li's son."

"Then why did you leave him?" His voice sounded calm, but I could tell that inside his emotions were in turmoil. He knew that I'd been married, so he had to know I was no longer a virgin. Maybe foreigners didn't care so much about this, only the backward, feudal, superstitious Chinese.

I hesitated, not knowing what to say.

"Spring Swallow, God forgives all sinners. You can trust me, and Father Edwin, too, to help you," he said, squeezing my hand for reassurance.

I spoke rapidly, trying to explain. "Wenyi's father arranged the marriage, but I discovered after the wedding that his son was dissolute. He spent most evenings out drinking and gambling away his father's money. When I refused him, he . . . forced me." I rubbed my stomach. "That's how I got pregnant."

Ryan looked very upset. "I'm so sorry, Spring Swallow." He paused to calm himself, then asked, "Did he hit you?"

"No, he just didn't care about me. Actually, he's not my husband anymore."

"What happened?"

"He gave me the letting-go-the-wife letter. So now I have no husband, just a baby on the way."

Ryan shook his head, looking deep in thought. "Father Edwin told me about your hard life . . . but I had no idea that your husband was that bad to you. Spring Swallow, you deserve a better man than him, one who will love and appreciate you."

I knew that Ryan really had himself in mind for this. That was why he often seemed so awkward around me—because he liked me as a woman. He planned to be a priest, but he had feelings a priest isn't supposed to have. Unlike Father Edwin, who had always been kind to me but nothing more.

Ryan blushed, then asked for a fresh pot of tea and filled our cups.

He took several quick sips, then asked in a neutral tone, "Did you tell Father Edwin about your pregnancy?"

I shook my head. "I'm afraid. . . ."

He squeezed my hand again. "I understand." Then he remained silent for long moments as if deep in thought about matters of life and death.

Just then a middle-aged man nearby spat on the ground and yelled, "Whore! White-ghost-fucking whore!"

A younger man immediately joined in the attack. "White ghost, stop corrupting our women and go back to your country!"

"Yes," said the older one. "Get away from our women and get out of China!"

Ryan immediately stepped between me and the two men, steered me away from the dangerously growing crowd, tossed a few coins onto the table, then lifted me into a rickshaw.

When we got back, Ryan left me off at my room, but he seemed to avoid me. I assumed that he did not want to be around a woman with a past like mine, especially now I was carrying a "fatherless" baby. I went back to my room and cried. It seemed I had lost one of the few friends who had ever been kind to me.

The following days when Ryan and I ran into each other at church, he didn't say much. Not that he was ever impolite, just suddenly somewhat distant and formal. His sudden change of behavior bothered me. Because I started to like him and even hope that maybe we'd have a future together.

Two weeks later, when embroidering in my room, I heard knocking on my door and Ryan's voice calling my name. He came in, closed the door, pulled a chair to sit across from me, and took my hand.

"Spring Swallow, I apologize if I've been cold to you."

I put down my embroidery and looked at him. He seemed to have lost weight. Hair tousled, his cheeks were hollowed and there were dark circles under his eyes.

"It's okay. But, Ryan, are you all right?"

"I've been struggling. . . ."

"About what?"

"I finally have an answer. I've decided to abandon my priesthood." He caressed my hand. "Spring Swallow, will you marry me?"

Before I could respond, he went on, his voice urgent. "Spring Swallow, please marry me. Then your baby will have a father. I'll love the child as my own."

For a moment I was too stunned to respond.

He tilted my face to look into my eyes. "Spring Swallow, you haven't answered. Will you marry me?"

"But I've already been married. Not just once, but three times!"

He seemed to ignore my declaration, but asked, "Do you not like me?" His smooth brows knitted.

"It's not that, Ryan, I like you . . . a lot."

"Then what's the problem?"

This priest-to-be in front of me was so naïve. He just thought that if two people like each other, they'd get married and live happily ever after. How should I explain?

"Ryan, we really don't know much about each other. . . ."

In fact, what I wanted to say was he had no idea who I was, what I'd *really* gone through. However, I believed I understood this foreigner. . . . He was like a clean, clear pond through which you can see everything straight to the bottom.

I said before he had a chance to respond, "Ryan, tell me more about yourself."

He smiled. "Of course. I'll tell you anything you want to know so you can decide if you want to be my wife."

"Why did you decide to be a priest—no wife, no children. . . ."

"My brother is a businessman and my parents always wanted one of their children to be a priest. So I grew up thinking it was my calling to be celibate and serve God with all my heart and mind. When I was in seminary I found that I have an ability for languages and they needed missionaries for China. So here I am as a deacon. God brought me to Father Edwin's church—but then he also brought me to you."

"But what will you do?"

"Spring Swallow, as long as we pray to God, there is no problem that cannot be solved. . . ." He paused, then went on. "When I first saw you, my world changed. I fell in love with you completely. For a while I tried to suppress my feelings and stayed up late every night praying that God would restore my vocation. But He did not choose to do so. So I believe He has accepted my change to a secular life."

He smiled dreamily. "Now I feel that God is blessing us."

Feeling too embarrassed to look at him, I lowered my head. But my hand was still held in his.

Ryan said, his expression very tender, "Spring Swallow, you looked so fragile, vulnerable, and sad the first day I saw you, my heart just melted. I believed it was love at first sight. I've never experienced a feeling like this before."

I looked and met his grayish blue eyes. "You've . . . never been in love?"

"No, before I met you, I only wanted to serve God. I still want to serve God, but I longer want to be celibate. So, Spring Swallow, will you marry me?"

It felt very strange to have a barbarian ask to marry me. But did it matter that he was a foreigner? I'd even been married to a ghost!

As I felt too embarrassed to say yes, Ryan leaned close to me and whispered. "Let's go back to my room."

"But, Ryan . . ."

It was the first time I saw him smile mischievously. "Don't worry too much, Spring Swallow, everything will be fine. Don't forget that we're in God's hands. I just know that He wants us to be together."

It was the first time I'd been invited into Ryan's room. The small space had several bookcases, a bed, and a wooden desk covered with more books and manuscripts. The walls were bare except for a rosary that hung above the desk and a wooden crucifix over the bed. After Ryan locked the door and took down the cross, I knew what would happen next.

Holding me tightly, he began to kiss me, very tenderly at first, then increasing in intensity. Had I fallen in love with this man? I was not a hundred percent sure, because Shen Feng still lingered on my mind. As I responded to Ryan's growing kisses and caresses, disturbing thoughts whirred through my mind. Would Father Edwin object to our reunion? Was I a slut for letting Ryan, a foreigner, touch me? Was I just using Ryan to have a father for my child, as I had with Wenyi?

When Ryan finally released me, he gazed at me lovingly and asked, "Spring Swallow, do you love me?"

I nodded, for I did like him, very much. But I also felt guilty that I still thought about Shen Feng.

He looked very happy. "So, you'll marry me and make me the happiest man on Earth?"

I looked at his glowing face and nodded again.

On that day, Ryan and I became lovers. The fact that our relationship developed so quickly made me feel uneasy. I was surprised that an aspiring priest who'd never been with a woman before could turn into such a passionate lover. It was obvious to me, if not to him, that he'd been starving for a woman's love. After all, God's love does not keep you warm at night.

Ryan and I secretly met and made love in different places—mostly in a small inn in the Front Gate area, sometimes even the park near Beihai Lake at night. He preferred not to do this again in his own room unless he absolutely couldn't suppress his desire. I didn't ask why, but guessed he respected his church and deemed it sacrilegious to act out any carnal pleasure there.

We continued to be lovers, even as my belly expanded. Ryan decided he could not put off telling Father Edwin that he would not become a priest. He feared that Father would not want to bless our marriage. Though I had no doubt that I should marry Ryan, at times I felt that I was being unfaithful to Shen Feng—even though he was dead. The Chinese say a woman is her husband's wife when he's alive, and his ghost's wife after he dies.

So when Ryan told me that he was about to tell Father Edwin, I asked, "Are you really sure . . . ?"

Both his expression and voice were firm. "Spring Swallow, I love you. Better I tell Father Edwin myself than wait until he figures it out."

"But what if Father tells us we both have to leave Our Lady of Sorrows—then where are we going to live? How will we make a living?"

"You know, Father Edwin is a very kind and considerate man. I believe he'll even agree to marry us in the church."

A long silence passed. Then, suddenly, Ryan looked extremely worried. "Spring Swallow, are you sure you're not still legally married to Old Li's son?"

"Li Wenyi gave me an official letting-go-the-wife letter. That's what Chinese do when they are in a hurry to be rid of a wife without losing face. All he had to do was state that I'm not fit to be his wife or a mother."

"Good." He finally looked relieved. "Then I can ask Father to marry us soon."

"But, Ryan, now that you're expected to become a priest in less than a few months, you think Father . . ."

"Don't worry, even if he is bitter, there's really nothing he can do to stop us."

Fortunately, Father Edwin was not bitter, only disappointed. Ryan told me that when he informed him about our decision to marry, he didn't look shocked; perhaps he sensed it was coming. We were relieved not only that Father was gracious about our "betrayal," but that he didn't say anything about my pregnancy, nor how our love affair had started under his very eyes in his church.

"God would not stop true love from flourishing." Father paused to scrutinize Ryan, then me. "Be sure to be faithful and cherish each other all the rest of your days."

We both nodded. We loved each other, but I didn't think we really could promise that it would be undying. I thought of my love with Shen Feng. We had pledged "undying" to Heaven and Earth, but he had died anyway. However, I hoped this would be different, for Ryan was not a revolutionary, but a man of peace, so I could at least hope for a quiet life.

Father Edwin and Ryan agreed that it must be a Christian wedding. Then they started to talk to each other in rapid English so I had no idea what they were deciding. Maybe they were talking about my shameful past, so I thought it was just as well I couldn't understand. Later Ryan explained to me that to be married in the Church I had to be baptized and confirmed. Father Edwin actually had baptized me back in the old village; though I had long ago lost the certificate. Fortunately, he remembered. So all I had to do was go with Ryan to the cathedral to be confirmed by the bishop.

Ryan had told Father that he would give me religious instruction, but in our private time together we somehow always ended up doing other things. Given my condition, it was obvious that we should have a discreet, private ceremony.

Of course, I felt happy knowing that I was about to be married, but I also felt some apprehension. My three former marriages had not ended well. A Chinese man would be terrified of catching my bad luck if he even looked at me. I would be the all-destroying star and avoided like a leper. So I considered myself very lucky that I had met a foreigner who wanted me.

* * *

Two weeks later, Ryan and I became husband and wife in a very simple ceremony presided over by Father Edwin. Besides Father, only a few guests were present—the cook, the cleaning lady, and three of Ryan's seminary friends. Because Ryan was a foreigner, during the ceremony we did not have to bow to Heaven and Earth, or inform our ancestors of our union. Nor was there any kowtowing and offering tea to the elders, even Father Edwin.

Ryan wore a gray suit with a red silk tie while I wore a white-lace western dress with pink floral embroidery, which I rushed to finish for my big day.

When Father Edwin read the "till death do you part," my tears fell. That was exactly what had happened to Shen Feng and me. So although the phrase expresses hope that the couple's marriage would last till they die, in my experience, death, like a cunning fox, is always lurking around the corner ready to catch you off guard.

Ryan wiped my eyes with his handkerchief. "Be happy, Spring Swallow. I love you."

So I murmured softly, "Me too."

After that, the maid's little boy brought rings on a red velvet cushion and we placed them on each other's fingers.

That evening, the chef served a special dinner with a few guests at the church's dining hall. We drank wine and ate roasted chicken, stewed beef, scampi with cream, pudding, and a small wedding cake.

Our wedding night was spent in Ryan's room, which had been decorated for the occasion in red for good luck. We made love under a red bed cover and cuddled against each other as we fell asleep on the red pillows—decorated by me with a pair of Mandarin ducks for marital happiness.

Father Edwin told us we could have a week's holiday for our honeymoon. When Ryan asked where I'd like to spend our week together, I suggested Soochow. Though it was a place of bitter memories, it was also famous for its beauty. When I was there I had never had the chance to visit its scenic gardens, or even its famous little pagoda on a hilltop. I hoped now to replace my old unhappy memories with new happy ones.

But most of all, since I did not know where life would take me next, I wanted to find Little Doll.

PART FOUR

⤜25⤛

Returning Home
Is Heartbreak

Before we left for our trip, Ryan studied the map of Soochow and read up on its culture and history. Excited about the "Venice of the East," he wanted to visit all the famous sites: the lavish gardens, the Cold Mountain Temple, and Tiger Hill with the Auspicious Light Pagoda. But I had more than fun in mind in going back to Soochow. Most important to me was picking up Little Doll. Though I had not said anything about her to Ryan yet, I planned to have her come live with us. I also would figure out a way to go by myself to Aunty's house because I was curious to see what had happened to it. Then I would go to the mountain to make offerings for Leilei and Shen Feng.

Though I felt excited to be returning to Soochow, I was not at all eager to run into Old Li, or my mean aunt, or my mother-in-law back in my old village. Despite the trouble that they had caused me, I realized that I no longer needed to worry about being caught by the villagers or turned over to the police. Since I now had a living husband, and a tall foreign one at that, they would be more afraid of me than I was of them.

Although I trusted Ryan as my husband and a man of God, I

was not ready to tell him everything about my past. He knew I'd been married before, once to a ghost and the second time to Li Wenyi, but I'd said nothing about my revolutionist husband. I was determined to put all this behind me and have our honeymoon be the start of a happy life with the decent man who would soon be the father of my—though not his—baby.

On the train to Soochow, I kept thinking of the saying *jinxiang qinggeng qie*—we fear going back home because we don't know what we will find. In ancient times, most people could only afford to go home once or twice in their lifetimes. On their way home, they'd wonder what would have changed. Their little children had now grown to be unrecognizable young men and women. Parents might have died and the neighbors moved away. In our memories, people and things remain the same. But after twenty or thirty years, though they seemed to pass as quickly as a horse jumps over a ravine, we might not recognize anything from our old life.

I thought of the famous poem by He Zhizhang:

> Leaving home when young and retuning when old.
> My accent is the same but my sideburns are white,
> The children don't recognize me,
> Giggling, they ask me where I came from.

When our train finally arrived at Soochow station, Ryan and I alighted, then squeezed through the crowd on the platform. I was not surprised that we attracted stares, some curious, a few hostile. Unlike cosmopolitan Peking, where mixed couples were not unusual, in provincial Soochow we stood out. Outside the big cities, when people see a Chinese woman with a Westerner, they assume she's a prostitute or a slut. Only loose women with insatiable sexual desires would be attracted to a Westerner, because they need the big, hairy barbarians to satisfy their demands in bed.

Because so many people had alighted from the train, we had to wait a while for an empty rickshaw. In the distance, I saw a middle-aged man holding a package as he dashed inside a pawn shop, looking embarrassed. I wondered what he would be pawning, some valuable family heirloom, or his wife's jewelry? As I watched, several men walked out from a gambling house; a few looked happy, but others were gloomy.

I suddenly realized why the pawn shop was right next to the gambling house. After people gambled away all their money, they could make a quick stop at the pawn shop, then back to the casino to lose more. This made me think of Li Wenyi. I wondered what had become of him, his father, and Ping. I reflected on how fortunate I was now to have a caring husband and be rid of the Li family. But my happiness was not complete, because I still worried about Little Doll.

Finally, a tricycle rickshaw pulled up in front of us and we climbed in. Even though it was our honeymoon, Ryan and I were so tired after the long trip that as soon as we arrived in our hotel room, we went to sleep.

The next day, I took Ryan for a stroll along the rivers of Soochow. Fortunately, it was now autumn and the weather, like my new husband, was calm and refreshing. We stared at our still reflections, envying the fishes that didn't seem to have a care in the world, as they wriggled their tails and gurgled trails of bubbles. After a leisurely lunch, we toured the Master of Nets Garden, appreciating the lush, fragrant vegetation, imagining we were back in the Tang dynasty drinking wine and reciting poetry together. As the soothing autumn breeze gently massaged our faces, everything seemed right with the world.

Our last stop was Lion's Grove Garden, one of the four most famous in Soochow. Ryan and I were pleased that this one was not so crowded so we attracted few stares. We strolled at a leisurely pace, side by side along winding paths, beside ponds, over bridges, under pavilions, until we reached the lion-shaped rocks for which the garden is named.

On the way back to the gate, we stopped in a small gallery. From a scroll I read Du Fu's poem "Tribute to the Hermit Wei Ba":

In this life, it is rare for good friends to be together,
We are like the stars rising and setting in the sky.
Only on this night do we share the light of the same candle.

Youth was quickly gone; now our sideburns are white.
Tomorrow, once again, we'll be separated by tall mountains,
How fleeting and fickle are life and human affairs!

Although I had not read much poetry, somehow this one brought
tears to my eyes. I was relieved that Ryan didn't notice my emo-
tional state, for he was a few steps ahead of me looking at other
masterpieces. These lines seemed to echo my own life, even though
I was nowhere close to the poet in fame or achievement. With all
that I had been through, I felt my own youth was disappearing
quickly. The mountain I had climbed so often while living in
Aunty's house was now a place of loss, reminding me of Shen Feng
and Leilei. And even Aunty had tried to end her and Little Doll's
lives there. The tall mountain was impassive as it looked down on
the fleeting and fickle lives below.

I considered Du Fu luckier than I, for he had the chance to re-
unite with his old friends, sharing delicious wine under the same
candlelight. But my Shen Feng was gone. Since I had no idea where
he was buried, I couldn't even make offerings, or tell him not to
worry about me, for my new husband was a good man. And the
other people who were close to me—Leilei, Purple, Aunty Peony,
Little Doll—they were all gone from my life. Just like Du Fu in his
poem, we were stars rising and setting in the sky, separated by tall
mountains.

But now, under Heaven and above Earth, I had my foreigner
husband, Ryan, and my to-be-born baby. So I would be sure to
watch over them both. I strode up to Ryan and took his arm in
mine. My new husband looked very happy and I was too.

"Spring Swallow, have you seen something nice?"

I stared into his eyes and gently nodded.

The next day, Ryan took me for a boat ride on the famous Taihu
Lake. When we arrived at the pier, several boatmen crowded
around us, eager for our business. In his fluent Mandarin, Ryan ne-
gotiated a good price with a sturdy young man smelling of the lake.
When my barbarian husband helped me onto the swaying boat, the

other boatmen cast us disapproving glances, as if saying, "Ha, a white ghost stealing a Chinese girl!" Or so I imagined.

So I turned away from them and looked at my husband's eyes, which seemed to reflect the blue water of the lake.

He said, "The city will look very different from the lake. I think of the poem about King Wu's wife, like the West Lake, equally beautiful from any angle."

"I never had a chance for a boat ride like this. Thank you for bringing me here."

"Spring Swallow," he said and smiled, "it's good that this is your first boat ride. It will be something unique to remember from our honeymoon."

The small boat had a low table and plain wooden benches. From the picnic basket Ryan had been carrying, he took out food, drinks, and napkins, then laid them on the table. To my delight, he'd brought some of my favorite foods—dumplings, pork buns, pickled cabbages, scallion pancakes, and fragrant tea.

I asked, "Ryan, you didn't bring any Western food for yourself?"

"I'm happy to eat whatever you do." He smiled.

Ryan made a signal to the boatman to cast off. I felt the boat swaying gently in the water. At first the constant motion reminded me of my unstable life, but then as I relaxed I found it soothing. Neither of us spoke as we savored the delicious dishes and appreciated the scenery. Like a pair of embroidery scissors, our boat cut through the turquoise lake scattered with leaves and pink petals. Here and there white pagodas stood like lumbering warrior women standing guard over the ancient city.

I turned back to look at the lake. In the distance boats drifted slowly along, their turquoise roofs matching the sky and water. Beside us whiskered carp swam, perhaps hoping for crumbs thrown over by passengers.

Ryan's gentle voice rose next to my ear. "Spring Swallow, see how the fishes are happy?"

I replied, feeling very clever, "You're not the fishes, so how do you know that they're happy?"

"I'm not you," he smiled mischievously, "so I don't know if you know the fishes are happy. But you're not me, so how do you know that I don't know that the fishes are happy?"

Of course I knew Zhuangzi's famous dialogue because Father Edwin had taught it to me—so I assumed Ryan learned it from him too.

Ryan gently put an arm around my shoulder. "All right, let's be as happy together as the fishes."

So we stared at the happy fishes wagging their tails and blowing bubbles, which now looked to me like question marks. Perhaps they were asking, "Young miss, what are you doing here with this white ghost?"

Just then, we felt a few drops from an overhead cloud. Then a much larger boat passed next to us. It was painted lavishly with pleasing floral patterns. In the back was a wide deck, while in front was a cabin, its large windows decorated with embroidered curtains and silk tassels. Outside under a canopy sat three girls, elaborately made up and wearing colorful silk gowns. Silver hairpins held their hair up in buns. Next to them were several men, one in an expensively tailored business suit, the others in traditional Chinese gowns. The drizzle veiled the girls' faces, rendering them beautiful and mysterious, like immortals from a high mountain far, far away.

Ryan looked intrigued. "It seems we are about to be treated to a concert!"

"Good that we're going to hear some free music," I answered nonchalantly.

On the nearby boat a slick-looking middle-aged man cast an obsequious look at his important-looking guests. His voice carried to us across the water.

"Honorable gentlemen," he said with an ingratiating tone, "Miss Dingdong is going to sing for you an excerpt from the Peking opera *A Tale from the West Pavilion*."

The rich men's eyes, like little beggars' hands, kept searching the girls' faces and bodies. Suddenly I realized what this was—a "pleasure boat." A floating whorehouse.

I'd never seen one before, but I had heard about them. The girls on these boats were called *liuying,* "drifting orioles," or drifting prostitutes. Because they entertained on boats and didn't have a fixed residence, they were looked down upon. The lucky ones might save enough money so that one day they could afford a home and a stable life.

Ryan's voice interrupted my thoughts. "It must be nice for the girls to perform on such a beautiful boat with such a respectable audience."

I didn't have the heart to deflate a naïve foreigner's illusion.

The "host" spoke again, his voice betraying years of heavy drinking and smoking. "Gentlemen, as you know, the *Tale from the West Pavilion* is about undying love. The heroine Yingying and the young scholar fell in love at first sight at a temple. This happened a thousand years ago in the Tang dynasty. No marriage would be possible without a matchmaker and the approval of one's parents. However, because of Yingying and Zhang Sheng's true love, their maid helped them to escape the feudal system and finally marry."

"All right"—he made a sweeping gesture—"now let's enjoy some beautiful music from our equally beautiful girls. Miss Dingdong's voice is heavenly, I can guarantee it will make your ear oil flow."

To enthusiastic applause, a girl wearing an embroidered turquoise *cheongsam* began to play a sentimental tune on the flute, her slender fingers fluttering back and forth like butterflies. A girl in red earnestly plucked the four strings of her *pipa*. The prettiest—Miss Dingdong, I assumed—breathed out a melody as she gestured with one hand and clicked wooden clappers with another. The soft music and the slight drizzle over the misty lake gave everything a dreamy quality. Cool breeze swayed the girls' hair and dresses. One could imagine that they were fairies descending onto this dusty world to soothe us mortals with heavenly music.

The west wind blowing as the geese fly south.
Accomplishment comes, but late,
The hanging willows fail to detain the trotting horses.
I hope my carriage will catch up to his,
And the forest grasp the fading sun. . . .

The song was about the bittersweet nature of life, but Ryan, oblivious to the lyrics' meaning, listened happily with his body swaying to the music.

I guessed things with Ryan and me would be fine. Anyway, what more bad luck could there be? I believed I was finally having some good luck by marrying Ryan. Before I could stop him, he waved to the other boat and, to our surprise, the girls waved back. But the men cast us annoyed looks, probably uncomfortable being observed.

I turned my head away from these women with their misery wrapped in luxury. Likely they were village girls whose looks had drawn the attention of gangsters who had kidnapped them to be entertainers and sex slaves. It occurred to me that they would be surprised if they knew that the foreigner next to me was not a paying customer but my husband.

I was relieved when the pleasure boat finally passed us and moved ahead, yet the sadness of Dingdong's singing—and of her life—continued to linger in the air.

Ryan was still happy about the encounter. "How auspicious to hear this heavenly tune during our honeymoon!"

I snapped. "Ryan, don't you understand?"

"Didn't you enjoy it?"

"Ryan . . ."

He looked surprised at my irritated tone.

"Couldn't you hear what she's singing?"

Now my husband looked puzzled. "No . . . what's she singing?"

I decided not to explain that the girls were prostitutes, not performing because they enjoyed it but because they had no choice. I could not blame Ryan for enjoying the singing, or even looking at the pretty girls. It made me realize that his naïveté was due to his goodness that made him overlook much of the evil of the world. Until I met him, almost everyone I'd depended upon had betrayed me. But Ryan had not experienced treachery as I had, and so had an optimism that I decided I should protect.

"It's nothing . . . I think I was a little seasick. I'm okay now."

Ryan leaned to kiss me. "Don't be upset, it's our honeymoon. I promise I'll be a good husband and make you the happiest woman on Earth."

"You have already."

He pointed to the fishes. "See? Like the fish we'll be very happy together, you just have to trust me, and life."

I nodded. I hoped life from now on would be as simple for me as it seemed to him. But after all that had happened, I could not be as optimistic as he was.

I thought of Nalan Shengde's poem:

> If our love is forever like the first time we met,
> No one would be abandoned like a fan in Autumn,
> In an instant the heart can change,
> But we never blame ourselves,
> Instead, only the easy changing of our heart.

I knew this poem was about how the human heart becomes fickle after the purity of early love. The feelings between Shen Feng and me were also pure, but then he'd passed away. Now I shared the same feelings with Ryan, but what would our future together be? Did I dare hope that my bad karma was used up?

My new husband placed his hand on my belly. "Spring Swallow, don't worry, I'll love your baby as I love you."

❧26❧

Back to the Mountain

The boat ride, although lasting only two hours, seemed an entire incarnation. As we sailed along in the light wind, I thought of my name, Spring Swallow, and how my life so far was only drifting in the breeze, but never alighting for very long. So when we came along the dock I hoped it meant that from now on I would live on solid ground. When we tied up at the dock, Ryan took my arm and helped me from the swaying boat.

"Spring Swallow, are you happy about the boat ride?"

"As happy as the fishes in the lake."

We both laughed.

After the boat ride we just strolled around at random, enjoying the sights and each other's company. We found a small garden and walked in. Nearby was a group of people flying kites. One father patiently held his son's arm, instructing him how to launch the kite into the air. Another one proudly watched his daughter as she held the string of her butterfly kite that was high up in the sky. The sight of the children enjoying their kites was very touching to me. There were many different shapes: bat, scorpion, lotus flower, dragon, phoenix, Monkey King, Moon Goddess, the characters for good luck and double happiness.

I lost myself in this innocent world of kites swaying hither and thither in the gentle breeze. They seemed to be making friends with each other, happy to be so high up and so free. But all had someone to keep them attached to the Earth.

Just as the kites were lifting my mood, my eyes met something that spoiled the happy feeling. A young man with a scorpion kite moved his string back and forth like a slippery eel, trying to entangle a rabbit kite.

I pointed this out to Ryan, who commented, "It looks like this guy is trying to cut off the other kite's string."

"But why?"

He pointed to a group of young men surrounding the one with the scorpion. "See those men cheering over there? I believe they're betting on whether he can cut the string."

My heart sank. I turned away so I didn't have to witness the pointless meanness of the young men. The world can suddenly turn ugly. Just when you're enjoying a pleasant outing watching children flying kites, others try to ruin the fun. But maybe that's life: in the end, everything is about gambling. Wasn't my own life one gamble after another? All I could hope is that my new marriage, my fourth, would be my last, lucky bet.

Upset by the gambling in the clear blue sky, I nudged Ryan's elbow. "Let's go."

My eyes continued to wander. Across the street stood a small group of people waiting for the bus; above them hung two huge movie ads—*A Girl Should Marry* and *The Merry Son-in-Law*. Next to the two movie ads was a poster for Diamond Brand clocks with the saying: "Accurate, Dependable, Beautiful." Were these ads here to reassure me that I'd made the right choice to marry—even for the fourth time—and that my husband was both merry and dependable?

Maybe I'd made the right choice, but it would take some time before I could be sure. It worried me that Ryan had made a big sacrifice—giving up his aspiration to be a priest. Would he come to regret this or, worse, decide to leave me to be a priest after all? Ironically, I also felt sad that Ryan was such a good man. Because to me, good men often came to bad ends. Like Shen Feng, who had given up his young life for a good cause—China's future.

Finally, a bus arrived. The group across the street climbed on the bus; then it sped away. Now the sidewalk was empty, as if the people had never existed. I didn't know any of them, of course, but it brought to mind how someday we will all be gone. But nothing we can do about it—just go on living, appreciate my new husband, and cherish my baby.

As if reading my thoughts, Ryan told me that he would always love me and our baby. I was touched that he said "our" instead of "your" baby.

He went on. "Spring Swallow, you know I'd do anything for you."

"You've already done enough." I smiled.

The next day Ryan told me that he needed to take some time out from sightseeing to visit the new priest who had taken Father Edwin's place in the little village church. I was overjoyed because this would give me the chance to see what had happened to Aunty's house—and also to visit the mountain to pay my respects to Shen Feng and Leilei. So two days later we set out together by cart. I had already explained that since he and the new father would mostly be talking in English about church matters, I would prefer to walk around by myself to revisit the places I had known.

After passing many of the sights that had been so familiar to me, I finally approached our house. My first look was disappointing—the house was now dilapidated and the doors and windows were covered by planks. Had the police realized it was deserted and boarded it up? Or had they only come after it had been ransacked? Though the planks looked very thin, I dared not break them off to look inside. Would I see Aunty's dried corpse, crawling with worms?

I blinked hard, trying to get rid of this disturbing image. But I had seen her boarding the train for Peking with the opera singer, so most likely she was still alive.

I walked around the house and saw a gap between two of the planks covering the back door. Though nervous about what I might see, I could not resist peeking. Most of the furniture, tools, framed embroidery, and the altar were still there but looking forlorn and ghostly, as if they had given up hope that their owner would return to revive them. Though my years there had not been entirely happy, now I felt sad to remember when the house had been full of life—we girls embroidering, practicing, bickering, scolding, laughing. My life was much better now, but thinking of the past filled me with melancholy. There was nothing more for me here, so I turned and headed toward the mountain.

I easily found Leilei's shrine, but in my absence it had become grown over with weeds. I pulled out the weeds, lit incense, and recited a sutra for her to have a better rebirth.

Next, I braced myself to climb higher up the mountain, a little nervous now, hoping no bandits or ghosts would be hiding out or wandering around. I'd never felt entirely calm up here since Shen Feng and Purple had told me that the reason few came here was that it was haunted. I'd had enough of ghosts with my first marriage.

No person—or any other kind of being—disturbed me, however, and I soon reached the top, then walked to the area where Shen Feng and I had corresponded. No traces were left of our writings. The messages were gone, probably having been washed away by the rain. Perhaps Heaven was telling me it was time to forget Shen Feng and move on with my new life with Ryan. For a moment, as I stood here, it almost seemed my time with my mountain husband was but a dream, a figment of my imagination.

I doubted that I'd have the chance to come here again, so I burnt some more incense and whispered to Shen Feng's spirit.

"Dear Feng, Spring Swallow comes here to pay you her sincere and loving respect and say good-bye. Now that you're in the other life, I hope there are no more revolutions. Because I always hope we'll have another chance to meet in our next life.

"I have to tell you that I met another man, an American missionary. So you don't need to worry about me—I have someone to take care of me. And my baby, not yours I am sad to say.

"Since we last met, many things have happened to me, but I'm not going to bore you with them. Now I am concentrating on taking good care of myself so I will have a healthy baby. I was pregnant before with your baby, but he has gone to Heaven, so maybe he is with you now."

After I finished, I felt myself restored by the mountain's energy.

In the stillness, it seemed somehow that my connection with Shen Feng was not altogether lost.

When I was about to descend, I spotted what looked like a few incomplete characters on a rock. When I realized one could be *feng,* or "peak," I felt a chill splash down my body. The handwriting seemed like Shen Feng's. But most likely it was from another mountain climber who had written the word "peak" to witness that he'd been here. For a moment it seemed as if my dead husband had come back as a ghost to leave me a message.

Later, when I arrived back at the little church, Ryan was deep in conversation with Father McClatchie, the new priest. I was pleased that he seemed to be enjoying himself, despite my having gone off on my own secret mission. I was not sure why I had not told him I had visited the old house—just too much of my life there I did not want to have to talk about. Ryan asked me how my walk was but did not inquire about the details. After we chatted with Father McClatchie for a few minutes, we started on our way back to Soochow.

27

The Good Luck Mahjong Parlor

The following morning when Ryan asked me where I'd like to go, I suggested Old Li's Golden Thread Embroidery store.

"Are you sure you want to go back? They might make it unpleasant for you."

"It's possible, but they can't do anything to me now. And there's someone I want to see."

Ryan looked upset. "You mean Old Li and his son?"

"No, a little sister there whom I left behind."

Now he looked stunned. "You have a little sister and you just deserted her?"

"No, of course I don't mean a real sister." I touched his hand. "Her name is Little Doll—she was the youngest girl who worked for Aunty Peony. We care about each other like sisters."

"Then why did you leave her behind and come to Peking alone?"

I sighed. "Ryan, you would have needed to be in my situation to understand. Because I feared there might be danger on the trip, and I didn't want to drag her into it. Now that I am safe with you, I'd like to find her and take her with us back to Peking."

"But why would you want to take her with us to Peking?"

"I left her a letter promising her that if I could, I'd come back to get her."

"You know," Ryan frowned, "Father Edwin is not very happy that I gave up the priesthood for you. But he was gracious enough to marry us and let us continue to live and work at Our Lady of Sorrows. So I'm afraid if we bring one more person . . ."

I was disappointed by my husband's response. But maybe I was really asking too much from him, to not only be the father of my baby, but also take in an orphan girl. Moreover, Little Doll was a stranger to him and not even my real sister.

But I did not want to give in. "Little Doll can help out at Our Lady of Sorrows. Besides, doesn't your God teach love and compassion?"

Ryan had no answer, but I could tell he was not happy having another person between us. Soon we climbed into a tricycle rickshaw and rode in silence toward Golden Thread. After we paid and got off, I had a big shock. The store was gone!

"Something wrong?" asked Ryan.

I nodded and pointed to where now a sign said, GOOD LUCK MAHJONG PARLOR.

A middle-aged couple stepped inside eagerly, while at the same time a dejected-looking man came out with his head lowered. So it seemed the good luck was for the owner, not the customers.

"You're sure this is the right address?" asked Ryan.

"Yes"—I pointed to the vinegar store to the right, and the store selling tea leaves to the left—"I remember these two stores."

"Then what are we going to do?"

"Let's go in and see what we can find out."

Once we stepped inside, all eyes were on us, even though the sound of the clashing tiles continued as hands kept busy with "dry swimming" on the mahjong tables. Against the wall in the middle was a huge fish tank, inside which several elaborately colored fishes leisurely swam back and forth, oblivious to the dramas at the gambling tables. The fish, however, were here mainly for good luck—the word for "fish" sounds like the word for "plenty." Framing the fish tank were two hanging scrolls in red. The one on the right said,

GUESTS DRIFT IN LIKE CLOUDS, while the one on the left, BECKONING MONEY AND WELCOMING TREASURE.

I almost chuckled. Of course the fish and the couplets were meant for the owner's luck, not the customers'.

One muscular man, obviously a bodyguard, hurried toward us. "Please leave, we don't entertain white ghosts here."

Maybe he thought that Ryan was a missionary bent on spoiling their business by preaching to their customers.

I smiled. "Mister, we're not here to gamble but ask for information."

He gave both Ryan and me a suspicious, dirty look. "What information?"

"Was this place an embroidery shop in the past?"

"Yes, so?"

I noticed many eyes still lingered on us—with curiosity, envy, disapproval. I imagined the envious ones thinking, "*Wah,* a white ghost boyfriend! Lucky girl—she'll go to the U.S. or England someday."

"What happened?"

"Why do you want to know?"

"Because I have a friend who worked here in the past."

"Who's your friend?"

"You won't know even if I tell you, so please just tell me what happened." This tough guy was as annoying and inquisitive as a gossipy woman.

"Ha, ha, ha! Because the Golden Thread's young master needed to pay off his gambling debt, that's why!"

"How much?"

"Ha! May I ask why this is any of your business? He owed so much that finally his father had to give us this place. And he still owes some more. Are you their relative? Did you come to pay off the rest of his debt?"

I ignored this and asked, "What happened to the workers?"

Actually, I was just interested in Little Doll's whereabouts.

"How do I know, or should I care?" Suddenly he looked angrily at Ryan. "Who's this white ghost? A spy?"

"No!" both Ryan and I exclaimed simultaneously.

"We're husband and wife," I said.

"Husband and wife? You think barbarians are better than us, eh?"

This exchange must have intrigued the customers, because now playing had stopped while everyone stared at us.

One pock-faced, middle-aged man shouted, "Husband not bad looking; too bad he's a ghost. Pretty Chinese woman should benefit their own people instead of a barbarian." He made a sweeping gesture with his arm. "Am I not right, brothers?"

The den roared with happy laughter. A few threw down their tiles, sounding like small explosions.

"Things are getting out of hand. We'd better leave!" Ryan grabbed my arm and pulled me outside.

We ducked into a nearby alley and I turned my head away, hoping that Ryan would not see my tears.

He put an arm gently around my shoulder. "Spring Swallow, they won't hurt us."

"No, it's not that. Now I have lost Little Doll forever!"

"Don't worry. She is probably still with the Li family somewhere. I am sure she will still have a roof over her head and food to eat."

Through my tears, I looked up at Ryan's innocent face. "But they might sell her to help pay off their debt!"

He looked stunned, not realizing that this was common in China.

"Who'd they sell her to?"

"A rich household as a maid or a concubine, or worse, to a prostitution house!"

Ryan looked horrified.

I sighed. "If that's happened, I don't think I'll ever see her again in this life."

He shook his head.

I went on. "The new master might also give her another name, so it'll be impossible to track her. . . ." I started sobbing loudly.

"Don't give up hope," Ryan sighed, wiping away my tears.

"If I had taken her with me, none of this would have happened!"

"Don't blame yourself, Spring Swallow. You've already had such a hard time surviving. I believe in miracles, so I'm sure we'll find her someday."

"When will this someday be?"

But my husband, smart as he was, opened his mouth and then closed it again without saying anything.

Soon our all-too-short honeymoon was coming to an end. Ryan and I were sitting in our hotel room discussing how to spend our last two days, when a telegram arrived for him. We were both nervous because telegrams are almost never good news. Ryan tore it open and read aloud that Father Edwin had taken ill and needed him to return right away. The doctor had said it wasn't serious, but Father said there were business matters that he needed help with.

I told Ryan that if I did not keep trying to find Little Doll I would never forgive myself, so I would need to stay in Soochow another day or two to try to get some news of her whereabouts. My husband did not look happy about this, but he really couldn't argue. So I helped him to pack and told him I would go to the station to see him off.

Except a few small gifts for Father Edwin and the church's staff, we hadn't done a lot of shopping. So we packed quickly and went early to the train station to avoid a long queue for the ticket. Then we took seats in the waiting area. Ryan began to study the train schedule, so I told him I'd get him some food for the train ride.

"All right. But don't take too long, because I like you to be close to me. I'll miss you."

"Don't worry, Ryan. Please, when you see Father Edwin, send me a short telegram saying how he is. And wish him speedy recovery from me."

As I walked toward the snack stand, I passed a small group of people peering at a poster pasted prominently on a pillar. I thought it was probably a *xunren*—a notice of a missing person—so I decided to take a closer look, wondering if it might be about Aunty Peony, Purple, Little Doll, even the Li family.

When I got closer I saw that it was not for a "Missing Person," but a "WANTED MAN." When I saw the name I almost screamed out loud and my head began to spin.

The wanted man was Shen Feng!

But my former husband Shen Feng had been dead for months. So this had to be another man with the same name. The voices around me buzzed in my ears like angry insects.

"What did he do?"

"I'm sure he'll be captured soon and executed!"

I forced myself to squeeze through the crowd to read the small print:

> Shen Feng, male, twenty-nine, is wanted for treason.
>
> The reward for information leading to his capture is 30 ounces of silver.
>
> Shen, last known to be living in Soochow, is a traitor, having fought to overthrow the government. Since the revolution was defeated, Shen and his group have not been seen. They might be hiding in a Buddhist temple or a church.
>
> Anyone who spots him or his collaborators, or has information about their whereabouts, must report to us immediately. He is known to be armed and dangerous.

As my heart knocked hard against my ribs, a question kept swirling in my head: Was my mountain husband dead or alive? Then I looked more closely at the blurred picture. The man both looked like Shen Feng and didn't at the same time. He had his square jaw and broad forehead. But the eyes were downcast, so I couldn't tell if they were as bright and penetrating as Shen Feng's. Besides, he'd had a full head of hair, while this man was completely bald with a scarred scalp.

My mood flip-flopped between believing he was indeed my Shen Feng and hoping he was someone else. Though I'd read in the newspaper that "Shen Feng" had been executed, I supposed that it could have been about another revolutionary with the same name. Though he looked worn down in the picture, I now had to admit to myself that he *was* my revolutionary husband, suddenly returned from the dead to haunt me in my new life.

As another wave of dizziness hit me, I leaned on a pillar.

A middle-aged, maternal-looking woman asked with a concerned expression, "Are you all right, miss? You want some medicinal oil?"

I shook my head. "Thank you, but I'm fine. I think it's just too crowded here."

When I finally regained my composure, I slowly walked back to Ryan, wondering what I should tell him about this. But if he thought the real reason I was staying behind was to find Shen Feng, he would be totally heartbroken. And what would Father Edwin think of me? Such a flippant, irresponsible girl whom he shouldn't have helped in the first place, not to mention let Ryan marry me. So I decided not to tell Ryan, unless I had to.

If Shen Feng was really alive and in hiding, I was the only one who knew where he might be. Now I remembered the scraped-off message on the mountain—maybe he was trying to reach me, but then feared someone else would see it and turn him in.

I loved Ryan, but if Shen Feng was really alive and I could find him, I couldn't leave him without a proper good-bye. However, I was afraid that if I did find him, I would not have the power to resist him, that our love would be rekindled. What could I do? If I stayed with him, I might get arrested and executed. Now that I finally had a secure life with a caring man, I did not want to lose it.

Then another thought hit me. Maybe when Shen Feng saw my bulging stomach he wouldn't want me anymore.

∼28∼

Two Husbands: One Witnessed by God, the Other by Heaven

Finally, the train arrived at the station at 11 a.m. My farewell with Ryan was a little tense, but affectionate. Back at the inn I went to my room, changed my clothes, and immediately set out for the mountain, buying some food and candles on the way. It was a long way to the mountain, so I hired a bicycle rickshaw to bring me there.

After we arrived and I had paid the scrawny cyclist, he asked, "Miss, what are you going to do here all by yourself?"

I said, my tone half-joking, "I'm going to jump off the cliff, turn into a ghost, and come back for you, hahaha!"

As expected, he shut up and quickly rode away.

I didn't begin to climb right away, but stood at the base of the mountain to take in the surroundings. I could see Aunty's house in the distance, looking forlorn and forbidding, with no people in sight. I decided that this time, when I came back down from the mountain, I would prick up my courage to break in and take a look. Then, I began my ascent, pausing only to make three quick bows to Leilei's shrine.

As my feet began to crunch on the dry grass and twigs, I imagined Shen Feng when I first saw him, his silhouette set against the morning sun, and his flute's bittersweet tunes floating to me in the crisp air. He lowered his flute and our eyes met. Then I imagined him hurrying to me, scooping me up in his muscular, revolutionary arms, and swinging me around until I felt dizzy with happiness. After that, I thought of him carrying me inside the cave, gently putting me down, impatiently pulling off my clothes, then taking me passionately. My imagining was suddenly interrupted by a surge of guilt. How could I think about being with another man when my honeymoon with Ryan had barely ended?

So I willed myself to focus on my climb. When my sore feet finally reached the top, reality painted a completely different picture. There was no Shen Feng, nor his beautiful music. Just the morning sun—warm, soothing, but totally impersonal. I hurried inside the cave, only to find it as empty as a poor family's rice vat.

I lay down on the ground, thinking about Shen Feng. Could Heaven really bring him back to me? Maybe the poster I had seen was an old one and he really was dead. I realized that there must be hundreds of men with this same name in China. That meant that at this moment, there would be many Shen Fengs who were dead and many alive. Could I let myself hope that *my* Shen Feng was among the living? And if he were, what would I do?

I thought of the line from Du Fu's poem "Tribute to the Hermit Wei Ba":

> Tomorrow, once again, we'll be separated by tall mountains,
> How fleeting and fickle are life and human affairs!

I suddenly felt hopeless.

Exhausted, I did not realize that I had fallen asleep until a strange noise awakened me from my deep oblivion. It sounded like a starving animal or a badly injured tiger. My initial thought was to escape. I hadn't gone through so much to end up as a meal for a wild beast. Then I became even more frightened—what if it was a wandering ghost? After all, this was a haunted mountain where no one dared come, except two outcasts from society—a runaway ghost bride and a wanted revolutionary. Maybe in the past Shen

Feng and I had been so consumed by our passion that we never noticed all the hovering beings from the other realm.

But it was still broad daylight, not yet the opening hour for the Gate of Hell to release ghosts into the land of the living. But if what I heard was not a ghost, then it must be an animal. And if it was wounded, it would not be able to hurt me. So I stood up and cautiously felt my way farther into the cave, straining my ears to trace the source of the sound. I lit my candle, but it let off only a feeble light, so I had to advance very cautiously.

As I walked I realized that the cave went much deeper than I had ever realized. Shen Feng and I had always met near the front, where there was some light. The path got narrower as the whimper got clearer and my heart beat faster. My nostrils were ambushed by a faint but nauseating stench, making me feel queasy. Common sense told me I should turn around and run before I got myself into deeper difficulty. But my curiosity and stubbornness kept me poking along. Finally, I saw something—a person, lying on the ground, sick or wounded, it seemed.

The voice was of a man, but without *qi,* as if he had one foot already inside the Gate of Hell.

"Someone . . . here?"

I didn't respond, but I was sure he could hear my heavy breathing echoing loudly inside the womb of the dark cave.

He struggled to speak again. "If you're going to kill me, get it over with. . . ."

Though the once-powerful voice was now but a whisper, I had no doubt to whom it belonged.

Shen Feng.

I dashed to him, knelt down, and reached to tenderly touch his cheek.

"Feng, it's me, Spring Swallow."

He stared into my eyes. "Is that really you, my dear wife?"

"Yes." I wanted to say "husband" but just couldn't.

Silence passed, followed by soft sobbing reverberating in the cave.

"Feng, are you all right?"

He shook his head. "No, Spring Swallow, I'm dying."

"Please, Feng"—I put my hand over his mouth—"don't say bad-luck things, you're not . . . you'll be all right."

Then I felt a sudden panic. Despite all I had seen, I was only nineteen and death had always seemed far away, yet now it was right in front of my eyes. In the flickering candlelight I could barely make out my mountain husband's face, but I felt his fear.

"Spring Swallow, a revolutionary who tries to reform China cannot be superstitious. So I'm not going to lie to you or to myself. The truth is that I'll not see this world or your beautiful face much longer. . . ."

"Feng, please . . ."

I touched his sunken face and he took my hand with his skeletal one. What torture was he suffering for his damned revolution?

"Don't be sad, my wife. At least Heaven has granted us one last chance to meet on this Earth, inside our love cave."

It must have taken great effort for him to talk, for he was now gasping for air.

"Spring Swallow, please hold me and let me feel you. . . ."

So in the dark, we cuddled against each other, feeling each other's warmth—and pain.

Long silence passed, and he said, "Please let me see your beautiful face. . . ."

I picked up the candle, then held it up. When I clearly saw Shen Feng's face I screamed out loud. Not only had he lost all his once-thick and luscious hair, his scalp was covered with burn scars. His cheeks were so sunken that I was sure if I poured water it would form a puddle. Then I saw that he had only one eye left—the other one was an empty socket!

I burst out crying.

"Feng, what have they done to you?"

He reached his emaciated hand to touch my lips. "Don't be sad, my dear Spring Swallow, for this will soon be over. . . ."

"No! Please stop saying that, I beg you."

"Don't feel sorry for me. I did my best for China. And now I have seen you once again. . . ."

I gently covered his lips so he couldn't continue talking about his approaching death and breaking my heart. But he tenderly removed my hand. No one could resist a tender man.

He was about to say something, but I spoke first. "Feng, let me give you something to eat to help you regain your energy."

I offered him a bun and some weak tea from my thermos. But to my great sadness, after taking just one bite, he stopped.

"Please, Feng, eat more, please."

He shook his head adamantly. "I want to hear what happened to you after I left for the revolution."

This was the question I had been dreading. "I will tell you soon. But I want to hear what happened to you first."

He didn't respond. It must be too painful.

So I said tenderly, "You don't have to if you don't want to."

Of course I wanted to know everything, but I also dreaded hearing more.

"Spring Swallow, I want you to understand me and my goal, but I also don't want you to suffer because of me. To make it short, I've been horribly tortured. My comrade too. . . ."

"Your comrade?"

He nodded, then pointed to a dark, semi-hidden corner. "He too was tortured, but I managed to help him escape with me; but then he died a few days later. I was not strong enough to dig a hole to bury him, so I put his body over there in a cleft in the rock and covered him as best as I could with small stones."

No wonder there was this stench. I did not want to think about the horrible ordeal my mountain husband and his comrade had gone through. But I was all too aware that his time had nearly run out.

"Feng, let me carry you down and get you to a hospital."

"No"—he vehemently shook his head—"I'm not going to die in a cold institution—"

"Who says you're going to die?"

"Spring Swallow, please don't pretend. Look at me; I'm but a rotten piece of meat, a broken skeleton. You can smell death oozing from my pores."

He slowly lifted his pant leg and revealed what was underneath—black flesh oozing blood and pus.

I covered my face to hide my tears and willed myself to calm down. "Feng . . . I'm sorry, so sorry . . ."

Now I realized that the rotten smell was not from his buried colleague, but from his leg. I took out the handkerchief, trying to bandage his wound, but he shook his head and pushed my hand away.

"Spring Swallow, this is kind of you, but useless. All that is left for me now is to die in peace, with you. Here on this mountain where we met and became husband and wife, witnessed by Heaven and Earth."

He reached into his pocket and took out the handkerchief I'd given him as the token of my love, now worn and stained.

Tears coursed down my cheeks as Shen Feng spoke. "Spring Swallow, I've always carried your love with me. This handkerchief kept me going during many difficult times."

He paused to suck in the cave's stale air, then went on. "If I'm lucky, there's time for you to tell me what happened after I left for the revolution. For me, there's not much to say—I failed, was tortured, and am now about to slip into the great Unknown. However, I die believing my revolutionary comrades will someday succeed after I'm gone."

Shen Feng took another gulp of air. Suddenly his remaining eye brightened, radiating hope. "Against the emperor's wish, the historian Sima Qian was determined to tell the truth, so the emperor ordered his hand cut off. Sima's son also persisted in telling the truth and had his hand chopped off too. Later, all Sima's offspring lost their hands also—until finally the emperor passed away. The truth was finally told because of this family's courage."

He looked at me with a brave expression. "Spring Swallow, if we had a son, he'd do the same for the revolution, for China's future."

I really didn't know how to respond to this. How did you reason with a man who admires a family in which their children's hands were cut off for generations, for a truth no one now can even remember?

He spoke again. "Spring Swallow, when I am gone, please come here sometimes to remember me, to tell me about your life, and recite a sutra for me. Who knows, perhaps somehow I'll be able to hear you."

I knew it was pointless to try to stop Shen Feng from saying unlucky things, so I just nodded as he poured out what had been stuck inside him. But I couldn't stop my tears from flowing, and Shen Feng lifted his emaciated hand to try to wipe them away.

"There are too many tragedies and tears in this world, Spring Swallow. After I'm gone, try to live a simple and happy life. . . ."

I nodded, grabbing his hand and kissing its many scars.

Some silence passed before I blurted out, "Feng, I'm pregnant."

A few sparks shot out from his remaining eye. "It can't be mine, can it?"

Of course he knew the baby couldn't possibly be his, but he still wanted to keep up hope, no matter how faint. I shook my head, but couldn't say a thing to comfort him.

"Feng, you know it can't be . . ."

"Then who is the father? Tell me the whole story so I can go in peace, knowing you are safe."

So I did, but not that I had lost the baby who would have been his son. A boy who might have carried out his father's patriotic dream. I did tell him about Ryan, that he was good to me, but not that we were married. Strangely, instead of feeling guilty lying, I felt I'd be betraying both Ryan and Shen Feng if I'd told all of the truth. I believed that the lie was a much better "truth" for all three parties—Shen Feng, Ryan, and me.

Shen Feng touched my cheek, then pulled me with the little force he could muster, so I was nestled against his bony chest. He smoothed my cheek and hair, sending shivers down my spine. I knew this would be our last few minutes together.

My mountain husband said, his voice thin as wisps of smoke, "Spring Swallow, listen to me, marry this foreigner as quickly as possible so your baby will have a father and you a husband; then have more babies. . . ."

He paused, then went on, a half smile hanging on his ghostly face. "What's his name?"

"Ryan McFarland, a missionary from America."

"So, a foreigner who works in a Western church?"

I nodded. "Feng, in my mind, you're my true husband, as only our marriage was witnessed by Heaven and Earth."

I felt I was being untrue to Ryan, but he would never know. Shen Feng was my first, a love match, and I wanted his last time on Earth to be as happy as possible.

His expression broke my heart.

I asked hesitatingly, "Feng, are you . . . all right with this?"

He nodded. "Of course I'm very jealous of the other man, Spring Swallow. What husband wouldn't be? But even if I could be well and healthy, it's no life for a woman with a revolutionary as a husband."

I gave him another sip of the tea, and he asked, "Spring Swallow, did you come to Soochow and up here to find me?"

I nodded. Of course I was not going to tell him that I was also in Soochow for my honeymoon. But I was not lying, I did come here for him.

Shen Feng squeezed my hand, but without much force.

Moments later, he spoke again. "Can you do one last thing for me?"

"Of course, Feng, anything I can do."

"Help me go outside the cave."

"So you're willing to go down the mountain and to a hospital?"

"No"—he shook his head—"so I can see the sun and feel its warmth one last time."

"Feng, I beg you, let me take you to a hospital, and you'll recover. I'll take very good care of you, promise."

He didn't respond to my pleading, but insisted all he wanted was to go outside. With one rotten leg and the other, which he probably hadn't moved since he'd come here, I had to half-drag him outside. When the bright sunlight first struck his eyes, he flinched back, looking startled. I helped him to lean his back against a boulder so he could face the breathtaking view before us. The sun's rays shone through clouds, turning everything golden— trees, leaves, flowers, rocks, sand. A flock of geese flew over, high up in the sky, calling to each other in melancholy tones.

We remained silent for the few moments we had together enjoying the scene fit for immortals. Seeing that Shen Feng had closed his remaining eye to let the breeze soothe his face, I felt touched to see him have a moment of pleasure, probably his last.

Then he lifted his head and asked me to help him stand so he could walk a few steps closer to the edge.

"But it may not be safe for you. Why don't we just stay here?"

"Don't worry, Spring Swallow, we'll be fine. It's a beautiful, peaceful day, no rain, only a gentle breeze. There won't be any danger."

I still didn't feel comfortable. "But, Feng, why can't we just sit here?"

"Because I want to have a better look at Soochow off in the distance, its rivers, you know, everything."

I could not deny him what might be his last wish, so I used all my strength to help him stand and take faltering steps toward the edge. I held on to him as we enjoyed the breeze grazing us like a massaging hand. Suddenly the sun's rays landed on Shen Feng and gilded his whole body, so that for a brief moment he seemed to transform into a saint. I knew this meant he was slipping away from this terrible world, and again I felt tears sting my eyes. He looked almost content, as if willing to accept whatever lay before him. We held each other even more tightly.

Suddenly I felt his body shake as he released himself from my arms, followed by, "Farewell, my dear wife Spring Swallow . . ."

When I realized what had just happened, I found myself totally alone on the peak.

❦ 29 ❦

An Unexpected Encounter

My mind blanked for a moment; then I dashed down the mountain. Sharp rocks and twigs kept cutting my arms and feet, but I didn't care. During my plunging descent, the image of Shen Feng loomed in my mind, his shattered body—blood-soaked, skull cracked, brain splattered. . . .

I kept shouting, "Feng, why did you do this to me, why?!"

I looked down but didn't see him. I couldn't tell if he'd fallen on the ground or in the nearby river. When I was halfway down, drops of water began to shower on my head and face. At first I thought it was my tears, but then I realized it was the sky pouring big drops of rain. Like sharp pebbles, they hit hard on my face and back, hurting me. I slowed down and held on to branches so I wouldn't slip and fall.

I could hear my own sobbing competing with the hissing rain, and my desperate screaming. "Feng, why did you leave me like that?"

In the heavy, hissing rain, I strained my eyes and ears, but my lost husband was still nowhere to be seen. Now the sky had darkened and the weather turned chilly. I pulled my thin jacket across my chest and continued to plod along the muddy ground. The world was now obscured by a veil of rain, hiding everything in the distance. I tripped on a large rock and fell. . . .

I must have passed out, for when I woke up I found myself lying, head downward, on the mountain slope. The rain had stopped and it was now twilight. Head throbbing, I put my hand to my forehead, which felt warm to me, as if I was developing a fever. Eager to get down the mountain before it was totally dark, I forced myself to stand up. If I was trapped here overnight, I'd either get a chill, be attacked by wild animals, or even worse, by ghosts.

Then what about Shen Feng? I didn't want to believe that he was already dead. If he was severely injured but still alive, I *had* to keep looking for him. I couldn't just abandon my first love.

With worries and horrible images swirling in my mind, I soon reached the foot of the mountain. But in the dim light remaining I could not see any sign of Shen Feng, so I feared he had fallen into the river and washed away downstream. Feeling hopeless, I dragged my sore feet toward my old house, which loomed in the distance like a huge, wounded beast. When I arrived, I tugged at some loose planks until they fell to the ground like lifeless snakes. The knob turned easily and I entered, my heart beating like a swinging pendulum.

Though I'd once lived here, I felt like a thief breaking into a rich person's mansion. A strong, musty smell ambushed my nostrils. But I also felt comforted by the house's nostalgic familiarity—the embroideries on the walls and the long wooden table where we'd worked. I went right over to the kitchen, hoping that somehow I could find a little food there. Luckily I found some bits of dried meat and salted fish. They weren't very appetizing, but I was tired and hungry, so I gobbled them down. After that I went outside to relieve myself, then back inside to my old room. Quickly pulling off my wet clothes, I crawled naked under the tattered covers of my dusty cot. I pulled the thin blanket up to my chin and sobbed until I fell into a deep, troubled sleep.

When I woke up the next morning, my headache was gone and there was no sign of a fever. I went to the kitchen to finish off the leftover dried food, then put on my still-damp clothes and went outside. Though I was curious to check once more on Aunty Peony's secret chamber, I was more concerned with searching for Shen Feng. I knew that the chance he was still alive was slim. But if somehow he had survived, there was no time to waste, so I quickly set out for the mountain. On the way I said a prayer to Ryan's God, begging him to grant a miracle that Shen Feng had not fallen to his death but was only injured and waiting for rescue.

I walked around the base of the mountain, scrutinizing the area carefully, but there was no sign of Shen Feng, not even blood, or a scrap of clothing. I knew that most likely he had fallen into the river and been borne away. So I walked downstream along the river for a while but finally had to give up the search.

I could not help but hope that somehow Shen Feng had recovered and had gone back up the mountain to our old meeting place. So I decided to make one last trip up the mountain, so I would not always wonder. But unfortunately when I reached the top, I realized that my revolutionary husband was gone and somehow I had to accept that I had lost him forever. All I could do now was to go inside our cave and make a little shrine for him, as Purple and I had for Leilei. I recited a sutra twice, first toward Heaven, then toward Earth. When the cave fell silent after my recitation, I walked out of it and this part of my life forever.

Exhausted by three physically arduous and heartbreaking trips in just two days, I rested for a while before I headed back down the mountain. When my feet finally touched level ground, I went straight to Aunty's house, then back to my room. I didn't have the energy or the will power to go back to Soochow, so I decided to rest here for one more night, then make my way back to Ryan in Peking.

In the middle of the night, a strange noise woke me up. I guessed it was a stray animal scavenging for food. But what if it was a homeless person looking for shelter? Or a wandering ghost from the haunted mountain? Shen Feng's ghost, even? Suddenly, I was as awake as if cold water had been splashed on my face. I got up from my cot but couldn't make out anything in the dim living room.

Maybe it was a small animal after all. As I started to relax, a hunger pang hit me. When I walked into the kitchen to look for the last bit of dried meat, something bumped into me.

"*Aiiiya!*"

As I screamed, another voice joined me in a panicky "*Aiiiya!*" We blurted out, "Who is it?!"

I grabbed a candle, lit it, and looked.

It was Little Doll, looking as startled as me!

"Oh, Heaven, how come you're here?" we screamed at each other.

Under the candlelight, Little Doll looked like a little beggar. Wearing a dirty top and pants, hair disheveled, eyes dull, face sunken, she looked even smaller than ever, as if she'd lost twenty more pounds.

"Little Doll, what happened, why are you here?"

She kept staring at me without saying anything. So I helped her to sit down on a chair and went to start a fire to boil water. Her voice rose from my back like an angry ghost's.

"Sister Spring Swallow, why did you leave me?"

I went to sit next to her and put my arm around her shoulder.

"Little Doll, please forgive me. I really had no choice."

"Why no choice?"

"It's too complicated to explain now. But I will later. If I had taken you, it would have been dangerous for both of us. So, I thought you'd be safer with the Li family. So, how come . . ."

"But you left me alone. . . ." My little sister started to cry.

"Little Doll," I said very gently, "we're together now and won't be separated anymore."

Her teary eyes stared into mine. "Promise?"

"Promise."

Little Doll extended her pinky and hooked it with mine.

"After you left"—she wiped her tears with the back of her hand—"Golden Thread was cursed, so its business dropped. Mr. Old Li believed it's because of you."

"Why me?"

"Because you're his all-destroying unlucky star." She paused, then continued. "After you left, Li Wenyi gambled away everything. Then loan sharks came and splashed red ink on the shop windows and dirty words that scared away all the customers. Old Li had a stroke, and Golden Thread went bankrupt. They couldn't keep me anymore, so they made me leave."

"Did they give you money?"

She nodded. "One month's salary and some embroidery tools. I also had some savings."

"When did this happen?"

"A while ago. That's why I came back here; I had no other place to go."

"How did you get in?"

"One of the boards was loose, so I crawled in."

Hmmm . . . Little Doll was actually more resourceful than I'd thought.

"What have you done since you had to leave Li's house?"

"Selling my embroideries on the streets." She smiled proudly. "Some people buy them because my works are cheap and they feel sorry for me. One time a woman paid me double what I'd asked, but another time I was robbed."

"How did that happen?"

"A group of beggars snatched the cloth bag where I put my money."

"That's terrible! Did they hurt you?"

"No, but they laughed and threw stones at me so I couldn't chase them."

I sighed. "Sorry, Little Doll. But from now on, I'll take good care of you. Did you leave the dried meat and fish in the kitchen?"

"Yes, every day after I finish work, I go to the market to pick up leftover food. Mostly vegetables, but once in a while I can find some meat."

"But where were you last night?"

"Yesterday when I finished, it was already dark and I was too tired to come home. So I slept on a street bench and worked late today."

Now I looked at my little sister in a different light. "Little Doll, I'm so proud of you. Do you know you've been self-sufficient and independent?"

"What's that?"

It'd be too hard to explain, so I said, "Don't worry, I'm just so happy that we meet again."

"Me too, Sister Spring Swallow. But I've already told you everything about myself, so tell me where you've been. Why did you leave without a good-bye? And then what happened?"

So I told Little Doll almost everything, except what I thought might upset her, or that she was too young to understand.

When I finished, her eyes were round, as big as two plums. "So you now have a real husband?"

I nodded. "He's very good to me, and he will be to you too."

Little Doll suddenly exclaimed, "Oh, I almost forget, wait here, Sister Spring Swallow, I'll be right back!"

She dashed away and came back in no time, handing me a bag.

"What is it?"

"Open it and you'll see."

I opened the bag and couldn't believe my eyes—my jacket with the imperial undergarment attached.

"Heaven, how did you get this?"

"After Old Li's stroke, one time when Sister Ping asked me to bring food to him, I saw him holding this on his lap. I recognized your jacket because I saw you wear it many times. I didn't like him to touch anything of yours, so when he fell asleep, I just took it. So now it's back to you."

Did Little Doll know how valuable this was? Had she turned my jacket inside out and seen the imperial garment? Judging from her expression, she had no idea. And I was not going to tell her the whole story.

So, I simply said, "Thank you so much, Little Doll. I really love this jacket; it keeps me warm."

Suddenly she dashed to her room, then returned with a note that she handed to me.

"Where did you get this?"

"I saw it underneath the door. I tried to read it but don't understand. I did recognize Sister Leilei's name and '*Along the River*' on it, though."

"Leilei?" My heart started to pound as I read the note:

To the people in this house:

I know my lover Leilei lived here, because I brought her home here a few times. Maybe you don't know that she's dead, so don't keep looking for her.

We planned to marry but had no money. She said she could sell her embroidery for big cash and already had a rich buyer.

But this rich buyer murdered her!

Leilei asked me to hide behind a tree to be sure that he didn't just grab the scroll and run away. I saw the buyer take out a stack of money and hand it to her, but she asked for a lot more. The man got very angry and pushed her so hard that she fell into the river. The man was very big, so I ran away.

I never saw Leilei again, so I am sure she's dead.

Don't call the police—the man must be a gangster!

But I needed to tell you so you won't stir up trouble by asking around for her.

The letter was unsigned. This was typical of Leilei—after she agreed on the price, she asked for more. And it got her killed! I felt very sad for her—a woman who never realized that she brought her troubles on herself.

My emotion must have shown on my face because I was interrupted by Little Doll's voice. "Sister Spring Swallow, are you all right?"

I looked up at her innocent face and had no heart to tell her the truth about Leilei, so I just said, "It's nothing important, Little Doll."

"You look so pale! You want me to cook you some soup?"

"Thank you, Little Doll, but I'm fine, really."

Then she seemed to cheer up. "So, Sister Spring Swallow, are we going back to Peking to live with this Mr. Ryan in the Western church?"

I nodded and she clapped with excitement.

"Good, so we're going to see this foreign ghost soon!?"

I gave her a disapproving look. "Little Doll, his name is Ryan. And when you meet him, you better address him respectfully as Uncle Ryan."

"Yes, Unkle Rai An," she said with a dreamy expression. "Unkle Rai An must be a kind, good-looking man."

"What made you say that?"

"Because I just know he is."

I didn't know how she "knew" this, but I liked her logic anyway.

∞ 30 ∞

Another Unexpected Encounter

The next day, when I arrived at Our Lady of Sorrows Church with Little Doll, Ryan looked displeased.

He pulled me aside and said in a heated whisper, "You never answered my telegram! I've been extremely worried about you!" He looked over at Little Doll. "And who is this?"

I gave him a warning look and whispered back, "This is Little Doll. Remember I said I'd bring her to stay with us? She has no other place to go."

I knew Ryan was not happy about this, but he couldn't really object, not as a Christian and the Lord's loving servant.

So Ryan greeted her in Chinese, but my little sister was so shy and a white ghost so strange to her that whenever he asked her questions, she'd avert her glance and burst into nervous giggles.

Eventually, I knew they would have to get used to each other. In the meantime, I took Little Doll to meet Father Edwin, who was gracious in welcoming her to "God's house." He called for the maid and told her that the newcomer would be sharing her room, but also helping her in her work.

Gradually Ryan and Little Doll became more comfortable with each other, and he even seemed to be starting to feel some affection for her. Father Edwin was very kind to my little sister, giving her some money for new clothes and reassuring her that the church was her home as long as she wanted to stay. Little Doll, in turn, did errands for Father Edwin and sometimes Ryan. My little sister was content to have a place called home where everyone was nice to her. She helped the maid with her chores without complaint and assisted me with the embroidery that we sold to raise money for the church.

Ryan taught Bible classes and catechism, as well as helping with church administration. I tried my best to take good care of him and also the baby growing inside me. Eight months pregnant, my belly was pointed, so I believed it'd be a boy.

When I asked Ryan if he'd prefer a boy or a girl, his answer was, "A girl, so she'll look exactly like my beautiful wife."

I didn't consider myself beautiful, but nevertheless felt flattered to hear this from my husband. I was happy to be married and expecting. I still thought of Shen Feng and was troubled that I had failed to find his body. But I could no longer hope that he was still in this life.

To ease my mind, during prayers in church I would mention him in my thoughts and would silently say a sutra for him on occasions like the day we'd met, the date of his death, and, of course, the Qingming Festival. I'd also been thinking that I should look for Aunty Peony since I had promised Little Doll that I would try to get our "family" back. And I also hoped that somehow I would meet Purple again but had no idea of how to look for her.

The Lunar New Year was approaching. For our celebration, Ryan suggested taking Little Doll and me to a Peking opera performance to be held in the Compassionate Light Temple. I asked Ryan if he minded going to a Buddhist temple. He shook his head and went on to explain that it was the tradition for Chinese operas to be performed in the temple courtyards in the hope of attracting followers by providing free entertainment. Moreover, before the performance, the actors would carry out an elaborate ritual, praying and making offerings to the theater gods to ensure a smooth performance. I was pleased my Catholic husband appreciated Chinese customs and did not mind going to a rival religion's temple.

Little Doll asked with curiosity, "Unkle Rai An, you mean there are other gods besides yours?"

"Little Doll," Ryan laughed, "are you hungry? Why don't we have our afternoon tea now?"

My little sister exclaimed, "Yes, my stomach is rumbling like the opera drums!"

This worked—Little Doll forgot to pursue the question that was too complicated for her Unkle Rai An to answer.

On New Year's Eve we took the bus to the southern part of Peking, not too far from the famous Altar of Heaven. On the bustling street were many shops, some displaying red banners with lucky couplets for the New Year:

Firecrackers send away the old year with a bang.
The ten thousand things renew themselves.

Heaven grant us many more years,
Soon springtime will fill the universe with happiness,
And luck will knock on your door.

Along with the banners, red lanterns hung from rooftops added a festive touch to the street. Spring might be coming, but for now the people were covered in thick coats, steam coming from their mouths. Most looked happy, but not all. The latter were scurrying from house to house asking to "borrow" money, so they could celebrate the New Year with new clothes, sumptuous meals, firecrackers, and gifts for their children and their elders. It was feared that refusing to give money on the New Year would bring bad luck.

At the church we'd had a Western dinner, but now the aromas floating in the air made me yearn for the traditional New Year's feast: hair seaweed with dried oyster, because *facai haoshi* sounds like "prosperous business will make a fortune." There was also *hongyun dangtou,* a large fish head covered with red chilies to symbolize "big fortune right above your head." Then a course of *dazhan hongtu,* marinated chicken wings meant to symbolize spreading your wings for a bright future, and, finally, kumquats to represent gold coins.

Here and there red envelopes of lucky money were being passed. Even the poor felt obligated to do this when children would wish them "endless money and treasures enter your house," because otherwise the magic of their good-luck sayings would be gone.

Long lines formed in front of shops selling new clothes, because old clothes trap the worn-out *qi* of the year that is ending. For our special New Year's outing, I'd spent two weeks making new clothes for all of us. For Little Doll's and my jackets, I'd embroidered flowers, birds, and lucky characters. For Ryan's Chinese coat, I had embroidered a dragon for success and positive *qi.* He seemed happy wearing his new Chinese clothes with his new Chinese wife, about to see a Chinese opera.

On the street, a few pedestrians cast us curious glances. But none looked hateful that I was with a foreign ghost, maybe because on Chinese New Year, a time for good luck and happiness, no one was supposed to think or say anything bad. Besides, Ryan seemed somehow to blend in.

Now we were at the green-roofed Compassionate Light Temple. Around the entrance hawkers were shouting out for us to buy food for the performance:

"Sweet soy bean, good for health and immunity!"

"Fried doughnut and sugar plum—balance your *yin* and *yang!*"

"Fresh scallion pancake, the best in town!"

"Stinky tofu! If not stinky, your money back!"

Other vendors were selling incense to offer inside the temple, bamboo baskets, toys, and tiny wooden stools for children to sit on during the performance.

Little Doll was completely fascinated by all of this. Ryan offered to buy her a snack or a toy, but she couldn't decide if she wanted stinky tofu, sugar plum, a small basket, or a tiny, painted kite. Finally, Ryan purchased all of them, so now Little Doll was happily holding her basket with the sugar plum and kite inside while she ate stinky tofu smeared with hoisin sauce. Ryan, pretending to find the stink unbearable, covered his nostrils and walked apart from us. This made Little Doll giggle nonstop.

Pressed in by the crowd, we were soon inside a spacious courtyard. In the middle a huge bronze incense burner fogged the air with billows of smoke. Even here there were more items on sale—incense, small Buddha and Guan Yin statues, and other amulets like beads and talismans. Actually, because it was New Year's, everything was free—but donations were expected. Ryan bought some colorful beads for all of us.

When I asked why he was now wearing Buddhist beads, he replied, "The Chinese say, 'When entering a temple, kowtow and offer incense, when entering a foreign country, follow its customs.'" He winked. "I'm just being Chinese."

As we continued to move with the crowd, we saw a large, makeshift stage set against the saffron temple wall. Because we had tarried on the shopping street, the performance was already in progress. To the right side of the stage, a small assembly of musicians was playing ferociously—flute, *erhu,* moon guitar, *pipa,* and a few other noisy instruments I didn't recognize. On the stage itself, actors sang in high-pitched tones as they moved about, assuming ritualized postures. People either stood or sat on wooden stools, eyes intent and mouths ajar. The three of us squeezed our way toward the front, our feet crunching on discarded watermelon husks and chicken bones. The seats were filled, so we stood off to the side.

I leaned toward a middle-aged woman next to me and spoke to her in a low voice. "*Taitai,* what's playing now?"

She turned to look us over, then pointed to a wooden plaque with red characters next to the stage: THE YANG FAMILY WOMAN WARRIORS.

She spoke with a heavy Shanghainese accent. "Now all the men in the Yang family have been killed on the battlefield so Grandma Yang is leading her daughters to fight."

She glanced at Ryan, then back at me. "Miss, does your white ghost friend know that the female Yang members onstage are male actors disguised as women?"

"They're men?"

"Of course." She pointed a pudgy finger at a tall, handsome woman on stage. "See this one who plays the young daughter-in-law of Old Lady Xie?"

Onstage, the women warrior was prancing and singing, her armor sparkling heroically.

"She's really good—is she famous?"

"She? Ha, it's a him! You never heard of Snoring Cane?"

Two women in front turned to stare at us. "Shhh . . . lower your voices."

But the woman ignored them and went on excitedly. "Snoring Cane is a man who can play a woman even better than a real woman. He's amazing, isn't he? He's most famous for *The Drunken Concubine* and *Picking up the Jade Bracelet*. You really never heard of him?"

I shook my head. The name did sound familiar, but I didn't know who he was.

"Miss, then you're really lucky to see him tonight. Because he'd quit performing, but couldn't turn down the temple's invitation, because it would be bad karma. This way he'll gain more merit by performing during New Year. This is his last performance, so I came all the way from Shanghai to see him."

"Why did he quit performing?"

She smiled knowingly. "They say he met a very rich woman. So he retired early."

I nodded, although I didn't care about this opera singer's rich lover, or his early retirement. I glanced over at my family and saw that Little Doll was now sitting on her uncle's shoulders, looking very happy to have a full view.

Ryan was astonished when I told him that the woman warrior was, in fact, a man.

Onstage, Snoring Cane continued to show off his martial arts prowess, waving a long spear while wearing heavy armor with four flags. Thunderous applause exploded amidst shouts of *"Hao, hao!"* ("Wonderful!")

But when the performance finished and all the actors were bowing, a woman's voice rose above the cheering crowd.

"Dead man, go to hell!"

The insult was followed by a barrage of rotten meat and vegetables, obviously aimed at the opera singer Snoring Cane. Fortunately or not, they missed their target. This unexpected outburst caused an uproar. People looked around for the person who so bitterly hated this actor whom everyone else loved so dearly. But most of the audience seemed too busy arguing with each other to notice the old, shabbily dressed woman tottering her way toward the exit. I nudged Ryan's elbow. "Who would do something like this?"

"Must be some crazy fan with a crush on the performer. But, of course, he won't care about her."

That made sense. But somehow I had a feeling that I'd seen this woman before. I asked Ryan to stay with Little Doll for a few minutes during the intermission. Before he could question me, I'd already squeezed my way through the crowd and hurried outside the temple. I kept searching among the bustling crowd, until finally I thought I'd spotted the one who'd just thrown garbage at the opera singer. She was now moving from one vendor to the next, seemingly begging for food. So it seemed that Ryan was right, she was just a crazy fan. Finally a middle-aged vendor wrapped a pancake in newspaper and handed it to her. Grabbing the food without thanking her benefactor, she walked to a corner, stooped down, and began to eat voraciously.

I waited patiently until the old woman finished her food; then I went up to her.

"Aunty Peony . . ." I gently called out.

Though she looked up at me, she didn't seem to recognize me. With sunken cheeks, cloudy, bloodshot eyes, and dirty clothes, her beauty was gone. But not her arrogance.

"Who's that?" she asked, her tone harsh and suspicious.

"It's Spring Swallow."

"Who's Sprint Wallow?"

Did she fail to recognize me, or just pretend?

She kept staring at me until I suddenly realized she was partly blind.

"Can you see?" I asked very gently.

"A little."

"What happened to your eyes?"

She chuckled. "Ha, you don't know?"

"I don't, what happened?"

"I'll tell you if you take me for a good meal."

It was a strange request, but to be sure she was Aunty Peony, I agreed.

"All right, let's find a place."

She stood up, put her arm around mine, and we began to walk.

Soon I spotted a simple restaurant, led her to a table, and we both sat down. The place was wet and dirty with cigarette butts, and broken beer bottles littered the floor.

When the waiter came, she ordered like a rich boss. "Give me dan dan noodles, concubine chicken, pan-fried pork dumplings, stir-fried pork intestine with chili paste, steamed fish with black bean sauce. And some beer."

Soon we were talking and eating. Her chopsticks kept hitting her bowl, making an urgent, irritating sound. Finally, after she finished everything and had washed it all down with two pots of tea, she rubbed her bulging belly, looking satisfied, if not happy.

"It's been a very long time since I had a chance to eat like this. You are kind." She paused, then added, "And rich."

I ignored her compliment but asked, "You really don't know who I am, Aunty Peony?"

"Hmmm . . . maybe I do, but you look very different. Did you work for me in the past?"

I nodded.

"How come you look so fat? Hair down like a slut, wearing a Western dress—you a whore now?"

But I was not angry. Aunty Peony was after all Aunty Peony—rude as ever. She could at least see well enough to notice my bulging stomach. But I was not going to give away any details about my present life. Anyway, I was dying to know what had happened to her.

"What happened to you, Aunty Peony? Why did you leave us?"

She sipped her tea and sighed heavily. "Can't you see that I'm going blind?"

"I'm so sorry. What happened?"

"It was all my years of embroidering, from when I was a child. But I never told anyone. Why do you think I let you redo *Along the River*? Not because you're better than me—don't even dream about that—but because my eyes started to blur and I couldn't tell the difference between the subtle shadings. Now all I can see are shadows, silhouettes, and faces—though very blurred."

She gulped her tea, then went on. "But my young lover told me he loved me no matter what. That he'd always take good care of me, since I can't see well and am older than him. Now you see the effects of his honeyed words and slippery tongue! I left you all to start a new life with him here in Peking. That's what comes of believing a man's lies."

I gazed at her in bewilderment as she went on. "He told me how he loved and admired me, so I let my guard down and gave him my whole life's savings and all my imperial treasures. After that, he ran away with a pretty girl much younger than me."

She paused, looking morose. Her bloodshot eyes wandered around the small restaurant. "In the past," she said, raising her voice, "I'd never have eaten in the same place with these losers. I used to eat with the emperor!"

A young man at the neighboring table laughed and said to his friend, "Hahaha, what a crazy woman! Ate with the emperor! I bet she didn't even have the chance to eat with the emperor's dog!"

"Or rat, hahaha!" his friend blurted out.

The two laughed more, then resumed eating their greasy food.

Aunty continued with her boasting spree. "Huh! I'm the only one who knows the secrets of a thousand beauties! In the palace I only ate with chopsticks made of ivory, from bowls of the finest white tallow jade, and rubbed my hands only with the most delicate oil scented with a hundred different herbs—"

I cut her off. "Then what happened . . . ?"

"My mouth is dry. Buy me a drink so I'll be able to tell you more."

The waiter brought her another bottle of beer, which she finished in several big gulps.

"So I ended up begging and stealing on the streets. You know, some people are generous, but most are so stingy that it kills them to spare you a few coins. So I steal. And I never feel guilty. . . ."

"Why not?"

"Because it's fair that after I had everything stolen, I steal in return."

I knew this half-blind and crazy woman in front of me was indeed Aunty Peony. But, smart as she was, how did she end up in her present pitiful state?

"Aunty, do you have a place to stay?" I blurted out, then immediately regretted it. I couldn't possibly take her to live at Our Lady of Sorrows—though now Aunty Peony was indeed a lady of sorrow.

She cast me an are-you-stupid-or-what look. "I stay right here."

"What do you mean?"

She pointed to the direction of Compassionate Light. "In the temple here, where else?"

Of course there would be lodging for homeless and old people in a Buddhist temple.

"Aunty Peony, why don't you go back to your house in Soochow?"

"I don't even have money to buy a train ticket—will you lend me some?"

I ignored this. "Tell me about the person who cheated on you."

"Oh, you don't know? The one I threw rotten meat and vegetables at—the singer, that bastard, Soaring Crane!"

Now something clicked. I remembered. Soaring Crane—not Snoring Cane as mispronounced by the woman in her heavy accent—who got the bad review I read in the newspaper. And Aunty was the rich older lover mentioned in the article.

"Aren't you afraid he'll call the police to arrest you for attacking him?"

"You think he dares? He stole all my"—she leaned toward me and said in a heated whisper—"imperial treasures!"

I remembered when I had searched Aunty's secret chamber and found that everything was gone. So this is how they'd ended up—stolen by a crooked opera singer.

"But . . . what can he do with them? If he tries to sell them, he'll get caught."

"But he can."

"How?"

"His most ardent admirer is a gangster, so he'll buy them."

"But the police have spies everywhere—what if they find out?"

"Ha! You don't know that gangsters' best friends are the police?"

It took me a minute or two to digest all this. Then I wondered, "How could this Soaring Crane make you give him all your prized possessions?"

"He has the sweetest honeyed lips and tongue, not to mention that he's very handsome and good at you-know-what. He told me that I was so beautiful and talented that he could never love another woman. So I told him everything about myself, my years in the palace and the emperor's treasures. I always paid for the hotel rooms, expensive restaurants, and bought him lavish gifts. He'd told me that the theater owed him a lot of money and that he'd pay me back when he got paid."

"Aunty, you kept this secret from us. How did you and he see each other?"

"Sometimes I went to Peking to see him, but most of the time he came to Soochow."

"How come we never got to meet him?"

She cast me a disgusted look. "There're lots of things about me you girls had no idea about, stupid."

Before I could respond, she went on. "I spent most of what we made on him. He kept saying he wanted us to get married so he'd take good care of me and my treasures. So I took everything I owned and moved in with him. After a few days he disappeared, and my treasures with him. I had a little money hidden away, but pretty soon it ran out. With my eyesight nearly gone I couldn't embroider anymore. So here I am, living at the mercy of this temple."

Listening to Aunty, I couldn't help but think of the saying "Smart for whole life, stupid for one moment."

"Why didn't you call the police to expose him?"

"Because he already sold everything to the gangster. I'm sure he's gambled it all away by now. I'd just be asking for trouble."

I felt so sorry for her that I asked, "Aunty Peony, do you want to come and live with me?"

She didn't respond, looking down at the empty dishes. I suddenly realized that during our entire conversation, she'd never once asked about me. Why I was here in Peking; what I'd been doing; how I'd survived since she'd left; what had happened to the other girls; did I still embroider?

I sighed—even destitute she was as cold as ever. But I should not have been surprised by this. I'd never known her to care about anyone else. Except Soaring Crane, of course. It was ironic that she'd been cheated by the only person she'd ever loved and trusted. Or maybe that was selfishness, too, wanting to be with someone young, famous, handsome, who had promised to take care of her.

She gave me a curious glance. "Why did you invite me to live with you—you want to learn my secret stitches? Pay me back for all I've done for you and the other girls? But the answer is no, because I'm not homeless. Anyway, where do you live?"

"I'm married to a man who works at a Western church. I help out by doing embroideries for the church to sell."

"Ah, so you're still living off the skills I taught you. I always knew you're the smartest among the girls. Not like the stupid Leilei who got herself killed by running away trying to sell *Along the River.* Or Purple, that whore!"

I decided not to tell her about Leilei, so I asked, "Purple? Do you know where she is?"

Aunty spat. "She threw all my teaching down the toilet! Worthless, ungrateful girl; should have been a prostitute to begin with."

"How do you know that?"

"Compassionate Light Temple receives many different newspapers. One lady reads to me from the *Soochow Daily.*"

Purple in the newspaper? That did not sound good. "What'd it say about Purple?"

"Even though she was a whore, she wanted to be a nun instead. So she left the turquoise pavilion for a temple. But inside she was still just a whore. When she fell in love with a monk, the abbot kicked them both out. The newspaper said they were sent to another temple in Manchuria to do hard labor to work off their bad karma."

She must have guessed what I was going to ask, because she quickly added, "Since then, nobody knows what happened to them. Maybe they couldn't stand the harsh weather and committed suicide together. Who knows?"

I tried to digest this disturbing news. Was this what really happened or was there more to the story? I felt I should try to help

Purple, remembering her kindness in taking me to Aunty's house. But with a husband and baby on the way, I could not travel to the far north to look for her. I could only pray for her and her lover.

Finally, I said, "Aunty Peony, Little Doll is with me and my husband—you want to see her?"

She vehemently waved her bony hand. "No, she'll hate me—like all of you do. None of you appreciate what I did for you. I'm not that stupid. Just leave me alone. Anyway, I have my plans."

"What are you planning?"

"Why are you so nosy? It has nothing to do with you anyway." She stood up abruptly. "All right, I'm going back to where I belong."

"How can I see you again?"

"Ask for the death room in the temple, you know, where all the old people are." She laughed.

"What do you mean?"

"You're the smartest one, so go figure it out. But even if you come, that doesn't mean I'll see you, you understand?"

When I tried to help her walk back to the temple, she pushed me away.

"Go back to your husband and the worthless doll. And don't you pity me. I know this area like the back of my hand. You understand?"

∽ 31 ∾

The Fate of an Imperial Embroiderer

With a heavy heart, I quickly walked back to Compassionate Light Temple. Entering the courtyard, I was alarmed to discover that it was now empty. The makeshift stage was dark, looking forlorn and dilapidated like an abandoned farmhouse. It was then that I realized I'd been gone for almost an hour and my husband and little sister must've gone crazy trying to find me. I just hoped Ryan hadn't gone to the police to report me as a missing person!

In the distance, an emaciated, middle-aged man was sweeping the ground in front of the stage, occasionally picking up dropped objects—bits of food, a pen, a few coins.

I went up to him and politely asked, "Mister, did you happen to see a foreigner with a young Chinese girl?"

He stopped sweeping to look up at me. "You mean white ghost?"

I nodded.

"Yes, you think he's going to do something bad to the girl?"

I chuckled. "No, mister. That foreigner is my husband and the girl my little sister; please tell me where they are."

"Miss," he said, and now looked at me differently, "why marry a foreigner? Chinese men no good? That's why my twenty-seven-year-old son still can't find a woman to marry!"

"Please, mister, just tell me if you saw them?"

He pointed to the temple's exit. "I believe they went out there."

Although his suggestion was basically useless, I thanked him and quickly walked toward the entrance. When I passed the bronze incense burner, I saw that donors' names were etched on its round belly. Did these people all have such bad karma that they were desperate to reverse it by giving money to a temple? But actually all of us could use more good karma. Maybe when I had more money, I'd have Father Edwin's, Ryan's, Little Doll's, and my name etched here too. One caught my attention: Peony. Could this be *my* Aunty Peony who had donated to have her name inscribed hoping to gain merit?

My musing was interrupted by Ryan shouting my name. "Spring Swallow, please don't scare us like that in the future!"

He grabbed me and hugged me tightly, as if fearing even the incense's smoke would lift me up and carry me away. Finally, he released me, looking upset and happy at the same time. Then it was Little Doll's turn to hug me.

"Sister Spring Swallow, where have you been? We looked for you all over! Unkle Rai An was very upset; he thought you might be kidnapped."

Ryan chimed in, and his voice held a scolding edge. "Spring Swallow, promise me that you won't wander off like that again!"

"I promise," I told him, meaning it.

"Where were you? What happened?"

We all went to sit on a bench near the gate and I told them about running into Aunty Peony and hearing the sad story of her life since leaving us. I also told Little Doll that I would take her to see Aunty very soon.

Ryan didn't look very enthusiastic about the reunion, and told me, "Spring Swallow, you should stay away from her."

"But I promised Little Doll I'd try to get our family back together. Heaven let me run into Aunty, so—"

"You're a married woman now. A married woman's responsibility is with her husband, not her aunty, especially since your so-called aunty is not even nice to you and is now mentally unstable. So you and Little Doll should stay away from her."

This was the first time Ryan had been so firm. It made me a little scared, but his concern touched me.

"But, Ryan—"

"If you go to see her, there'll be nothing but trouble. As your husband, I have to warn you."

"Then what am I going to do, just let her be?"

"Exactly. And don't worry about her—she has the temple to care for her."

And that ended our conversation.

After my unexpected encounter with Aunty Peony, life went on uneventfully. Little Doll and I continued to embroider, and Ryan taught Bible class and helped run Our Lady of Sorrows with Father Edwin. Although I was planning to visit Aunty Peony again, at least to bring Little Doll to her, I was not going to discuss this with Ryan.

Just a week later I had my chance. Father Edwin had sent Ryan away to interview prospective new seminary students. So the next morning, I hailed a tricycle rickshaw and took Little Doll straight to Compassionate Light Temple.

Instead of sounding like a huge, noisy circus, now the temple courtyard possessed a quieter, melancholic air. Also, it was not until now that I noticed the many smaller temple complexes beside the main *Daxiong Baodian,* the "Grand Heroic Hall." I had no idea how to look for Aunty. I dared not take Little Doll inside any of these halls, because they all looked mysterious and intimidating, especially the *Daxiong Baodian.* So we waited till we saw a nun heading toward one of the complexes, carrying a plate of food.

We hurried to her, and I asked, "Please, *shifu,* can you tell us where the nursing home for women is?"

"Who are you looking for?"

This time Little Doll answered eagerly, "We want to see our teacher, Aunty Peony."

To my surprise, a shock shadowed the nun's face. "Oh, her . . ."

"Doesn't she live here?"

"She did . . . but no more."

"What do you mean—what happened?" Aunty was lucky to be housed by a Buddhist temple, so why would she have left for another place?

"She's your teacher and you don't know? It's all over the newspapers!"

"But we don't usually read the papers."

"She's a murderess! She's in jail," the nun blurted out.

Little Doll and I exclaimed, "What!?"

"Yes, it's horrible."

"Aunty Peony a murderess? Who—"

"The famous Peking opera performer Soaring Crane."

"But he was here last week. We heard him perform."

"That's when it happened. After the performance she went to his home. We heard that they had a big argument and she stabbed him many times. By the time he got to the hospital he was dead. This is a terrible thing for the temple and the nuns. Very embarrassing."

"Where is she?"

"They arrested her right away. Now she's locked up in the Tian Shan Women's Prison outside the city."

"What will happen to her?"

"There will be a trial, I guess."

I really did not want to talk to her about Aunty any further, so I thanked her profusely and pulled Little Doll away.

But the nun called, "Poor little girl! Wait." She picked up a sweet bun from the tray she was carrying and handed it to my little sister.

"Here, little girl. You're too skinny; try to eat more."

Next she stared at my pregnant belly, then gave me two buns and two dumplings wrapped in lotus leaves.

"Take these, you two may be hungry on your way."

We thanked her again and hurried away. Though a cold wind blew from the gate, I felt the warmth of the nun's kindness to us.

Outside the temple, between bites of her bun, Little Doll asked, "Sister Spring Swallow, what are we going to do now?"

"We are going to where Aunty Peony is. This may be our last chance to see her."

Half an hour later, Little Doll and I arrived at the Tian Shan Women's Prison. In the distance, the elongated building looked like a huge, indolent snake ready to wake up and attack. We walked another five minutes in the cold before we reached an iron gate guarded by scowling police. I checked inside my cloth bag and was relieved to see the lucky money envelopes given to me and Little Doll during the New Year were still there. After one of these envelopes discreetly changed hands, we were led inside. I could not even have imagined what it was like—dark, gloomy, and stinking of death, impending or actual.

At the reception area, a bulky man with a crude face looked up at us from his newspaper. I handed him another "entry fee." He looked at it and told us to wait.

When he reappeared without Aunty, he told us, "She said she won't see any visitors because all people are worthless."

I showed him the snacks given to me by the nun. "Can you tell Miss Peony that I have some food for her?"

"All right, I'm the one who decides whom she'll see or not see. Hahaha! Come, follow me."

As Little Doll and I followed him along the gloomy corridor, from the dark, filthy cells, eyes stared at us, silently expressing resignation, bitterness, and misery. No one complained, cursed, or spat; they simply ignored us, waiting resignedly for the inevitable. Their silence was much sadder than angry protest would have been. There was no hope in this place.

I asked the man, "What's going to happen to Peony?"

"Don't know yet, probably a death sentence. They might give her an easy death because she's old and crazy. But maybe not—the judge is an opera fan."

Little Doll started to cry, so I patted her shoulder, trying to calm her.

The guard turned to look at me. "But who are you, young miss, and what's she to you?"

Fortunately, I didn't have to answer this question, for just then we reached Aunty's cell. He took out a big metal ring, found the right key, then threw open the door with a nerve-wracking clang, and then let me and Little Doll in.

"Fifteen minutes."

"Oh, please, can't we have more?"

Aunty Peony answered for him. "That'll be enough."

So the man left with another loud clang of the gate. The harsh sound seemed to terrify Little Doll. For now we were prisoners, too, locked into this confined space stinking with human sweat, urine, and excrement.

Little Doll, cheered by the sight of Aunty, ran to her and passionately hugged her.

"Aunty Peony, so good to see you!"

Aunty pushed her away. "Stop talking so loud and acting so excited. Behave like a lady, won't you?"

Looking crestfallen, Little Doll went to stand by me.

In place of the rags she had worn when I had seen her at the performance, Aunty now wore a baggy gray prison uniform that matched the equally gray and dreary prison walls.

She spoke. "I told the guard that I don't want to see anyone, so why did he bring you here?"

Before I could say anything, she turned to Little Doll. "And you, how come you can grow so big; who's wasting their food on you?"

In the past, I'd have laughed at this preposterous comment, but now I only felt sad. But not Little Doll. She looked happy that her aunty had addressed her.

"Aunty Peony, I'm fine and having a good time! Now I'm living with Sister Spring Swallow and Unkle Rai An, who is a very nice foreigner and very good to me. I even embroider small things to make money. Thank you, Aunty, for teaching me."

Aunty scoffed. "Thank me, what for? Don't you girls realize you all caught bad luck from me?!"

I ignored this. "Aunty Peony, I brought you something." I took off my jacket and handed it to her.

She waved her bony hand. "Don't pity me. I'm not cold, and even if I was, I don't care. So keep your worthless jacket for yourself. Or"—she pointed to Little Doll—"for this stupid girl when she grows even bigger."

I didn't know why she kept saying that Little Doll was big, because, in fact, she was anything but.

I leaned to whisper to Little Doll. "I have to talk to Aunty Peony privately, so why don't you stand over there and cover your ears."

Little Doll giggled as she complied, though I suspected she would try to listen anyway.

I patted her shoulder and said tenderly, "Don't forget to keep your ears covered—and turn your back. I won't take long. You can have another bun when we're done."

"Aunty Peony," I asked in a whisper, "was it because Soaring Crane stole your treasures that you killed him?"

"Yes, he ruined me completely. Then he ruined himself gambling it all away!" She spat on the ground. "I should have stabbed him even more, hahaha!"

Before I could say anything, she went on vehemently. "He ruined me with his charm, so I ruined him with my knife. Not my fault—it was his karma. He took all my imperial treasures; I took his life. We're even. He lost his voice; I lost my embroidery. Everything is gone!"

"Aunty Peony, it's not all gone."

She cast me a suspicious look. "What do you mean?"

I opened my jacket and showed her what I had sewn inside.

Aunty's eyes were round as two big coins. "Oh, Heaven! How did you get this? I thought I'd lost it."

"No, Aunty. I found it where you'd hidden it in your pillow."

She reached out with her bony hand and stroked it. "How could I have forgotten where I put it? It was my token of love for the emperor!"

"The emperor?" I already knew about this but hoped to learn more.

"Yes, the emperor. I was sixteen and he was twenty-six; we loved each other dearly. I embroidered this for his thirtieth birthday. But he died shortly afterward."

"How?"

"Poisoned, I'm sure. People inside the palace died mysteriously all the time. Princes, princesses, imperial consorts, eunuchs, maids, anyone you can think of . . ."

Of course, I couldn't think of such people—I'd never met a prince or princess, or any of the others. I tried to imagine life inside the Forbidden City and Aunty's life and love in that vanished era, and assumed that she was imagining the same.

Little Doll had taken her hands off her ears and seemed to be trying to hear our conversation, so I spoke in a whisper. "Aunty Peony, you better hide this in case the guards here—"

"No, they won't. The people here are idiots. They can't tell the difference between an imperial garment and a rag."

She frowned and shook her head. "Don't worry, after all that has happened to me, I'm not going to lose my treasure again. No way, unless I die." She held it against her cheek, then put the jacket on to conceal it.

Just then the prison guard reappeared. "All right, time's up. If you like, come again tomorrow."

He held up his hand and rubbed his fingers together. "You're welcome anytime here."

I didn't want to be welcome in a prison. Of course, he wanted me to return so he could get another "entry fee."

As Little Doll and I were walking out, I turned back and said, "Aunty Peony, we'll come again soon."

"No need. I'm happy that I finally had my revenge, ha!" Her eyes were blank and her voice cold.

"But, Aunty—"

She cut me off. "It's no good for Little Doll—or your baby—to absorb the bad prison *qi,* you understand? Not good for you either. So no more visits."

Little Doll exclaimed, "But I want to see you again, Aunty Peony!"

I turned away from my little sister so she could not see my tears.

∞ 32 ∞

The Letter

That night, thinking about Aunty, I tossed and turned on my bed and couldn't enter the dream village. Since Ryan was still away, I decided I would visit Aunty Peony again in the morning. I feared it might be our last chance to see each other—I doubted the judge would really let her off for being crazy. This time I decided not to bring Little Doll. She'd had her chance to see Aunty one last time and I worried about the effect of the grim prison atmosphere on her impressionable mind.

To my dismay, when I was at the prison's reception area, the guard from yesterday was not there.

When I asked his replacement for Aunty Peony, I was told, "She's no longer here with us."

For a moment my hope soared; could she have been released? But then reality intervened. They would not let a murderess go free. Yet I could not help but feel a slight trace of hope.

"Where is she?"

"Miss . . . she's no longer on this Earth."

"What . . . ?"

"She's dead."

"Are you joking?"

"Death is no joke here."

"But I just saw her yesterday and she was fine!"

"Here, one minute they're as alive as a fish thrashing in a bucket and the next as dead as the last emperor."

"So Peony is . . ." I couldn't finish my sentence.

"Dead."

"How . . . did that happen? Was she . . . executed?"

"Oh, no, she hanged herself."

He spoke as casually as if saying, "Oh, she just ate a bun."

He went on as if talking to himself. "But strangely, with a jacket we didn't know she had."

I felt an explosion inside my gut. Legs wobbling, I tried to steady myself but instead collapsed on a nearby chair.

"You all right, miss?"

"I'm all right, thank you for letting me know. Where's her body?"

"No relatives, so she's taken to be buried with the others."

"But where? What others?"

He cast me a curious look. "You don't want to know, miss. Are you her daughter?"

"No, I was her student for many years."

"Well, then, I guess this should be for you."

He took a soiled sheet of paper from his desk and handed it to me. "I don't want it here anyway. Bad luck." He spat on the ground to rid himself of this bad luck.

There was no reason to stay, so I said, "Thank you, I'll leave now."

"Good, and I hope you never have to come back."

"I hope so too."

I waited until I was on the bus to go back to the church before I unfolded the note and began to read. My heart galloped like a wild horse as I opened it and saw my teacher's handwriting, once neat but now clumsy:

> My Embroidery Girl Spring Swallow,
> When you read this, I will no longer be with
> you on the Ten Thousand Miles of Red Dust.
> Don't feel sorry for me. I have decided to end
> my life with my own skillful hands rather than be
> executed by a man with dirty, bloody ones. You

gave me back the undergarment I embroidered for my love. Now it will serve for me to end my life. I must thank you for bringing it back to me. Otherwise, I'd have to bite off my tongue, or hit my head against the wall to crack my skull.

Now my last thoughts will be of my true love, the Son of Heaven.

After I'm gone, I'm not your mother or your relative, so don't bother making offerings or paying respect to my spirit. I never had any daughters, so I never treated you and the other girls like one. However, you better take good care of your baby—and of Little Doll too. I didn't bother being nice to her, but she's still very attached to me. You owe me a lot, so do what I tell you—treat her just as you will your own child.

I had some good luck in this life—I was the best embroiderer and the only woman the emperor truly loved. But for my next life, I have no idea. Probably no more emperors and no more embroidery.

I thought nothing was left of my life. But then you brought me the gift I had embroidered for the emperor and I felt alive again, for a few moments. Now I want to join him in the only place where we all meet again.

I have no regrets, as I hope you will not when it's your turn—it comes sooner than any of us think.

Your Aunty Peony's last words

I read the letter over and over as the bus rattled and shook on the bumpy road back to Our Lady of Sorrows. Tears coursed down my cheeks, attracting the stares of other passengers. She was gone. My teacher, this woman with magical hands and a mysterious, forbidden past, was now only a memory. No offspring, no family, no friends . . . Nothing left even of her exquisite creations, now in the soiled hands of a gangster to feed his arrogance.

Soon after I came home from my unhappy journey, Ryan returned from his trip. Though I greeted him affectionately, he could tell something was wrong. I explained to him that Aunty Peony had passed.

"I'm so sorry, Spring Swallow. I will go with you to her funeral."

"But there's no funeral."

I sighed and told him the sad story of Aunty's end. When Ryan understood that she had committed suicide, his face turned pale.

"How terrible, no last rites, no Christian burial!"

Of course I knew such thoughts would have been far from Aunty's mind. She'd be much more upset if she knew that she would not have a proper grave with good *yin* feng shui. But I appreciated Ryan's concern for her soul. He suggested we go to church to pray for Aunty, which I thought was the least I could do for her. That and caring for Little Doll, which I would have done even without her telling me to.

I told him I was worried that she would not be properly buried.

"We can't bury her in the churchyard here. Father Edwin would never allow it. Suicide is a mortal sin."

"Then what can I do?"

"We can keep praying for her. But you're pregnant. Try not to be too upset. Her soul is in God's hands now."

If so, I was not sure why she could not be buried here, but this was just one of the many strange ideas that foreigners have.

That night I slept fitfully. Disturbing images rose in my mind: Aunty hanging with her tongue bulging. Thrown into a mass grave on top of other corpses of those with no one to miss them. Her body, once wrapped in embroidered silk, urgently desired and lovingly caressed by the emperor, laid to "rest" with the bodies of criminals, gangsters, homeless beggars, and other outcasts. . . .

Then I dozed off and had a dream.

Aunty seemed to be standing before me, but looking well, as she had when I first met her. She lifted up her hand, the one I'd watched so many hours as she taught me embroidery. She opened her mouth, but at first no words came out, though she seemed desperately trying to tell me something. Then I seemed to hear her speak, faintly but clearly, reminding me of what she had written in her last letter: "After I'm gone, you don't need to make offerings or pay respect to my spirit. I could have treated all of you better but I didn't, for various reasons. Don't worry about me anymore. Now, you must take good care of your baby—and of Little Doll too."

I woke up, my face wet with tears, but also relief. I had decided what to do.

The next day when Ryan was at work, I grabbed a thick wad of cash and went back to Tian Shan Women's Prison. The guard who'd been there the day before recognized me.

"I thought you were done with this place."

"Mister, I have a great favor to ask you."

His face twisted into a frown but broke into a smile as I held up my wad of money.

"What do you want, miss?"

I told him what I wanted: for him to go to the burial ground and place Aunty's head to the south, so she would be able to look respectfully north toward the emperor. Then, of course, protect her modesty by covering her over with earth.

"Well, I can't really leave here now, but . . . maybe the other guard will let me go for a while. But, of course, that will mean more work for him." He looked at the pile of bills I had handed to him.

The message was pretty clear, so I reached into my purse and held out a few more bills that rapidly disappeared into his rough fist.

"I can't go myself, not in my condition, too much bad *qi* for me and the baby. But you better really do it. Unless you want to meet her again—as a ghost."

He looked alarmed at this possibility, so I was pretty sure he would not dare to offend the dead by leaving Aunty Peony as she was.

Epilogue

To my complete joy, my new baby Bobby McFarland arrived on a beautiful day in spring, at turns kicking, screaming, and smiling. I truly believed he was sent by Heaven to heal my heart, which had been broken so many times in the few years I'd been on this Earth. I felt a fulfillment that I had never felt before. To my relief, Ryan enjoyed the baby as much as I did. Our life together was uneventful, but happy.

Though my life was forever changed for the better, I still thought about the old days.

I had none of the imperial embroidery left, but perhaps this was best, as it seemed to have brought tragedy to so many. Maybe it held some of the same curse that brought down the emperor and the entire Qing dynasty. As for Aunty Peony, I thought of her and her meticulous teaching every time I sat down to embroider. At the same time, I was also glad that our karmic connection had run its course. Having done my best to get her a burial that would put her spirit at peace, I felt released from my debt to her.

I decided not to try to look for Purple in the far north. Perhaps she really had entered the Empty Gate to detach completely from the dusty world. If so, I did not want to disturb her seclusion. However, to let her know that I still cared for her, I sent a letter to the temple where Aunty told me she'd become a nun. I ended the letter saying I hoped to hear from her, but if she didn't want to reply, I would understand and wouldn't be offended.

I never heard back from her.

The death of Leilei was no longer a mystery. Since she was not really a nice person and we'd never been friends, I didn't really miss her. But Heaven had thrust us onto the same path for a short time, so I felt it my sisterly duty to pray for her unhappy soul.

Though I still missed my mountain, or revolutionary, husband Shen Feng, I came to accept that my life now was better than life with him would have been. When I thought of him, I would remember Du Fu's lines:

> Tomorrow, once again, we'll be separated by tall mountains,
> How fleeting and fickle are life and human affairs!

To show my gratitude to Ryan and Father Edwin, I became more active in their religion, willingly doing all the Christian things like attending mass, singing hymns, studying the Bible, and helping with charitable work. But, after all, I was a Chinese from a village, so I discreetly set up a small altar in the kitchen to burn incense for Leilei, Aunty Peony, and, of course, Shen Feng. Ryan told me that as a Christian I had no need for such superstitions, but I pointed out that it was to pay respect to the kitchen god so we wouldn't have a fire in the house. Even as a devoted Christian, he couldn't argue against the safety of his home and family.

I'd never expected my skill as an embroiderer would be acknowledged outside the church, but I was wrong—happily so. A missionary who visited Our Lady of Sorrows took one of my large works back to America, where it got noticed by an important person at a department store. They wanted me to supply them with works on a regular basis—and they paid much better than Heavenly Phoenix.

Then one day a museum in America decided to have a show of my work, inviting me to the Gold Mountain to demonstrate *Soo* embroidery. I was able to accept because it would be in two years, so little Bobby would be old enough to travel.

Ryan and Little Doll were ecstatic, and Father Edwin congratu-lated me.

Little Doll clapped happily. "Sister Spring Swallow! Can you bring me with you so I can be your little assistant?"

Ryan and I both laughed at her enthusiasm.

I said, "Of course, we'll all go, little sister."

Ryan planted a kiss on my forehead. "Spring Swallow, you're now internationally famous!"

Of course I was not going to argue against a genuine compli-ment, let alone from my beloved husband and the loving father of my little boy.

Since I'd become very busy keeping up with orders from Amer-ica, Little Doll happily busied herself helping me and playing with little Bobby. Ryan became attached to my little sister, and finally of-ficially adopted her. Now Little Doll was Dolly McFarland. How-ever, I wouldn't let her call me Mama—I was not yet old enough to have a fourteen-year-old daughter!

I was very proud that not only had I fulfilled my promise to care for Little Doll, but also gave her a father and a little brother. In fact, I felt even happier about this than being invited to America. I was very grateful to Old Heaven—known to foreigners as God—for putting us all together.

From time to time, I would look at the only picture I had of Aunty and the girls—the one we'd taken together during our trip to Peking. Aunty Peony sat in the middle with an imperial air. Leilei's and Purple's eyes seemed to be wandering, searching for something far away, perhaps happiness, which unfortunately they would only find in the Western Paradise and the Empty Gate. Lit-tle Doll was not even looking at the camera. Maybe she was think-ing, "When will we finish this so I can have some tasty buns?" As for me, I looked alert, as if expecting attack from all sides.

Staring at the picture, I could only remember two times that Aunty had smiled happily during the whole time I'd known her. Once for this picture and the other when I'd taught her how to pronounce English, the exotic chicken's intestines.

Now Aunty seemed to stare at me from the picture, admonishing, "Spring Swallow, though you're the smartest girl, don't forget you've learned everything from me. Only from me did you learn the secrets of a thousand beauties, you understand?!"

I nodded to her in the picture as tears mixed with joy and sadness rolled down my cheeks. . . .

SECRET OF A THOUSAND BEAUTIES

Mingmei Yip

ABOUT THIS GUIDE

The questions and discussion topics that
follow are intended to enhance your
group's reading of this book.

Discussion Questions

1. What do you think about the Chinese custom of marriage to a ghost?

2. Spring Swallow is married four times. What do you think about this?

3. *Secret of a Thousand Beauties* is set in a time where China is trying to become a modern country. How does this affect the fates of the five embroiderers?

4. What do you think about Spring Swallow? Is she brave, determined, and unselfish? Or is she an opportunist?

5. Describe Aunty Peony's character, her love affairs, and her attitude to the girls she takes into her home.

6. Had Shen Feng survived the revolution, should Spring Swallow have gone back to him?

7. What do you think about the women taking vows of celibacy? Were they right to break this vow?

8. Several of the characters believe in ghosts. Do you believe in ghosts? If there are no ghosts, what do these characters actually believe in?

9. Ryan had almost completed his training to become a priest, but instead fell in love with Spring Swallow and married her. Do you think this was proper, or should he have suppressed his feelings and maintained his vocation?

10. Ryan accepts both Spring Swallow's baby by another man and Little Doll. Do you think this will affect his relationship with Spring Swallow in the future?